BOUND BY DESTINY

CROWNS OF MAGIC UNIVERSE

COVEN OF SHADOWS AND SECRETS SERIES

ASHLEY MCLEO

MERAKI PRESS

Editing by Owl Eye Edits

Cover art by Hannah Sternjakob

Ebook ISBN: 978-1-947245-95-2

Paperback ISBN: 978-1-947245-96-9

Audiobook ISBN: 978-1-947245-97-6

FOREWORD

This book is part of the Crowns of Magic universe. In this universe, characters and storylines cross over, but the series and standalone can be read independently from one another. The reader just gets a fuller picture of the world by reading all of the books.

Other series in this expanding universe include:

The Winter Court Series - start with A Kingdom of Frost and Malice

Curse of the Fae Prince - a standalone

GLOSSARY

* *Abscondita* Coven - a coven hidden in the woods of England tasked with keeping information about the *Vindix* and *lapis caelesti* safe.
* *Arcacustos* - the eight members of the ultra secretive *Abscondita* Coven.
* the Beinecke - a library at Yale
* the Covenant - the supernatural ruling body of the human world. It's made up of three individuals from each supernatural order (example: three vampires, three witches, three phoenixes and so on).
* the Darkborn - people in the human world who follow the Princes of Hell. Some are Hellblooded, but not all.
* Eyes of Darkness - one of seven portals linking the human world and Hell. All were closed until the events of *History of Witches* transpired.
* Hellblooded - individuals with demon blood. They are usually born in the human world and are forced to register by the Covenant.

* Hellborn - individuals who were born in Hell. Nearly all of these creatures are demons.

* Isila - another realm where magical beings live. It's comprised of nine kingdoms (four fae kingdoms, mage, dragon shifter, elf, vampire, and wolf shifter). Many characters in the Coven of Shadows and Secrets have direct ties to Isila's courts.

* *Lapis caelesti* - the sacred stones made by angels thousands of years ago and given to seven witches to protect. They are great sources of power that can defeat the darkest evil.

* Luxiter - an orb that allows its holder to light-travel. Few can make these items.

* Ordo Aeternum - Also known as the OA, Ordo, or the Order. An elitist group of supernaturals who believe those of magical blood should rule the world (many believe they should enslave humans too).

* Ouroboros - The symbol of the Coven of Shadows and Secrets. It is a snake, formed in a circle, eating its own tail.

* Wolvea - royal wolves of Isila

* *Vindix* - the chosen seven individuals who can claim and use the *lapis caelesti* to their highest potential. The *Vindix* all have witch blood in their line.

* *Volar* - the spell that activates a luxiter

* Vow of Intent - an vow between supernaturals where the person loses their magic if they break it

* *Irekita.*- a spell that opens a locked or warded door

* *Burresku* - to protect something inside one's body, such as a child, when the body is under stress.

CHAPTER ONE

GUNNER

MY BONES SAGGED—HEAVY AS LEAD, WEAK, AND UNMOTIVATED, exactly like the rest of me. No matter how hard I tried, I just couldn't shake the Prince of Sloth's power.

That oily blackness that clung to my blood vessels spread everywhere now. New Orleans had gone dark, and people lounged in the streets, gorging themselves on whatever food they found, drinking to excess, and sleeping on the sidewalk.

Old Ones, have mercy. I didn't know how the *Vindix* were gonna defeat Sloth. Let alone how they'd beat six other princes. The thought of such a huge feat exhausted me, and I paused in the hallway I'd been ambling down with no rhyme or reason. Though it was hard to find the energy to do so, walking the halls of Prince Belhor's castle cleared my mind a touch. For a few precious moments, I thought about my friends, family, the coven, and most of all, Harper.

An image of the clever and feisty redhead filtered through my clouded mind and made my heart clench. I shoulda kissed the hell out of that she-wolf before Luca and I went to Ireland to get Silas. Shoulda told her how she made my heart skip a beat.

Will I ever see her again?

A howl outside the window drew me out of what would have been one hell of a self-pity spiral. I crossed to the hallway window, pulled back the ornate damask curtains that woulda made Pa shudder, and peered outside.

"Aw, no." The hellhounds, like the ones in New York City, prowled down the street, snarling and snapping at the sin-enchanted people of New Orleans.

The monsters loomed larger than a true wolf, and even bigger than me when I shifted. Worse, a dozen of 'em roamed this street.

I swallowed down fear as the pack of monsters approached a group of gals. One of 'em wore a white dress and a pink sash. No doubt they had been in the city for a bachelorette party. As they'd been here when the city fell, they too were under Sloth's spell and boy did it show. The hair that they'd no doubt taken great care to make look good stuck out all over the place. Cuts grazed their bare legs, and one gal looked to be missin' half her skirt. The ladies were so out of it and plastered that they didn't notice the hellhounds, not until the one in front snapped at the would-be bride's heels.

One girl shrieked, and the bride jumped, which only antagonized the hellhound. It struck, biting into the girl's leg and shaking.

She fell and cried, but her friends scattered, too scared to be in the presence of hellhounds.

And I just stood there. Watchin' her cry, knowin' the hellhound's poison was spreadin' through her. If I hadn't already known that somethin' was wrong with me, the sheer lack of desire to help the bride would have hit it home. But I, like everyone else in the city, was under Sloth's spell, so I didn't move. I felt pain for her, but also didn't care to do a thing about it. Apathy was sheer hell.

I pulled back the curtain, knowin' that even if I wanted to help the girl, I'd never be able to leave the castle. If I tried, Sloth would bear down on his sin and probably put me in a coma. So, there was nothin' to be done.

Pa would be so disappointed in me.

Heck, I was so disappointed in myself. But I shuffled off all the same, down the endless hallway that looked straight outta some teenage vampire show. I was still feelin' sorry for myself when I went down some stairs and turned a random corner, only to find myself faced with two demon guards standin' before a door. Light shone from a stained glass window behind them. They were guardin' something outside?

"What are you doing here?" one grunted. He was the rhino-demon type, ugly as all get-out and big as a house. Alert too. Since I'd been here, I'd concluded the demons weren't under Sloth's influence. Maybe by the prince's choice, or maybe hell's blood just acted like a protectant, but I was sure that humans and magical beings like me were affected. Lucky us.

"No reason." I shrugged. "Wanderin'. Sloth said I could."

"*Prince Belhor,*" one corrected me.

"Yeah, that. Can I go outside?"

The guards shared glances but stepped aside.

"The witches are working out there," rhino-boy said. "Don't get in their way."

Witches?

"All right," I replied as if somethin' hadn't stolen my interest.

On the other side of the doors, the castle walls rose around me, tellin' me I was in a courtyard of sorts. A lush one at that. Aside from a thin gravel path, the outdoor oasis crawled with green plants. Here, one could almost forget where they were. That was until they looked up and saw the black towers, one of which held an eerie light blue flame that was probably 'round my height. That flame had been flickerin' day and night since the castle rose outta nowhere.

My gaze dropped back to the garden and tryin' to be in the moment, I inhaled and savored the fresh air. Though I'd become pretty desensitized to the sulfury scent of Hell permeatin' New Orleans now, whenever I saw Prince Sloth, I remembered I was steepin' in the stink. The city was probably worse too. Trash lined the streets and people definitely weren't washin' like normal.

Out here, though, the air smelled fresh and nice and sorta invigoratin'. The plants and fresh air might save my sanity, so I made a note to come here as often as I could.

"Push!" a male voice with that distinct Louisiana twang called out from somewhere in the garden.

I straightened as a tree shot up from the ground. Ripe dark purple plums grew on its limbs, hangin' heavy and temptin' as all get out.

"Hold!"

The tree stopped growin'.

Okay, that had to be from the witches. Not followin' the guard's orders, I strolled down the path at my frustratingly slow and steady pace, lookin' for the witches.

It took all of a minute for me to find 'em. The pair had turned away from me and were sizing up another tree with lemons hanging from the branches.

"Why are you two the only busy people in this castle?" I asked, tryin' to make my lips form my usual easy grin.

The pair whirled, and the man's blue eyes narrowed. "What're you doin' in the courtyard?"

"The guards let me come out here." I shrugged and the guy's broad shoulders loosened. "Not like I have a lot else goin' on. Unlike you."

Did they work for Sloth? Or were they here against their will, like me? And if so, how did they have enough where-with-all to use magic? While I could feel my magic rollin' through me, Sloth's hold over me was so intense, I couldn't use my power to shift.

"He releases our magic for this. Only in this courtyard." The lady, a pretty Black gal of around twenty or so, gestured to the area. She wore her long hair in braids that flowed over her shoul-der. Her face glowed with the exertion of performin' magic. Her accent told me she wasn't from around these parts, more like the West Coast. "The prince gives us seeds, and we're supposed to grow food from them. Then we go back to our rooms."

That explained the plum tree.

"Almost makes me wish I was an earth witch," I drawled. "I miss magic."

The woman's dark brown eyes softened. "I miss it too when he stifles it." She exhaled. "What's your name?"

"Gunner. I'm a wolf."

"Alpha?"

"How'd you know?" It wasn't like I was exudin' alpha energy. Far from it. Slug energy was probably rollin' off me.

"If you weren't, I'd bet you would lie around all day. Dan and I are strong with our magic too. I think it's how Sloth detected our magic and decided to use us." She held out her hand. As she came closer, I got a better whiff of her and stiffened. Somethin' about this girl reminded me of . . . someone. But I couldn't put my finger on who. "I'm Rhianna, by the way."

I pushed aside my olfactory distraction as we shook. "Good to meet the both of you."

I meant it too. I'd been in the city for a smidge over a week, and with no one to talk to, I was gettin' down. A wolf needed friends. Touch. Communication. I didn't get a lick of that here.

"So," I gestured to the tree again, "does he have you making food for outside the castle?"

Dan shook his head. "Just inside."

"How long were y'all out there before he brought you here?" I asked.

As I'd been captive in a smaller mansion when Sloth first took the city, I was pretty sure neither had been around back then.

"Two days back," Dan drawled before a yawn overtook him. "They caught me tryin' to grow food for my old neighborhood. Took me from my family."

My heart broke for the guy. My pack and my family were safe in Isila. Thank the Old Ones.

"You saved your children, Dan." Rhianna patted his shoulder. "You did the right thing."

Dan didn't reply, so Rhianna turned to me. "I've been here five days. They picked me up around Loyola, where I go to school. Or, at least, where I *went* to school. They saw me also growing fruit because there's already a food shortage out there. When I arrived at the castle, I didn't leave my room for the first two days. Then when Dan came, the prince had his stooges put us together to work. What about you?"

"Little over a week."

Rhianna's eyes bulged. "But the castle rose five days ago."

"He had a mansion before that, and I was there—got the pleasure of seein' Bourbon Street fall. Guess he thought he needed more room."

Rhianna snorted. "Why were you in the mansion? Seems like you might be important."

"I'd been chasin' someone allied with Prince Belhor, and he opened a portal to escape me. My dumb butt ran through it and—poof!—here I am."

Not for the first time, I wondered if Silas was still 'round these parts. Or if he'd gone back to his damp cottage in Ireland. Even with all the rain, I'd give anythin' to be there too. Not with Silas, of course, but any place not smothered in a sin was better than here.

"You some kind of magical cop?" Rhianna asked.

"Dark artifact hunter," I answered. "Sometimes demon hunter. Though the guy I chased is fae."

"Right," she huffed out a dry laugh, "that's a lot."

"Yeah, it kinda is." I scuffed the ground with my shoe.

"Did you hear the latest news?" Dan asked.

"What's that?"

"We were gettin' directives from the prince when news that another city went dark came in. Don't know where because Belhor dismissed us right quick. That means each Prince of Hell has a territory now. Seven cities for seven princes."

Dan's words took the air out of my lungs. The princes had claimed their kingdoms. What was their next move?

Did I need to do some rootin' around?

"Guess I should be goin', so you two can get back to work. I don't want those demons comin' out here and razzin' ya."

"Us either." Rhianna pulled back her long braids.

As she did so, her scent intensified. My eyebrows knitted together. Who in the world did she remind me of?

"You okay, Gunner?" Rhianna asked.

"Yeah, it's. . ." I shook my head, not wantin' to wear my thoughts on my face. In a place like this, that was dangerous. "The sin is cloudin' my head."

She nodded understandingly, so I gave 'em a wave and left the courtyard, puzzled as hell over what had happened.

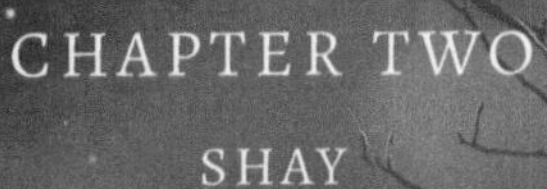

CHAPTER TWO

SHAY

Hᴀɴs's ᴄʜᴇsᴛ ʀᴏsᴇ ᴀɴᴅ ꜰᴇʟʟ sʟᴏᴡʟʏ, ᴀʟᴡᴀʏs ɪɴ ᴀ ᴘᴀɪɴꜰᴜʟ rhythm. Sometimes he screamed, sometimes he moaned. Once he'd even had a seizure. But never did his eyelids open.

A week had passed since our heart attack-inducing escape from the Blood Court, and despite Hannah's ministrations and many sleepless nights, there'd been no improvement. He'd barely even shifted in his sleep.

I swallowed, watching Hans breathe, taking in the color in his face—or, more accurately, the lack thereof. Not for the first time, the memory of the vial I'd taken to Isila shattering in my pocket came to mind. I shuddered. Had we not had more of the Elixir at the manor, Hans would have died trying to protect the rest of us from Queen Narcissa's wrath.

My chest tightened. If he'd gone down for us, I wouldn't have been able to live with myself. I would be forever thankful that Nicolas Flamel saw fit to give us three vials. Should I ever see him again, I planned on giving the ancient alchemist the biggest hug.

Still asleep, Hans moaned, jolting me out of my thoughts. I

waited, hoping for more than the pained sound, that he'd wake this time, but no. Like the first time, and the second and third, that gut-wrenching moan filled the infirmary, and his eyes remained shut. I supposed it could be worse. I didn't want to hear him scream again. Or have another seizure.

With every checkup, every potion brewed and spell cast, Hannah kept telling me that the moaning was a good sign. He was fighting the curse running through him. That he still felt something *at all* was important. She always tried to assure me there was hope. Despite her efforts, I felt no hope. Negative hope, even.

If Hans didn't wake up, I wasn't sure what I'd do. If he *did* wake up, what would happen between us? Would he be interested in me while he was in such pain? After sitting at his bedside for days, one thing had become clear: I didn't think I could live without him.

My gaze drifted to Queen Narcissa's dagger, which Hannah kept in a glass box on the healer's countertop. Luca had studied the blade many times and deemed the curse contained in the metal to be of mage origin. He also claimed that since he was a powerful mage, he might be able to break the curse.

Hannah and the rest of the *Arcacusto* witches possessed little experience with mage-cursed objects. And while those in the Coven of Shadows and Secrets *were* well-versed in dealing with cursed objects, we rarely dealt with ones created by mages. Those of that magical order generally kept to Isila, and their objects did too.

Luca was our best hope. *Hans's* best hope. And he knew it, for the Italian mage had set to studying the curses created by his magical order with a fervor I'd never seen.

My chest tightened and tears threatened to spill from my

eyes. I wiped them away before they fell. I'd cried more in the last week than I had in my entire life. Hans was worthy of my tears, but I couldn't do it again. Wouldn't. I needed to be strong for him so that when he woke with that curse—*that poison*—pushing through him, he could lean on me.

"Shay?"

I turned to find Meredith waiting at the door, her expression unreadable. Calculated to be a mask. I'd broken down too many times for the others to dare show their own emotions around me.

"Yeah?"

"We're meeting in fifteen minutes in the war room."

The war room. The room with the large table and the pretty tree, bedazzled with gemstones. I wondered if the *Abscondita* Coven ever thought their peaceful gathering place would be called a war room.

"Want to come?" Meredith asked. "Hannah said she's happy to sit with him."

"I'm fine." The only times I'd dared to leave Hans was when I'd had to relieve myself. It showed too. I stank so bad that not even the dried herbs in the infirmary could cover up my smell, and dark circles ringed my eyes. Despite being given an actual bed next to Hans's, I hadn't slept well in the healer's quarters. "Fill me in later. I need to call my mom back."

I was using Mom to get out of work but didn't care. Besides, it was true that she'd been calling me incessantly since we'd come back from Isila. Not that I could blame her. The world had gone down the gutter, and I was her only daughter.

Meredith nodded. "You got it. Should I bring you lunch before we disappear for an hour or two?"

"No." I exhaled as if she'd asked me to run a marathon and

not eat something. To me, they both sounded equally unappealing. "I'll get food when I'm hungry."

A lie. We both knew it was a lie.

"Okay," Meredith replied softly, "see you later."

"Later." I waved, and she disappeared, leaving me alone with Hans again.

CHAPTER THREE

MEREDITH

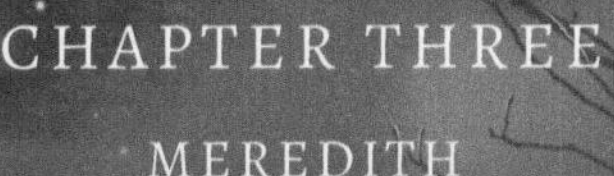

RAIN PELTED MY LITTLE CIRCULAR SHIELD OF MAGIC AND MY BOOTS squished into the sodden grass as I searched for Rabi outside, all the while recounting what I learned during the meeting.

Sydney. Envy took Sydney.

A long, tired exhale parted my lips. Envy had just reinforced the vastness of the world. And with that revelation, another one came: I still needed to find two specific people in this big, messy world.

The holder of the Emerald of Earth and the Sapphire of the Sea. The final *Vindix*.

Would the Covenant have a clue as to where they are?

If so, that could be one good thing to come out of an upcoming meeting with the Covenant, the magical ruling body for our world. A meeting that was happening in a few days' time.

"I just hope they're ready to act once I find them." I twirled the hemp bracelet I wore around my wrist—a new tick of mine when stress came calling, which lately was all the freaking time.

The bracelets were one of Hannah's clever ideas, something she said she used to do as a child. Under Hannah's instruction, Harper, Tana, and I had created hemp bracelets, woven our stones into the material and then tied them tight on our wrists. Enchantments kept the fibers braided tightly and the stones in place. The bracelets were far more secure than slipping the *lapis caelestis* into our pockets, or even wearing them as a necklace, which could easily be ripped from our necks. They weren't cute, but they did the job, and we'd made one for Hans too, just in case. That way, no *Vindix* would lose their *lapis caelesti,* and it kept our hands free for fighting.

Fighting, Goddess, save us. Even if I found the final two tomorrow, and they were completely prepared, we would not be ready to fight the Princes of Hell.

Hans was still comatose, cursed to endure horrific pain if he awoke.

Harper floated through the manor like a shade. She hadn't said a word during the meeting. Just kept looking out the window, waiting for one of the ghosts she'd sent out to return with information on Gunner.

As for me, I understood why my stone might be important to keep from the princes, but not how to best *use it.* Although I'd been happy to simply maintain control of the Opal of Heaven before, now something told me I'd need my *lapis caelesti* for more. But what?

Then there was Rabi. He hadn't even agreed to join us, and no one wanted to ask him to make a decision. After all, the vampires enslaved the man for years. In contrast, he'd been free for just over a week, and we were asking him to fight in a supernatural war against the Princes of the Underworld?

It wasn't fair to him, and a large part of me hated myself for wanting to push him. Yet, here I was, searching for Rabi and hoping for an answer. A *yes, I'll join you*, if I was being honest.

Benedict reported seeing Rabi wandering around outside, but the air witch was no longer in the manor's front yard, so I rounded the side to the back. As I cleared the building, I found him. Rabi, his white markings from the Enchanted Pool still gleaming against the dark ebony skin of his raised arms—as if he still needed the reminder of who he was. Tana also stood in the vast backyard, or the garden as the elder *Arcacustos* called it, practicing magic. Tana laughed as Rabi created an umbrella of air that kept the rain off them and allowed her to form a fire dragon. The fiery creature circled above the pair, maw opened in a silent roar.

My heart warmed. I wasn't close to either Tana or Rabi, but they'd both come here broken people. I'd never forget the day I'd spied Tana in the woods, dark hair gleaming and amber eyes alight, as if from her inner fire. She'd been terrified, but fierce, and her fire burned brightly even when she couldn't fully control it.

Rabi had been terrified too when we'd saved him from Isila. Well, abducted him, really.

Now though, they were smiling. I wouldn't assume they were healed, but as a once-broken person myself, I knew smiling was often a first step.

Feeling creepy for watching them, I stepped out of the shadow of the manor and waved. "Hey guys!"

Tana let out a scream and spun, her hand to her heart. When she saw me, though, she dropped her arms to the side. "Och, Meredith! You put the fear in me!"

I grinned at her turns of phrase, all the more charming with her Scottish accent. She was Greek by birth, but the girl had been raised in Scotland, and it showed in her speech and mannerisms.

"Did you see my dragon?" Tana cocked an eyebrow.

"It was very impressive. You've improved a ton."

"Haven't I?" she beamed.

While I'd been in the vampire kingdom, Tana and Harper had remained here, working on magic. Truth be told, they'd both needed the practice. With Harper not even knowing that she had witch powers, I used to worry that they wouldn't be ready in time, but they'd both improved by leaps and bounds.

"How's practice going?" I came to a stop a few feet away, beneath the air shield Rabi created to keep the rain at bay, and shoving my hands in my pockets for warmth.

"Brilliant. Rabi showed me his magic," Tana replied. "He's quite powerful, isn't he?"

Indeed. I'd seen his power in action, and I wasn't the only one to recognize his potent magic. The vampires had not drained him of blood so that Rabi could use his magic to entertain at their court. Now, hopefully, he'd be using the gift inside him for so much more.

The air elemental remained quiet. Since I'd joined them, he didn't seem to want to meet my eye. That was not unusual. He hadn't warmed to those in the Coven of Shadows and Secrets. Or the elder witches living in the manor. The only person Rabi seemed to enjoy being around was Tana. In every other way, he acted like a deer among a pack of dogs, skittish most of the time.

"I'm glad to hear moving realms hasn't affected your magic," I said to Rabi.

He lifted his gaze from the ground, only to give a single nod and look back down.

Tana cleared her throat and stepped forward. "I'm a wee bit peckish. I'm going ta heid inside." She winked at me.

A slight look of alarm crossed his face, but he nodded goodbye to her, and Tana left us alone in the rain.

I turned to Rabi and clocked his discomfort at being alone with me. I swallowed. Was I a monster for asking this of him? For asking him to join the *Vindix*? Or would I be more of a monster if I did not ask yet again?

No clear-cut answer presented itself, no matter how long I questioned myself. I wanted to give Rabi his space and allow him to heal. Unfortunately, though, seven cities had already fallen. Time was not a luxury we possessed. Not with millions, even billions, of lives on the line.

"Can we talk?" I forced out.

Rabi met my eyes, his dark brown ones still so full of pain. "Yes. I think we should."

"Let's walk," I suggested, sensing that standing around might make him feel like he had to make eye contact which might make him more uncomfortable.

He nodded and fell into step with me, his borrowed tennis shoes squelching in the grass as we walked closer to the forest. His hand continually brushed the fabric of his jeans. Rabi had arrived in clothing from Isila and was still getting used to the jeans and tops Tobias and Stuart had loaned him.

"Are you feeling better? More secure at the manor?"

Squelch. Squelch. Squelch. I inhaled the damp scent of the earth and tried not to dwell on the long pause between us.

"As much as can be expected, I suppose."

"Right. Well, if there's anything we can do to make the transition easier, don't hesitate to speak up."

Goddess, I sounded like a hotel concierge!

Despite how stupid I thought I sounded, I detected the

barest hint of a smile on Rabi's face, so I pushed onward. "You know no one here will hurt you, right?"

"I believe that," he replied. "Though, from what you've told me, I'm not safe here either."

"That's a tall order for anyone on the planet right now."

He cast me a confused glance at my slang, reminding me he truly was from a different world. Isila could connect to our realm via portals, but it wasn't like Earth.

"No one is safe," I amended.

He stopped, turned to me, and I mimicked his actions. "I understand that and have come to a decision about joining you and the rest of the *Vindix*."

I breathed out an exhale. "You have?"

He drew in his own deep breath. "I will join you. Help you." He cast a hand around the garden. "If this world is to be my new home, I don't wish to find myself in the same situation I've been in all of my life—owned by vicious royals. So I will help you stop them."

"Rabi," my voice was tight as relief flooded me. I'd barely slept for days, not knowing what he'd choose. "I can't tell you how happy I am to hear that."

No trace of happiness appeared on his face. "However, I do not have my sacred stone—the Amethyst of Air, as you called it."

I'd been wondering about that. I hadn't felt the Amethyst, but he had his talisman, which was how I'd recognized him in Isila. I'd spent hours wondering if I should just ask about the Amethyst. Tobias had warned me time and time again to take it slow, to wait for Rabi to give information as he saw fit. Rabi would need time and space and understanding to heal from what he'd been through. If that were ever even possible.

"That's okay," I replied, trying to be positive. "I can find it. I'm a seeker witch, so that's kind of my job. Do you know anything about it? Or the side of the family who passed it down?"

The two stones that found replacement families—the Diamond of Souls and the Pearl of Hell—were already accounted for by Harper and Hans being among the *Vindix*. On the flip side of the coin, Rabi's family line had to have held the same *lapis caelesti* for thousands of years. I only hoped that they remembered how important it was and that he recalled something about them.

"I heard very little about my family," he answered. "My mother was a blood slave. A human one. My father was a witch. I believe his line would be the one to investigate."

"Do you know where he lived? Maybe your mother mentioned it?"

Rabi swallowed. "Not really. My mother used to speak of a place called New Orleans but vaguely. The vampires compel slaves to forget their lives, but it's impossible to erase an entire life. Lots of slaves remember bits and pieces, like their full names and important memories. Mother was enamored by the place, so it had to have been important to her. She mentioned being there with my father too."

My stomach sank. It was a clue, but unfortunately, New Orleans was one of the cities taken by the Princes of Hell. I wasn't sure which prince, but I was not keen to enter their territories before I must.

"What's your father's name?" I really hoped that he knew it.

He met my gaze, and no fear lined his dark features or sparked in his soulful eyes. As if claiming his spot and his future was already changing the man. "Louis Rosser."

"I'm going to look him up, if that's okay with you? He might know where the Amethyst is. Heck, he might even possess it himself."

Rabi gazed into the woods. "I think that's a good idea."

CHAPTER FOUR

HARPER

Weak morning light drifted into my room, fighting through the incessant rain and cold to thaw a freeze that penetrated all the way into my soul. I curled into a ball on my large four-poster bed, complete with a plaid canopy, not ready to face the day yet.

Gunner was still missing, and with each passing day, I broke a little more. My emotions screamed a truth I had barely dared to let myself consider. A truth that, months ago, I would have found preposterous.

But truths were just that, and this one hit me hard: I was falling for Gunner Bryant—chatterbox, alphablood, and previous pain in my butt.

I'd sent three spirits out to find him. Aya sent six. None had returned, and I no longer sensed my tether to my trio. Of course, I hadn't been able to feel it since they'd disappeared through the manor's wards, but Aya had been so sure that it was there. That I was strong enough to keep connected to them.

While I appreciated her confidence in me, *I* wasn't so sure I deserved it.

I grabbed a pillow and pulled it close to my belly for comfort. I didn't like to think that Gunner was gone. Though it made no logical sense, I thought I'd feel such a thing—somehow—and I did not feel his absence. But where did he go that he could not call? To send a text? Sure, the Internet out here was spotty, but things still came through . . . I swallowed the lump rising in my throat.

I needed to get out of bed and occupy my mind. Otherwise, I'd make myself crazy.

So I pushed up, only to find myself face to face with a ghost. A small scream left my lips before I smothered it with my hands.

"Miss Harper." The ghost took off his opaque hat and inclined his head. His attire would have looked at home in 1930s New York. "Apologies for startling you."

My hands dropped from where they covered my mouth. As much as I wanted to cuss out the ghost for almost making me wet the bed, now I recognized him. One of my trio.

"Did you find Gunner?"

"I did, miss."

"Alive?"

"Yes."

I waited, but the ghost did not seem inclined to speak further. My hands landed on my hips. "Then where is he?"

"New Orleans, more accurately, he's in a very dark place."

My heart stuttered. A fallen city. The very same one that, last night, Meredith had told the group that we might find information on Rabi's family. Was this yet another act of convergence? Of fate pulling the *Vindix* closer and closer together so we could work as a team? How did Gunner fit into the convergence, though? He wasn't a *Vindix*, though he was connected to three of us.

"What do you mean by dark place?" I asked, pulling myself back on track through sheer force of will.

The question of why he had not contacted me—or anyone—was solved. Those in the fallen cities remained isolated. In the Princes' of Hell's kingdoms, no phones worked. Not even older technology, like a telegram, worked. Either that or no one had tried, and I found that impossible to believe. If there was a single way to make contact with the outside world, people would find it.

"Dark in the sense that it is the darkest part of the city. The palace of a fallen prince."

"Old Ones protect him." I pulled my blankets tight around me. "Who's holding him hostage?"

We'd made guesses which prince ruled where, but the only city we knew for certain who ruled it was Los Angeles. The rest of the cities remained mysteries.

"Prince Belhor, Prince of—"

"Sloth," I finished for him, then sat up straighter. "I need to ask another favor of you. Of any and all the ghosts I'd sent out."

"Which is?"

For the first time, the ghost looked annoyed. I supposed that was understandable. I'd only sent them out into the world to find Gunner. He probably thought I'd release him from duty after completing his task. That he could go back to his perfect ghosty life or whatever.

However, the idea of ghosts infiltrating the fallen cities and retrieving information, well, that changed the game.

"Can you go to the fallen cities that are not LA and New

Orleans? And can you tell me who rules them? Maybe start with London, since it's close?"

He stared, those transparent eyes seemingly judging me, and the chill in the room deepened. The seconds stretched on, and my trepidation that the ghost would deny me mounted before he let out a long huff and gave a single nod. "I will go. Mind you, it will take time—a few days at least, but I will go."

I leapt from the bed, intent on hugging the ghost and stopping inches short of doing so. He seemed to understand my intent though, and the lingering annoyance on his face vanished.

"Thank you," I breathed. "This will help us."

"I know," the ghost said, "and I still have descendants who walk this earth. They don't remember me, but I do this for them, as much as you, Miss Harper."

"If you want, I can tell them what you did. After."

His face lit up. "I'd like that." He put his hat back on his head. "I should be going." He vanished through the wall, on yet another quest for me.

With a new fire burning inside me, I dressed and went in search of Luca. The *Arcacustos* would expect me to study and train, but I hoped to convince Luca and the rest of S&S to go to New Orleans today. Gunner had suffered long enough.

The manor was quiet, but after being here for so long, we all had routines in place. Luca was no exception, so I strode right for the kitchen and found him alone, sipping on a coffee and eating toast. Both scents warmed me somewhat, briefly reminding me of home and simpler times.

"Good morning," Luca said at my approach. "You're up earlier than usual."

"A ghost found Gunner," I said by way of greeting. "He's in New Orleans at Prince Belhor's mansion."

Luca's dark brown eyes widened as he set his cup down. "You're sure?"

"That's what the ghost said. I don't know why he'd lie." I inhaled. "I sent the ghost out again, to learn which Prince of Hell rule each city. Figured we'd need a leg up when we went in, guns blazing."

"Brilliant," Luca mused. "And very lucky they'll do as you say."

I shrugged, playing it off as if the ghost had not initially seemed inclined to deny me. "I think it's a sign. Meredith said Rabi's father might be in the same city. Maybe it's that convergence she keeps talking about."

I said it like I wasn't sure, but I believed in the theory of convergence of the *Vindix*. After all, Hans and I had been in S&S for years. Meredith found the coven too, and Tana had shown up at this very manor. The *Vindix* were truly drawn to one another, which should make Meredith's job easier. That was when you didn't factor in things like one had been a slave in Isila.

But even that . . . Meredith had been called to that court. Was it a matter of fate working in our favor? Even if the path fate spun was not an easy one, it lit the way.

"It might be," Luca agreed.

"We should plan a trip to New Orleans today then," I said, my voice rising with excitement. "We could be there at sunrise, find Rabi's father, then save Gunner!"

"No."

"No!" My fists clenched. "Why not?!"

"Harper, we cannot run blindly into a Prince of Hell's territory. We need a *real* plan." Luca sighed, which only heated my blood more. "Not to mention, if we're going to infiltrate a kingdom and defeat a prince, Sloth's might be the one to begin with. The easiest—based on his sin. And most importantly of all, we'll need Hans to do so. Hans at his full power, which means we also still need to convince Richard Brons to give Hans back his wizard magic."

That was too much. Hans was still in a coma, the effects of an otherworldly curse pummeling him. Since being placed in one of the rooms on the lower level and magically imprisoned, Brons had not cooperated. Besides that, I wasn't sure we'd be able to defeat any prince without *all* the *Vindix* present. Defeating Sloth hadn't even been on my radar. Only helping Rabi find his stone and saving Gunner—mostly the latter, if I was being honest.

"What if Hans never gets better?" I hated myself for asking the question. Not only was Hans a coven member and a *Vindix*, he was a friend. Still, someone had to be realistic here.

"He will. I've been researching mage curses and found something promising. I'm heading to the infirmary after I finish breakfast."

"Gunner has been there for over a week!" My voice rose with each word. I was becoming frantic, so unlike me, as was reflected in the surprise on Luca's face.

"I'm aware. I was there the day he disappeared, and I care for Gunner too, Harper. But I cannot risk the other members of S&S, and certainly not the *Vindix*, to charge into a dark kingdom without forethought. We must plan, and I'd like to speak with the Covenant before we go too."

Old Ones! No longer able to handle the conversation, I spun. "Fine. Tell me when you're done sipping coffee and ready to really get things done!"

"Harper, I—"

I slammed the kitchen door behind me, and the sound echoed in the empty hall. No longer could I listen to Luca, no matter how practical his reasoning. I needed action, and a way to move this mission along.

So I sought my mentor Aya, a different plan already forming in my mind. One that, if I pulled it off, would make it impossible for Luca to deny me again.

CHAPTER FIVE

TOBIAS

A RENTAL CAR SLOWED TO PULL OFF THE PAVED ROAD AND ON TO the entrance of the long gravel drive that led to the *Abscondita* manor house. Hidden in the woods, I stepped out, sure that they'd already spotted me.

Serena waved out the window. Behind her, the midday sun peeked through the clouds and dappled light shone on her ebony skin. Unmarred skin, I noted, and hoped the rest of my sister was the same. Hoped that she'd escaped the Blood Court without issue and injury.

Communication out of the manor was now restricted. Luca conversed with Covenant officials, but the rest of us made minimal contact with those we loved. In the time we'd been back, I'd only spoken with my sister once, when Serena had called and informed me that she had returned to our world. I'd told her to get Giselle and come here to safety. Once we were all together, we could catch one another up on matters.

"Wasn't expecting a welcome party on the side of the road," Serena called out, an easy smile on her face that made me relax a touch.

"The *Abscondita* Coven strengthened the wards. Many times, in fact," I replied. We'd infuriated the royals of the Blood Court *and* the Princes of Hell were our primary targets. We could assume that we were targeted by them too. That was a lot of threats which meant this place needed every protection possible.

Funny to think that at one point, we'd only been concerned about the Ordo Aeternum, a faction of radicalized supernaturals who thought those with magic should rule and rule cruelly.

Though they joined the princes. Perhaps those from the underworld have shown the members of the OA a thing or two since allying? I bloody well hope not.

I slipped into the back seat. "You have to be escorted on to the property by someone marked by the coven. Someone like me." Miriam had done it herself, though I didn't feel the magical mark she'd placed on me. I supposed it didn't matter, as long as it worked to let us on to the property.

Serena put the car in drive, and as she eased onto the gravel road, Giselle turned to me, green eyes twinkling.

"Things are heating up, are they not, Tobias?" Her blonde hair was tucked into an elegant bun that suggested nothing ever got to Giselle. In truth, little did. My maker was remarkably grounded and always held her cards close to her chest.

I gave a single nod. "I have much to fill you in on, but first, Serena, you escaped unharmed, right?"

Serena winked in the mirror. "Of course, brother. Were you worried?"

"Yes." Our own escape from the vampire kingdom had ended in disaster.

"Well, that human you sent to warn me got there in time. I took one of Aldéric's horses and ran out the opposite gate before it closed. Snow in the mountain ranges delayed me, but once I reached the Autumn Court, I spoke with the prince there, and he allowed me to use his portal."

"Prince Kerian?"

"The same charmer," Serena replied.

I exhaled. I owed Kerian quite a debt for helping my sister.

"Good. Well, I'm relieved that you escaped, Serena." I turned toward my maker. "Also that the queen didn't seek to target you while she was in Paris."

"I know why," Giselle answered, her tone dipping.

"Pray tell."

"The queen's mate died."

I sucked in a breath as understanding slammed into me. To escape the vampire kingdom, my mate had hurled a locket filled with riot fire at the vampires—the king in particular. Such a fire caught early, burned unnaturally hot, and was incredibly difficult to put out. Meredith had struck true, and now King Vladistrica was dead.

"This is not good," I whispered.

"No, it's not," Giselle replied. "But let us stick to one issue at a time, Tobias. Or at least, the issues that are in the same world as us."

"What if Narcissa hunts us here?"

"She might, but not until after her mourning period. In the vampire kingdom, that lasts six months."

"She'll do it herself?" In the grand scheme of things, six months was nothing to a vampire, but if someone killed Meredith, I'd hunt them to the death. No ritual would ever stop me.

"When the mourning period is over, Queen Narcissa will want to be the one to find and kill her mate's killer herself."

Giselle eyed me with sorrow. "When that day comes, we must worry. But not until then."

We had six months. It was better than having to look over our shoulders every second now. At the very least, Giselle was right. I needed to use this time to focus on the threats that were closer to home.

As we neared the manor, the trees cleared, and I spied Rabi sitting on the front steps, eating a sandwich. The *Arcacustos* had released the *Vindix* for lunch then. I hoped Meredith would come find me.

"That's the one from the ball, isn't it?" Serena asked.

"He is."

"How's he adjusting?"

"As well as expected for someone who has only been a free man for a little over a week."

Rabi was quiet and stuck to himself. When he was not alone, he was with Tana, or researching in the *Abscondita* library. Despite his traumatic upbringing, he seemed to be adjusting. There was only one person who put him on edge: me.

"I should tell you he's not very comfortable around our kind," I admitted before either of my family members could exit the car. "Especially knowing that we're part of the vampire royal line. He hasn't been hostile, but I can tell that I put him on edge. I assume you will too."

The bright expression that Serena wore dimmed. "We'll keep our distance unless he initiates contact."

That was all that needed to be said, so we opened the car doors. The moment my family and I exited, Rabi's shoulders tensed.

I waved, trying to diffuse the situation before one could

begin. "Rabi, this is my sire and my sister, Giselle and Serena. They plan to help us find the sacred stones."

Rabi swallowed, but the scent of fear that the wind had picked up and stuffed up my nostrils only strengthened. I was sure my sister and our maker smelled it too.

"Hello," he replied, his voice strangled.

He was staring at Giselle. Had he seen her at court during one of her visits?

"*Enchanté*, Rabi." Giselle inclined her head, doing her best not to appear intimidating. As she had many years of acting under her belt, she succeeded.

"I'm glad you got out of that kingdom," Serena added. "What a horror show."

Rabi's bushy eyebrows drew together as he worked out what a horror show was. "It was my life."

None of us spoke. We'd all been to the Blood Court many times and seen the slaves. While it was upsetting and wrong, I'd never done a thing about it until recently, and there were still so many more slaves there.

Guilt built inside me. Desperate to avoid the unpleasant sensation I gestured to his sandwich. "It's lunch time?"

Rabi nodded.

"You wouldn't know where Meredith is, would you?"

The air elemental shook his head. "She ran off the moment the *Arcacustos* let us out of the library. Seemed to have—"

Before he could finish his sentence, the door to the manor burst open and my mate appeared, and my heart gave a hard thump. As if she could feel her effect on me, a victorious smile bloomed on Meredith's face. "You're here!"

She bounded down the steps and veered to Giselle. I hid my smile, proud that my mate was honoring vampire code and seeking the eldest among us first.

"*Ma chérie*, we must branch out your color palette," Giselle murmured as she kissed Meredith on each cheek.

Meredith laughed. "Black forever, Giselle. Though, if you're offering to take me shopping *and* pay for the damage, I might be convinced to purchase a few other colors."

I snorted. As if Meredith needed to worry about money. We were together, and I had enough for many lifetimes. Still, I supposed that, for her, wealth would take getting used to and a shopping trip was more about bonding, anyway.

"Consider it a date, darling." Giselle twirled in hand through the air. "After we've dealt with the hellspawn. An afternoon of champagne for you and haute couture for the both of us will be well deserved."

My mate grinned and went to Serena, who folded Meredith in a warm embrace. When she pulled away from my sister, Meredith shook her head. "I'm so glad to see you. We were worried."

"No need to be," Serena assured her. They'd bonded quickly, and their growing relationship warmed my chest.

Meredith came to me next. Her delicious scent made me want to steal her away as she kissed me on the lips, then nestled into my side and held up a folded piece of paper. "I spent half of my lunch hour fighting with the Internet—they really need to upgrade—but I found it."

"What's it?" I asked.

Before she answered, Meredith turned her two-toned gaze on Rabi. "I have an address for Rabi's father."

The wizard stiffened. "How?"

Seeing as he had never used the Internet, Meredith's feat must've seemed incredible to him.

"It's not in the library, but there's a thing in this world called the Internet and it's like . . ." Meredith let out a thoughtful hum, "like one enormous book with a lot of the world's knowledge. It has information on people too. I searched for the name you gave me, and some information about your father came up. He lived with a woman who shared his last name."

"A wife?" Rabi asked.

"I didn't do any research on her," Meredith replied. "Does that change you wanting to go meet him?"

The wizard fell quiet before he shook his head. "He was bound to have some sort of family. And we need the stone. So no."

His tone was not convincing, but there was nothing to be done. Rabi spoke the truth. We required the Amethyst of Air, and if his father had it, then we needed to make contact.

"Okay." Meredith smiled at Rabi. "Good. The sooner you have that stone in hand, the sooner you can practice. Not that you need to practice much, I guess. You already know your magic—and that you're powerful."

While Rabi had not committed to joining the *Vindix* until yesterday, he *had* given us displays of his power. The trees surrounding the garden were still recovering—save for the one that he'd toppled. I wasn't sure I'd ever seen such a powerful air elemental, be they witch, fae, or other.

Rabi spoke softly when he answered. "I appreciate that."

"I wish I was in the same boat," Meredith said. "If my powers were at all connected to my stone, I'd feel better about this. But aside from the Opal of Heaven being important because it's the Pearl of Hell's opposite—and we need to keep it out of evil hands—I feel useless. Once all the *Vindix* are found, I won't have a place."

"Of course you will!" Serena said. "Fighting alongside me!"

"And me," Giselle added with a confident smirk, "it will be a family affair."

In more ways than one. My elder brother, Raphael, was on the opposing side of the oncoming war. I didn't like to consider what would happen when we met again.

"Excuse me?" Rabi came three steps closer, confusion clouding his face. "Are you saying that you don't know how to use your stone?"

"Not really," Meredith replied. "Hans's mother, she's a queen in Hell but not bad, I promise—well, she told me the Opal is best kept away from the princes. They would want to lock it up. Destroy it too, if possible."

"Remind me what it does?" He didn't look like he needed a reminder, he looked like he knew, but Meredith obliged.

"The Opal can counteract the Pearl, which controls others and causes madness. It also brings joy back into the world. But how do I *practice* that? It might be something I have to do at the spur of the moment."

Rabi cocked his head, and his gaze bounced between me and Meredith. "But your mate is a vampire who can compel others, is he not?"

"Wha—*ohmygod*, we're so stupid!" My mate spun to gaze up at me, her eyes bulging. "*Tobias!* You can compel someone, and I can try to use the stone to reinstate their free will! Maybe their joy too? Can compulsion make people sad too? Actually, who cares? For where we're going, freewill is enough!"

I blinked, unable to understand how we had not seen it before. How short-sighted we'd been. In LA, we might not have needed the Opal to keep us safe from the sin of pride, to keep us in our own minds. The kingdom had been so new and the first of its kind, so perhaps it was less guarded? Or Lucifer simply had a light hand on his sin? Or maybe he didn't think he needed it, as filled with pride as he surely was.

I thanked all the gods ever to exist that we hadn't needed the Opal the day we'd infiltrated LA. Until we'd found Queen Lilith, we hadn't possessed a single *lapis caelesti*, anyway.

The *Arcacustos* assured us that the *lapis caelesti* would help fight the demon's sins and after more researching, everyone was inclined to believe the sins would fill those new kingdoms.

I supposed I should look at Lucifer not using his sin in his kingdom as a rare stroke of luck.

And with my maker before me, I spotted another stroke. While I was skilled in compulsion, Giselle was a league above. Being that much closer to the vampire king and queen in the Laurent bloodline made her far more powerful than me. Giselle could mind control as easily as blinking.

If Giselle took away someone's free will using compulsion, and Meredith broke them out of it, well . . . that might change the game.

Prince Orien, Prince of Wrath, had used his sin in New York to devastating effect. People had raged. And when he'd used the Pearl, people had gone mad, even throwing themselves from windows.

What if Meredith reversed such inclinations? What if she could provide a bubble free of the intoxication of sin for the coven until we killed the princes? She might even shield an army.

"Love." I gripped my mate's hand. "We need to find an *Arcacusto* and tell them that you'll be training with my family this afternoon."

CHAPTER SIX

SHAY

"RIGHT NOW, THE IDEA IS TO CONTAIN THE CURSE, RATHER THAN break it." Luca's fingers tapped the counter in the infirmary. Between us, Hans lay sleeping.

I blinked and cast a glance at Hannah, who stood at the foot of the bed.

She, too, looked bewildered when she asked. "And how do you suppose we'll do that?"

I'd never heard of containing a curse before. While a part of me thought it sounded improbable, even dumb, this was Luca freaking Moretti proposing the idea. He'd spent days researching curses, even going as far as light-traveling back to the S&S tomb in New Haven and rifling through Yale's extensive supernatural library because the *Abscondita* Coven had scarce information on mage curses.

"I don't think you two can do anything," Luca answered. "But I might be able to."

"Explain."

"As Rabi said, a mage gifted the vampire queen her dagger, and I'm sure that the curse's origin is in mage magic. Not fae or elven or dragon, which makes a difference, seeing as I'm a mage with direct ancestry to Isila. To the most powerful family there too."

Hannah's eyebrows shot up. It wasn't common knowledge that Luca was a bastard-born son of King Tyra, the most powerful mage in Isila.

"It's likely I'm stronger than whoever cursed the blade. That I can, at the very least, contain the magic flowing through Hans."

"Will that reduce his pain?" Hannah asked as her hand circled the wooden bedpost. It had to be odd for her, asking healing questions to someone who had no practice in the magical art. But then again, nothing about Hans's condition was normal.

"*If* I can contain the curse, there's a chance that his pain will reduce. It might also make the curse easier to attack or eliminate—once I figure out a way to do so."

Hannah cleared her throat. "I suppose it's something. Which is better than what I've been doing. I hate seeing my patients in constant pain."

"We should try," I agreed. The echo of that night when I'd awoken to his shriek, only to do nothing to help, haunted me. "If there's any chance it can help him, or even minimize the pain enough so that he wakes up, then it's worth it. When he's able to talk, Hans can help us to better help him."

I didn't really know what I was saying, but I was desperate for Hans to wake up. To look alive again. *To be him.*

Hannah cleared her throat. "It's worth a go."

Luca gave her a soft smile. "I'd like to try it now. Is that okay, given any potions he's received? Nothing will interact negatively?"

"I'll stand by in case something bad happens, but he should be fine. Or at least, the same as he is now."

So not fine at all I almost said before I bit back the retort. Hannah had worked tirelessly to bring Hans back from the brink of death. She didn't deserve even an ounce of anger. It wasn't her fault that she wasn't well-versed in mage magic. Why would she be? There were so few mages in this world that studying it over other types of magic would make as much sense as her studying nephilim magic. That was to say, none.

Luca pulled a chair up to Hans's side. I remained seated in mine, the one between my bed and Hans's. The one molding to my butt cheeks with how much I'd been sitting in it of late.

"What should I do?" I asked.

"Hold his hand. Be there for him," Luca said. "I can't be sure this won't hurt and, if he wakes, he'll need a friendly face."

I swallowed and hoped Hans saw me that way. After I'd kissed him, I'd gone all weird and then we'd basically been running for our lives. What did he think of the kiss? Had he even thought about it at all?

Stop being so selfish. My inner voice sounded so much like my mother's it grated, but I ignored that too. *It doesn't matter right now. Be there for him.*

I gripped Hans's hand and leaned closer. Hannah positioned herself near her workbench, within reach of a hundred different remedies in case we needed them. With everyone in place, Luca closed his eyes and laid a tanned hand on Hans's chest.

I couldn't see Luca's power, but the air shifted when he began to pour magic into Hans. It warmed, and the air hummed, as if Luca was expending so much energy some disappeared into the air before it latched on to Hans.

I shot a glance at Hannah, who met my eyes. She shrugged a shoulder, as if to say *I don't know either, just be ready.*

An exhale parted my lips as I searched for a sign that whatever Luca was doing inside Hans was working. So far, I saw no difference. My stomach began to churn, and in an effort to keep calm, I dropped my gaze to Hans's tattoos. He'd been collecting his ink for years. Some images were so young, so unlike the Hans I knew now. Like the d20 die I assumed harkened back to his D&D days. Some images, however, were pure Hans.

The wrench signifying his love of working on cars. The runes, which I assumed were real magical runes and not just something he'd picked up—though I couldn't be sure as I could not read them. And my favorite, the image of a small home nestled amongst snowy drifts. He'd once told me that it was his family home in Romania.

I hope he can go back there. I hope . . . oh!

The skin beneath my hand warmed and that heat seemed to ripple across Hans's finger bones. I cast a glance at Luca and sucked in a breath. When had he started sweating so much?

Luca gave a sheepish smile. "I called the poisonous curse out of that hand, and you . . . Well you felt it, didn't you?"

"I did," I replied, and my mouth went a bit dry. "Have you done most of his body?"

"No. Only his head, and I'm now working up this arm." Luca's chin dipped to the one closest to him, his hands still on Hans's chest, mage magic still pouring into the hellblooded wizard. "It's a slow process."

"Where are you going to store the curse?" My heart rate

spiked as I considered the many vulnerable places in the body. Where would be the most dangerous? The least?

"Once I have it under control, I'll move it into his femur," Luca said. "To keep it away from the most vital organs, in case my containment fails at some point."

"But what about walking?"

Luca exhaled and sweat dripped from his chin. "Hannah?"

"Perhaps lower? In the calf? I'm thinking in case . . . The worst happens. But not the foot. Given the nature of the curse, he may not be able to walk if the containment is not foolproof."

In case the worst happened? Would the curse somehow explode, and his leg would need amputation? What the hell!?

I was about to say something, but Luca nodded. "Believe me, ladies, I'll be putting the strongest barrier I can around the curse. It's just uncharted territory."

I swallowed my negative remarks. The thing was, they were both doing the best they could for Hans in an impossible situation. That Luca had actually moved the curse was astounding. If containing the curse helped Hans wake up, that was infinitely better than a perpetual coma. I hoped he could walk. And that he wouldn't lose a limb.

Stop, I told myself, halting my thoughts. *Do not spiral.*

"I'll work downwards," Luca said to himself.

Hannah and I fell into silence as Luca pulled the curse from Hans's body, his blood, maybe even his bones.

An hour passed, then two. Luca worked as fast as possible, but by the time we neared two and a half hours, he'd still only managed to pull the curse from Hans's torso. That much seemed to be exhausting the mage too. He wasn't merely glistening. No, sweat soaked Luca's collar and armpits. I was about to suggest that he take a break—if that was even an option—when Hans's eyelids fluttered.

I gasped, pointed at Hans's face. "Did you two see that?"

"See what?" Luca panted as he worked on Hans's lower abdomen.

"His eyelids. They fluttered."

Hannah's face brightened. "It might be working then."

"Heavens! I hope so!" I trained my gaze on Luca. "You're doing great, but are you going to need a break?"

"I'm not sure I dare. I might only have it in me to try and contain the curse once."

Pulling it from Hans wasn't even the hardest part. Heavens, Luca was a trooper.

"I'll get you water," Hannah said, eyeing the mage again carefully. "Food too. You'll need to keep your strength up."

"Thank you." Luca glanced down the length of Hans's long legs. "That's a good idea. We might be here for hours longer."

CHAPTER SEVEN

MEREDITH

Sweat dripped down my face.

"Climb that tree," Giselle barked, the magic of compulsion thick in her voice as she pointed to a tree across the backyard, far enough away to give me a fighting chance to test our theory.

Stuart, our latest test subject, spun on his heel and marched for the tree. On the sidelines, Miriam, Gloria, and Claire watched with frowns on their lined faces. They'd each had their turn at being compelled, and not one of the fiery matriarchs had enjoyed it.

Worse, I hadn't been able to free a single one from Giselle's powers. I was failing.

Maybe this doesn't work at all? Or am I that bad at using the Opal?

"Concentrate, love," Tobias called out. "You can do it."

I rolled my shoulders back and focused on Stuart.

To say I'd tried everything was an understatement. I'd verbally and mentally commanded people to stop doing whatever the vampires were making them do at that moment. I'd touched the compelled person. I'd rubbed the Opal on them. I'd leapt in front of them and thrust the stone out like some crazy superhero.

After all those attempts, one thing was clear: my natural magic was not in line with what the Opal wanted me to do. It shouldn't come as a surprise, I supposed. Seeker magic dealt with things, not people. And while my hedge magic had grown over time, I'd only known I was a witch for a few months and was definitely still a beginner in the realm of hedge magic.

But this was important, so despite the crushing weight of disappointment that had long since settled in my belly, I focused on Stuart, still shuffling toward the tree, nearly there and about to climb it. Could the poor guy even climb trees? If not, he'd hurt himself.

I squinted, and, once again, tried to speak mind to mind with Stuart, like a vampire.

Stop! Stuart, stop! You don't have to listen to her! You're your own man.

He touched the tree, the same one where Benedict was bathing himself among the branches, lifted his leg and began to climb. As the tree was wet from the near constant autumn rains, Stuart slipped, but that did not deter him. He hiked that leg up and tried again. Benedict glared down, and my spicy familiar rolled his eyes. Even he was getting fed up with my failures.

Now with familiar desperation mounting inside me, I pushed out my wrist on which the Opal rested. *Stuart, stop climbing. You don't want to. You're afraid of heights!*

It was a sheer bit of evil genius on Giselle's part, getting the elder witches to tell her what they disliked and feared. She'd used those very fears in each compulsion. To make it more obvious that she had complete and utter control. As if anyone would have doubted such a thing.

Stuart slipped again, back to the ground and fell on his butt.

I sighed and, reaching for my hedge magic, tried a different tack. I pulled pure hedge magic and thrust it at Stuart. It hit him in the back, and as my magic struck, I held the Opal tight and commanded him to stop, yet again.

And for what felt like the millionth time, nothing happened.

What the hell am I supposed to do?!

Tears pricked my eyes. I wiped them away before they fell, feeling defeated and so stupid. Maybe if we'd figured this out sooner, I would be able to do this already. Or we could have sought a specialist in breaking compulsion. Did such a person exist?

"Stop, Giselle," Tobias said.

Stuart froze in trying to climb the tree and let out a booming laugh as if it were all one big joke. Maybe to him it was. I only saw my parade of failures.

Tobias appeared at my side. "Meredith, love, I have an idea."

"Good, because I'm flat out." I cringed at how whiny I sounded. Besides hating to fail, the stress of everything I had to do was getting to me, but I needed to suck it up. Too many people depended on me, on what I might be able to do —what fate might intend for me. I would *not* be a whiny baby.

"I'm going to compel you."

My brows furrowed. "Tobias, I can't even pull someone else out of a compulsion. How am I going to help myself?"

"You're not. You're going to come along with me as I

compel another person. I'm going to take you as a sort of side-along experiment."

"Uh, can you do that?"

"I've never tried, but we're mates. If anyone can do this with me, it will be you, Meredith." He squeezed my hand. "And if this is successful, I'm going to show you that there is always a weakness to be exploited. That way, you have an idea of where to begin."

"Do it." There was too much to lose not to try. "Show me."

Tobias twisted to the vampires and witches watching us. "I need another volunteer to be compelled."

Miriam stepped forward; her steel-blue eyes narrowed on my mate. "I'll have another go. But don't you dare try and make me climb a bloody tree."

"I wouldn't do that," Tobias assured her.

I repressed a snort. She might be a tough old bird, but the witch had little muscle. I doubted she'd get more than a foot off the ground.

"You should know, Miriam, that I won't be the only one in your mind," Tobias told her. "I'm going to compel you both and then bring Meredith inside to show her how to break a compulsion from the inside out."

"Very well," Miriam replied. "If you think this will work."

"I do." Tobias rolled his neck. "Perhaps not with Meredith's normal magic, but with the Opal, she can do this. She only has to be shown how the obstacle, which in this case is compulsion, works first."

Miriam said nothing. She only gave Tobias a stern look that indicated she was ready. A moment later, her eyes went vacant.

"Open your mouth as wide as you can, stick out your tongue, and cross your eyes," Tobias commanded.

Miriam did as he instructed, showing his full control of her. In her right mind, Miriam would never do such a thing. Probably not even in the privacy of her own room.

"Now, Meredith." Tobias's voice was like a caress. "Are you ready?"

"As I'll ever be."

He gave me a reassuring smile he had not bothered to give anyone else, and all my worries lifted and everything around me clouded.

Meredith?

Yes, I replied.

I'm going to loosen my hold on you and then take you with me into Miriam's mind. Are you ready?

I am.

The moment I said so, the sense of flying overcame me. A second later, Tobias was showing me something I'd never seen before. A wall of sorts, one made of pure steel.

This is my control on her mind, Tobias said. *Obviously, I can make it stronger or weaker, depending on how much I wish to control her. Not every vampire can do so, but I can. Giselle and Serena too. The princes' control will be of a high level and possibly look similar.*

I studied the wall. He'd made his compulsion absolute and with this in place, Miriam would do nothing unless Tobias bade her. Unlike other compulsions where I'd learned people could go about their day and appear normal. In those, they'd only follow the instructions a vampire gave them, if the situation arose. He'd been smart to create something so unbreakable. The princes' control would be absolute too.

But how am I going to break in?

We're mates. I had a feeling I might show you something I've shown no one, and you being here tells me I was right.

I jolted. Right, he could hear everything.

Tobias smirked. *Something you want to tell me that you don't want others to hear?*

Since we're in Miriam's head, let's keep things PG. Miriam would kill us if we started getting spicy in here.

Tobias laughed and then guided me to the wall, up close and to the far right. *My compulsion appears absolute, but there has to be a chink in all armor. Otherwise, Miriam could not do anything without me. Not even draw breath.*

I blinked. *Where?*

Down.

I did as he said and felt my head following the movement. A reflex, I supposed. A weird one, considering that I was not physically here, but whatever. It didn't matter because at that moment, I saw what he meant. At the bottom of the wall was a hole big enough for a mouse to wiggle through.

Is that the reason sometimes people's eyes cloud over when they're compelled? I asked. I'd seen it done a few times now, and that always varied.

No, cloudy is the default state, but if a vampire wants the person to look normal, they can alter the appearance of their eyes. We often do it because we want to hide our control.

You learn something new every day, I said sarcastically, as if this wasn't all new to me.

And you're about to go deeper into your studies. I think you can tell the Opal to attack there, and you might be able to break Miriam free of my powers, Tobias said.

Riiiiiight.

Awareness is a large part of the battle. I'm leaving now.

I shuddered and was back in my mind, alone.

"You can do this," Tobias said, still nearby. "I think this is what you need. Envision that hole. Tell the Opal to seek the weakness. To break it open."

The air buzzed with anticipation. I swallowed and closed my eyes, hoping that I didn't fail them again as I brought up the image of the tiny hole at the bottom of the metal gate.

All right, Opal, there's a weakness in that compulsion, near the bottom. Find it and break it, so Miriam is in her own mind. I'll show you.

In my mental image, I zoomed in on the hole and saw myself pointing at it. *There. Break through that.*

I expected nothing to happen. I expected to open my eyes and find Miriam standing in front of me like a statue again, slack-jawed, her tongue sticking out, and cross-eyed.

What I did not expect was for the Opal to warm, and for a jolt of magic to shoot up my arm and a tendril of gold magic to connect Miriam and me. I gasped as the tendril wrapped around her, and suddenly, Miriam was frowning again.

"No success in taking her inside?" she asked.

Tobias was grinning like a fool. "On the contrary, Miriam. You were freed by my mate."

"Finally," Benedict drawled, still up in the tree branches.

I glared at him, but the cat looked unbothered and started licking his belly again.

Miriam's blue eyes went wide. "I didn't feel abnormal."

"You were standing there looking silly for a while," Stuart told her, which made Miriam scowl. "And the magic came from Meredith. She used the Opal of Heaven to break a vampire's compulsion."

"I-I can't believe that worked," I admitted.

Serena jumped in. "But it did. You *can* do it. You needed that proof to yourself."

"And now, you must go again." Giselle stepped forward and rubbed her delicate hands together. At that moment, she looked so much like a supervillain that I took a step back.

Goddess, my mate's maker could be scary as hell when she wanted to be. "You must break every compulsion we can show you. In every person here. You must practice in as many ways as you can until you can do this in your sleep. Then we can focus on you practicing to shield with the Opal before anyone has time to take control."

As annoying as that sounded, and as tired as I already was, she was right. In a way, the Opal and I needed to bond. I needed to understand it as much as I'd needed to see how a mind might be blocked off—controlled.

"Let's keep going," I said, ready for round two and willing to work for as long as this might take.

Luca had gotten off to a strong start in controlling the curse on Hans, but things had slowed. *Dramatically* slowed.

Darkness fell at around half-past six, which was typical for England at this time of year. Dinner was served, which we did not attend. Minute by minute, the manor quieted, and yet, we were still in the infirmary. I'd left twice to pee, whereas Hannah kept Luca in food and water. Luca, however, hadn't moved from Hans's side, and it showed.

Sweat drenched the coven master and about an hour ago, his arms had begun to shake from the magical effort he was expending. Had it been anyone else, I suspected they'd have given up hours ago. But not Luca. *Never Luca.* He'd do his best to make sure we pulled Hans out of this coma.

Throughout the process, many moments of doubt overcame me, but I tried to maintain a positive attitude. Luca was working so hard, and I supported him as much as possible.

"Do you need more water?" I held out the water bottle so that he could sip from the straw.

"No, I think I'm close." Luca's hand floated above Hans's

foot, the other hovering a few inches away above his calf. "Once I'm sure this foot is clear, I'm going to contain the curse. Shouldn't be much longer."

"You got this." I beamed, shoving down my doubts and tightening my stomach so it wouldn't roil. This needed to be over. Hans needed to wake up and be pain free.

Or close to pain-free? Heavens, I hoped this would work like Luca thought and Hans would get better, but the truth was, no one knew. What if Luca missed some of the curse, and Hans still experienced pain?

"Okay, I'm beginning the containment process." Luca exhaled.

"We're here for you." Hannah came to stand right behind the mage to hold him up in case he passed out, which, judging by the looks of him, might happen.

I grabbed Hans's hand, ready to provide similar support if this all went to hell, and the curse exploded through him again. No one wanted to consider what that might mean, what it could do to Hans.

Luca inched his hand above Hans's foot toward the other. Both arms trembled, but thanks to the short distance, it took only a few minutes until they were side by side. Luca closed his eyes.

He mumbled words in a language I did not know. Considering I knew many, I had a hunch that Luca was speaking the language mages spoke in Isila. Whatever that was, it sounded odd. Harsh and cold and at odds with Luca's lyrical Italian accent.

Please, let this work. I tipped my head up to the ceiling, imagining the sky and the heavens, filled with archangels and lesser angels, all beings that performed amazing feats. Granted miracles. I hoped they'd grant this one.

If my father were here, I'd demand it of him, but I had heard nothing of the Archangel Uriel since the day he'd battled Prince Orien of Hell. I didn't expect to either. My father came down from the heavens because I was his blood, but angels, especially archangels, did not traverse realms lightly, and Heaven was a different realm, much like Isila.

Beneath my hand, Hans shuddered, snapping my attention back to Luca.

"What happened?"

"The curse knows what I'm doing," Luca ground out. "It's been fighting me for an hour, and it tried to surge up Hans's leg. I caught it, though."

Panic rose in my chest, hinting that I'd been much more dedicated to making this work than I'd allowed myself to admit. "What can I do?"

"Calm Hans. Talk to him."

I blinked, stunned by the recommendation. Hans had been comatose for over a week. Sure, I'd spoken to him—in private —but how could me talking to him now help?

"It helps," Hannah urged, clearly having read the doubt on my face. "Patients in a coma have claimed to hear things others have said. Center him, Shay. I'll assist Luca with anything he needs." She held the water out and though Luca was fighting with the curse; he took an obliging drink.

I turned to Hans, squeezed his hand and noticed his tight jaw, the muscle there fluttering. My pulse quickened, and I leaned closer, hoping he sensed my presence and that it gave him a sense of not being alone.

"Hey, Hans, we're almost done here. I can't wait for you to wake up. So much has happened." I swallowed, feeling foolish and also like sharing the manor's gossip wouldn't help at all, but Hannah shot me a stern look, so I plowed on. "Meredith had a breakthrough today with her stone. She's shattered the vampires' compulsion a bunch of times now."

Rooms had come down here before dinner to tell us the good news. She hadn't looked as beat as Luca did now, but it was close.

"That's going to help us. Heavens, I can't wait for you to wake up." I loosened my grip on his hand, and my own drifted up his arm. In the motion, I swore that Hans's jaw loosened a touch.

"*Keep going*," Luca growled. "I'm almost there."

I chanced a glance at him, took in the tomato red hue of his face, and returned to Hans.

"Rabi also joined the *Vindix*. I haven't spoken with him, but Meredith says he's quiet and has taken a liking to examining appliances around here. Mechanical stuff. I wonder if he'd like cars too. Maybe you two can bond over it?"

A sharp cry of pain left Luca, jolting me out of my seat, just as Hans began to shake in the bed.

"What's going on?" I asked, terror rising. He looked like he was having a stroke.

"It zapped me!" Luca yelled. "I still have it. Almost— *there! Ha!*"

A flash of light burst through the room, so blinding I had to look away. When the stars in my eyes receded, I sought Luca.

He was leaning back in the chair, panting, but also grinning from ear to ear.

"You're sure it worked?" My attention bounced between the mage and Hans, who still had not woken. But surely, he wouldn't right away? Right? That had to take some time. I hoped it wasn't too long. I felt ready to jump out of my skin with anticipation.

"Positive. The curse put up a good fight. It took everything I had to close the sphere."

"Sphere?"

"I sealed the curse in a magical sphere. A small, warded area, if you can imagine?"

"Wild."

"What did you think the containment would look like?" Luca let out an exhausted laugh.

I shrugged. "I wasn't thinking that much into that part." I refrained from adding that I'd had serious doubts we'd even get there. "I was more worried about you and Hans."

Hannah nodded her agreement. "I should do an examination. Check his vitals. Scoot on back, Luca."

The mage complied, and Hannah moved in to do her job. She'd checked Hans's vitals daily and more often while Luca had been working. In the last few hours, Hans's numbers had often revealed stress, but it hadn't been enough for Hannah to stop Luca.

I waited, hoping for good news. After about ten minutes, a smile broke out on Hannah's face. "Heart rate is good, so is blood pressure, respiration, and temperature. As far as I can tell, he's fine. Better than before, to be certain."

A long exhale left my lips, and I stared down at Hans again, relieved to hear good news for once. "Thank the heavens."

"Agreed. I—"

Hans's eyelids fluttered open, wrenching a scream up my throat.

I threw myself over him, my heart ready to burst. "Hans! Oh my god! You're awake!"

A low groan filled the room as arms pulled me off Hans.

"He hasn't moved in over a week, Shay!" Hannah scolded.

I pulled back, aghast at what I'd done. "I'm so sorry, Hans."

He winced, pain visible in every minor movement as he tried to stretch his arms and legs and tried to crane his neck. His gaze landed on the Pearl of Hell, sitting on his bedside table.

The men had changed Hans out of street clothes and into soft sleeping attire that had no pockets for the Pearl. Most of us believed Hans would want to know where his *lapis caelesti* was the moment he awoke, so we'd made sure it was in his line of sight.

Though, as he took it in now, I didn't see relief on his face. Rather, Hans's eyes widened as if he were seeing a ghost.

"How do you feel?" Hannah asked, her voice softer than before. "What's your pain level?"

"P-p-pain level?" The words croaked out of Hans's throat, likely dry from disuse.

Luca came to the same conclusion, for he stood and went to the sink, filling a glass of water and returning to press it to Hans's lips. The hellblooded wizard drank.

"That's enough for now," Hannah said when half the water was gone. "Go slow."

Luca withdrew the glass, an apology in his eyes. "Are you in pain?"

Hans cleared his throat. "Yes. It's everywhere. Throbbing." He shook his head, wincing again. "But wasn't I stabbed in the back? Why do I hurt so badly?"

Luca gave him the rundown on the dagger, and that the curse was still in Hans, just contained. Hannah swooped in and made sure that Hans understood feeling poorly was to be expected after being bedridden for so long. Also that even though the curse was contained, his body could still be feeling the aftereffects of the curse nestling in his tissues for so long. Or perhaps Luca missed some of the curse. Luca nodded at that last point, though he'd seemed certain that he'd gotten it all, but Hannah was managing expectations, which was a large part of her job.

Through it all, Hans remained silent, taking it all in. And when they were done, he turned to me.

"And you're here."

A statement, not a question.

"I am."

"Why?"

The loaded words rang through the infirmary. What did I say to him? That I hadn't left him for more than the time it took to relieve myself? That I would have stayed here for a month longer? No. As long as it took for him to awaken?

That not being by his side had been impossible, and that I had feelings I could no longer deny?

"I needed to make sure you were okay," I settled on. "Hans, you risked your life for all of us. I couldn't ignore that." I swallowed down a telling lump in my throat. "I liked to check in on you."

Hannah's stare pressed into me. Everyone in the manor knew I'd been here night and day. That I'd slept in the bed next to Hans's bed. That I'd cried for hours over his condition. Thankfully, though, Hannah did not tell the truths that I'd carefully omitted, but rather turned to the counter and plucked a vial from a holder. The liquid inside was bright pink.

"Drink this," she said. "I fed you through an IV, but these potions are better at replacing nutrients and helping you regain strength."

Hans took the vial with a trembling hand and downed the

vial in one gulp. He handed it back to Hannah, and then looked at me again, as if surprised to find that I was still there.

Unsure what to do with myself, I became very interested in the folding of my hands. Did he not remember the kiss? That alone would have tipped me off that something changed.

Then again, I had acted distant right after that. I was such an idiot sometimes. Why did I let embarrassment get the better of me when I *knew* what I wanted? *Who* I wanted.

"What's happened since I've been out?" Hans asked.

"Quite a lot," Luca replied and began telling Hans about the last week and then some. By the time he was finished, Hans was blinking hard.

"So, all the kingdoms have all fallen. Gunner is gone, and the new *Vindix* has joined us."

"Those are the high points," I said.

"And Brons?"

None of us expected that he'd ask about the captive wizard right away. How silly of us. Hans had risked his life to get Richard Brons back here so that he could have a shot at retrieving his wizarding magic back from Brons. Of course Hans was going to ask about the Covenant Seat.

"Captive," I said. "Held in Josiah's old room."

"I want to see him." Hans tried to sit up but collapsed back into the bed with a yelp.

My heart leapt into my throat. "Can I help? I can use my angel light to burn away any lingering effects?" I didn't dare say I could burn away the curse itself. I wasn't that strong. Or maybe that wouldn't work, anyway. But angel light did alleviate some pain. Could that work here?

"I'm hellblooded." Hans glared at me. "Remember what happened last time?"

Now I did. Heavens, what was I thinking in offering my power?

"She's concerned." Luca stuck up for me.

"No, he's right. It was stupid."

The ire dropped from Hans's face. "I'm sorry Shay. I'm irritable."

As one would expect if he was still in pain. I needed to give him space. Time.

"I understand."

"Do you think you're strong enough to see Brons?" Luca asked.

"I'm not sure I can walk, but I'm not tired, just aching. Do you have a wheelchair?"

"'Course I do." Hannah disappeared into a large storage closet. A moment later, she wheeled out a chair that looked to be a hundred years old.

"Uh, is that safe?" I asked.

"I take care of my tools," Hannah replied. "And it's rarely used, so it hasn't had a lot of wear. I'm sure it's fine."

The process of transferring him over was slow and laborious. Hans wasn't a small man, and every slight movement caused him great pain, but finally, he sat in the chair.

He looked up at me, his chest heaving from that small effort. "Wheel me, Shay?"

"Of course." I positioned myself behind him, trying to tamp down the ridiculous spark of joy that had ignited in my chest upon his request.

CHAPTER NINE

HANS

The stairs would be the death of me.

Shay and Luca were trying their best to be careful and smooth when carrying me and the ancient wheelchair down the steps. Despite their efforts, every jostle shot stabs of pain through me that I did my best to hide.

Was this what I'd been experiencing for over a week? If so, I was grateful that I'd been in a coma. No one could endure this for so long—and something told me I had not done so. That what I'd endured was *far* worse and that my brain would not allow me to remember.

A mercy considering how horrible I felt. Particularly in my shin, where Luca had contained the curse from Queen Narcissa's dagger. The area around the curse felt like I was being stabbed with a hundred knives.

Still, this, all of this, was better than sitting in the infirmary. I'd never been good at being passive, and seeing as I'd been in a coma, I figured I'd done more than enough of that. I needed to do something and gather my strength, and not just to beat this curse.

No, the curse was only one of my worries.

I'd sensed the Pearl the instant my eyes had opened. It tried to grab ahold of me, to take charge. While I'd been languishing, the Pearl had been waiting, biding its time. Maybe even growing stronger. Aside from battling my curse, I needed to remain in control of the most notorious of the *lapis caelesti*.

"Last one," Luca grunted as we neared the bottom of the staircase. He'd taken the lead in getting me downstairs, and, I suspected, much of my weight. Always a gentleman.

The chair leveled out as Shay stepped off the staircase and let out a long breath. "That was tricky. We might want to get Tobias for the way back up. It's late, but he'll be awake."

"I can find him," Luca said. "Unless you wish for me to stay with you, Hans?"

I checked for my magic and found it flaring to life. My demon magic was as strong as ever. If Brons still had access to his magic and attacked, I'd be able to handle him.

"Get Tobias," I said. "Shay and I will go. You're okay with that, Shay?"

Momentarily, she looked taken aback, but a smile formed on her face as she nodded. "Of course."

"Good luck." Luca waved as he left.

Shay wheeled me toward the room where Josiah had been held captive before we'd given him a chance to turn spy and redeem himself. I wondered if anyone had heard from him since we returned from Isila. If he'd had news. Or if, like so much of the world, he'd gone dark too. For his sake, I hoped not. Jo might have made bad choices when it came to protecting his girlfriend, but I'd always liked the guy. I wanted him to be redeemed, not hurt. Or worse, dead.

Shay stopped the chair in front of Brons's door. "Knock?"

"We'd better," I replied. "Who knows what he might be doing in there all alone with only himself for entertainment."

She let out a disgusted laugh. "Please don't say that. I don't want any dirty thoughts featuring Richard Brons's leathery old ass."

I laughed too, but it devolved into a painful coughing fit.

"You okay?"

"Yeah," I lied, my throat burning. "You caught me off guard with your dirty mind."

"*Oh please*," Shay trilled. "I may be half angel, but I'm far from a saint."

I grinned, pleased that she was rolling with it even though I could see the concern in her eyes. Except for that period of time when she couldn't even look me in the eye, Shay had always excelled at smoothing over sticky situations.

She knocked, and right away Brons answered. "What?"

"Are you decent?" Shay asked. "We need a word."

"Whatever."

He didn't ask who was at his door. It was possible that he recognized Shay's voice. I had no idea how often people questioned him since I'd been in a coma.

Richard Brons lounged in an armchair in front of the fire and judging by the way his face went cold when Shay wheeled me through the door and shut it behind us, activating the wards once more, he hadn't been expecting me to be part of the visiting party. He wasn't the only one surprised. Richard Brons, usually so put together as befit a Covenant Seat, looked awful with bloodshot eyes, sunken cheeks, and wrinkled clothing.

And goddess have mercy, the stench. I wrinkled my nose. The room smelled like BO and takeout left to rot on the counter.

Seeing as there were no plates or bowls, I had to assume

the smell came from Brons himself. Had he bathed at all since being dragged through the portal?

"So?" Brons hissed, gaze landing on me as he stood and rounded the armchair, only to lean against the back of it. A fire burned in the hearth behind him, the firelight dancing on his egg-bald head. "Have you come to finish me off? Like you and your friends did to Egor?"

Ah, now his disheveled state made sense. In all that had occurred since I'd woken, I had not given a second thought to Egor Drago. Brons and the vampire spy had been lovers, surely Brons had been thinking about Egor.

"No one is finishing anyone off," I said, glad that Shay was keeping distance between us and the wizard. Every small motion he made caused a new whiff of rancid BO to flutter across the room.

"Like I'd believe you." Brons gave me a scathing once-over, as if seeing me for the first time. "Why are you in that chair? And why do you look like death warmed over?"

Has he not looked in the mirror?

"I was injured while fleeing the Blood Court. Carrying you out of range of a fiery death, I might add."

I vividly remembered hauling Brons toward the portal, my heart racing as the queen of the vampires chased us, but that was the last thing I remembered. Luca had painted a good enough picture though, for me to understand what had happened after and since then. I was lucky to be alive.

"You should have left me there. Left me to mourn the man I loved." Brons's face crumpled, and I felt bad for the guy.

If he hadn't insisted on making me an enemy, and forcing me to make a Vow of Intent, we wouldn't be at odds. But my demon blood had been too much for Brons and Egor and so many of those on the Covenant. Shay's mother included.

"I am sorry for your loss." I meant those words. I despised Egor, but I also knew what it was like to lose people. It always hurt. Even if those people were still alive—like Nicoleta. Actually, *especially* when they were still alive.

Trying to stay on task, I put the thoughts of my younger sister, now an official Princess of Hell, from my mind. "But I won't deny that I've come here with an agenda."

Brons snorted. "Of course you have. No humanity in you whatsoever."

My power crackled deep inside me, begging to be released on the man who continually insulted me. It took more effort than normal to restrain the demon magic. Maybe it was stupid to come here when I was not at 100%.

"He's not the monster you think he is." Shay came around the chair, her chin high. "Why would he be fighting for this world if he was? Hans has demon blood, yes. He's been open about that—"

"Not always," Brons interrupted. "He hid his true self for years."

"From people like you!" Shay pointed a finger. "And people like me too. People who would judge him for it. If I can see to his true heart, why can't you? Why can't you see that everything he's done has been to protect people? Not to help the demons who are taking over our world."

"So he's playing the long game." Brons shrugged. "He has the time. As a demon of the royal line, you'll have a longer lifespan, won't you hellblooded?"

"Maybe." I leaned forward in the chair and my joints barked. I did my best to mask the agony that every movement pushed through me. "But we're not here to discuss *me*, Richard. I won't beat around the bush a moment longer. I want my witch magic back. Want it so that I can be at full capacity when I fight the Royals of Hell. And while I know you hate me, if you had any shred of decency, you'd release it back to me."

Brons's eyes darkened, and he pushed off the armchair, toppled it, and ran at me.

"Hey!" Shay shouted, pulling the wheelchair back to the door, but Brons was too fast.

In an instant, he stood in front of me, his hands on the arms of the wheelchair. The stench of him overwhelmed me, but I dared not look away. His eyes had taken on a crazed sheen and this close, he was trembling violently.

I held up my hands, trying to diffuse the situation. Brons only snarled.

"If you think for a second that I'm going to give you back your magic, you're delusional. You're an abomination. In fact, I should begin paying you back for what you did to Egor right now." He pulled a fist back, about to punch me but the motion of Brons removing his hand from the wheelchair, shaking the chair in the process was enough to send a deluge of pain through me, and my demon magic rose to protect me, to strike before more pain came.

Brons fell to the ground shrieking in pain as my magic hit him. I gasped, trying to catch my breath, trying to control my powers of torture, but they were in free flow.

"Hans! Hans stop!" Shay shouted and rounded the chair to stand over Brons, her eyes wide with horror. "You can't kill him. The transfer has to be willing!"

"I'm—*not*—trying—to kill him!" I roared each word, a triumph to push past my lips. "I can't control it!"

Shay sucked in a breath. Somehow ignoring the screaming man on the floor and how insane I must have looked, she lowered to look at me in the face. "You can. I know you can.

Breathe, Hans, and control your magic. You're stronger than it."

Then she did the unthinkable and took my hand. Even at her slight touch, pain shot down my arm, but it ran its course quickly. Shay was being so gentle, so calm.

"Breathe. Fight it. Control it."

I inhaled and exhaled a shaky breath. Again. Again. All the while, I ignored Brons's screaming. It was a wonder that no one had shown up yet. Then again, this room was so warded they might have soundproofed it too. I hoped so.

Shame welled, threatening to bubble out of me. I hated this magic, hated that now, in my weakened state, I couldn't even control it anymore. Hated that the Pearl might overtake me too. How was I *so weak?*

"Breathe," Shay chanted again, her voice like a song in a time of war.

I breathed in and out five more times, all the while looking into her eyes. Needing her as my anchor. She nodded, seemingly understanding what was going on in my screwed-up body and mind, and squeezed my hand.

"You've got this Hans. Master it."

I swallowed and dipped into my magic, trying to seize control. It wasn't easy, and it wasn't fast. I did not know how long Brons laid on the ground screaming and trembling beneath the onslaught of my power, but at the very least, minutes passed before I seized my power.

I wrestled with it and pulled it tighter, into a ball deep inside me, much like the curse. When it was contained, I gasped.

The screaming stopped.

"Good," Shay whispered and then turned. "Brons, Hans didn't mean for that to happen. And you shouldn't have threatened him. We're going to go. We'll come back later to revisit this conversation."

"Go drown yourselves," Brons rasped. "I'll never give it back. I'll die before I do."

"We'll see," Shay said, and before I uttered another word, she wheeled me backwards.

I stared at Brons as the door to his prison shut, terrified that I'd destroyed my last chance of getting my power back.

CHAPTER TEN

HARPER

Heavy mist crept over the village graveyard, the cold moisture sticking to my cheeks as we walked through, looking for the best spot to practice.

"Here is good," Aya spoke as if she'd woken up minutes ago, which wasn't too far off.

Just shy of eight in the morning, no one had been awake long. The air was cold and misty, and I could feel the rain building, threatening to drench us all.

Aya insisted a place like this was optimal for calling ghosts. Even more so, when we'd seen how misty it was, and she'd practically applauded. According to her, mists indicated a thin veil between worlds. What better time to call a ghost?

I asked for this. Asked to be pushed harder, I reminded myself as I rubbed my frozen hands together. *We might need this.*

"My umbrella is worthless in this country," Giselle's French accent cut through the quiet, imperious as usual. "Why anyone would live here is beyond me."

"I don't disagree. France is superior. But you lived here for a while," Serena countered, pulling a hood over her naturally coiled hair.

"Before I came to my senses." Giselle's nose lifted into the air. "At least I got Tobias out of it."

We'd brought the vampires for added protection, just in case demons or their allies were still skulking around the village. It was the first time in a while that I'd left the protective wards of the *Abscondita* Coven manor. Miriam deemed the *Vindix* were too important and needed protection, so as everyone else was sleeping or busy training or teaching magic, Giselle and Serena had drawn the short straw of guard duty.

"Remember what we've been doing." Aya came closer, an old school thermos of tea clutched in her wrinkled hands. "You know how to call spirits. Outside the manor wards, it will be easier. Here especially." She gestured to the nearest grave, one adorned with a Celtic style cross made of stone so old that the writing was all but gone. "For an army to rise, you need to push yourself. Try for eight ghosts."

Eight. She'd told me once that was the record—at least the record for any witch in living memory. Of course, spirit witches were rare, so I tried not to let it get to my head that I was close to that number already. My record was six.

But there were tales. Tales that the *Vindix*, who possessed the Diamond of Souls, could raise *an army* of ghosts. And moon above, could we use an army right now.

So here I was, trying to set a record in spirit magic when I'd learned I possessed the power only a couple of weeks ago. Gunner would claim it was typical Harper behavior. He wouldn't be wrong. I'd always been an overachiever.

"Try." Aya laid a weathered hand on my shoulder. Though I'd only known the Nigerian witch for a short time, I leaned into her touch, comforted by it. By her. "I believe you're capable of so much more than you let yourself believe, Harper."

"Thank you," I looked down. "Did you bring the salt?"

"No salt circle today," Aya said. "It's a precaution, but when you use your magic in the real world, you won't have time to draw one."

"Today is a day to try new things, huh?" I snorted, uneasy about not having the salt circle.

"If not now, when?"

Considering the world was in shambles, and I was about to dive headlong into the muck with S&S and the *Vindix* Mer had found so far, I needed to be flexible. Adaptable. Stronger.

"Alright." I rubbed my hands together again, desperate to drive away the chill before brushing my new bracelet with one hand. I'd been a hold out on transferring the Diamond of Souls and the diamond that acted as a talisman into the bracelet. For one, I thought the bracelet ugly, but there was no denying that it was comforting to see the stone at all times. More importantly to me, I'd destroyed my mother's family earrings.

Thinking about my mother, and subsequently my father, made my chest hurt. Were they still possessed by smoke demons? Were they even still alive? In California?

I wished I could go back to the day I'd failed them, the barbecue that should have been my coming out as the pack's soon to be alpha but instead ended in disaster. I'd failed every single wolf there.

"Harper? Ready?" Aya prompted, bringing me out of my despair, a state I was becoming far too familiar with for my liking.

"I am," I replied and tried to sound strong and sure, like an alpha heir *should* sound. "Here goes nothing."

I summoned my power. So normal, so comfortable now,

though this time it felt *a little* different due to the lack of salt. Though it wasn't different enough to scare or dissuade me, I pushed on, whipping the magic into a frenzy above the gravestones.

"I require you, souls of the dead," I spoke clearly into the cold morning air. "Who will heed my call?"

A ghost floated down from the sky. Obviously, I understood they probably would not pop out of the ground as though they'd just been waiting inside their graves. Still their entrances, some grand, some hesitant, always seemed so random. The ghost came closer, but before she could reach me, two more simply appeared in front of me.

Three. And it had been so easy.

I pushed my power harder. My white, shimmering magic glowed silver in the morning mists, but I did not ask a spirit to come again. Aya claimed if you had to repeat your request, they were less likely to take you seriously.

It took another full minute before two more ghosts appeared, hand in hand. They appeared around the same age —ghosts could appear at any age they chose—and as Aya had told me, ghosts didn't form romances in death, but these two had a certain pull between them, so I assumed that they'd been lovers in life.

I only needed three more.

A bead of sweat dripped from my temple. I hadn't even realized I'd been growing warm, my heat trapped in my rain gear. But at least I wasn't shaking. The first few times I tried to level up, I'd shaken so hard.

More. The Diamond heated on my wrist. The ghosts surrounded Aya and me now. They shared amused glances, perhaps wondering why I needed so many of them. Or what I was doing here at all.

They'd get their answers. Once I succeeded.

The bead of sweat turned into a trail, and my face turned hot, but still nothing happened. Come on! My teeth clenched, and I dug deep inside, pulling the power out of me, using the Diamond to summon.

Two more ghosts appeared with the others.

"She's quite insistent, isn't she?" one newcomer asked. He presented as an old man smoking a pipe and wearing a fancy jacket. Apparently, I'd interrupted his leisure in the afterlife.

"And I'm not done yet." My hands trembled as I summoned more power. Demanded more. I had to. I had to push even harder for an army.

Old Ones, is it possible?

The question entered my head when not one, but three more spirits appeared. I gasped.

"Very good!" Aya clapped her hands. "Let go. Take a breather."

"And pray tell us why we're here?" one ghost chirped. "I was quite busy, you know?"

"Ah yes, the spirit scene must be riveting," Giselle teased.

Though she and Serena had been acting as lookouts while I practiced, apparently, they couldn't resist watching too. I couldn't blame them. After all, I'd *shattered* the record for spirit callings!

"You're going to have to call the witchy Guinness Book of World Records, or whatever the equivalent is, Aya."

My mentor chuckled, her dark brown eyes shining with pride. "I suppose I will. If there's one to call after all this."

My good mood withered, and I was back to business. I turned to the ghosts. "Thanks for coming."

"What do you need?" the old man with the pipe asked.

"Nothing at the moment," I said.

Half of the ghosts scowled at me.

"I am practicing for war. I might have to call an army of ghosts soon. Any tips to make it easier?"

At the question, the ire fell from their translucent faces. Aya had taught me this trick. Ghosts didn't like to be called if we had nothing in mind for them to do. Sometimes, they didn't want to do the task either, but it was best to offer them one. If you couldn't, then always ask their advice to satisfy their pride.

"You did a marvelous job," the woman who'd arrived hand in hand with a man spoke. "For the, uh, war, maybe speak of that when you're calling?"

Not a bad idea. I tucked it away. "Thank you. Anything else?"

A smattering of advice spewed from the ghosts. Some sounded like good advice. Other bits, not so much. I didn't care how to best pickle cabbage, not when I had a war against demon princes riding my butt.

When the ghosts fell silent, I gave a shallow bow, respecting them and their time as I'd been taught. "Thank you for appearing and letting me push my magic. I'm going to try again, but can you guys not come? I'm practicing calling unfamiliar spirits."

They agreed. And said they wouldn't tell any of their ghost friends a witch was calling for aid and that they should come. Appeased that my next attempts would be based on my merit, we parted.

I sighed and turned to Aya. She beamed.

"What?"

"You're a natural. I didn't have to intervene once when you spoke with them, placated them, listened to that horrible advice with a straight face." She rolled her eyes.

"Who in the world would go diving off the Cliffs of Dover?"

"That's probably how he died." Serena laughed.

I didn't doubt it.

"Thanks." I took the thermos Aya offered, unscrewing the top with trembling fingers. The hot tea slipped down my throat, warming me from the inside out. The shaking lessened somewhat. "Now what?"

"Now, you try to break the world record yet again."

I TREMBLED AS I FINISHED MY ELEVENTH ATTEMPT AT CALLING ghosts to use for an army. Each time, I shattered the record again and again and again.

But as noon neared, my limbs grew heavy. My movements sluggish.

"Two more," Aya encouraged. "Get to twenty-five. Then we'll return to the manor."

I swallowed as the ghosts waiting before us stared at me. Half seemed impressed, the others aghast. No one had done this to them before, nor to any ghost they knew.

Soon, though, they'd understand why. Around attempt five, Aya had suggested we start recruiting, so I'd told the ghosts why I had called them. Most wished to stay, to fight, but that wasn't what today was about. Today, I'd stretched myself to the max, and proven I grew stronger by the day. As a result, my confidence soared.

Two more.

I pulled from a deep well of magic inside me. My magic glimmered in the graveyard, still misty as hell though the sun had risen behind gray clouds. At least it hadn't rained.

My breathing thinned as power surged from me, and the hair on the back of my neck rose in anticipation.

Not three seconds later, two more ghosts appeared on opposite sides of the growing crowd of specters. I loosed my magic, sure that if I'd needed to continue for another second, my wobbling knees would have buckled.

As a wolf, I was used to pushing myself physically. Magical expenditure was different, but equally taxing.

"Amazing," Aya praised me. "You've done so well today, Harper."

"Thank you. But I think I need to return to the manor. It's time for lunch."

"Tell the ghosts what's happening, and we'll leave," Aya agreed.

I gave the spirits the spiel. That war charged toward us. That I might need them again, if they were near the veil when I called. That we were trying to save not only supernaturals but everyone on Earth.

Indignation rang through the air and most pledged their allegiance to our cause. If they heard my call, they'd come, they'd help us fight.

I prepared to release the ghosts when Giselle let out a long, eerie hiss.

"Serena," the blonde vampire pointed to the right. "Scent."

"I smell something. Like a wolf . . . Oh!"

From the mists, ten figures appeared, not twenty feet away.

"So, there you are," a man who smelled a lot like a wizard grinned. "We've been looking for you." He shot off a crimson round of power, right at me.

Before I mustered a retaliation—from witch magic, or by shifting, I didn't care—Aya pointed to the ghosts.

"Shield her!" Shimmering magic flowed from my mentor

and suddenly, a shield of ghostly magic surrounded me. The others, though, remained outside, Aya included.

"No!" I pounded on the shield. "Let me out!"

But the ghosts did not. They'd taken to heart my place in the war to come and the barrier did not dissipate.

Aya remained standing in front of me, attacking and deflecting. As there were ten of them and four—no, three—of us, she didn't stop every attack, but the barrier held strong. It was impenetrable to the spells and bullets our adversaries hurled at it.

The rest was down to Giselle and Serena. I'd seen vampires fight before, but this pair was something else. Watching Giselle, there was no denying how ancient and powerful she really was.

The Laurent matriarch took down a vampire, then a shifter, and two witches in rapid succession, while her daughter tangoed with two vampires, ripping off one head and punching a hole in the heart of another before decapitating him too.

After five minutes, four adversaries remained. One of them was the shooter who'd stayed back, hidden behind a gravestone. I wasn't sure it mattered—Giselle and Serena would get him—until I watched the shooter change guns.

"What the hell?"

He shot. The bullet flew past Giselle and slammed into my shield. The sound it made when it pinged off was unlike the others that had hit the shield, and it only took me finding the bullet in the grass to figure out why.

Wooden bullets?

My heart stopped. What were wooden bullets but teeny-tiny stakes?

"Giselle! Serena! The shooter has wooden bullets!"

A stream of French left Giselle's lips and judging by the tone, I had to assume that she'd cursed up a storm.

More wooden bullets flew at the vampires, some straying close to Aya, whose only protection was a regular shield that she'd conjured. The bullets made it more difficult for our vampire protectors to face off with the remaining three fighters, but once Giselle got close enough, she held up a hand.

"Stop!"

The fighters stopped in their tracks, two of them each with one foot in the air. Moon above it was good to be a vampire with powerful compulsion.

"Serena." Giselle jerked a proud chin to the vampires in her thrall. "I'll take the last."

Her daughter began decapitating, and Giselle ran toward the shooter, darting left and right out of the way of bullets as she went. I thought she'd rush him, that she'd want to scare him a little, but once she got close enough, the shooter stopped and dropped the gun.

She'd compelled him.

"Ask him where he's from!" Aya shouted, her words labored from the fighting and protecting me.

Giselle didn't respond. She stalked the rest of the way to the man, picked up his gun and pointed it at his head. In the graveyard's quiet, I heard her ask, "Who sent you?"

"The Ordo," the man replied.

"Are there more of you?"

"We're the last guard in the area."

"How did you know we were here?"

"We didn't. We patrol the village and this is just part of the rounds."

"Will more come?" Giselle asked.

"Not unless we call for them."

Giselle turned to Aya. "Anything else?"

"We have our spy for inside information," my mentor replied.

I was about to say that we hadn't heard from Josiah since the others returned from the vampire kingdom, but the gun went off, stopping my words. The man slumped to the ground as Giselle tore the gun in half with a sneer.

Somehow, despite the blood spattered across her face, she still looked beautiful. Terrifying, but beautiful. *Remind me never to get on her bad side.*

Giselle turned. "We must leave and tell Olga and Tana. They'll need to come quickly in case humans stumble upon the bodies."

"It's unlikely. Locals don't come here anymore, but I agree." Aya waved a wrinkled hand. The shield of ghosts around me separated into bodily figures again.

One female ghost gave me a sheepish look. "Sorry we didn't listen to you, but you were so weak already."

I bristled at that, even though I couldn't argue the point. Exhaustion clung to my bones, and I needed to eat. So, I put aside my pride. "Thank you, but you can leave now."

"We'll be listening for your call," another ghost said.

They disappeared into the ether, my silent army, waiting for my summons.

CHAPTER ELEVEN

GUNNER

THE DOOR TO THE ROOM FLEW OPEN. A SOLDIER WITH BLACK BAT wings and a scrunched-up face stomped in, a finger pointed right at me. "Wolf, get up. You're coming with us."

It was early as hell, and I'd been loungin' on my cot, unmotivated to do much of anythin' besides picture Harper's face and remember better times when my chica and I were laughin' and flirtin' all day.

"Why?" I drawled.

"My prince wants you."

I stiffened. I hadn't seen the prince since I'd arrived in New Orleans. And thanks to his powers, I sure as hell hadn't been makin' a fuss or tryin' to escape, even if that would've been the smart thing to do. Why would he want to talk to me?

"Up." The demon soldier lifted a gun, pointed it at me.

The monsters had been havin' a lot of fun playing with the firearms—new weaponry for them. They practiced shootin' daily, though I hadn't come across a range in the castle. That the demons now had access to guns didn't bode well for our side.

I shifted off the cot and slid my feet into sneakers. "Lead the way."

The soldier snarled but turned his back on me and marched down the hallway. We'd made a couple of twists and turns down the dark but luxurious corridors, none of which I'd seen before. Still, as we approached a red door, the hair on my arms rose. We'd arrived.

Soldiers stood on either side of the door, but they opened it at our approach. No waitin' for me to see the prince. I guessed I was special.

"Inside." My escort gestured for me to enter.

Steelin' myself, I entered the throne room. The Prince of Sloth lounged on a throne of gold and light blue. Today, he wore flowy light blue robes that matched the throne and most of the room. I hadn't been in here yet, but light blue must be Prince Belhor's favorite color or somethin'. His long black hair was pulled back, and his face seemed more relaxed than when I'd seen him before. Probably 'cause he wasn't doin' any conquerin' today. He'd already done all that and, true to his character, he just chilled.

None of that surprised me, but what did surprise me was that the witches I'd met a couple of days ago were there too, standin' before the prince. My heart rate kicked up. Had I gotten Rhianna and Dan in trouble by talkin' to them?

"Leave us," the prince said, and the soldiers in the room marched out, closin' the door behind them. The prince was so sure of his power over us that he didn't want any muscle behind him. I hated the guy but had to admire his bald confidence.

"Gunner," Sloth drew my name out, all lazy like. "Approach."

I took a heavy step. My feet felt like lead so close to Sloth, so I all but shuffled forward the rest of the way to stand next to Rhianna. She didn't look at me, and to be safe, I didn't look at her either. In a place like this, especially as a prisoner, indicatin' you had a relationship, no matter how slight, with someone could end badly.

"I have a job for you, wolf." The prince stretched his black feathered wings.

"What's that?"

No use in sayin' I didn't work for the guy. Especially when I was curious about what he'd use a prisoner like me for. I didn't have earth magic to grow food. And I suspected the only reason Prince Belhor was keepin' me around was as bait for S&S. After all, my friends had broken into Prince Lucifer's kingdom and killed certain heirs of darkness while they plundered two *lapis caelesti*. Both Lucifer and Orien, the latter bein' the prince who'd gained the stones in the first place, had to be furious 'bout that. No doubt the baddest brothers in hell wanted revenge. My capture made that easier.

"These witches have made a case for the people of New Orleans, my subjects. I'm sending them out to propagate fruit trees so the people don't starve until I can come up with a more permanent solution to the food issue."

So people were already goin' hungry. That hadn't taken long. How could Sloth not have considered this when he claimed a kingdom? I'd bet that in the underworld, his brothers had helped their laziest brother out on the logistics of rulin' a kingdom. Here, though, that didn't seem to be the case. I hadn't seen or heard of another prince. Was it every demon for himself up here?

"The witches are leaving the castle today," Prince Belhor continued. "You will go with them as protection."

What in the world could I do while bogged down with Sloth's magic?

"Just me?" I asked.

"I have other wolves waiting. They require an alpha to lead them. Once you mind-link with them, you become their alpha, no?"

My mouth fell open. He wanted me to claim a pack? But I already had one. My family's pack in Isila.

"Gunner?" the prince prompted.

"But I'm already part of a pack."

"You're not the alpha."

"Well, no. My pa is."

"But you are an alphablood, capable of commanding a pack, so you will do that. You will gain ten wolves who, while in the city, will look to you for leadership."

I didn't like that. Didn't like the idea of turnin' my back on my real pack. Then again, the wolves—wherever Sloth was keepin' them—weren't at fault here. Maybe they'd lost their pack and were now packless? My gut clenched. Bein' a lone wolf was the worst thing that would happen to my kind.

Still . . . I didn't want to betray my people.

"I won't be of much use." I shrugged a lazy shoulder. "Your sin has me not wantin' to move, so I can't see myself leadin' anything or anyone."

"As I did while the witches grew food, I will loosen my sin's hold on you for the duration of your outing."

I blinked. "I gotta say, I'm surprised. Why not send your soldiers?"

Sloth's face twisted in a way that told me all was not well in the kingdom. "You will have an aerial guard of three demons, but you and the wolves will deal with any threats on the ground. It's all that I can spare."

The main upside to an aerial unit was that they saw far—a bird's-eye view. Why would we need that for such a task?

One possibility struck, hard and fast. Was there fightin' in the city and the aerial guard would be on the lookout for violence approachin'? If so, the fightin' had to be a real issue, maybe an actual militia? I hadn't heard the sounds of fightin', only the demons practicin' their shooting. If people were fightin' back, how did they have the energy? Were Sloth's powers weaker the further away you got from the castle?

This might be my chance to escape. No matter how I might feel about claiming a pack and, in doing so, betrayin' my old pack, I had to do this. Outside, there might be answers. In here, I was worthless.

"Fine," I said. "When do we go?"

"Now." Sloth waved a pudgy hand and, though no soldiers stood in the room, the door opened.

I stiffened. He hadn't said a word and yet they'd come. He must be able to speak with them telepathically. Had he been doin' that the whole time I'd been here? How far did his influence reach?

As questions ran through my head, the smothering magic of his sin lifted a bit. I rolled my neck, relieved to feel more present, more like me. The sin wasn't gone. No, Sloth's dark, oily, nasty magic was still there, ready to pull me back into the docile dog I'd become should it be necessary. But I felt much more like myself.

"Once you mind-link, the effects of my magic will lessen in the other wolves too."

"Aren't you worried we won't come back?"

The prince of darkness smirked. "I've protected my kingdom, wolf. You can only go as far as the boundary, and if you do not return by nightfall, I will send soldiers after you. If you test me, you will not win. And you'll find yourself a few wolves short in your new pack."

Even if I didn't know them yet, just the idea of losin' a pack member was enough to make me reconsider crossing the prince. An alpha protected his pack at all costs.

Plus, Sloth kept another ace up his sleeve. I'd seen the possession of Harper's father—a powerful alpha—and so many in his pack with my own eyes. While I wouldn't be thankful for anything this prince did to me, he wasn't hittin' as hard as he could. Maybe it woulda been too much work. No way to be sure, but I needed to remember that, to play this smart-like.

"We'll be back before dark," I said.

"Silas will show you where they're being kept." Sloth gestured to the door.

Silas! I spun, my gaze locking on the white-haired fae entering the room. The fae of Winter who I'd once called a friend. I growled, and next to me, Rhianna stepped away.

"You know each other?" she whispered.

"That backstabbin' fae is the reason I'm here."

"Well," she murmured, "this should be interesting."

The fear in her voice was unmistakable, and though I hated makin' her feel unsafe, rage still coursed through me. Burned, more like. Silas was the reason I was here. The reason I hadn't seen my friends in far too long.

Haven't seen Harper.

Free of the prince's influence over my mind, my desire to see my favorite she-wolf multiplied tenfold. Already, my desire to see her had been strong, stronger than I would have imagined, given the feeling of sloth in the air. A part of me wondered if that was 'cause of the isolation I experienced most hours of the day, but another part knew that wasn't it. Harper and I had grown close, and I wanted more than a friendship. I thought she did too.

"Gunner," Silas said as I approached with the witches right behind me. "I'll show you three to the pack so you can be on your way."

"Did you trap those wolves too?" I sniped as we left the throne room and Sloth's watchful gaze.

"They're local," Silas said. "No need to trap them when His Majesty's magic is so effective."

There was also no hint of remorse in his voice. Cold as ice.

"His Majesty, huh? Si, I never thought you'd be such a traitor."

Silver eyes flashed up at me, hurt brimmin' there before Silas's lips curled into a sneer. "I did what I had to do for me. For my people."

The question of what that meant nearly flew off my tongue when I slammed my lips shut. I didn't give a hoot what Silas was doin'. The moment I could bring him to justice, I would.

So I said nothing as Silas led me and the witches through the castle. He stopped at a locked door,

"Open it," Silas instructed the guard on duty, one of the rhino-demons.

The guard did so, and the door swung open on a groan to reveal stairs. Even from where we stood, the musty scent of wolves was thick in the air. We descended the steps, so many of 'em I wondered how deep we were goin'. There weren't true basements in this city—then again, this whole castle was protected by magic, so maybe it was an exception. Not a speck of sunlight penetrated down here. Only torches lit the way down.

That the Sloth was keepin' wolves down here and me upstairs—under guard, but still in a decent enough room—

was proof that Prince Belhor saw me as a lure. As if I needed such proof. I didn't trust that demon as far as I could throw him.

"Here they are," Silas said as we reached the bottom step and gestured to the cages.

Ten wolves in human form stared back at me. Six men, four women, all of 'em filthy as hell and spaced so they couldn't touch one another. Rank smelling buckets were their only companions in their cages.

Old Ones have mercy on them. It would have been horrible to be down here, locked away and unable to hold hands for comfort.

"Your new alpha." Silas gestured to me. "Submit and we will let you out. For a while."

I stepped forward. "I'm Gunner."

"You follow the demons who took our home! We don't want you!" A brown-skinned woman in her forties thrust a rigid finger at me.

The blood left my face. "I don't. I'm captive, same as you."

"Then why aren't you down here?" A man rasped as though he needed water. "Why do you look clean and smell normal?"

"I—"

"He's a valuable captive," Silas answered. "And no one said you may ask questions. We need you to mind-link to Gunner. Now."

Moons above. I wanted to pummel Silas even more, but those demon guards stood behind us, and they would remain as a guard until they handed us off to be babysat by the aerial unit.

"Silas, let me." I turned to the wolves again. "I'm not a follower of Prince Belhor, but I am someone he thinks he can use. Like he's doin' now." I gestured back to the witches. "Them too. The prince wants these witches to go out and grow food. Apparently, people are already goin' hungry. If you're locals, you might even know some of them."

I didn't like playin' the guilt card, but in this instance, I would. No matter if I learned more about what was happening out there, people needed food. "We need to protect the witches while they work 'cause somethin' is happening out there."

None of the wolves said anything. A good sign.

"I know it's not ideal. Heck, I have my own pack that I miss, but the prince wants us all to mind-link. You may all be from the same pack and know each other, but if you want outta those cages, even just for the day, you'll need to accept me as alpha. You have to submit and allow me to mind-link you. Once you do, the effects of the prince's sin will lift from you too."

The silence echoed in the basement, and from what I could tell by their narrowed eyes and sneers, the wolves were still mad as hell. Not that I blamed 'em. As much as I wanted to get out into the city and see what in the blazes was goin' on, defecting from your pack was a big deal.

The minutes ticked by, and I prepared try again, to go at this from another way, when one wolf, the forty-somethin' woman stood and bowed ever so slightly.

It wasn't the traditional way to express submission, but seein' as these people couldn't shift, I wasn't offended. One by one, the others followed her lead, standing and bowing, until every single wolf had accepted me as alpha.

"I'm gonna mind-link now." I hoped it would be as easy as Pa always claimed it was. He said that once wolves submitted to an alpha, creating the mind-link came naturally. I needed to be let in.

I stretched my powers out, the ones I used subconsciously to mind-link with my pack. It took more effort than I thought it would, but I was pretty sure that was on me. No matter how much I wanted to leave this castle, to take my first step into maybe findin' freedom, it was impossible to ignore that creating these new links meant severing ties with my old pack. It meant I'd claimed a pack.

I would no longer be my father's heir.

But I had to do what I had to do. I had to survive, so I pushed through that block and entered the wolves' heads one by one. They submitted again, and we clicked into place. The bond of a new pack formed.

When the last member submitted, I prayed Pa hadn't felt it, that he didn't think I was dead after I severed our connection.

I swallowed down the many emotions, all of 'em negative, wellin' inside me. My new pack didn't deserve my drama, so right now I needed to be strong for them.

I placed a hand over my heart. "I vow to protect you with my tooth and claw."

"We vow to follow and protect you with tooth and claw." The echo rang through the room, and though tears shone in many of their eyes, I recognized relief there too.

"It's done." I glared at Silas, then the demon guards. "Let 'em out."

CHAPTER TWELVE

TOBIAS

MEREDITH'S FACE NESTLED INTO MY CHEST AS I PULLED HER CLOSE. "I wish you didn't have to go."

I swallowed. I didn't wish to attend the Covenant meeting either, but S&S was entwined with the demon princes and after the attack in the graveyard this morning, no one believe the *Vindix* should go anywhere that didn't involve them doing one of two things: finding more *Vindix* or fighting the princes. So Luca, Shay, Serena, and I were journeying to Seattle alone.

Shay had taken the most convincing. It was, of course, Luca who'd persuaded her that we'd need the nephilim when we informed the Covenant of Egor's death. A firsthand testimony from a nephilim went much further than that of two vampires. Or even a mage.

Unfortunately, that wasn't the biggest news we'd share. No, today we'd also be telling the Covenant about the *Vindix* and their fated mission, which the *Arcacustos* were not happy about. But Luca had always had a silver tongue, and the *Vindix* might very well need the help of the Covenant. So the elder witches relented, on one condition—that the identities of the

Vindix remained a secret until it was absolutely necessary to reveal them. A stipulation that I was all too happy to follow. I did not want anyone trying to target or use my mate.

"I'll be back before darkness falls," I assured Meredith.

"But what if the meeting goes on and it takes days to get things done? Luca said it might."

"Then we'll return to Seattle tomorrow, and the next day, and the one after that. But I am not spending even one night away from my mate."

We possessed luxiters. There was no reason why I could not return to England on a whim. Not that seeing my mate was a whim. More like a necessity.

Given the current climate, I was very aware of how lucky we in S&S were. Globally, travel was discouraged. To attend this meeting, many in the Covenant had needed to drive or fly on wing. Oftentimes for days. Some of the wealthier elected officials had hired private jets with pilots who were willing to break the flight ban that, in light of Hell coming to Earth, now spanned the globe. Most Covenant members could not come. The world was in chaos, and to bring elected officials from every corner of the globe was impossible, but the members had done their best to get as many leaders in one place as possible. They'd even chosen to meet in a part of the world that had, thus far, experienced fewer horrors than most. I only hoped it stayed that way—that the convergence of so many powerful leaders would not attract attention.

"I'll be waiting." Meredith pulled back and stood on tiptoe. Her lips found mine and heat rushed through me as she gave me a very thorough goodbye.

"Whenever you're done sucking face, we're ready," Shay shouted from where she stood with Luca and Serena, ready for travel. Giselle, Stuart, and Benedict waited nearby for Meredith to return. My sire and Stuart would be working with Meredith today, helping her hone her skills as a compulsion breaker. To my relief, my mate had caught on to that power, and the Opal of Heaven strengthened her daily. The rest of the *Arcacustos* were out back with the other *Vindix*, training in the magics of spirit, air, and fire.

Only Hans wasn't training today. It was too painful for him. Though Luca had contained the curse days ago, it still seemed to radiate through Hans. He walked and functioned, but not like normal. I suspected Hans's condition was more the reason for the scowl on Shay's face than my lengthy goodbye with my mate.

"Be safe," Meredith whispered. "I love you."

"I love you too." I kissed her again before we broke apart, and I joined Luca's side.

"Link up," Shay commanded, and I took Luca's hand as Serena grasped my other one.

Meredith remained before us, eyes shining with tears. My heart constricted, feeling her pain. Since we'd become fully mated, we had not been separated by so many miles. As our mate bond was still new, it was bloody difficult to stay away from her.

"We'll be back soon," I promised.

"I'll take good care of her." Giselle slipped next to my mate and put her arm around Meredith's shoulders.

Had my maker not been present, I would not be going at all. Only knowing that wards, a coven of powerful witches, *and* my maker all protected Meredith made me feel safe in leaving.

Safe, but not happy.

"Thank you, Giselle."

"We're going now," Shay pressed, her tone more irritated than before.

I wanted to snap at her but held my tongue. Something was going on between her and Hans, and I thought I knew what. Had I been in such a situation, I would be irritable too.

"To the SAM in Seattle," Shay announced before speaking the magic word.

The luxiter lit up, and suddenly we were being compressed and blinded by white light. I squeezed my eyes shut, willing the travel to be over. As convenient as luxiters were, they were also uncomfortable.

Nearly a minute ticked by before the light dimmed and our feet slammed into cement. Hard rain pelted my face. As I opened my eyes, the Seattle Art Museum materialized. I smelled the water in the nearby sound.

"Over here." Luca gestured us away from the museum and to a boarded -up dingy bar.

While no demon prince had claimed this city, and few demons ranged this far north of Los Angeles, the humans still knew something was afoot. Their news channels reported on the sightings of monsters and many people had gone into hiding.

The sidewalks stretched before us, empty. The city was eerily quiet, though I felt eyes watching us from above. I imagined people peering through their apartment or office windows, wondering who the people were who had appeared out of nowhere. If we were friends or foe.

To be a human in this new world would be utterly terrifying.

Luca approached the bar and placed his hand on the door. "Luca Moretti."

The door shimmered and opened.

"Who set up the protections?" I asked.

"Artem," Luca answered as the door swung open on creaky hinges. "He drove across the country. Ran into more than one horror along the way and knew they'd need extreme protection."

"Horrors are becoming quite the trend," Serena said as we entered a dim bar that reeked of cheap beer and peanuts. My sister wrinkled her nose. "Please tell me this dump is a front."

"Of course it is." Luca shut the door and put his palm flat against it. Magic swirled, re-activating whatever spell the Covenant had put on the door to keep unwanted people out. "The safehouse is in the city's underground. This is the entrance. Follow me."

The coven master led us through the bar, all the way to the back and to what looked to be a janitor's closet. Again, he placed his hand on the door and spoke his name. Runes flared on the wood, reminding me of Hans's home and the markings he used to keep his property safe.

Was that house still standing? Was mine?

Only a few weeks had passed since I'd stepped foot in my New Haven home, but it felt far longer. So much had happened. So much had changed.

"In and down." Luca opened the door, and I found I had been right. It was a janitor's closet.

And, it seemed, an entrance to the underground tunnels of Seattle. From where I stood, I could smell the musk, the damp, and the feces of mice and rats that thrived in the underground of any city.

We descended into the tunnels, and at the bottom, Shay summoned light, and we followed Luca down a tunnel. He wended his way through the underground system. There were no signs of footsteps in the dirt to follow. There weren't even scents, aside from those that were natural. Whomever spelled these tunnels had done so intentionally to wipe away any sign that the Covenant members had been here.

Five minutes ticked by, then ten. I was about to inquire if Luca had taken a wrong turn when he stopped. "We're here."

Serena looked up the tunnel, then down. "There's not even a door."

"Not one you can see. But Artem told me I'd sense it, and I do." Luca twisted right. *"Irekita."*

The password that doubled as a spell left his lips and the wall of the tunnel disappeared so that we gazed into a room filled with supernaturals.

"Luca," Artem Kovalenko, a Ukrainian caster wizard in his sixties, was the first to notice us. The red beret he often wore was perched atop his head. "You're the last. Come in."

"Apologies if we kept everyone waiting," Luca replied as we strode into the room. "Did I get the time wrong?"

"No. Most of us arrived days early and have been staying down here. There are beds, in case of an emergency."

"This is quite the setup." Luca eyed the room.

Despite being underground, the safehouse resembled an English hunting lodge in decor, complete with a fire burning in the hearth, leaving me to wonder if the smoke was simply magicked away. Worn armchairs, candles, and even a bar cart completed the look. There was, however, one notable differ-ence from a leisure lodge.

A table that sat at least thirty ran the length of the long room. A place to meet, to discuss the future of the supernatural world.

Perhaps now the human world as well.

The magical world could not hide again. We were well and truly out.

That sentiment multiplied when a man in uniform entered the room from a hallway that led to what I had to assume was the sleeping areas. He wore a midnight blue uniform and a white shirt beneath. Four stars and various military insignia decorated the dark blue jacket.

"The Covenant has been in talks with world leaders. The U.S. Army needs to have knowledge of our plans so they can help, if possible." Luca swallowed. "They are unprepared to deal with magical threats on their own. Today, only one branch of the U.S. armed forces could make it, but they will relay the messages to other powers."

I'd thought the militaries around the globe would need to get involved, but had I ever believed I'd be in a meeting with a four-star general? Never.

"*Shaylina!*" a shrill, accented voice cut through my astonishment and suddenly, I was being pushed aside. "Shaylina! You're safe!"

"Hi, Mom." Shay exhaled as her mother, the strong-willed nephilim Seat, Angelina Ramos, pulled her daughter into a hug. "I told you I was back."

"Two days ago, darling!" A sob wrenched out of the woman, and Shay's eyes widened. I knew from Meredith that Shay was not close with her mother. Such a show of affection, of worry, must be rare.

"I didn't know you'd come today!" Angelina pulled away from her daughter and brushed aside Shay's curls.

Shay's face softened. "I didn't either. Not until a few minutes before we left."

"Well, I am glad you did. Come sit by me." Angelina took her daughter's hand and led her to the table.

"Yes, I suppose we should begin," Artem said. "I'll get the

others." He disappeared to the back, leaving us to take our seats.

Luca veered to the end of the table, to the side nearest to the hearth. I positioned myself between Luca and Serena. The human general appeared at a loss, which was likely strange for a man of such a position, so I patted the seat next to me. "This is open."

The general's eyes narrowed. "What are you?"

Ah, so he was here, and he would work with us, but he did not trust us.

"Vampire."

Though the general kept his expression neutral, I could hear the uptick in his heartbeat.

"We won't bite," Serena said with an enchanting smile that showed off her extended fangs. I refrained from rolling my eyes at the show she was putting on. "Not unless you want us to, that is."

The general chose a seat at the opposite end of the table, far away from us.

The others filled the room and took their seats. As they entered, I noted their magical orders, and recognized some by name.

Raven-haired Liliana Valori represented my order, though I did not see the third, and the only other living vampire Seat since we'd killed Egor.

Two wolves had made it, one necromancer, and Nina Tyche represented the phoenixes, one of the rarest magical orders.

Susan Chappel was a middle-aged witch of prodigious skill. Her presence meant that two witch Seats had made it to Seattle, and as Brons was locked away in the *Abscondita* manor, the third would not be coming. I wondered if Artem and Susan worried over Brons. Or if they disliked him as much as I did. I did not recognize the others in the room, but overall, there were more people present than I'd expected.

The table was full when Artem returned and took the final seat at the end of the table, next to Luca. "General McNair? Would you like to move down here? Luca has vital information for our cause."

I glanced down the table. Would the human dare approach the monstrous vampires?

"I can hear as well from here," the general replied.

Serena sniggered, which earned her a look from Artem. A look that turned into a small, amused smile as he no doubt concluded what had happened. I was willing to bet the general hadn't accepted him easily either. Or any of us, for that matter.

"I'll take the minutes," Susan Chappel announced as she set a piece of paper and pen on the table, twirled her hand, and the pen righted itself, preparing to note down what was said and done.

"Luca," Artem began, "why don't you begin with telling us what you can about your coven's involvement in fighting Hell's takeover?"

"Get comfortable." Luca leaned forward over the long wooden table. "It's quite a long story."

LUCA SPOKE FOR AN AGE, INTERRUPTED ONLY BY GENERAL McNair, who did not seem to understand that Luca—while not a Covenant member—held great sway in the room. But perhaps most shockingly of all was the fact that no one balked at the news of Egor's death. It seemed he was as unpopular among the Covenant as he was in my own estimation.

When the coven master was done, he leaned back in his chair, the wood creaking as he did so, and folded his hands. "Questions?"

Nina Tyche, the phoenix representative, spoke first, her eyes glowing in a way that happened only when her kind was quite riled. "So this group—the *Vindix*, as you call them—will have to defeat the princes, but the rest of us need to be ready to protect and fight when the barriers erected around the cities fall. So destroying those domes is a priority for the rest of us. That's the gist of it, no?"

"It is," Luca agreed and turned to the human. "Is it possible for the army to join forces with supernatural armies?"

Once the Covenant members left this space, they'd mobilize forces. And while the humans had said they would help, that was before. Before Luca had explained everything we knew, which was quite a lot more than anyone else in this room.

General McNair lifted his chin. "We have already surrounded two: DC and New Orleans. The military is trying to break through the magical barriers there. However, I must speak to the president about being outside other cities."

The wolves under Lucifer's control that ranged outside of LA had probably kept the armed forces away. I wasn't sure why they weren't outside Las Vegas yet, but they needed to form a presence there too.

"As many of the affected are American cities, it's not out of bounds for us to ask that the army mobilize to *each* fallen city," Luca pressed.

"I realize that," the general replied. "However, I'm not of the rank to make promises. Not about this. I have questions, though."

"Go on." Artem tented his hands on the table.

"Will guns kill them? Bombs?" the general asked, his tone somewhat smaller. I didn't think it was one a man of his stature used often.

Luca exhaled. "Hit most demons in the heart and head and bullets will work the same as they would on humans. Or most creatures, really. There are exceptions, like vampires and shades and demons who have no form, but the magical community will be present to help with those. What the humans cannot handle, we'll target."

When faced with a threat like the one we were facing, there was only one true way forward. Kill or be killed.

Artem jumped in. "Small magical forces are already stationed outside each US city, trying to break down the walls. We've been steering clear of the military, for obvious reasons, but once we get the go-ahead to work together, we will."

"We'll need loads of healers too," said Cuan O'Malley, an Irish wolf Covenant Seat living in the States. "For when the walls fall. Who knows how many people are injured inside?"

"Healers will be paramount." Artem echoed Cuan's point.

Susan flicked a wrist. She'd been taking the meeting's minutes with an enchanted pen and was presumably adding 'find more healers' to the list of necessities.

"Does anyone have information on the international cities?" I asked, thinking of London in particular. I had not called it home for many, many years, but to think that it had fallen to a demon prince made me see red.

"You mean the outside forces, right?" Cuan asked, blue eyes narrowing.

"Of course."

To my knowledge, we hadn't been able to reach anyone inside the wards the Princes of Hell placed over their kingdoms.

"I'm in communication with those in the UK and outside Venice," Angelina spoke up. "Forces are waiting. Human and magical. More in the UK but . . ." She shrugged. "The Italians are doing what they can. The infrastructure of Venice limits the means of defense."

"We need to gather information on Sydney too," Luca said. "As much as we can get while global communications are still working."

"As best they can," General McNair amended.

Thus far, the web had been attacked no less than five hundred times. The fact that the Internet was still up at all was a miracle. Same with phone lines.

We had to be prepared to lose them at any second.

"Are there magical means of communicating?" the general asked. "Ones that will not fail. At least for those in this group? Once we leave, things may change quickly."

Everyone looked at Artem. As a caster wizard, he'd be the most likely to know how to enchant items for communication.

But he shook his head. "I have no spell for this. We can only hope that communications hold up and be prepared for when the walls around the cities fall."

When. My chest tightened. No one here doubted that the wards around the prince's kingdoms would fall. They did not doubt that my mate and the other *Vindix* would succeed.

And if they did worry about failure, they did not dare whisper a word of their doubts.

Artem looked at Luca. "Is there a way to purchase more of those . . . luxiters, you called them?"

"Fascinatin' objects, them," Cuan added, his eyes lighting up, presumably at the prospect of getting his hands on one.

"Shay?" Luca asked.

"I don't know," Shay admitted. "The person who creates

them is in hiding. Or he'd planned to go into hiding when I last spoke to him. I can visit and see if maybe he changed his mind?"

"That would be helpful," Artem said. "If one day flight is out of the question, they might be the only option we have to move large numbers of people. Even if we have to move an army group by group, it would be easier than the alternative."

Walking. Miles and miles of walking to get to the princes' kingdoms. And in some cases, sailing. We could only hope the princes did not bring down the world's infrastructure as thoroughly as we feared.

Shay swallowed. "Even if he makes them, though, they take time to create."

"Ask," Nina echoed Artem's sentiment. "It's the best we can do."

"I believe the president needs one of those luxiters you have on hand," General McNair spoke up, clearer, more forcefully this time. "If anyone should have one, it's him."

My eyes widened, but it was Shay who bit back first.

"You think so, *do you*? Has he been fighting this battle for weeks? Does he even plan to come out of his hole to fight?"

The general's jaw worked from side to side and though he sat far away, the frustration rolling off him in waves perfumed the air. I very much doubted that such a high-ranking general met derision from someone who looked as youthful as Shay.

"Interesting," Shay shot back. "If he does not fight, he does not get one."

"This is no way to begin a partnership," McNair spoke levelly but the tension lining his face gave away his frustration.

"Maybe not," Luca interjected before Shay spoke again. A smart move as the nephilim appeared ready to explode. "But the president could not use a luxiter as they are currently configured anyhow. And we need them for the reasons we've lined out. The *Vindix* need them."

The general could not argue with that, so he folded his arms over his chest.

Crisis averted.

For now.

CHAPTER THIRTEEN

GUNNER

Wolves surrounded me, soothin' my soul despite the demons flyin' above and the destruction crowdin' every street.

I'd mind linked with these ten wolves. Strangers. And though I'd severed my ties with my own pack, *my family*, and I felt horrible 'bout it, there was no denyin' that the feelin' of being around wolves again couldn't be beat.

Though bein' outdoors, and not under Sloth's sin, came a close second.

I veered right and rubbed my furry side against a pole. The demons above didn't stop me, didn't even blink an eye, but the wolves in my new pack gave me a lotta side eye.

They suspected what I was up to.

Markin'.

It might be a slim chance, but if S&S broke into the city, and Harper, or even Toby, was with 'em, they might catch my scent. If they did, they could follow it and find me and help free me and my new pack.

"Stop here," Rhianna called out as we approached a garden

of withering trees. "These are orange trees that need some love. We'll be here a while."

The witches got to work, and my wolves spread out around them, ready to protect should we need to.

Alpha, one heavyset gray wolf spoke in my mind. His Southern accent rang out, heavy and thick, like the air in NOLA.

Gunner, I corrected him 'cause though I'd been born to be an alpha, the designation didn't sit right yet. Not from them, these wolves who I didn't know from Adam.

Alpha Gunner, the male corrected, still sounding hesitant. *Is marking wise? If they figure out what you're doing, they might not let us out again.*

I have friends who can help us. But they gotta find me first.

Even as I defended myself, my stomach sank. Not 'cause I didn't trust S&S to come for me—if they found my location, that was. No, I felt bad 'cause these wolves had been enjoying their time outside, around other wolves, and not under Sloth's influence. And though I had a good reason for doin' what I did, they were right to be worried. If I was caught, Sloth would keep us captive at the castle—my pack in cages, Sloth's sin riddlin' our bodies.

I shuddered, rememberin' how under Sloth's powers, we'd barely had had the energy to walk down the street. The world was in an awful state, but I was happy we'd been let out to defend the witches from whatever Sloth was worried about roamin' the streets.

What that somethin' bad was, I had no idea. The humans who'd seen us were docile enough.

Then again, humans weren't the only ones in the city. Hellhounds patrolled the city, though we hadn't seen any today. And, of course, a wide range of demons too. Back in the throne room, I'd gotten the sense that Prince Belhor might be able to speak telepathically to his kind. And maybe that was true. What could equally be true was the idea that Sloth didn't have a super great hold over all his subjects.

The gray wolf continued to watch me. I got the feelin' that those gray eyes didn't miss much. Maybe in his old pack he'd been a beta, a lookout for his alpha.

What's your name? I asked.

His eyes widened as they found mine. *Rubin, Alpha.*

Seriously, just Gunner.

He nodded.

Are you from 'round here?

Originally, but I've been living in Cajun country for a while. Came into the city for the day. Worst decision ever.

Your family is still out there?

They are. Thank the Old Ones.

The princes had only claimed cities. Though demons might drift into the less populous parts of the country, folks seemed safer out in the sticks.

Anyone else in our pack familiar with the city? I asked Rubin. If so, they might help us get to the boundaries of the city. Even though I felt bad about markin' and puttin' my pack at risk, the tradeoff was high if S&S came lookin' for me.

Rubin twisted toward the brown female wolf on his other side. In her human form, she had long brown hair and dark eyes. A pretty thing, no more than twenty-five. *She's from here.*

I linked the female into our conversation and soon enough learned that her name was Lola, and she'd lived here for ten years. The rest of her family lived in Missouri, and she'd had a pack in New Orleans before Sloth took over, but most of them were outta town on a wolf retreat, huntin' and such. Only Lola and a few others had stayed back 'cause they had to work. She didn't know where they were or if they survived the city's fall.

I wanted to reassure Lola and Rubin and each and every wolf under my care that we'd find those they loved. Those to whom they really belonged.

Alpha Gunner? Rubin shook, trying to get my attention again.

What's up?

We're with you if you want to find the barriers around the city. We—

BOOM!

An explosion cut Rubin off. Rhianna screamed, and Dan moved his body in front of her as each wolf in the pack whipped around to where the sound came from.

I sniffed the air, but no gun powder or reek of burnin' anything hit my nose.

Look, Lola lifted her paw in the air.

I looked up, up, up and to the left and saw what she meant. A glow filled the air, though it dissipated by the second.

I think someone tried to bomb the barrier, Lola whispered. *Is the military there? Magic would look different, wouldn't it?*

I wasn't sure but thought she might be onto something. Hope rose inside me. If the military was out there, that had to mean magicals were too. Maybe, soon, the wards that trapped us all would shatter, and we'd be able to fight back.

CHAPTER FOURTEEN

HANS

With each tentative step, my jaw tightened.

Goddess, was it possible to end this pain? It remained as ironic as it was infuriating that a man with the power to torture others with a single thought was enduring constant pain unlike any I'd ever known.

Despite Luca's magical intervention, some of the curse had evaded him. Around the area of confinement, my leg burned—every nerve ending on fire. Still, if the pain had only been there, I could have functioned normally. But somehow, a portion of the curse remained in my bones, so deep I was sure it had been trying to hide from Luca's power. Perhaps it recognized him because it was mage magic, and he was a mage. I had no bleeding idea. All I knew was whomever had cursed that dagger possessed extraordinary magic, paired with unfathomable foresight.

None of Hannah's potions or balms or spells had done much to help. No breath work or positive thinking dented it. Only one thing really worked.

Shay.

Her presence, her light—and not the angelic kind—worked its own magic. Though the pain was always there, it dimmed in her presence.

And while I enjoyed being around Shay, and was grateful for her effect on me, I still needed to fix this. After much rumination, I suspected the first step would be to fill the gaping hole inside me where my wizard magic should be. As I was, no matter what cures people foisted upon me, they weren't dealing with a *whole* person, but a half. Maybe less, considering I still had not quite come to terms with my demon magic.

Hence why, while the others attended the Covenant meeting, I was dragging myself to Brons's room again. No doubt he would spit at the sight of me, but I remained determined to get my magic back. Not only for my sake, which would have been motivation enough, but for that of the world. I was a *Vindix.* The defining characteristic of this archaic group was that we were all witches. Surely, I would need my witch magic to help finish off the Princes of Hell?

Somehow, I have to convince Richard Brons to return my caster powers.

I reached the stairway that led to his room, and one by one, lowered. Each time my foot hit the next step, it felt like I'd jumped on a dozen knives. I hissed and tears pricked my eyes. It might have been smarter to wait until the others returned from the meeting, but sitting in my room, in pain and alone, sounded like torture.

Plus, a prideful part of me wanted to do this without help. To heal myself. To be whole when they got back. Sin or not, pride motivated, and I would use it.

By the time I reached the bottom, sweat ran down my face. Grasping the wall with one hand, I wiped perspiration from my brow and fought to reclaim my breath. I couldn't let Brons witness my weakness. He'd only use it against me.

Straightening, I continued to the door and knocked.

"What?" a bitter voice within called out.

"It's Hans," I replied. "I've come to talk."

"No."

Heaving a resigned sigh, I pushed the door open and caught Richard Brons, one of the three Covenant Seats for the witches, leaping off his bed and hiding.

"I won't speak with you!" Brons called out. "You're a savage."

The demon magic inside me surged, as if it wanted to show him how monstrous I could become. I shoved that dark power down, down, down, smothering it quickly. If this was to work, I needed to prove I was not just my demon blood. That I could choose to be good—as Shay had told me so many times, even if I did not believe her every time.

I thanked the Goddess that I'd had the foresight to leave the Pearl of Hell in my room. Though I hated to part from it, the Pearl's influence was too strong, and I was currently too weak. If Brons were to attack me, I didn't need the Pearl piling on him.

Dark powers subdued, I stepped deeper into the room. It smelled as bad as the last time I'd been here. Goddess, didn't Gloria know a cleaning spell or something? I was a much younger caster, and I knew plenty of such spells.

"Richard, I want to apologize for my actions the other day. I was not myself."

"Or you were more yourself than you wish to admit," the wizard grunted, still not showing his face, still hiding.

I paused about halfway to the bed, wanting to be closer, but not wishing to get too close—lest he saw that as aggression. I'd already entered against his wishes and had attacked the guy on my first visit—when he'd been defenseless, no less. I couldn't blame his fear of me, and sitting on his bed seemed a step too far.

"I went through a lot at the Blood Court and lost control of my demon magic," I admitted. "I should have waited until I was wholly myself, but I miss my powers. Can you stand so we might talk about this like civilized men?"

Richard Brons barked out a harsh laugh. "*Civilized?* The hellblooded are not civilized. Or have you not heard what's happening outside? What *your kind* is doing? Filthy monsters!"

"I'm aware of what they're doing," I replied, brushing off the commentary on 'my kind'. In no way did I expect to erase his prejudices today. I only needed him to see that keeping my magic to himself did great harm, and not just to me. "I'm one of the chosen ones who is supposed to stop it."

He stared at me, silent as the grave. Silent, but seemingly unsurprised.

"Did someone already tell you?"

"A crone might have mentioned it."

The *Arcacustos* kept the knowledge of the *Vindix* safe by keeping our secrets. That one of them had told Brons the truth, screamed at how dire things were getting in the world—how much they, too, believed I needed to be whole for the war to come.

"Then you know what I'm to do. Who I'm to fight. Though I might share a magical order with the Princes of Hell, they are the veritable monsters."

"As are you." Brons sneered and waved a tanned arm in my direction. "No matter how calmly you stand or how levelly you talk. These things are not mutually exclusive."

Anger flared. How was he so blind? So stubborn? Why did he insist on withholding something that wasn't his when his selfishness affected so many?

"I am part monster, but this monster has a job to do and if I don't, millions will die," I said, trying not to convince him of my goodness, but to appeal to his sense of humanity.

Brons shot up, his face gaunt and a trembling finger thrust at me. "Don't pretend like you care about others dying. I saw how you and your friends hurled demon fire! I watched them die!"

The truth hit me. Despite Brons's hatred of me, this might not be about me at all. Or not as much as I believed.

This was about Brons's lost love. And how I'd been, at least partially, responsible for Egor's death.

I stared Brons in the eye. "I care. And I won't lie and tell you I liked Egor, but I *am* sorry for your loss. For your pain. That he had to die so needlessly." I inhaled, repressing the urge to tell him that Meredith hadn't thrown demon fire at all, but riot fire given to her by a witch. A witch, like Brons. "Had the king and queen given us what we wanted, no one would have been harmed. I never wanted to harm Egor. I promise you that."

His lower lip trembled. Had I elicited something other than hatred in the man? He might never call me a friend, but could my apology change his mind? Get him to see that this was bigger than me or him or his lost love? Bigger than anyone in this manor. Or even on this entire island?

"Richard," I began again, "I—"

"Get out." He turned his back to me. "I do not compromise with monsters."

CHAPTER FIFTEEN

SHAY

My legs and back ached under the strain of pushing back my chair.

For hours, we'd been sitting in the underground meeting chamber in Seattle. Hours in which we'd debated the literal fate of the world.

With a human, nonetheless.

I wondered how often that had happened throughout history. Would this be the new normal?

After what so many humans had seen, what they'd likely been through at the hands of the Princes of Hell, I didn't see how the magical community could shove the truth of our existence back into the dark. If I didn't have so many more pertinent issues on my mind, I'd love to daydream about what the new world we were about to embark on would be like.

"Shaylina, a word?" my mother called.

During the meeting, I'd noticed her stealing glances at me often. Strange to be the object of such intense attention. When I was younger, I would have craved that attention. A small part of me still did. Another part knew that Mother should have focused more during the meeting—that our kind and those of other supernatural orders would depend on her leadership in these coming days, weeks, months, or even, I shuddered to think, years.

Members of the Covenant had swarmed my friends, occupying them, so I turned to my mother and forced a wary smile.

"Of course."

She led me out of the meeting room and down a narrow hallway. For the first time, I spied basic sleeping chambers—places for people of importance to hunker down and wait out the storms. Unlike the meeting room, these spaces were sparse, emergency quarters only. Small space or not, my skin prickled at the injustice of the world right now. What the people in the fallen cities wouldn't give to be living where they'd be safe and sound.

"In here," Mother said, opening a door.

Her room was very small, easily filled with a collapsible cot and a small side table littered with personal effects that defined my mother: a tube of designer lipstick, a soft pink cashmere shawl I'd seen her wear a hundred times folded in a neat square, and a cell phone. The screen was dark, no texts of calls coming in like they usually did. For the first time in years, no one in her business empire needed her.

"What's up?" I asked when she motioned for me to join her on the cot.

"Shadows and Secrets is highly involved in the war to come," my mother took my hand as she spoke, "but I wish for you to stay here. With me."

I blinked. Of all the things I expected my mother to say, a plea for me to remain with her was not anywhere near the list.

"Why?"

"Why? You're my *hija angelical,* Shaylina! I've feared for your safety since the day Los Angeles fell." Tears—real, honest to Heaven, tears—filled her eyes. Even if her eyes had been dry, I'd have known how deeply she felt. Mother had slipped into Spanish and that only happened in two occasions: when she was furious, or when she was upset. Basically, when she felt raw.

My lips parted. "I can't."

"But *you can!*" Her voice cracked. "There are plenty of people to fight. You don't need to. Not against those monsters."

The demons. Heavens, I should have expected this. We were nephilim, after all.

I met my mother's eyes and flinched at the pain there. Had I been selfish not to consider her feelings this whole time?

She has been calling more often. A lot more.

But during her calls, she hadn't asked me to come to her or to stop doing what I did. With Hans at death's door, I never would have considered such a thing.

"Mom, I can't. I have to stay with S&S. That's my job and people I love—people you love too—are affected by this."

"I love no one more than I love my daughter."

I sucked in a breath, and she did not fail to notice.

Her face fell. "Shaylina, I've been hard on you. It comes from a place of love. A place of wishing for you to be better than me. To live up to your full potential."

As an archangel's daughter, so many people thought I was capable of far more than was possible.

My mother scooted closer, and the canvas cot squeaked beneath our weight. "I wouldn't be able to take it if you fought and died at the hands of the demons, my love. Your light is too precious. You're too precious to me."

My heart ached. Heavens, how I'd yearned to hear such simple words from her. Words that weren't what I could do better or how I could do better. How I could remind people I was an archangel's daughter.

I'd always wanted to be *enough*, and now I was. And yet . . .

"I can't stay here, Mom," I said. "Just like you can't."

"I'm different," she replied. "The nephilim elected me. I must go out there and help, but you . . ." She swallowed. "You're the only person I truly love."

Tears slid down my cheeks, and I fell forward, into my mother's chest. My mother pulled me closer and stroked my hair as I cried. For once, she said nothing, just let me feel and be and when my tears were done, I exhaled before rising.

"Mom," I breathed, feeling wrung out after all that had happened these past days. "I'm sorry, but I can't stay here. I have to go back to England to make sure that—someone is okay." I swallowed the name that almost snuck out, but my mother was cunning.

She exhaled. "You worry about the demon."

"Hans isn't a demon," I retorted, my usual rigidity when around my mother returning despite the moment we'd shared. "He's a hellblooded wizard."

I half expected her to say they were the same to her, but instead, she nodded. "May I ask you something, Shaylina?"

"Sure?"

Why was nothing in this conversation going as I expected?

"Do you love him?"

All my breath left me in one go. Yet again, another blow I had not seen coming. And as the question swirled in my mind, I found there was only one answer. But could I tell my mother?

I met her stare, sizing her up, and when I did, her face softened.

"So, you do." She exhaled.

"I do," I agreed.

She looked down before meeting my eyes again. "Then he must be exceptional if you love him."

The wall I'd built around my heart crumbled. Since she'd learned his blood status, it was the first time I'd heard my mother say something nice about Hans.

"Thank you," I whispered. "I hope he feels the same."

Mother's eyes widened. "Well, of course he does! I've seen how he looks at you, Shaylina! And if he doesn't love you back, then, I don't know what is wrong with that man."

A laugh burst from me. Who was this woman and what had she done with my mother?!

"You're too much."

"I'm always the right amount." She rolled her shoulders back. "If you love him, I'm sure he loves you. He'd better treat you right."

Treat me right. I was certain Hans would—if he loved me. Not that I felt comfortable asking him about that. Not while he was in so much pain, anyway.

If only Brons would give Hans back his magic.

An idea sparked something inside me. Mother and Richard Brons had been elected the same year and served many terms as Seats for their magical orders. Could my mother know something about Brons that might help us convince the wizard to give up Hans's magic?

"Mom, not to change the subject, but I have something important to ask you."

She nodded, as if to say *go on.*

"Do you remember the Vow of Intent that Richard Brons made with Hans?"

"Of course."

"Well, Hans broke his promise to save his sister."

"A stupid move," Mother said.

Yes. Hans had shown time and time again that his demon blood did not define him, but Nicoleta was a horrible person and had not deserved to be saved by her brother. Not that Hans would agree.

"Yes, well, now Brons has Hans's wizarding magic, and we need it back. As we mentioned in the meeting, Hans is a *Vindix*, and he needs to be at full strength."

Her eyebrows pulled together. "Are you saying that you have information on where Richard Brons is?"

Oops, my big mouth. But I'd already said as much so, in for a penny, in for a pound, I supposed. "Um, yes?"

Mother remained silent for a few seconds before a low chuckle rang out of her. "I can't say that I care about the man much. But what in the world would you need to ask me in relation to Richard Brons?"

This was going far better than I'd expected.

"Do you have any information about him that I might use as, say, *leverage*?"

Her full lips parted. "Are you blackmailing him?"

"No." What we were doing—had done to him—was worse. My mom did not need to know that. "But I need information to convince him to release Hans's magic back to him. Willingly, of course."

"Shaylina, that *is most definitely* blackmail."

I blinked. "Well, you asked if I *already* was. We're not, but I guess I'm not above it. Hans needs his magic."

Not just to beat the Princes of Hell either. Like Hans, I

believed that if he was at full power, his pain might be lessened. Also, I hoped that if he had his wizard magic, I might be able to help him more.

"It's against the law," Mother mused, "but you're right. You and S&S need his magic more than Richard Brons."

I envisioned gears spinning in her head as a slow smile spread across her face.

"He has a young niece in Phoenix whom he loves dearly. Alicia. Threaten her, and he will give it up."

My stomach pitted at the resurgence of the mother that I'd known all my life. She was brutal, and though that was what I needed in the moment, I hated bringing an innocent into this.

But for Hans, I would.

"Thanks, Mom," I whispered, trying to ignore the sensation of spiders crawling along my arms.

THE LUXITER'S LIGHT DISAPPEARED AS IT DEPOSITED US ON THE manor's lawn. Damp air filled my nostrils. We were back, and I was dying to see Hans.

Luca broke apart from the group, his brown eyes weary from the meeting and all the decisions it had entailed. "I'm calling it a night. I suggest everyone else get as much rest as you can. In two days, we're leaving for New Orleans."

"Two days? Why not tomorrow?" I asked. "Harper is already dying to leave. She won't like waiting another day."

"I'm aware," Luca replied. "But after speaking with General McNair, I believe it's for the best. We already have to go to the city for Rabi's stone. Of course, we're going to rescue Gunner while we're there. If we can also bring down the wards around the city, or make a hole in it, the armies can move in. For that to happen, the general requested an extra day. I don't think it's too much to ask."

When he put it that way, no, it wasn't. Still, Harper was gonna be *pissed*.

"Also, I'd like to give Hans more time to heal." Luca cleared his throat. "If that's possible."

I had not mentioned the conversation with my mother. If anyone deserved to know about our possible leverage over Richard Brons, it was Hans.

"*Okay*," I muttered. "But you're gonna be the one to tell Harper 'cause I'm not about to deal with that attitude."

Luca gave a dry laugh, but didn't argue and as a group, we aimed for the door.

The relative warmth of the manor engulfed me, and I heaved a long sigh. With its many dark hallways and witchy ambiance, this place didn't exactly feel like home, but I had grown used to being here. Comfortable, in a way.

Luca climbed the stairs to our rooms. The vampires branched off. No doubt Tobias was going to find Meredith, whereas Serena made for the kitchens. While I was starving too, I needed to see Hans first.

I climbed the steps to the part of the manor where the S&S members stayed. It was late in England, and considering Hans was still in a lot of pain, I suspected I'd find him resting. Maybe even sleeping.

One would think the idea of waking him up would be a deterrent, but after my conversation with my mother, all I wanted to do was lay eyes on Hans.

I approached the door quietly, listening hard for any sound of life inside Hans's room and catching faint notes of music. I tilted my head. The song struck me as strange—new age. So unlike Hans.

Intrigued, my fist fell against the door three times, and the music silenced.

"Yes?" Hans called out.

"It's Shay," I said. "Checking on you."

"Ah." A long pause filled the space between us. I tried to imagine what Hans was thinking about my late-night visit. "Come in."

My heart leapt, and I pushed the door open to find Hans sitting on the bed, still in jeans and a t-shirt, his phone next to him.

"What was that song?" I asked, shutting the door softly and hovering near the entrance.

"You heard it?"

"Only when I got close."

His cheeks took on a pink hue. "Music to raise your vibration. I found it on an app and hoped it would ease the pain."

"Did it?"

"Not really."

My heart sank to my knees. "I'm so sorry."

"It's not your fault."

I searched for something positive to say, settling on the first thing I thought of. "The meeting went well."

Hans patted the bed. "Tell me."

I glided over, heat flooding me as I got closer to him. Did he feel the same way? It was difficult to tell. Every few minutes, he'd wince from the pain, and I was pretty sure he was masking it most other times.

I eased down onto the soft bed and relayed what had happened at the meeting. Hans took everything in while I spoke, which had to have been for an hour straight. Near the end, his eyelids began to droop, his energy was waning— something that had become more common.

"So," I said, trying to wind it up and allow him to rest, "we're leaving for New Orleans in two days."

Hans jolted. "Two days? To get Rabi's stone?"

"And Gunner," I said. "Harper won't accept anything else."

Hans swallowed. "Then I must be ready."

"We hope you will be. But if you aren't, I can stay here with you."

Luca would be mad, but to be honest, I didn't care. Hans was all that mattered. And he needed someone to be with him.

"I'll talk to Brons tomorr—aaah!" Hans hissed and gripped his thigh as his lower leg spasmed and black tendrils of magic began to spin out of him.

I leapt up, and my stomach pitted when his face fell.

"I'm sorry Shay," Hans ground out. "When the pain strikes like that, I can't control my magic as well. I think, if I can get my wizard magic back, it will help. I'll be more stable. *More me.*"

I nodded, unable to deny his words. I hoped the same. And seeing him in pain now, I clearly saw what I needed to do to make it happen.

"It's fine." I smiled. "I was startled, but I should let you rest, anyway. Try to get some sleep myself too. I'll see you tomorrow, okay?"

"Good night," Hans replied, easing back onto his bed. "Thanks for coming by."

I left Hans's room, though I didn't go to my own room. No, I couldn't bear seeing him in pain any longer. And while I hadn't shared my plan with Hans, it started in the same way his did—albeit with a bit more malice—by blackmailing Brons into releasing Hans's magic.

CHAPTER SIXTEEN

HANS

MY STOMACH GROWLED, INSISTENT AS THE AGONY THAT RIPPED through my bones and pulsed in my leg. I didn't want to walk to the kitchen but couldn't wait any longer to eat. I shoved off my bed, wincing at the stabbing sensation that shot through me at the slight motion and swallowing the groan climbing up my throat.

How would I be able to help in New Orleans when I could barely move across my room?

I should see if flying is easier.

I hadn't summoned my wings, let alone tested them. The blade had hit so close to the feathered appendages that apparently, they had vanished during healing—or so I'd been told. Were they damaged? Terror at the idea kept me from finding out.

I pulled on a shirt, jeans, and socks, but opted to leave off the shoes. The less I had on my body at the moment, the better.

Presentable enough, I exited my room and jolted as I found Shay sitting in a wooden chair across from my door.

"Uh, hi?"

She beamed, and some of the red-hot agony pummeling me dimmed. I didn't know why she was here, but her presence helped. "I didn't want to wake you, but I have great news!"

I blinked. "I'm all ears."

"Brons agreed to give you back your magic!"

My knees buckled, but Shay caught me before I fell.

"Whoa," she whispered, her sweet scent teasing my nostrils even as she helped me straighten. "You okay?"

"You convinced him." I paused. "It was you, right? You look entirely too smug for it not to have been you."

She stuck out her tongue. "Yes, I convinced him."

"How?"

Yesterday, Brons insisted that he would not even speak to me again. Releasing my magic? I'd been certain it would never happen. And yet, Shay had gotten him to see the light.

Shay looked at the ground. "Cause I'm nephilim, and so adamant about supporting you that he had second thoughts?"

Yeah, no. She was not convincing me of that one.

"Shay?" I pressed as her cheeks took on a delicious pink tone that I hadn't seen since the day after she kissed me. "What did you do?"

An age passed before she met my eyes. Her own were steely. "I blackmailed him."

"What?!" My heart pounded; an uncomfortable experience that made my blood throb harder. *"How?"*

"At the meeting yesterday, my mother told me Brons had a niece he loved in Phoenix. I might have brought her up."

A laugh burst from me, and it felt amazing. Freeing. It felt so good it almost made me tear up.

"Stop laughing!" Shay hissed. "I'm not proud of it, but he was so freaking stubborn! Stupid too. He knows what's going on out there, and he can't give you back what's yours because he hates your kind? Like, *come on!*"

"I'm not denying that." My lips curled in a self-satisfied smirk that she'd ride so hard for me. "I find it ironic that a nephilim resorted to blackmail when a hellblooded didn't even consider it. A twist of expectations."

"I would say blame my human blood, but to be honest, even if I was a full-blooded angel, I'd do it again. And again. As many times as it took to get you back to yourself." Shay's chin lifted in defiance, as if she needed that around me. "Now, do you want your magic back or not, Hans?" She gestured in the direction of Brons's room, and though I had more questions, I went with it, falling into step with Shay and making our way to the lower level of the manor.

As ever, the steps were murder. While I did my best to hide my pathetic winces, I was sure Shay saw them. She saw far more than most people gave her credit for.

The woman beside me was brilliant. And ruthless when it came to those she called her own. Apparently, I counted as one of those people.

The memory of the night she'd kissed me came rushing back, and my lips burned with need to feel hers again. If this went well and the pain crawling through me lessened, we'd be able to talk about it. Even revisit that moment.

Goddess, I hoped so.

"One more flight," Shay said as we reached the steps leading to Brons's room. "You good?"

"I can handle it."

Barely, but I was a prideful man, and lately I'd leaned on others far more than I'd ever considered possible. A few steps wouldn't kill me.

Famous last words. Halfway down, my legs were trembling, and by the time I reached the basement level, sweat glistened on my brow.

Shay pretended not to see as I wiped the sweat away and took a few deep breaths. When she turned to me again, there was no concern in her eyes. Calculated, that's what this was. For her and for me.

She might have already made a deal with Brons, but until my wizard magic was flowing through my veins again, he could renege. Especially if he sensed weakness. I might feel like a stampede of vampires had run me over, but I wouldn't give Brons that satisfaction.

I stepped up to the door with Shay. She knocked, and unlike the last time I'd come to call, Brons opened the door. He scowled.

"Come in." He left the door open as he turned and walked into the room that still reeked of body odor.

We entered the room, and something caught my eye. Something that hadn't been in the room yesterday. A luxiter.

I turned to Shay and gestured to the priceless object. "Why does he have one of those?"

Her cheeks went pink, but she lifted a nonchalant shoulder as if trying to minimize what she was about to say. "I can light-travel further than I used to." Her tone was low, so Brons didn't hear. "And he needed greater incentive."

Still, that magical object might have been used by the *Abscondita* Coven. Those in S&S. Or even the Covenant. Someone far more in need of it than Richard Brons, which, in my opinion, was pretty much everyone. And did S&S know of her choice?

Whatever the answer, I didn't question Shay further in front of Brons. No doubt it had taken Shay hours to convince him to do this, and I would not be ungrateful.

"Where should we do this?" Shay asked, likely to fill the empty air.

Brons lowered himself into a chair that faced another. "Here."

A good choice. Though I'd never experienced magic being returned to me before, I understood from reading that such a transfer of energy often rendered the giver and the receiver unconscious.

I lowered myself into the chair across from Brons, refraining from sighing with relief as my muscles got the chance to relax. Soon, this would be over. Or so I hoped.

"You know what to do?" I asked.

"Of course I do." Brons sneered back at me as he held out his hand, the same one I'd grasped when we'd made our Vow.

So he wanted this done quickly. Fine by me. I grasped his hand as he did mine, ignoring the cringe from the wizard across from me. He hated touching my hellblooded skin.

"Remember, Brons," Shay's voice was lower as she stood to the side like a referee, "any funny business, and I'll attack."

His eyes snapped up to her. "Don't think I've forgotten a single one of your threats, Miss Ramos."

"Good." Shay's lips curled up in a cold semblance of a smile. "Get on with it."

Brons snarled, but his fingers dug into my skin, sending stabbing pains up my fingers and through my arm. I exhaled through my nose, trying to ignore the agony, knowing more would come during the magical transfer.

"Goddess, hear me," Brons spoke loud and clear. "Dissolve the bind between this man and me, returning his power to him. Returning his magic that I give freely."

This time, no wind surged around us, but my hair still lifted and the skin on the back of my neck prickled as the air in the room shifted and Brons closed his eyes. As we'd already made a pact with each other that involved the Goddess, she was more likely to listen. And seeing as Brons released a groan, I suspected he sensed her, as I did in the air, but far more deeply for him.

Richard Brons opened his eyes. They glowed from within, a brilliant gold color.

My stomach lurched. Yes, the Goddess was here. Listening.

"Do you, Hans Novak, wish for your wizarding magic back?" Brons asked.

"I do," I said without hesitation.

Light wreathed our hands. It came from neither of us, but from a power we were both connected to, one so much bigger than both Brons and me. The Goddess—the creator of magic as witches now knew it. Like before, the illumination seeped between our fingers and then blossomed to fill the dark room. The Covenant Seat ground his teeth together and the surrounding light intensified until I exploded.

A scream wrenched its way up my throat as my power stormed inside me like lightning. I tried to retract my hand, but no, the process had begun, and Brons and I were bound until it ended. I sat there, my jaw clenched tight as my magic flooded my system and ignited every frayed nerve ending I'd been living with. The edges of my vision darkened, and I hoped this would end soon. Within seconds. I was sure that was all I had.

So when Brons wrenched his hand away with a yowl, and I was still conscious, I knew it hadn't taken long. The breaking of the Vow and the bind had merely felt as if it had lasted hours and not minutes. Or even seconds.

Despite the short time period, I swayed in the chair. Gentle hands caught me.

"Hans, are you alright? Do you need to lie down?"

I sucked in a breath, unaware that I'd been holding it before—or maybe I'd been unable to breathe through all the sensations. When I gulped down enough air to speak, I answered her.

"I'm fine. Let me sit here."

Brons was whimpering, but Shay just stood behind me, taking my weight and keeping me sitting upright as the stars in my vision receded and the magic that had pummeled into me settled into my bones.

Minute by minute, the pain lessened. Tears pricked my eyes at the realization that I'd been right. The emptiness inside me had amplified the pain that now only remained in my shin, the localized area where Luca bound it.

Could I deal with that?

I had to, I realized, and I should be grateful. Though I might not be able to walk or run, I could probably still fly. I had options, whereas before, I'd had far fewer.

"Free me," Brons hissed.

I lifted my gaze from where I'd been staring at my hands, trying to center myself. The wizard's eyes burned up at Shay.

"You promised that after I gave it back, you'd tell me how to use the luxiter. I want to leave."

Shay snorted. "We don't want you here any longer than necessary. However, as we *also* discussed, your memory of this place will need to be modified. You know too much about the people here." Shay took a step around the chair, closer to Brons. "And I need to get Hans to his room. You're still second priority, Richard, so prepare to wait a few hours."

"Trash," the Covenant Seat spat. "I demand—"

"Oh, shut up," Shay said. "You'll be out of here by tonight.

In the meantime, I suggest you clean up, so whoever you plan to meet with doesn't have to smell you."

Brons looked like he'd been slapped.

Shay held out her hand to help me up. "Let's go."

I SLAMMED ANOTHER PIECE OF BACON INTO MY MOUTH AND debated taking Shay up on her offer of vanilla scones. I wasn't a sugar guy, but I was so ravenous I found I did not care.

Since my magic had returned, the hum of energy rushing through me had not ceased. That, along with the reduction of pain, had amped up my hunger levels to monstrous proportions. This was the second plate Shay had brought to my room.

Would the magical hum ever stop? Or was this my new normal? If so, it would take some adjusting. My power hadn't been like this before. But then again, I wasn't the same person either.

"How's the pain?" Shay asked from where she sat in the armchair across from mine. The fireplace was burning brightly, fending off the morning chill of the manor.

"My leg still aches." I scooped up a piece of toast and devoured it. My appetite increased along with my power level. "But the rest of me is fine. Normal."

Shay frowned. "Food didn't help at all? Or time? Not that it's been all that long . . ."

It had been less than an hour since I'd gotten my magic back.

"Food helps, but not in that way." I patted my stomach.

She let out a soft, thoughtful noise. One I'd heard many

times during S&S meetings or when someone needed Shay to translate something.

"I wonder if—"

A knock at the door stole her words. Shay turned. "Yeah?"

"It's Meredith. Can I come in?"

"Yes," Shay replied.

I snorted. "Not like this is my room or anything."

Shay didn't answer, and at that moment, Meredith entered, her eyes lighting up at the sight of me.

"Hans, you look so much better. Almost glowy." Meredith's eyebrows inched closer together. "How do you feel?"

"Better."

"He's still in pain," Shay piped up.

"*Manageable* pain," I amended. "In my leg."

"Which you're going to need if you want to come to NOLA. I'm sure we'll be doing some running for our lives." Meredith said as if she were talking about arranging a game night or some other mundane event. "Hannah can bring potions; they might be more effective now."

Shay cleared her throat. "I have an idea I'd like to try. I was gonna wait until he was done eating the manor out of house and home, but," Shay turned to me as Meredith came closer and leaned on the side of her roommate's armchair, "how do you feel about me trying to burn the curse from your leg?"

I stiffened. "Burn it out?"

We'd tried that once, and it had been agony. Not that my leg wasn't already agony but compared to what I'd been living with most recently, I could deal. As long as I was careful.

Careful.

I swallowed. That wouldn't work. I was a *Vindix*, the foretold leader of the group, though I had had little chance to act as such so far. Our mission was to take on the Princes of Hell.

To expel them from this world and retake the land for those who lived here. While there might be times we could take care, I wasn't sure that careful applied to that mission.

"It's a bad idea," Meredith said. "You told me last time your light hurt him. If the same thing happens, he might not be able to join us on the mission at all."

That would not stand. I was about to say as much when Shay shifted in her seat.

"He only had his demon magic last time," Shay retorted with confidence.

She was right. She'd thought this through. For how long?

"We should check with Hannah first," Meredith said. "What if your method sets Hans back? We need him, Shay."

"You think I don't know that!" Shay's eyes narrowed. "I was the one who sat by him every day! I convinced Brons to return his power. I know how important Hans is to the *Vindix* and to . . ." Her eyes cut up to me as she trailed off. My heart rate doubled at what I imagined she was about to say. "I think he can use his wizard magic as a buffer. Contain the demon powers, like Luca contained the curse. If anyone can do it, it's Hans."

My chest swelled with pride. Even if I wasn't sure she was right, Shay believed in me. Came to bat for me.

"Hans?" Meredith pressed. "You should have an opinion."

"*Really*? I wasn't so sure." My lips quirked up, and for the first time in a long time, I felt like my old self. Bantering with the girls when they tried to run the world.

Together, they rolled their eyes.

Yes, it was like old times.

I hid my smirk in my coffee cup. My initial fear when Shay suggested such a thing had dimmed. Possibility outshone it. Maybe Shay was right. My witch magic had always been strong. With it, I'd smothered my demon powers for most of my life. Now I'd say they were about equal, but I had far more practice with witching magic. Did I know an interior shielding spell?

It took only a moment for me to rummage through the lexicon of my mind to find something that could work. An oddity of a spell I'd picked up in passing during a long day of research in the Beineke's supernatural section.

The spell had been developed by a pregnant warrior witch who wished to give her growing child more protection while she fought. According to her records, she devised a spell before a large battle in which she'd been hit. She was injured, her magic shattered, but the spell did as she wanted, and her child survived. I might be able to use it to 'protect' my demon magic from Shay's angel powers.

"I have something I want to try. Now. While I still feel good." I pushed the plate away. No need to fill myself to bursting when I might vomit in pain.

Shay beamed, but Meredith didn't look so happy. Instead, the seeker witch gave a resigned nod. "I'll get Luca and Hannah. They should at least be with you during this."

"We'll be ready," Shay said as Meredith showed herself out. The nephilim turned to me. "Get on the bed."

My eyes widened. "*Excuse me?*"

"Okay, filthy mind," Shay's tone was light and teasing, though pink roses filled the apples of her cheeks. "You should lie down during this."

"Oh, right." I stood, wincing at the stabs in my shin.

Shay must have seen that I needed a moment to myself because she excused herself to use the restroom.

I settled on the bed, keeping my breathing level. As an expert caster, I didn't doubt my ability to get this spell to work.

The witch said the magic was not difficult, or revolutionary. It was just that no one had ever thought to create such a spell and use it in the way she'd done. The only thing I worried about was my demon magic retaliating. What if I expended energy and trapped it in a bubble of safety only for it to break loose and unleash on those in the room?

Shay's bright eyes filled my mind. She was so excited to try this, to help me again. And Luca and Hannah had already done so much for me.

I cannot hurt them. I must keep it inside, no matter the pain I might feel.

So, I closed my eyes and sought my demon power. As it had been so often of late, it was there, below the surface of my skin, though this time it was mingling with my casting and hedge magic. I saw them as different colors inside me. Casting magic was blue. Hedge magic was yellow. Demon magic was the deepest, darkest black. Somehow, all the colors lived inside me harmoniously, though I didn't think that under threat, or if I was holding the Pearl, that the demon magic wouldn't overpower the others.

The pregnant witch had not needed to do so, but I separated my powers out. Like how they were colored, they also vibrated differently. At the moment, my casting magic was humming at the highest vibration, my demon magic at the lowest, with hedge powers somewhere in between. They were easy to sort, though some resistance arose when I pushed all my demon magic deeper. I needed to move quickly in case it felt a threat and surged to the surface again. I had more power over it than ever before, but every single day, the dark magic inside me never ceased to shock me.

Exhaling, I cast the spell, thinking only of that swarm of low vibrational black magic as I did. *"Burresku."*

The moment I locked away my dark magic, it jostled, then pummeled its cage. It struck me then that the spell was like the barrier Luca had formed in my shin, just witching magic. Weaker too, as witching magic was when compared to mages, particularly those of Luca's standing. Had I been in my right mind before, maybe I could have done this for myself, but I hadn't been right at all. Breathing had been a struggle.

I bid my hedge magic to roll around the cage, thinking it might calm the demon powers. Shockingly, it worked. The dark magic stilled, content for the moment to be confined and near the hedge magic that was always around.

That done, I ran through the possible scenarios of how this might play out. By the time Shay returned, Luca and Hannah were two minutes behind her.

"Meredith sent us," Luca said and looked at Shay. "You're burning it out?"

"Trying to. He'd contained his demon magic, using a spell that he can access, so we don't think I'll hurt him like before. Can you two monitor him? And Luca, will you crack open your magical barrier? But slowly. That way, my light can catch the curse before it spreads."

Luca and Hannah shared looks of uncertainty, but after a moment, the healer nodded, and that seemed to be good enough for the mage. They took up positions on both sides of the bed. Shay stood next to Hannah, who had brought a small bag that clinked with glass. Probably healing potions, elixirs, balms, and the like.

"Ready?" Shay asked.

"No run down?" I teased.

"Unfortunately not." Her eyes softened on me. "Tell me if the light gets to be too much. I'll release it."

"I will."

At that, her hands glowed, and she laid them on my shin.

I jolted at the touch and the heat of her magic but slackened almost instantly. Was it uncomfortable? Yes, a bit. Was it anything like before?

Not in the slightest.

"You okay?" she whispered.

"I am," I replied. The faint discomfort had to be from the sheer nearness of her magic to my demon magic. Being opposites, they did not wish to be near one another.

But my witching magic welcomed Shay. It sang as her power wrapped around the cage Luca had built and the mage magic cracked open.

"I'm going to work fast," Shay said. "Once the barrier is gone, I'll burn. I can't go easy, or it will seep back into you."

"Do what you have to." I took a deep breath, fighting through the discomfort in my body and the sheer agony radiating from my shin as Shay worked on it.

I sensed the cage breaking. I could even differentiate between Shay's hot magic and Luca's cooler powers. The mage wasn't touching me like Shay, and his powers shimmered and flowed from his palms into my leg.

I took three deep breaths in and out as the pair worked together, their unique magics making me shudder and shake. Then, the dam broke.

"Retreat," Shay said as Luca's barrier cracked wide open, and her magic burrowed in like white fire.

I screamed and deep inside me, my demon powers pounded against the protections I'd put in place, begging to be let out, to fight the woman who was trying to help me, but causing pain in the process by releasing the curse.

Hannah squeezed my hand. "You're okay. We're here for you. Shay has this."

As rivers of sweat poured down Shay's face, I worried she might tire. And if she was tired enough, then the curse might slip past her. What if it wormed its way through me again?

I couldn't do that again. The leg was bad enough, but that kind of agony in my entire body . . . I'd welcome a coma. Welcome death.

"Harder," I wheezed. "You have this."

"Sure?" she panted, worried for me. Was I sweating too?

"Yes."

"Okay." She gulped down air. "Everyone, close your eyes."

I did so, and behind my eyelids, a blaze of yellow overtook the darkness. Heat filled the chamber, and Shay released a shriek. On my shin, her hands trembled.

"More!" I grunted. I swore the curse was disappearing. The pain that it created wasn't like the burn of Shay's magic. No, that needle-like pain was *lifting*. "As much as you have!"

"One more time!" Shay yelled as another flash of light filled the room.

My back arched. My hands gripped the sheets. My breath left me as I screamed.

But then, in the next second, when the light left and Shay's hands released me, the pain—*all the pain*—was gone.

I sucked in a breath and blinked my eyes open to find Shay staring down at me. Her light brown skin was red and blotchy with effort. Her face damp.

"I got it all right?"

"You did." With a trembling hand, I reached for her. "You're amazing, Shay."

She took my hand, her lips parting in a smile, and I was overcome with the need to feel those lips on mine. And not in a slight kiss like the one she'd stolen that night in the Blood Court.

I pulled her closer, curling a finger. "I have something to tell you. A secret."

Her eyebrows arched, but Shay played along, maybe thinking what I'd undergone addled my mind. Surprise, surprise, I was thinking clearly for the first time in far too long. She came closer, offering me her ear.

Instead, I took her by the back of the head and pulled her lips to mine.

"O—oh!" Shay exclaimed into my mouth.

Luca cleared his throat. "We'll be going."

I heard the door shut behind him and Hannah as Shay lowered on to the bed, and we lost ourselves in each other's lips.

CHAPTER SEVENTEEN

MEREDITH

MY SKIN BURNED WITH THE FIRE OF ANTICIPATION. SURELY, THAT meant I was insane or something.

Who gets excited to go to a Hell-dominated kingdom?

Well, *excited* wasn't the right word. Or at least not the *only* thing I was feeling, but it was in the mix.

If we were lucky, Rabi would find his *lapis caelesti* today. Seeing as he was already a powerful air elemental, that boded well for our side. Especially when we tried to infiltrate New Orleans to save Gunner.

I'd been practicing with my sacred stone for days, using the compulsion powers with Giselle, Serena, and Tobias as my adversaries. The Laurent bloodline possessed the strongest powers of compulsion amongst vampires, and now I could break through even Giselle's control over another.

Would I be able to shatter a Prince of Hell's power over others and restore free will? Would Prince Belhor have bothered to fill his city with his sin? I felt lucky that we knew he had occupied New Orleans when the rulers of the other cities —besides LA—remained mysteries.

If I was to fight any sin, the sin of Sloth would probably be easiest to cut away. Or that's what I kept telling myself. Today would be my true test.

Benedict sensed my unease. Along with Tobias, he'd joined me outside, but seemed content to sit in a sunspot and just let me breathe in and out. My right hand ran across his fur as, with the other, I adjusted the sling. Olga had designed the sling to allow me to carry Benedict through light-traveling. It reminded me of a front-facing baby carrier, a fact that Benedict did not like me bringing up.

Which meant that, of course, I did it often.

The door to the manor opened. As I'd been staring blankly in that direction, I witnessed the moment that Serena stumbled outside.

Stumbled. Vampires did not stumble.

"Uh, what's wrong with her?" I asked.

Tobias looked to his sister, and his eyebrows pinched together before clarity overtook his face. "A vision. Serena! Are you alright?"

"I was getting ready to join you when I saw something." She winced.

My mouth dried up. Serena had once been a witch, and some of her magic remained after Giselle turned her into a vampire. She had visions, and the last one she'd seen had related to me journeying to the Blood Court. I didn't remember it leaving her like this though . . .

"A powerful one," Tobias said.

"*Very.* I-I don't think I'll be able to go to New Orleans. I need to feed."

"Wise," Tobias said. There was no room for error in our mission, and I'd never seen a vampire in Serena's state. She must be incredibly depleted to admit as much. "But what did you see, sister?"

"Blood and water," Serena answered. "So much blood in the water. That's why I came rushing out. New Orleans, so much water."

"That's all?"

"That's all," she echoed my words, her usually vibrant tone hollow. "I'm sorry it's not more, but you needed to know."

Tobias nodded as though this wasn't the first time Serena had seen something so vague. If that was true, I was really glad I wasn't a seer. Seemed like a frustrating talent.

I wasn't sure how blood and water was going to help us today. Yes, New Orleans was wet and yes, I'd assumed we might spill some blood. How was it helpful?

"Go rest," Tobias said to his sister. "We appreciate you relaying the vision."

Serena swallowed and left, just as the manor door opened again, and the others began to pour outside.

"I'll tell Luca about Serena. Are you ready, love?" Tobias asked.

"Wish I understood more of what she saw, but yes, I am." I assured my mate and took in those who would venture to New Orleans with us. Hans strode hand in hand with Shay. I arched an eyebrow at my housemate, wanting to grill the heck out of her, but we hadn't had time today.

She'd spent the morning in Paris, looking for Flamel, only to find no trace of the Alchemist. Then Shay and Luca had traveled to Seattle to relay the bad news to the Covenant—that they would not be getting luxiters. Apparently, the magical government had not taken it well.

About as well as I'd taken it when Shay gave her luxiter up to Brons. I pushed the thought away before it riled me up. Shay had done what she'd done and, after some memory modification to erase the manor from his mind, Richard Annoying Brons had left this morning. Luxiter and all.

"Hans?" I asked, trying to focus on what was important and not what we'd lost. "Are you ready for this?"

Hans held up the Pearl of Hell. "Ready to give a Prince of Darkness what he deserves."

"Goddess, please tell me you heard that," Benedict murmured, his amber eyes shining in the sun.

"How about you, Rabi?"

I felt like I was mothering them to death or something, but I was worried. Hans was getting on his feet again, and Rabi was about to meet his family and find his sacred stone. That wasn't even considering this would be his first rescue mission.

But Rabi didn't look scared. Or gung-ho. Or any powerful emotion. The air elemental merely nodded, which was pretty normal for him. I had a hunch that his visible lack of emotions might be a result of having to hide his true self for all his life. Show too much fire or sadness or anger, and I could see the vampires in the Blood Court draining you, so they didn't have to deal with you anymore.

"Circle up," Luca said, taking control of the situation. "And close in tight. Considering we're nine people and a cat traveling, and some of us have not used luxiters yet," he glanced at Tana, who had insisted on joining the other *Vindix* on this mission, "we cannot be too careful."

Benedict leapt into my waiting arms, and I slipped him into the carrier. "Safe and sound, my little tot."

He hissed, and I fought back a laugh as I linked hands with Tobias and Giselle, noting the fierce look on Harper's face as I did so.

Harper had been vibrating with tension all morning, ready

to leave at a moment's notice. She seemed to have taken it personally that we hadn't acted faster. I did not agree. While I missed the heck out of Gunner and had worried about him too, having Hans at full power, and as a result, Shay willing to leave the manor, was invaluable in our efforts to save him. If there was one thing I'd learned in life, it was that everything was a tradeoff.

"I'll do the honors." Luca pulled out his luxiter before slipping the hand that held it into Giselle's other hand. I noted that he hadn't said a thing about Serena's vision and took that as a good sign. Maybe Luca thought it was as obvious as I did. "Brace yourselves."

I inhaled as Luca gave the destination and spoke the magical word that activated the luxiter. Before I breathed out again, light enveloped and compressed us. Benedict yowled, and I squeezed my eyes shut, waiting for the moment that we would be spit out.

When it happened, I tripped, but Tobias and Giselle tugged me upright, their vampire grace saving them from making fools of themselves like the rest of us.

I blinked away the spots in my eyes and took in the area. It reeked of sulfur so strongly, I couldn't even smell the Mississippi River, which flowed only a few blocks away. That stench was coming from across the river. Or maybe from the demons fighting the humans? If they were doing that? Goddess, how horrible would it reek inside the dome?

I hated that I'd have to find out.

Algiers Point, a neighborhood across the muddy river from the French Quarter and main business areas of the city, was now not only a place where people lived, but neighbors to a military site.

Prince Belhor had used the natural waterways of New

Orleans as an additional barrier to his kingdom. As if the vast black dome, one identical to the one Lucifer had put up in Los Angeles, wasn't deterrent enough for regular people. The dome rose high in the sky, gleaming black in the early morning sun of the South.

What did humans think of it? Had the military told them the whole truth already?

Even if the military or the human governments had not said a thing, I suspected people could guess. The dome screamed magic of the vilest sort. I considered LA, a city still trapped by Lucifer. We'd arrived there in the early days of demon occupation, and I hadn't been consumed by Lucifer's sin of pride. Would this city be different? Would it be like in New York when Wrath forced his sin upon others?

So many questions unanswered. So many variables left hanging.

"Where is the human military set up?" Giselle asked. "I can smell ammunition, but it's so quiet."

"That way," Luca pointed in the distance. "Closer to the highway bridges. I've been told they leave the homes alone as much as they can. Evacuation hasn't been a priority because no one knows where or when a city or town or even a rural area would fall next. Why move only to be attacked again? If we do end up being stopped or confronted, we mention Artem. Those in charge recognized his name now—even if they haven't acted in other measures."

"*Mon Dieu.*" Giselle shook her head. "This world is changing much too fast for my liking."

"Usually, I'd say that's a vampire quirk." Luca waved for us to follow. "But I quite agree. Humans likely do too."

Luca led us to the door of a small, single-family home. It looked pretty dirty, though I suspected that was due to the surrounding fighting happening, as all the homes had that sheen of grime on them. At the top of the stairs, he waved Rabi up to join him.

"Would you like to knock?" Luca asked, as if it was only him and Rabi.

The wizard shook his head, his shoulders hunched.

"I understand," Luca said. "Tell me if I'm overstepping." With that, the coven master let his hand fall on the door three times.

Though we'd expected the house to stay quiet, to have to coax our way in—if anyone was still there at all, we were wrong.

"Who's there?" a raspy female voice called through the door; her Southern accent thick. "I have my rifle ready. Be sure of it!"

Luca cleared his throat. "We're members of the magical community. Not demons, nor military."

A momentary pause echoed through the air before the woman spoke again. "Covenant?"

That told us the person behind the door was likely magical too. Hopefully, Rabi's grandmother, the owner on record for the home.

"Not precisely," Luca answered, "though we have spoken with members of the Covenant."

"Why are you here? Extraction?"

"No. We have someone who would like to meet you. The son of Louis Rosser."

The door flew open, and before us stood an elderly Black woman with wide brown eyes and her hair covered in a red silk bonnet. In her hands was the gun, still pointing at us, though when she spotted Rabi, she lowered the weapon.

"You look so much like him. Like my sweet boy." The woman looked like she'd seen a ghost. "You're really my

Louie's son?" Her eyes watered at the words, but she didn't move, demanding an answer from Rabi first.

Rabi too seemed stuck. Stunned. His lips parted, and he cleared his throat. "So I've been told. My mother gave me my father's name, and a search led us here."

The old woman's eyebrows knitted together. "Where'd you grow up? Your accent is strange."

"I don't believe that's a discussion best had on front doorsteps," Luca said.

The woman tore her gaze from Rabi and scowled at the mage. "That right? And tell me, have you been living through a demon occupation? A human military one? Tell me why I shouldn't be cautious about letting a group of strangers through my doorway?"

"You should," I spoke up for the first time, understanding that while this woman had a right to be cautious, she also needed to understand why we were here. She only needed to be told the right thing, and as I was the one to find Rabi, that responsibility was mine. "You and your family know better than most the dangers the world is facing, don't you?"

The woman looked at me, the light of wisdom edging in on the caution in her dark brown eyes. "Say what you mean, girl."

"Your family has been waiting for a time like this. Maybe you suspected your son would help save us. Him and the Amethyst." I gestured to Rabi. "But it's him, *your grandson*, that we're waiting for."

She exhaled. "*Vindix*. We thought—but . . ." She trailed off, a sob wrenching up her wrinkled throat.

I swallowed. Finally. *Freaking finally*, a family in our group knew who we were and what we were meant to do. Even if Rabi hadn't known, maybe his grandmother would have more information to help us. I stepped closer and laid a hand on Rabi's shoulder, all the while never breaking eye contact with the woman.

"That's who we are. I'm Meredith, keeper of the Opal of Heaven. And almost all of us are here. But we need the Amethyst if we're going to get anything done. We were hoping you knew something about it."

"I am knowledgeable of your stone. And that which my bloodline was entrusted to protect." The woman peered beyond me. I wondered if she sensed the power radiating off Hans, Tana, and Harper too. She lifted a hand, waved it, and a pulse of magic came off the house.

I blinked, not having sensed her wards before, and not understanding how. Given the feeling of lack in the air, they'd been powerful indeed.

"Warder," the woman explained. "The strongest my city has seen in near a century, not that it matters now." She turned and set the rifle down. "Come in. All of you. We have a whole lot to discuss."

I SQUIRMED IN THE ARMCHAIR I'D BEEN OCCUPYING FOR THREE hours. I wished I could say they passed in the blink of an eye, but I'd been itching to leave for at least two and a half of those hours. Through the discomfort, I'd forced myself to stay still, to answer the questions Lauretta posed when Rabi could not answer her—which was about half of her inquiries. The rest of the time, everyone in the room took in the decor—which was maximalist and eccentric—and tried to pretend like we weren't witnessing a somewhat awkward family reunion. Lauretta cried at her grandson's story. Cried again when she recounted the recent death of Rabi's father. She passed around a photo of the deceased Louis, whom Rabi was a carbon copy of.

Through it all, Rabi looked at a loss for words.

My heart went out to the guy. He didn't fit in this world and would never return to Isila—not that he wanted to, anyway. In short, Rabi didn't fit anywhere yet. Though I'd had an unusual childhood too, I couldn't imagine being such a fish out of water.

In my lap, Benedict stood and circled again. He'd done that at least ten times in the last hour, a tell that he was growing weary too. But he wasn't my primary concern.

When I hadn't been answering questions for Lauretta or Rabi, I'd been keeping an eye on Harper. My wolfy housemate, the patient, stoic one in our home, looked about ready to explode. To be so close to Gunner, and just sitting here, was killing her. I didn't think she'd last much longer before saying something she regretted, so when Lauretta and Rabi fell into yet another awkward pause, I leaned forward and cleared my throat.

"I realize that, in the grand scheme of things, you two haven't had any time to reconnect, but we came here for a reason, and—"

Lauretta snorted. "Wondered how long you'd let us go on."

I blinked. "You're not mad?"

"Course I'm mad." Her gaze drifted to her grandson. "My blood was enslaved. I never knew him and now . . . He's involved in a supernatural war that the poor boy is ill-equipped for."

I could say nothing to that. It was all true.

However, Rabi's face turned hard, and, to my surprise, he lifted a finger. "I may be new to this world, but I was raised in a deadly environment. To say I'm ill-equipped for war is to dismiss everything I've been through. Which is quite a lot."

Lauretta's face fell. "I didn't mean to imply you're not a strong young man, Rabi—"

"It matters not," Rabi waved a dismissive hand, "Meredith is right. We've lingered long enough and should be going. Every minute we're not battling the evil in this world, is another minute people here are captured and likely enslaved as I was. I will not abide by it."

Lauretta's lips formed an O before a cat-like smile crossed her face. "Then I suppose I should show you to my Louie's grave."

I stiffened. "You buried the Amethyst of Air with your son?"

"He is entombed," Lauretta corrected me. "Laid to rest days before those monsters took my home."

Of course. New Orleans was at sea level and the water table made burials precarious.

"Which of yous holds the Emerald of Earth?" Lauretta asked, appraising the group. She'd been speaking with Rabi almost exclusively and had no idea I hadn't found all the *Vindix*.

"No one," I answered. "That witch is still somewhere in the world. The holder of the Sapphire of the Sea too."

Lauretta frowned. "I see. The tomb is sealed up real tight. That stone'll need to be broken."

Luca stood. "I can help with that."

Lauretta assessed him, likely sensing the mage magic. "You'll have to do." She rose. "Let me take you there."

She shuffled from the crowded living room, and we followed, out the door and into the midday humidity of New

Orleans. I blew out a breath. It was autumn! How was it so sticky here?

"The cemetery is this way. A few blocks down." Lauretta gestured for Rabi to walk at her side and everyone else gave them space as we followed the old warder through the neighborhood. People peeked out their windows, but mostly, the neighborhood looked abandoned. No doubt they were all terrified.

When we reached the cemetery, the gate was closed, but Lauretta waved a hand, and it flew open. The nearby church stared down at us, and though I'd never been religious, unease prickled at my skin. And confusion.

"Is your family all buried, or kept, here?" I asked Lauretta.

"We sure are."

"Why? I assume you're all witches and," I nodded to the church, "that looks Christian."

"It is. And we are. But my family has been here for centuries, girl. We had to blend in. So we do what we must for appearances and later we perform a more private ceremony honoring the Goddess."

"Oh, right," I said, not having thought of the repercussions of a family staying in one place for so long and being like us. Especially such a Christian part of the country. I glanced at Tobias, who appeared unfazed. No doubt he had considered such things. Vampires had needed to play pretend for a long time.

Lauretta wended through the tombs, all above ground and stately. This cemetery, though small, appeared well-kept. She stopped in front of a tomb that at first glance appeared much like the others. A cross was atop, and a biblical passage on a plaque near the ground. There was no indication whatsoever that this tomb belonged to a family of witches.

Lauretta glanced about and once assured that we were alone, directed a piercing stare upon Luca. "Please try to be gentle. I—I don't wish for my son's corpse to be harmed."

Luca stepped closer. "I'll do my best."

"I can help too," Harper said. "Speed things along."

Luca arched an eyebrow. "How so?"

"I can ask a ghost to retrieve the stone. If you can open it a little, they can squeeze in and get it, and no one has to be dishonored."

Rabi bowed his head. "I'd like that. Please, try."

Lauretta's hand went to her heart. It was the first time Rabi had shown real consideration toward the father he never knew, and it clearly touched her. "Anything to avoid disrespecting my Louie. The Amethyst is on a necklace that we placed on him."

She thought Louis was the end of his line, the last air elemental too. But he hadn't been—he simply hadn't known such a thing.

Luca nodded. "Yes, let's try that, Harper. I'll create an opening, and you do your thing."

With the Diamond secured around her wrist, Harper closed her eyes. Seconds later, before Luca could so much as call his magic, the air shifted. Grew cold.

A ghost appeared in a blink. I stepped back. Aya had told us Harper was growing strong with spirit magic, but I'd not expected her to be this good, this fast.

"I need you to go into that tomb, when there's an opening, and bring back a necklace with an amethyst stone."

Apparently, the ghost only spoke to Harper because I heard nothing, but she looked at Luca. "He's ready."

Luca let out a soft chuckle and set to work, his magic filling the air and slowly, carefully, eating away at the material that sealed the tomb. Tightness grew in my chest, and again, Lauretta's eyes filled with tears. I hated what we were doing to her, to her son's tomb. A foul but necessary job as Lauretta wanted her grandson to be as strong as possible.

No one spoke as Luca worked and finally, he created an opening by shimmying the stones apart just a touch. "Now, Harper."

She guided the ghost into the tomb, and I held my breath, waiting. When the ghost appeared, he wasn't visible, but the necklace with the amethyst gem was floating in the air as if on a phantom wind.

Rabi held out his hand, and the necklace dropped into it. Wind blasted from him, knocking everyone—even the sure-footed vampires—to the ground.

The power of the Amethyst of Air radiated from Rabi, the true holder of the *lapis caelesti*. He tipped his head back to the sky, and his lips broke into a smile as air began to swirl all around us, gathering steam with each second, tossing up leaves and dirt and whatever else littered the ground.

I opened my mouth to congratulate him, just as an explosion rang through the air.

CHAPTER EIGHTEEN

HARPER

My hair flew forward as the percussive blasts of detonated bombs pulsed in my ears. Those in the graveyard gasped, some dropping low to avoid incoming debris, but I spun on my heels, ready to defend. To fight.

The reaction was a bit overkill. The bombs weren't that close to us, but rather on the bridge funneling into the busiest parts of the city. Hundreds, maybe thousands of soldiers and tanks covered that same bridge and the explosions they set free led their way, slamming into the dome around the city.

I exhaled my relief. So the humans were trying to break down the magical barrier. Lauretta had said that happened, but to watch it with my own eyes, feel the heat in the air, and smell the burn of magic, was a different story. It was really too bad they weren't making any headway.

I turned my attention to Luca. He, too, was watching the bridge. Beside him, the new keeper of the Amethyst of Air had stopped using his magic. It spoke to the strength of the explosion that I hadn't noticed Rabi's winds cease.

"Luca, we need to take advantage of the bombings," I said.

My heart rate spiked at the thought of finally finding Gunner. The wait had been necessary, but my heart didn't care. Thinking of Gunner being imprisoned shattered me again and again, and drove home the fact that I was falling for the alphablood who used to annoy me to the moon and back.

"We can use this as a diversion," I pressed when the coven master did not reply. "Surely, Sloth will send demons to watch over his wards. Other parts of the dome will have lighter security."

"We can't be sure, Harper," Luca replied, though he was still watching the explosives hammer the magical protections. "I think we should speak with the army. They might have a better lay of the land. We—"

"*No!*" I shouted. "Gunner has waited too long already. We're going in there, and we're going *now*."

I heard Shay suck in her breath, saw Tobias stiffen, and felt the unease washing off Tana and Rabi, but I did not care. Waiting was no longer an option.

"They do that twice a day," Lauretta spoke up. "None of their missiles have made a dent in the dome, but I have seen demons come through and fight, which makes me think the girl might be right. The demon prince might fortify that section, just in case."

"What do you know of the closest part of the ward?" Giselle asked. "Directly across the river from here."

"If you go as the crow flies, you'll end up looking out over Jackson Square."

"Right by St. Louis Cathedral, *non*?" Giselle asked, blonde eyebrows pulling together.

"That's right," Lauretta assured her. "Though I can't be sure the cathedral still stands. Only a few people got out of the Quarter before the dome appeared, and those who did, said buildings were fallin' hard and fast. In their place, a castle rose from the ground." Her face tightened, but the old witch swallowed and continued. "A cathedral might not be welcome under the rule of Hell."

"LA was demolished," Meredith added. "So you might be right, Lauretta."

"We'll see when we get over there," I said. "We should go."

"And *how* will we do that?" Tobias asked.

"Two of us have wings." Hans's black ones appeared as Luca spoke. "I don't imagine that we can boat across the river. Some of us might swim, but not all. And getting in and out of LA wasn't a smooth or easy endeavor."

No, I hadn't been there, but I'd seen the aftermath. Luca had nearly lost an arm.

"The luxiters?" I suggested. "Though that depends on the boundary of the dome. Do you know where it ends, Lauretta?"

"Right at the river. Any land is on the other side. Hell's lands."

Shay's shoulders slumped. "That won't work then. The luxiters don't work between realms. I'm pretty sure these kingdoms count as different from our world. Nicholas Flamel said so too."

"Flamel?" Lauretta's eyebrows shot up. "As in the ancient Alchemist?"

"We're acquainted," Shay said, and Lauretta gave her an impressed look.

"I can try smoke-travel," Hans suggested, and I was glad that he, at least, wasn't getting off track. "That worked within Lucifer's kingdom in LA, and since it's demon magic, I think it might work here too. Even between realms. I'm pretty good at it now too. In Isila, I got us within miles of—"

"Yes! Try it!" I was running out of what little patience I had.

Luca stared at me with exasperation. "Harper, I'd like to come up with a bit more of a plan. At least a meeting spot if things go poorly."

"Then hurry with it." My chin lifted in the air, and Luca turned to Lauretta and conversed with the elderly witch.

As they spoke, Meredith pulled Rabi and Hans aside, and the air witch worked with the Amethyst more. Judging by the wind whipping through the graveyard, he was a natural with his *lapis caelesti,* an enviable position but not unexpected. Rabi had already been powerful, strong enough for vampire royals to use him for his magic, rather than his blood. We'd hoped that he wouldn't have a problem with his stone, and it looked like that was the case.

After ten agonizing minutes, Luca faced the rest of us again. "We're going to make this simple and enter right behind where Cafe du Monde stands. Or maybe stood. If the building is still there, it will give us cover. Hans, over here, if you please."

He joined Luca and Lauretta as the witch pulled a phone from her house dress and showed the screen to Hans. "Is that enough for you to go by?"

"Better than nothing," Hans said. "I guess we're going now?"

Luca shot me a glance. "No better time."

My shoulders loosened a touch.

"We won't have time to make a bracelet, so keep your stone in your pocket." Meredith patted her own pocket. "Not around your neck. Wrath knew something about the Pearl and Opal, and maybe his brothers know about the other *lapis caelesti* too. A necklace can be ripped off too easily. Keep it safe."

Rabi slipped the gem into his jeans pocket.

"Hans, Meredith, Tobias, and I will go first," Luca said to the group as Meredith patted her carrier for Benedict. With narrowed eyes, the cat hopped inside.

"We'll get the feel of the immediate area," Luca continued. "And if Sloth is using his sin in the city. Once we're through, Hans will return for the others."

I bit my tongue to hold back the argument climbing my throat. Luca had chosen a powerful quartet to emerge first. While I fought as well as Hans, and better than Meredith, I'd save my battles for when they mattered. And what mattered now was that we were on the move.

Smoke gathered around Hans, thicker and faster than I'd ever seen, until it engulfed them. A moment later, they were gone. I held my breath, waiting.

Five seconds passed. Ten. Twenty. A minute had gone by, and my chest was growing tight, when Hans appeared again in a poof of black smoke.

"Clear. The rest of you, close in."

We did, and Lauretta took in Rabi one last time before Hans called his magic once more. Smoke filled my vision, and a tightness pushed in on me as I was lifted off my feet. Transported.

The moment the smoke cleared, I gasped. Four demons with protruding bulbous noses and bat-like wings lay sprawled on the ground, their necks bent at awkward angles and foul-smelling blood pouring from their wounds. That would have been enough to startle me, but the bodies of our enemies were the least of my concerns.

The air hung heavy and thick and oily, and the moment I stepped through the portal, that feeling sank deeper into my bones. I took a few steps back and slumped into a chair covered in powdered sugar—a remnant of happier days in the city.

"What's happening?" I barely recognized my voice. It sounded slower, like molasses.

"The demons were standing there talking when we arrived," Meredith replied. Why did she sound normal? "Tobias killed them. And Hans and Luca are going to strip two demons and act as guards to get us into the palace. One stroke of good luck."

"No, I mean with me. I feel . . . *Slow*."

Not lucky at all. Slow and heavy and *gross*.

"Oh, right." Meredith pressed a hand to me, and heat flooded my body. In her other fist, a faint glow told me she was holding the Opal of Heaven. A moment later, the heaviness lifted, and I had my answer.

So yes, Sloth had blanketed the city in his sin. Too bad for the prince, Meredith had been practicing with the Opal and compulsion proved similar enough to a demon's sin for her to break that enchantment.

"It didn't affect Tobias much, not like Hans, Luca, and me. Seemingly you too?" Meredith asked as more followed through the portal.

"Like a semi-truck." I nodded my head. "Tana, Shay, and Rabi might be feeling it too." Their eyes had glazed over.

"Vampires seem to be immune," Meredith mused, taking in Giselle's bright eyes as she went to help Rabi, Tana, and Shay. "At least those who are Laurents."

If she was right, I was glad for Tobias's and Giselle's presence. What if Meredith's use of the Opal couldn't hold indefinitely? We'd need someone, or two someones, with clear heads to keep us alive.

We'd entered Sloth's domain right where we were supposed to: at the backside of Cafe du Monde. From there, I didn't have a great view across the street to Jackson Square, but from what I could see, things weren't looking good.

As Lauretta predicted, no cathedral stood, and many other buildings had been reduced to rubble too. Central to it all, a dark castle rose from the French Quarter, a flame flickering from the tallest tower. I stared at the castle, a pit forming in my belly as people had staggered by, drunk, which seemed fitting considering the sin flowing thick in their veins. A few demons strode by too, oblivious to the dangerous newcomers in their domain.

I inhaled, nerves jangling, and immediately regretted that choice. Not only was the city a wreck but it stank like piss and rotting food and beer. My poor wolf senses.

"I'm ready." Hans stepped out of the deserted kitchen of the cafe, dressed in one of the deceased demon's fighting leathers. With the armor and his black wings spread behind him, he looked like he could be a cambion—a half human demon—in Sloth's army. He lifted one of the soldier's weapons, a vicious morning star. "Luca?"

Luca appeared a moment later, not as convincing as Hans, but that was impossible. However, the mage had pried a helmet off one of the dead guards, and we hoped that disguise would be enough to get to the castle in one piece. If not, compulsion and fighting skills were on our side, though we wanted to save energy where we could.

"Ready," the mage replied, fingers wrapping around the whip he'd taken from one soldier as we split into two groups.

I'd be under Hans's guard, along with Tana, Shay, and

Giselle. Luca would escort the rest. If asked *why* we were being escorted, we weren't sure what we'd say. Not knowing much of what had happened in New Orleans since the fall made it impossible to know what Prince Belhor valued, but we weren't so worried about that. The humans we'd seen were in no condition to be asking questions of anyone. And the demons who'd strutted by didn't look like anything we couldn't handle—especially seeing as there were few of them.

I hoped most of their kind congregated near the bridge, dealing with the explosions the humans continued to pummel the dark wards with.

"Act super slow and drunk," Meredith instructed, and I fell into an unnatural slump, hoping the act was good enough to convince demons the Prince of Sloth's spell gripped us.

"Pick up the pace!" Hans shouted, his voice deeper and rougher than I'd ever heard it as the show began. The act was on. He slammed the morning star into the side of the cafe, the sound reverberating through the air and making me shudder at how convincing he was.

"*Move, scum!*" Hans bellowed.

For extra effect, Luca cracked his whip, deliberately missing Tobias's back by mere inches. I wasn't sure when he'd learned to use a weapon of that sort, and I didn't want to know. No, I needed to stay focused on getting into the castle and saving Gunner.

So I dragged my feet and slouched and walked *far* slower than I wished as Hans herded our group across the square. Regular humans who spotted us coming diverted, hinting that though they were enchanted, some of their survival instincts remained intact.

Hans and Luca funneled us into the narrower veins that kept the French Quarter alive.

We walked by people slumped on the sidewalks, covered in food and spattered with alcohol. Judging by the rancid smell, most hadn't bathed in days.

Vomit climbed the column of my throat. I swallowed it back down with force, wishing, and not for the first time, that I could turn off my shifter senses.

"Hurry it up!" Hans shouted, as three weapon-less demons strolled closer, pushing two human women along in front of them. The demons twisted, saw Hans, and smirked. One winked, and they moved on.

We continued straight for the castle rising from the broken and filthy streets. Though beautiful in a dark way, I could only think of the castle as a blight on the land. And a prison. One housing a man I cared about.

What would I say to Gunner when I first saw him? That question had rolled through my mind so many times, and though I knew how I felt about Gunner, I wasn't sure if I should tell him.

"Clumsy idiot," Luca spat as Giselle fake-tripped and let out a cry with the perfect amount of confusion and fear lacing her tone. Had it been anyone else in the group, I would have thought the stumble was real. The streets were a disaster, after all. But Giselle was the epitome of grace, and vampires did not stumble.

Luca whipped the ground twice, and Giselle whimpered and scurried closer to Shay.

Shay. Though I hadn't said as much, I worried about her here. My housemate had told me how horrible it was for her to be in demon territory, and now I understood—to some degree. This place reeked and, along with the sin of sloth blanketing the city, a distinct sense of fear and hopelessness permeated the city. Darkness too. I suspected a nephilim would experience it ten times more.

I drew in a breath, trying to center myself and not get too off track. To remain focused on Gunner, when I caught a whiff of the alpha blood himself. I skidded to a stop.

"Move!" Hans bellowed, and forgetting to be entranced, I spun.

"I smell him."

Hans blinked. Then scowled. "I said move it, wolf." His tone was menacing, but as he spoke, his wings shot out. To anyone watching, it would look like a threat, but as the black feathers surrounded my face, Hans added. "Gunner?"

"He went this way," I whispered.

"Can you follow the trail?"

Thanks to my ghost, we were certain Gunner was kept in the castle, but this was too good an opportunity to pass up. It proved that he'd been let out at least once. Or maybe he'd escaped?

My heart rate kicked up. Not having to go into the castle would be the best option. One we hadn't considered much, but what if Gunner was out here? Walking around aimlessly?

"I'll follow it," I whispered.

Hans retracted his wings, inclining his head in a way that told me to lead covertly.

I shuffled up to the front of the group and began to scent.

CHAPTER NINETEEN

HANS

Harper followed Gunner's trail, a stroke of luck if there ever was one. The only issue was it had to look like Luca and I were in charge and with Harper out in front scenting that was a difficult illusion to pull off. After a few blocks, we came across another group of demons and earned a dozen strange looks, so I figured it was time to learn where the wolf was in her search.

"Watch the back," I growled at Luca as I approached Harper. "I need to get this wolf in line."

Once next to her, my wings spread, a natural barrier that might hide the fact I was talking to a wolf—rather than being hostile to her.

"What's up?"

"They walked through the city and stopped for extended periods," Harper said, her brows furrowing. "Did you notice the fruit trees? They're out of place here, where everything is so dark. And some of them don't even belong in Louisiana."

No, I hadn't studied any freaking fruit trees. I'd been too

busy making sure other demons didn't take too much notice of us.

"Why's that important? And what do you mean *they*? He's with someone?" I thought she'd been following Gunner. Not multiple people.

"There were other wolves and witches with him. Two of the latter. And the smell of magic was *everywhere*. At first I hoped that he'd escaped, but now . . . I'm pretty sure they were growing the fruit."

It only took a moment to understand why. The humans we passed by weren't motivated to do anything, let alone prepare food. I suspected Sloth had taken New Orleans before he'd worked out the many logistical issues of ruling a closed-off city.

"I bet Sloth made them."

"Hans," Harper whispered, and did her best to keep her lips still as I pulled ahead of her to make it look like I was leading the group. "There's more. One of the witches, her smell was different. Familiar, but not. Like I *should* know her, if you know what I mean."

My heart leapt. "*Vindix*?"

"We're still missing an earth witch. And Meredith is always talking about convergence." She swallowed. "I think they're heading for the castle. We're so close, it makes sense."

I'd read about convergence too. The *Vindix* would want to be together, to find each other. Likely in the past, in a smaller world, we'd have stumbled upon one another, but the world had grown vast in the millennia since the *Vindix* had last been together.

Every day it was getting more difficult to deny that fate existed and was pulling, or at least plucking, at the strings in this war between worlds.

"We need to tell Meredith," I whispered.

If a witch was growing food, it had to be at the behest of the prince. Otherwise, I was sure they'd have been caught. There were too many demons wandering the street not to be—especially when some of them could scent magic too. The castle seemed the likely place to keep a captive you wanted to use.

A sigh left me. For a few shining moments, we'd thought we wouldn't have to enter that dark castle. Now, it looked like we were back to the original plan.

I glared at Harper for the benefit of any demon who might be watching. "To the back, scum. I can't stand walking by you."

Harper fell in line, and I regrouped with Luca, whispering the development in his ears. His eyes widened, and he nodded and fell back, brandishing his whip at Meredith. He threatened her loudly but I knew the moment that he'd shared the secret too because she glanced down at the talisman on her finger, the ring that had told her other *Vindix* were around.

If we got close to the castle and a *Vindix* was there, Meredith would sense them.

With every step we took closer to the castle, the reek of sulfur grew stronger, and more demons roamed the streets amidst humans. Even with the increase in demons, though, I had to admit there were fewer guards than I'd have thought. Were they all by the bridge? Watching the humans try to break through a magical barrier with explosives? We'd heard a few more booms since being in Sloth's territory.

We rounded one last corner, and the castle came into view in all of its dark, black majesty. Foul though the demons of Hell may be, no one could deny that they didn't have style. Sloth embellished his new home, honoring its history with an occasional fleur-de-lis in addition to gargoyles and a light blue flag flying so high I could not make out what was on it.

My gaze dragged down from the flame burning at the top of the tower, and for the first time, I noticed a group near a vast door, likely the main entrance.

A group of wolves.

Harper let out a whine, and the hair on the back of my neck stood straight up. *No, is it . . .*

I scanned the wolf pack, two people standing among it, along with four winged demons, and saw him. Gunner, his black fur making him blend in with the castle walls.

He's here. Outside. This could be so easy.

Harper's step quickened, snapping me back to reality. I pushed past Tana, Giselle, and Shay, desperate to stop Harper. The level-headed wolf was being far too eager, too fast. *Too present* in a place where the sin of sloth hung heavy in the air. She was going to give us away.

I closed in, grabbed her arm, and roared, stopping her in her tracks. "I told you to walk on the right, wolf!"

My directive garnered attention from the four demons at the gates—but it also brought Harper out of her trance. She slumped and shuffled to the side of the road. When I turned to see if the demon guards suspected anything, I exhaled. They resumed their conversation.

But Gunner's silver wolf eyes widened as he took us in. I pointed my mace at him, hoping he understood we were here to get him. That soon, we'd attack. He needed to get out of the way.

Could he?

The humans here were lethargic and not in their right minds. Every now and again, the Opal's magic washed over me anew, ensuring we didn't fall prey to the sin of Sloth.

Gunner didn't look lazy and lethargic, though . . . His eyes shone bright and alert. As did the eyes of the humans standing with him and the surrounding wolves. Why were they immune?

"We need to act fast," Luca came up next to me. "You strike at a distance. I'll follow. If any survive the initial attacks, Tobias and Giselle will race forward and decapitate them. Ready when you are."

I did not hesitate as I drew up from the deep well of demon power. The torture magic writhed, furious I'd dampened it with my other power, but it still came, still flew from me at my bidding. The moment it struck the demons, they convulsed. One let out a shriek, but Luca cast his magic, silencing him.

All four fell, and to my utter astonishment, the wolves in the pack leapt atop of them, ripping their throats from their necks.

"What the hell?" I breathed as Harper broke from our group and ran straight for the wolves.

"Goddess, I can't believe we're about to pick up all those mongrels," Benedict said from somewhere around us. Meredith had let him out of her harness and the feline had been following us, invisible. "Aren't two wolves enough!?"

I barely registered the cat's quip, as the wolves parted for her, and Gunner transformed back into human form in time to catch her when Harper leapt for him. His arms wrapped around her, and they kissed with such passion that I nearly choked.

"About time," Shay said, restraint in her voice. I suspected only the need to remain as quiet as possible kept her from hooting and hollering.

"*Please.*" Meredith came to stand with us, her act of being under Sloth's thrall dropped. "Like you two are any better."

She smirked when Shay's cheeks turned a delicious shade of pink that I wanted to kiss off her.

"It's been obvious for quite some time they've had feelings for one another," Tobias added, joining us. "But is this the best moment?"

In answer, Gunner let out a whoop of happiness that had the rest of us grinning. That was until Luca marched closer to the wolves.

"Apologies to break this up," Luca said as we darted after him, "but we can't stay in one place for too long."

Gunner's eyes twinkled. "You're right. Anyway, if things get too heated, I might make a scene with what I wanna do with Harp."

"Hush!" Harper rolled her eyes, but a smile still graced her lips.

"We need to come up with an exit strategy," Luca said, redirecting the conversation yet again. "It will be more difficult if these other wolves wish to come."

"They're my pack," Gunner stated. "They're comin'."

My lips parted. His pack? But Gunner had escorted his pack to Isila. Had some returned? I was about to ask when Meredith sucked in a breath so long and sharp that it sent my heart rate spiking.

"You've got to be joking," she hissed as she held up her hand and stared at her ring. "It's warm! *It's warm!!!*" Her gaze scanned the wolves before landing on the other two people in the pack. After an assessment, she pointed to the woman. "You're a witch?"

The young Black woman eyed Meredith. "Uh, yes."

"What kind?"

"Earth."

I shook my head in disbelief. Harper had been right. "Convergence."

"Strikes again." Meredith beamed. "The more of us who gather, the more likely this sort of thing is to happen."

"Well, if you're right, and she holds the Emerald of Earth, we only need it to happen once more!" Harper glanced between Meredith and the woman, who, at the mention of the Emerald of Earth, stiffened.

"You know what that is, don't you?" Meredith breathed, probably, like me, barely daring to believe one of the *Vindix* would be caught up when we met them.

"I do," the woman replied. "My family has protected it for as long as anyone can remember. When we got it, that date is lost to time."

"I can't believe this is happening," I murmured.

"You're the others?" the woman asked. "The other *Vindix*?"

"We are," Harper answered. "Some of us anyway."

"We still need to find the person who can wield the Sapphire of the Seas," Meredith added. "But I think with you joining us, it might be easier than ever. Or at least, I hope."

The woman nodded, accepting her fate. I supposed if she'd known about her stone, and she saw the demon princes, our eternal enemies, were here, that wasn't a shocker.

Then, the woman opened the neck of her shirt and pulled out a necklace with a giant emerald in the center. "I've kept this close since my mother handed it down to me. She told me and my sisters stories about the *Vindix* growing up and the moment I showed signs of earth magic, she told me I was the one who needed to keep it close. At all times, she said."

"Thank tha' Goddess." Tana sounded close to tears.

"What's your name?" Meredith asked.

"Rhianna."

"Meredith. The Opal is my *lapis caelesti*."

Rhianna did not balk at the more formal term, which told me that she did know a lot about the sacred stones and, likely, those destined to wield them.

"I'm a seeker, and with the help of my ring, which is like a talisman for finding *Vindix*, I can sense you. You must have something on you, or on the necklace, that correlates with my ring." Meredith pointed to me. "Anyway, more importantly, this is Hans, keeper of the Pearl. Harper there has the Diamond. Rabi the Amethyst. Tana is our fire elemental." She acknowledged each in turn, targeting only the *Vindix* in the group, those Rhianna would want to set apart right away.

Luca stepped in when Meredith finished. "As much as I'm sure we'd all like to get to know you better right now, Rhianna, we must plan an escape."

Gunner arched an eyebrow. "Escape? We can do better than that, my man."

"Meaning?" the mage prompted.

"We're here. At Sloth's door, and we got six of the *Vindix*." Gunner swept a hand over the group. "We got S&S and some of my new pack too. And most importantly, the bulk of Sloth's forces aren't in the castle. They're by that black dome of terror —heard those demons we killed talkin' 'bout it earlier."

My blood chilled. "Gunner, what are you getting at?"

"It's obvious, isn't it?" Harper smirked and stared up at Gunner. "He wants to make a run at Sloth. Right here. Right now."

CHAPTER TWENTY

HANS

Given our dire need to move quickly and quietly, the group's outrage was far less than I imagined. Some stated they wanted to stick with the plan and run. Others, however, agreed with Gunner.

In the end, we put it to a vote.

Every single *Vindix* wanted to shoot our shot. Gunner and his pack too. So our side won easily. I only hoped we didn't look back on this moment and think ourselves foolhardy.

But when else would we have this opportunity? A chance to infiltrate a Prince of Hell's castle with someone who knew the building even just a little. *And* with a pack of wolves, albeit a small one, at our backs? To have these advantages and go up against a prince whose *defining feature* was being lazy?

Risky though it was, we were moving on Sloth today. I calmed those who'd voted to run by assuring them that if things got too out of hand, I'd smoke-travel us all out.

In human form, Gunner and I led the way into the castle, his wolves at his side, still in their animal forms.

I had wings. I had armor. We doubted anyone would question me as a guard. Luca didn't even have wings, so he used the helmet we'd picked up to hide that he wasn't a demon at all.

Luckily, the inside of the castle was as as empty of demons as the outside. As Gunner had said, Sloth had sent his minions to the barrier under attack.

But the Prince of Hell was here, Gunner assured us of that. As far as Gunner knew, Prince Belhor didn't leave the castle. He did little except rest and eat and command others to do his bidding.

I hoped Belhor would be napping when we found him. Was it honorable to kill a sleeping person? No? Did I care after all they'd put the world through?

Not one bit.

"Footsteps ahead," Gunner murmured. "Three pairs, I think. They're comin' our way and fast and from the hall we need to go down."

Luca let out a long breath. "We have to kill *and* hide the bodies."

"There are lots of rooms," Gunner said. "I dunno what's in all of 'em, though."

"We'll soon find out," I said as we made our turn.

Gunner had been spot on. Three demons, cambions by the looks of them. Their race of demon was characterized by human looks, save for the demonic eyes, wings, and some-times, horns.

"Hey!" one called out, his tone non-threatening. "What d'you got there?" He eyed the group, his gaze landing on Shay who shuffled a few steps behind me—still acting as though Sloth's sin affected her. "Delicious. Our prince doesn't want them all, does he? Cause I'd like to take blue eyes for a ride."

"I'll take the ginger," another said.

Gunner tightened. Apparently, the cambions didn't sense the tension mounting in the air, the threat growing inside me.

The Pearl grew hot against my wrist. I'd hesitated to use it, knowing my demon magic would be strong enough to level most people, but these guys were testing my willpower, talking about Shay and Harper like that.

"We can take one and then switch off?" the first guy leered at Harper. "She smells like a wolf. Never had one of them—"

Enough. I lashed out with my demon magic, and a shriek ripped up his throat, halting any more foul words. He fell.

The second cambion followed, and the third a long five seconds later. He'd been the only one smart enough to run.

Luca strode forward, silencing one with his blade as Gunner did the same, taking one of the cambion's own weapons to end his life. In the meantime, the third hellblooded had passed out from the pain I was inflicting on him.

My demon magic came as easily as breathing, and with the Pearl egging it on, even more so. Though now that I had my witching magic back, I found that I could better control the Pearl. At my full strength, the foul *lapis caelesti* no longer terrified me.

What I could do with it, however, did continue to make me uneasy. Others had gone mad with this type of power. For that reason alone, I still needed to treat the stone with great care and respect.

Luca killed the last soldier and pulled them into a room Tobias had scouted while Gunner and I were otherwise occupied. The last body disappeared, and only then did I realize everyone else was staring.

Rhianna looked ill, while Rabi and Tana stared at the opposite walls, as if nothing at all was happening. Pretending. Briefly dissociating.

The Pearl burned against my skin. I understood their distaste as I'd felt it about myself for years. And they were all new to this, new to fighting and the aftermath. I hoped they maintained focus through it all.

Thankfully, the others weren't as bothered. Harper, Meredith, and Giselle had remained alert, waiting, watching for other adversaries. And Shay was watching me, but not with revulsion. Was that pride in her eyes?

Get real. A nephilim would not be proud that I can even more easily torture someone.

"Can we go? The smell of their blood is making me want to lose my tuna," Benedict said, still invisible.

Meredith snorted. "You're not the only one."

"Then let's move," Luca muttered as he strode back into the hallway. He waved his hand and the blood on the ground disappeared. "Gunner says we're close."

"Real close," the wolf assured us.

I fell into step with Gunner, ready for another fight. For once, I let the power of the Pearl simmer, knowing that if I ever needed to indulge in its malevolence, this was the time.

We rounded a corner, and I locked in on our destination. Two guards stood outside a door, both turning to take us in.

"Who are you?" one asked.

"The pack's guard," I barked back.

"No you're not. My brother was in the guard, and you weren't with him." He raised a hand, and the air crackled with his power.

I extended my arm and struck first, pulling from my well of demon magic and using the Pearl to amplify. They fell, their mouths open in silent screams, eyes rolling back in their skulls, and before I could request a member of my group to finish the pair, Tobias blurred ahead, snapping one neck, then two. When he was done, his gaze met mine.

"It's terrifying, what you can do."

"And necessary," Shay retorted as we joined the vampire.

"I would not say otherwise, and you shouldn't take it as a negative, Shay." Tobias arched an eyebrow. "My kind is quite terrifying too, but *I* will not apologize for what I can do."

Shay's shoulders softened, and knowing she'd meant well, I brushed my hand against hers. For so long, I'd hated my darker magic. Hated the Pearl. Myself too. Shay had also needed to come to terms with that side of me and once she had, she'd assisted me in taking the last steps. She was protective of me, and the feeling was mutual.

"Focus," Luca breathed. "Prince Belhor likely did not hear his guards' dying, but there might be more inside. And we will have the upper hand only for a moment against him. Forget not what he is."

Not a normal demon, but a ruler of evil. Once of the seven princes from below. A monster.

Maybe, to some, even a sort of god.

"*Vindix* first," Meredith said, to which Tobias bristled. "Don't, Tobias. We need as open of a shot as we can get." She looked at the ground. "And Benedict, wherever you are, stay out of the way and invisible."

"A cat knows where he needs to be!" Benedict sounded offended, but it was the stony look on Tobias's face that worried me.

"You go behind the rest of the *Vindix*, Meredith," I added, both to mollify Tobias and because it was only sensible. "We'll semicircle around you and Shay and Luca will protect your six. All that you need to do is keep the sin from seeping into our heads and hearts."

Meredith nodded, understanding. She was skilled in many ways, but her primary use—her invaluable mission—was to use the Opal to make sure none of us fell prey to Sloth's powers.

"Tobias and Giselle, break down the doors," I said after we got into formation. "Then take any soldiers who might be standing nearby. I'll strike to disable the prince. The rest of you, do your worst and end him. We have surprise on our side."

The elementals and Harper shared glances. Among them, Harper was the newest witch, but Rabi was new to fighting and Rhianna—well, she didn't even know us. Still, she rolled her shoulders back, a witch who understood her place, if not the people who shared her destiny. I hoped that she was as powerful as she projected herself to be.

Gunner jerked his chin toward the wolves. "We'll stay at the door. Once you attack, I'm pretty sure Sloth will call more of his kind. He can do that telepathically. And they're fast. Real fast."

"Good call." No reason to barge in only to be swarmed from the back.

Shay and Luca hung right behind Meredith, prepared to defend our best hope of keeping our heads on straight. Somewhere at our feet, I was sure Benedict watched and waited to prove himself, though the snarky familiar had fallen silent.

"Now," I breathed.

The doors blasted inward, and the vampires rushed forward as half a dozen soldiers spun to face us, murder in their eyes. Two snaps told me that a pair met their ends at the Laurent hands, but that was the only jump on them that we got. Magic filled the air around the guards, a shimmering silver shield to protect them. As the surviving guards were busy fighting vampires, their magic inched slowly toward the end of the room to provide a shield over where Sloth lounged on an elevated throne, his mouth opened as two humans, one male, one female, fed him grapes. He wasn't even worried. That was his first mistake.

Determined to beat the shield and take Sloth down quickly, I directed my torture magic at him. It struck just as a grape landed in his foul throat. The prince screamed, the sound music to my ears, before it halted, and the prince straightened.

My mouth went dry. He really was made of stronger stuff than the rest of us. When his gaze landed on me, I shuddered.

"Ah, so you're the thief that took my brother's prize. One of our own." He sniffed the air. "Lilith's spawn, judging by your scent?"

The prince gave a lazy grin that was out of place in the room, as vampires fought demon soldiers at the sidelines, and air crackled with magic.

"Take my mother's name out of your mouth." I targeted him once more.

Again, a scream leapt from the prince's mouth, but he mastered himself quickly, and somehow turned my powers on those closest to him—the humans. They fell from his sides, bodies rolling down the steps, crying out in pain.

I released my magic and their screams stopped, but they remained panting, their faces red and contorted.

"Work smarter, not harder," Sloth drawled. "Isn't that what humans say? It's one of their better lines."

Through my indecision to strike again, to harm innocents, stiffness gripped me. Two humans versus one god of the underworld. Kill Sloth and thousands would get their lives back.

"If I remember correctly, none of your ilk were warders the

last time you came to save this realm. I wonder if you are now." The prince nodded to the humans. "Can you stop others from hurting those beautiful, weak humans?"

A soldier leapt from the fray toward the humans, sword raised. Sloth had to have telepathically told him to attack, but before he landed a blow, the air swirled with power and ghosts appeared.

I gaped. They weren't always visible, and that they were now indicated Harper wanted them to be. She wanted to watch Sloth see the specters.

"Protect," Harper shouted, and the ghosts, at least twenty of them, swarmed the humans, creating a shield of ghostly energy around them. A protection I was betting even a god couldn't break. "*Vindix* now!"

The hurdle of harming innocents was gone and just in time, too, for at our backs, snarls rose from Gunner's wolves.

"The pack needs help!" Luca shouted. "Shay!"

Before I worked out what to do next, my skin tingled. I sensed magic slithering around me. It wasn't the sin smothering New Orleans, but something darker and crueler, something—if I had to guess—all the brothers of Hell shared. I cried out just as the other *Vindix* did. He was going for us first, his staunch opponents. No doubt he'd let others take on our friends, as he had many demons at his disposal.

Pain lanced through me as his violent magic cut me to the core. I fell to my knees, heard them crack against the stone. The other *Vindix* fell too. All?

I forced my eyes open. Only Harper remained standing. No, Harper *and* Meredith, though the latter looked faint. I didn't know how, but I got the sense Meredith was shielding Harper, who was doing the same to the humans.

But I needed Meredith here. *To me,* I thought. *To me.* If I attacked, I could stop Belhor.

Not now though, not like this. I—

An icy wind whipped around me, only adding to the agony writhing through my blood and bones.

"*Subject!*" Sloth crowed. "I would like to see your magic upon them. Freeze them."

Freeze? Who was he talking to?

My answer materialized a moment later when Meredith growled. "Silas. You traitor!"

"I am," the fae answered, determination freezing over his voice. "But no longer."

Before I could compute what was happening, a portal opened by the Prince of Hell. Silas appeared in it, covered in blood. He must have been fighting the wolves.

The fae stepped through his own portal, side-stepping the fighting in the room in a single step. I watched, astonished, in agony, and frozen to the bone, as Silas pulled a dagger and slashed it at the prince.

He missed, but the attack startled Belhor, and his power over me lifted a touch. Taking my chance, I lashed out at him with my magic.

The prince screamed, and Silas flew backwards off the dais. His head hit the ground with a sickening crack.

"Now!" I roared, my voice guttural, and the elementals attacked.

Fire lanced. Wind swirled. Rocks pulled from the very walls of the castle pummeled. The force of the attack picked up speed as we shook off Belhor's effects and suddenly, the prince was in a storm of elements. Of pain too.

The clash of our magics shook the castle, and behind

Belhor, the rock wall shattered, crumbled. On the ground, the royal monster writhed, but did not die. No, he was no normal person.

"Harder!" I shouted, aware that more demons entered the room and now fought. How many, I could only guess. Tobias, Luca, Giselle, Shay, and—judging by the feline yowling—Benedict were engrossed in battle.

From the corner of my vision, Meredith collapsed but somehow pulled herself on to her elbows. She was up against her limit and if the holder of the Opal fell, we all fell with her. We had to finish this.

And finish it we did. The elements swarmed Belhor. My magic, that of my demon blood combined with that of the Pearl, and the power flew from me in waves, until finally, the prince stilled. I gasped, waiting for a battle cry. Or perhaps for him to jump up and attack once more.

But Harper was the only one who remained standing. She took a step forward.

"Wait." I cast a spell over the prince, one to detect life.

It came back with nothing.

I sighed. "Dead."

Rabi looked ready to faint. "Are you—"

Wails ripped through the air. I twisted, and my eyes widened as demons, over twenty of them that had been fighting the wolves and our friends, fell to the ground and writhed.

"Their master is dead," Luca rasped, watching a demon scream at his feet. "That death resonates through them."

"Will they die?" Hopefulness laced Meredith's tone.

No. The agony affected them for only about thirty seconds. Then the demons blinked and rose, ready to fight again.

Unfortunately for them, we were ready, and they were weakened. My friends and the wolves cut them down, leaving the room bathed in the stench of demon blood.

It was done, and even surrounded by death and blood and horrors, a collective sigh filled the room. My shoulders loosened. That was until Gunner uttered one word.

"Si."

Silas.

The alphablood crossed the throne room and knelt by Silas. Harper was with him in an instant, her face more wary than Gunner's, but still she went. Everyone waited until Gunner cleared his throat and rose again. "Dead."

"He redeemed himself, in the end," Tobias whispered.

"He did," Gunner agreed. If Gunner, as the one wronged by Silas, said such a thing, I could go with it. Maybe I'd even feel it one day too. "We're taking him back with us."

Silence hung in the air, and I wondered if anyone would deny Gunner, but never got an answer as a deafening *crack* ripped my attention from the wolf. Head swiveling, I took in the throne room but saw nothing.

"Look outside." Rhianna pointed out the window into the sky. The dome, previously shimmering and visible from anywhere in the city, was cracked, falling to pieces.

"Sloth's death means the end of his protections," Luca breathed. "The dome can't live without him."

"Which means the military will come soon," Giselle said. "A good thing too, from what we've seen of the city."

She'd barely finished her sentence when the sound of bombs being set off raised the hair on my arms. "We have to leave."

"We're taking the humans," Meredith said, and Tobias scooped up one human as Giselle took the other. Both humans passed out at some point, and I hoped for their sakes that they stayed that way.

"Hans, smoke-travel us to the manor?" Luca asked.

Once everyone surrounded me, and Benedict was strapped into Meredith's harness, I called my smoke.

CHAPTER TWENTY-ONE

SHAY

The wolves of Gunner's new pack and the two humans we'd picked up in Louisiana were tucked away in rooms to be dealt with tomorrow. The *Arcacustos* showed Rhianna the manor, and everyone was debriefed on the fall of Prince Belhor.

Tomorrow, Luca would meet with the Covenant and tell them what happened, and more importantly, *how* it had happened. While that was going on, Tobias and Gunner and whoever wanted to go, would take Silas's body to Ireland to bury him. Through it all, we'd wait and see if there was any retaliation from the remaining Princes of Hell. If they knew their brother was dead.

But that was *tomorrow*. Tonight, I had other plans. *Tonight,* my long-held fantasies would be made real.

I only needed to find Hans first.

I'd been combing the manor for at least ten minutes. Thanks to New Orleans wiping us all out, physically, mentally, and magically, most withdrew to their rooms. I was sure I'd even heard Harper's giggle from Gunner's room—something I'd be interrogating her about tomorrow.

But Hans? It was like he'd disappeared into thin air.

I came across Miriam, walking with a steaming teacup in hand. "Miriam, have you seen Hans?"

She stopped, her spine ramrod straight like it always was. "I saw him on my way down here. He was going to the library."

"I'll knock," I assured her when the elder witch looked ready to remind me that the library was off-limits to those who weren't *Arcacustos* or *Vindix*.

"Hmm, very well." She left without another word, and I made my way in the opposite direction.

The door was shut, but that wasn't anything new. It always was. Standing in front of the door, I drew in a breath, feeling the slightest edge of nerves creeping in. Before I could chicken out, I knocked three times.

Sounds came through the door and a moment later, it opened. Hans's eyebrows rose. "Shay. Is something wrong?"

"No, but I wanted to talk to you," I said. "If you're free."

He glanced back, and I got the impression I was interrupting something big.

"It can wait though," I backpedaled as regret seeped in. If Hans didn't even want to leave the library, how would he react to me seducing him? Was this not an appropriate time? Did I need to wait until the war was over?

But what if one of us doesn't survive? My stomach dipped.

"No, that's okay," Hans said, his assuring voice bringing me back and easing my worry. "I should get to bed anyhow."

He let himself out of the library, and we fell into step. As I couldn't come out and say that I'd been thinking about doing the horizontal mambo with him, I started out lighter. Best to test the waters.

"What were you doing in the library?"

"Trying to find if there are easier ways to kill the princes," he said. "We managed, but everyone was pretty drained after. I still am. Imagine if we had to take on two or more at a time. I'm not sure we'd succeed."

My lips pursed. "And you found?"

"Nothing."

"Oh. That sucks."

He gave a dry laugh. "To say the least."

Silence fell between us, and with every passing second, I doubted myself more. Had I misread the vibes between us over the last few days?

No, he kissed me. That's a solid fact.

But battle changes things. Did my timing stink?

I still wasn't sure, and by the time we'd reached the staircase leading to our wing, the muscles in my shoulders were hard as rocks. Each step felt like I was climbing a mountain, and I jabbered about something stupid to fill the silence between us. To soften the awkwardness growing inside me.

It didn't work, and by the time I stopped in front of my door, I was sweating.

Hans's eyebrows furrowed, as if he was seeing me for the first time since I'd drawn him out of the library. "Hey? Are you okay?"

"I—uh—Hans . . ." I cleared my throat, and an alarmed expression crossed his face. I excelled at flirting. Good at getting men to love me. Heavens, Hans and I had flirted so many times!

But now, I felt like a girl who had never even kissed a guy.

"Shay?" Hans came closer and the scent of the library, covering up his own manly aroma, came with him, filling my nostrils and making my knees weak. "Do you need me to get Hannah? You look pale."

"*Willyoujoinmeforadrink*?" The words tumbled out of me in an incoherent jumble.

Somehow, he made sense of them. "Sure. In the kitchens?"

"In here." I placed a hand on the doorknob. I'd prepared for this, had a bottle of wine waiting.

"Ah, yeah. I think I'd like that." Desire seeped into his tone. He remembered our kiss and maybe, even though I was acting like an idiot, he suspected this might lead to more.

If I didn't screw it up.

We entered my room, which as a result of my earlier stress cleaning, was sparkling. Hans noticed the enhanced cleanliness too, his eyebrows raising to his hairline as I kicked off my shoes and went to the sitting area and picked up the bottle. Two glasses sat on the table.

"Two actual wine glasses, huh? Why does this feel like a date?" Hans teased as he took off his shoes. We wore shoes in the manor, but as a general rule, no one liked to wear them in the places where they slept.

"I was hoping," I admitted, swallowed, "for alone time."

A gleam filled his eyes. One I'd seen before when Hans had left bars with other girls. One I'd always wished he'd bestow on me, though I'd never had the guts to follow through on telling him I was seriously interested.

I poured the glasses, held one out for him. Our fingers brushed as he accepted it, and the heat of his hand sent my temperature soaring. Hans watched me drink as he took a sip, long and deep. He set his glass down and stepped closer. Then, his hand landed on my wine glass, and he pried the glass from me, set it on the table, and hooked his fingers beneath my chin. When I met his eyes, I found a feral expression that had my toes curling in the thick weave of the rug.

"Are you sure, Shay? Sure you want more? More than what

we've done?" Hope filled his eyes, and I'd never been so sure that my emotions matched another person's emotions.

"I've never been more sure in all of my life."

"What about your family?"

He meant my mother. What would she say if we took our relationship to another level? Or even just fooled around?

"I told her you're important to me," I answered. "That I care for you. That I—I want you, Hans. I have for some time."

"Want me in what way?"

I exhaled. His eyes said he wanted me, too, but Hans had always been careful, so careful. Knowing what we were, and finding himself lesser than, he'd never pushed himself on me. For a while now, I'd known I'd need to be the one to take the first step to more. Now, I was ready.

"All of you, Hans. Everything. I want *everything* with you, and we could have it all. We might be perfect for one another, and too thick to see it all these years."

"Goddess, I've been dying to hear that." His lips lowered, taking mine in a sensual kiss that stole my breath. Both of his large, calloused hands wrapped around me, pulling me tighter into him.

I gasped. He was already hard, and already, I was wet and wanted him inside me.

I was a goner.

And he must have known it, because those hands, so adept at fixing cars and casting spells, found my hips and lifted. My legs wrapped around his hips, and he carried me to the bed, made and waiting—hoping for a little action.

Okay, *a lot* of action. I might be part angel, but in the bedroom, I was no saint.

Hans laid me down and leaned over me so that our kisses didn't break. I arched my hips into him, seeking that length and hitting it at the right angle. I moaned into his mouth, and his lips curled in a self-satisfied smirk.

An earned one at that. The man was well-endowed. I'd give him that.

"Rushing, Shay?"

"It doesn't feel like I'm rushing," I rasped. "More like we've been dancing around one another for years."

"Can't argue that." Hans climbed atop of me, and I envisioned his dark wings spread out as he took me. Heat pooled in my core and a delicious ache spread there.

"I want to see your wings," I whispered.

He froze, and I regretted my words. Hans had only just accepted his demon side. I didn't think he liked it—or believed I might find some parts of that side of him sexy.

"You're sure?" he asked.

"All of you," I said, and black feathered wings unfurled, blocking the manor's ceiling from my sight.

"And yours," he said, hands trailing down from my face, teasing the tops of my breasts above my shirt.

Heavens, I wanted my clothing to evaporate on the spot. I wanted his hands on my skin. Everywhere on me. In me.

"Leaving me hanging?" he whispered as kisses trailed down my neck.

I called my white as snow wings, a perfect juxtaposition to Hans's black.

"Goddess, you're beautiful, Shay."

In answer, I rose, and my hands drifted to his belt, undid it and then took to the buttons. Hans assisted and before I knew it, he stood before me in boxer briefs. Shirtless too. My eyes feasted on his body, his tattoos, on everything that was Hans Novak.

Wanting nothing more than to ignite his fire, I pulled off my shirt and, before it was gone, he helped with the pants.

"Scoot up. I want to see you," Hans growled and gestured to the headboard.

I imagined gripping that headboard as he took me from behind, and almost suggested it, but no. Not for our first time. This time, I wanted to look into his eyes, to see everything. It felt like we were on the edge of something blooming and magnificent.

So I shifted back, and he climbed onto the bed, the old springs creaking beneath his weight and making me giggle.

"Gunner is going to hear everything," Hans muttered.

"And Harper. They're together."

Hans smirked. "Something in the air."

"I'll say." I beckoned him closer with one finger, and our lips met again, softer this time, less desperate, though the kiss didn't stay that way for long.

It soon became clear that Hans and I liked things a little hotter. A little harder. *Rough.* Our tongues danced, and his hands massaged my breasts in strong, circular strokes.

When he reached for the bra clasp and undid it one-handed, I assisted by arching up. He pulled the torture device off, and I got to witness and relish in his reaction, how his blue eyes went round. How he licked his lips, as if imagining tasting my nipples—which was what he did next.

Hans sucked one peaked nipple, then the other, and I feared I might truly explode with the pleasure of it all as my hands wound through his long-ish blond hair. Then his mouth dipped, licking and sucking down my belly, closer to my core.

The insides of me fluttered in anticipation. I was betting Hans would be a rockstar with his mouth. Better than good, even, fabulous. But that wasn't what I wanted, what I'd been craving.

"Hans," I rasped, somewhat surprised I could speak at all with so much pleasure coursing through me. "I want you inside me. I want to do this *together.*"

His gaze pinned me from over the mound of my pussy, covered in sky-blue lace. He held there a moment before he winked.

I could have come right then and there, and when Hans peeled off my panties, I very nearly did.

"Let's see if you're ready," Hans answered and slipped a finger inside me. He closed his eyes as he did so, maybe feeling a fraction of the dopamine I was experiencing as my back arched.

Had he cast a spell over me? No one had ever had me so hot, so ready, so quickly. Usually, I savored foreplay, but today? I wanted the feast, wanted to feel our bodies together and the pounding of his heartbeat matching mine.

"Goddess Shay," Hans ground out. "You're perfect." He slid another finger in, happy to torture himself as well as me.

I was about to beg him to fill me in other ways when his fingers twisted and curled along the front wall of my channel. A gasp rang from my throat, and my pussy pulsed.

Hans chuckled, his black wings curling behind him as he dragged along my wall again, wrenching pleasure from me. "That's a good girl."

Oh. My. Heavens. I exploded, my core sucking at his fingers, wanting more but also begging him not to stop.

A soft cry left my lips, one that the coven members with sharp hearing would catch, but I didn't care. I only wanted more. Him. On me. Together.

Why had I ever fought it? He was so good. We were so good. And we fit like two puzzle pieces.

I rode out my orgasm on his fingers, and once it dimmed and the stars in my eyes had subsided, I reached for him. "Please. Join me."

This time, he didn't tease, didn't explore my body and slake off his needs. He withdrew his fingers from my core, licked them in a way that both made me want to die and throw myself at him, and pulled off his boxer briefs.

With his length long and proud and thick, he climbed up my body. The fullness of his tip pressed against my core, ready to thrust in. But he didn't. He held there, locked eyes with me. "You're sure?"

As if to emphasize something I no longer cared about, Hans rustled his black wings.

"I'm sure. I—" I paused, scared to admit what I'd felt when he lay in the healer's sanctuary half dead.

We almost didn't get this chance . . .

My heart cracked open at that truth, and I knew what I had to do. He was *here*. Despite what we'd been through, we were *alive*. If Hans rejected me now, then yes, I'd break, but I'd live having known that I told him the truth.

"I'm falling in love with you, Hans. And I want this more than I can say, want you inside me, want us together."

A soft breath left him. "I'm falling for you too, Shay. I have been for a while but was too terrified to admit it."

I pulled his lips to mine, and my heart exploded as he thrust into me, filling me. As if we'd been together a million times, it was easy to find our rhythm. Easy and out of this world, and as I ached for more, it didn't take long for another orgasm to swell. My core tightened, grew hot, as Hans moved in and out of me, his piercing blue eyes watching me, me watching him.

"I'm kind of embarrassed to admit this," he breathed, "but I'm close."

I laughed. "Let's fly home."

I arched, allowing him a deeper angle, and I swore his eyes rolled back into his head. I grabbed his hips, pulling him even deeper into me. I wanted us as close as humanly possible.

Angely and demonly possible? A laugh nearly ripped from my throat but was halted as pleasure exploded from me for the second time in less than ten minutes.

Hans roared as he finished, as we soared the skies together, our breaths mingling as one. Unable to stop it, my light burst from me too, encompassing us in a soft glow.

When it was over, he lowered and laid atop me.

"My light didn't hurt you, right?"

"Not at all," he replied. "It felt warm. Nice." He looked like he wanted to say more, but instead, he lifted his hand to brush a lock of hair from my face.

I froze, catching sight of something that had not been there before. "*Hans*, what is that on the back of your hand?"

"Huh?"

"The silvery-white circle on your hand! Look at it!"

Hans turned his hand and blinked. A white circle glowed there. My stomach swooped, and trembling, I lifted my hand to find a matching mark on my skin.

"Hans," I whispered. "It's a soulmate mark."

CHAPTER TWENTY-TWO

GUNNER

H*ER LIPS TASTED SWEET AS HONEY ON MINE AND IN THAT MOMENT,* I swore to the Old Ones, I coulda died a happy man.

Harper Ferenz wanted me as much as I wanted her.

What world did I even live in? I wasn't sure, but I didn't want to leave it.

But of course, all good things had to end, and our end came in the form of a bossy mage entering the snug lil' haven Harper and I had hidden away in while the others ate lunch.

"There you are! Can you two stop sucking face for more than a minute so we can all talk?" Luca glared.

Dude was grumpy. It was enough to make the pleasure in havin' Harper in my lap, my hands squeezing her hips, dampen. Had something happened?

She laughed. "Excuse me, but *sucking face*? Did Shay tell you to say that?"

Luca glowered. "No."

Harper arched an eyebrow. I couldn't help but notice how swollen her lips were. Swollen 'cause I had indeed been suckin' and lickin' and kissing' them for the better part of an hour. An hour that had felt like a dang minute.

"It may have rubbed off," Luca sighed in concession. "We've all been spending too much time together."

"The benefits of being cooped up in a manor." She shifted in my lap, and I pulled her in closer, not wanting her to leave. "Meeting, you say?"

"I return from the Covenant bearing news," Luca replied, his tone a touch tamer. "And everyone should be in on it."

"We'll be there," Harper assured him.

That was all Luca needed. The mage left, and Harper turned toward me again. I sighed, lovin' the sight of her, the feel of her—strong and also soft in all the right places—so close to me. "Lunch is almost up anyway. I can't imagine the witches are going to let the *Vindix* have the afternoon off when they gave us a long lunch."

"'Course not. We didn't just save a city or anything yesterday."

Harper smirked. "The only reason they're even being lenient on me is because they're getting to know Rhianna one on one, which I should be doing too instead of *sucking face* with you."

"Why ain't ya then?" I teased, though I didn't want her to leave. The morning had been hard enough with buryin' Silas. Though the fae had betrayed me, I still remembered the moments of friendship. I didn't think they were fake, and I doubted I'd ever forget them.

She shook her head. "Guess I'm too easily swayed by a pretty face nowadays." She leaned to kiss me again, fillin' my nose with her delicious scent of apples and sunbaked earth, before risin' and holdin' out a hand. "Let's go."

My favorite she-wolf had to drag me from the snug and

through the halls until we reached the meeting room with the large table and the tiny tree in the center.

Gems representing the *lapis caelesti* decorated the tree. My pack wasn't there. They weren't allowed in the war room, but they didn't care. They much preferred to roam the grounds. Still, the room was full of the members of S&S, the *Vindix*, and half the *Arcacustos*. Stuart, Hannah, Aya, Olga, and Giselle were the only ones missing. Oh, and Benny. He was in a state after the fight, limpin' and missin' patches of fur. Also, I was pretty sure he was in hidin' 'cause there were so many more wolves around, the poor guy.

Since we were the last to arrive, we sat in two spots side by side. As soon as we settled in, Harper's hand found mine beneath the table. She squeezed, and I couldn't help but think I had the dopiest of grins on my face.

"I recently returned from Seattle," Luca started up without a big show. I'd been in enough meetings with the guy to know that meant he had important stuff to cover. "They're aware of what happened in New Orleans yesterday and magical forces are now on the ground, alongside the human military."

"In the city?" Meredith asked.

We'd all seen the dome crack and fall, but we hadn't stuck around long enough after to know what was goin' on.

"In the city," Luca confirmed. "It appears we were right. Once Sloth died, so did his magical barriers *and* his sin. The humans and supernaturals in the city have come back to themselves." He swallowed. "Of course there will be lingering effects. Only time will help those."

"What about the demons in the city?" Hans asked. "The shrieks when we killed Sloth were horrible."

"Not like they didn't deserve them," Shay muttered.

My eyes caught on the ring of silver-white on the back of

her hand. Her soulmate mark. Hans had a matching one, and the pair had emerged from Shay's room this mornin', sheepishly showing the rest of us.

I'd known it all along. Swear, I had.

"No fighting that," Hans agreed, takin' her hand and kissin' the back of it as if they'd been together forever. Love was well and truly in the air in the *Abscondita* manor. "I'm curious if that only happened to a select few demons. Or all. And what state are they in now?"

"The demons screamed in pain at the front lines too," Luca answered, "But they also all lived, so the fighting continues."

"It would have been too easy if they died with Sloth," Meredith muttered.

"Yes, well," Luca shrugged. "That is not our fight. *We* focus on the princes."

Meredith chewed on her bottom lip. "You don't think we should return to NOLA to help?"

"Absolutely not." Tobias looked at his mate as though she'd lost her mind. "Like Luca said, you're needed to defeat the princes. Let the rest of the world handle normal demons."

It didn't sit right with me, but it was the truth. There were some things only a few people could do, and, in this instance, we were those few. The *Vindix* were the chosen. Riskin' the *Vindix's* lives when they still had six princes to kill wasn't a good idea. No matter how some of 'em wanted to stay and help, we had to be realistic 'bout that. As for the rest of us, many were tied to the *Vindix*—or adjacent, like my wolves. Where they went, we followed for support.

"Actually, our mission right now is finding the last *Vindix*, isn't it?" Rhianna asked. Unlike Rabi, the witch wasn't quiet at all. I liked that 'bout her. It spiced things up in the manor.

CHAPTER TWENTY-TWO

"Yes." Meredith agreed. "The keeper of the Sapphire of the Seas."

"And studying until then," Miriam Black said.

Rhianna rolled her eyes. "I've already learned everything in that library!"

Gloria snorted, as if she didn't believe it, right at the same time, Harper let out a wistful sigh. "Goddess, you're so lucky for that."

I squeezed her hand. My girl might not have known she was part witch, but she was a genius and keepin' up mighty well. I wouldn't have her downin' on herself.

A minor argument broke out between Miriam and Rhianna, and I watched, amused, as Rhianna seemed to be winnin'. Though Gloria was on Miriam's side, she grinned through the argument, seemingly amused too. Claire, the most even-tempered of the matriarchal trio, waited patiently with her hands folded on the table, though I caught a glimmer of amusement in those old Irish eyes too. I bet Miriam could count how many times she'd lost an argument, but with the earth witch around, things might be changin'.

Rhianna got in a good verbal jab, which sent Gloria roarin' with laughter. Harper turned to give me a smirk that sent butterflies swarmin' my belly when the door to the meetin' room swung open. Giselle strode in, her gaze snapping about the room until she found Luca.

"I have big news."

The air left the room.

"Don't leave us hanging!" Meredith looked 'bout ready to crawl out of her skin. "What did you hear?"

Giselle had been sent into the village that mornin' to watch and listen for information. Specifically for news that would tell us if the Princes of Hell knew of their brother's death.

"Nothing about Sloth." Giselle pulled up a seat and sat down as gracefully as a queen. "News of Venice."

Venice. One of the fallen cities. Nothin' had come in or out of it since it had been taken.

"What's the word?" Tobias prodded his maker.

"A group of people got out of Venice," Giselle said. "Some fled the city and made it far enough away to tell their tale. It's on the Internet. The radio. Everywhere."

"Not all?" Meredith asked. "What does that mean? Did some die on the way? Or did the demons catch them?"

"Neither," Giselle said. "It seems the person who broke them out remained around Venice. No one who left the city knows why, but that's not what I found most interesting."

"What's more interesting than that?!" Meredith asked, her brows pulled together in a V. "No one, aside from us, has left one of the taken cities while they're still under Hell's rule."

"The people broke through the dome using water. A great, vicious *tidal wave* of it."

A gasp rang through the room as Meredith rose, her face ashen. "That *has* to be the water *Vindix*. Oh my goddess! Maybe this is in regard to the blood and water! Serena?" Stoney's hand slammed on the table, shaking the gems hanging on the tree.

"Girl means business," I whispered, loud enough that only Harper, and maybe the vamps, could hear.

"Maybe," Serena answered. She hadn't spoken much of the vision I'd heard she had before New Orleans, which made sense to me. Felt pretty vague. "From what I heard, New Orleans didn't fit, and there's even more water in Venice."

"Everyone get ready." Meredith rolled her shoulders back and took the lead. "We're going to Venice, and we're going now while we still might have an advantage."

CHAPTER TWENTY-THREE

MEREDITH

It took way too long to get our butts moving, which was partly my fault, as Benedict insisted on coming, and I was not having it. Cue a huge fight. My familiar was already poorly off and limping. Plus, Venice was a city built on water. Benedict had admitted he couldn't swim well, for crying out loud!

Finally, though, I convinced Benedict that Venice was not the fight for him. That he needed to save his *prodigious* strength for bigger fights. A little soothing of the ego and my familiar, somewhat appeased, allowed us to light-travel to Italy without him.

I'd been to the city before, on jobs for the Ringmaster. Many others had traveled to the City of Water at least once too. According to what Giselle heard, the prince who claimed this land took the main island for his home, so first we landed on a small island nearby, to take in the lay of the land. Or water, as it may be here.

City of Water. I winced. Had I been stupid not to assume the holder of the Sapphire of the Seas might be here all along? As the seeker of the group, I *felt* stupid.

"Look around," Giselle said as she, Serena, Tobias, Harper, and Gunner ran off to scout the small island. The potential *Vindix* no longer walked the streets of the main island, so they searched for witches wearing a sapphire or a talisman resembling the other ones the *Vindix* wore.

I was glad to have Serena with us this time. She'd recovered from her vision and made the most sense to bring those who understood the *lapis caelesti* best.

I inhaled, taking in the scent of the seabed that permeated the air at low tide. It had smelled like this when I'd visited this strange and wondrous city during jobs too. At least some things didn't change.

"According to my sources, the dome opened right there. That's very close to where Piazza San Marco is located." Luca cast a spell that briefly marked the dome with a circle of light so the *Vindix*, all except Harper who was out scenting the island, could see the location. "It's no longer under patrol. I see no flying demons, do any of you?"

One by one, the rest of us agreed. Rabi being the last, as he conducted a procedure that he called 'feeling the air' for any invisible flying bodies.

"Now that we're here, where do you think the people went?" I asked as Shay came close and squeezed my hand.

Luca shook his head. "There are so many islands, big, small, and in between, it's impossible to say. This is one of the closest, but I don't expect our search party to come back with anything. If I escaped Hell's domain, I wouldn't risk remaining too close."

The minutes ticked by, and while I grew ever more impatient at being stagnant, I said nothing. The search party was strong and fast. They wouldn't keep us waiting longer than needed.

"So what happens when we find him or her?" Rabi asked. "Does our magic strengthen?"

"No," I said. "I mean, we are stronger together as we're meant to beat evil together, but it's not like the holder of the last *lapis caelesti* will amplify my magic. Or yours. Or Rhianna's. Or anyone's. At least, I haven't read anything indicating that."

Rabi's eyebrows pulled together. "We've already beaten one prince without the seventh. I wonder if we need them at all."

Thank the Goddess for our good luck in New Orleans. But I looked at it as just that—luck.

"Sloth is likely the weakest of the Princes of Hell," Rhianna chimed in. "He is—was—lazy by nature. In the stories my mother told me, Prince Belhor often benefited from his brothers' hard work."

I envied Rhianna. That she had parents who had helped guide her in her fate. When she'd seen the Enchanted Pool and the *Abscondita* Coven library, she hadn't been at all fazed. She'd taken it in stride, a destiny she'd known she would need to fulfill.

"We got right lucky," Tana agreed, her Scottish brogue thick. "I donnae think tha' others will go as easily. Even if we find tha' final *Vindix*."

I agreed, though I hated admitting such a thing, even to myself. Most of us were exhausted yesterday. What if we faced two or more princes at once?

One thing at a time. I brushed the gathering sweat off my palms against my pant legs.

Giselle reappeared, followed by Tobias and Serena and the wolves. Harper and Gunner shifted back to human form, and everyone had the same news. There were people on the island, all human and terrified. No one had bothered them.

"To the main island to see if anyone has information, then?" Giselle asked Luca.

"I think so," Luca agreed. "Hans?"

Smoke billowed from Hans's feet, and I held my breath as his magic took over and transported us across the water. When we landed inside the dome, everyone fell into a fighting stance. We could never be sure that where we landed would be free of enemies. As it was, the only enemy was the thick sin clouding the air, and as the apex of my thighs ached, I had an idea as to which prince ruled this land.

"This is Lust's kingdom," Shay breathed, her voice raspy. "Heavens, it's *so strong*."

A distinct edge of desire colored her tone and as she threw Hans a wanting look, I knew I had to act fast. I called on the magic of the Opal of Heaven and cast it out, like I'd practiced so many times against Giselle's, Tobias's, and Serena's compulsion powers. Fighting a sin worked the same way—though it took even more effort.

The moment my power took root, the heated expressions on everyone's faces dimmed, and the need inside me to climb Tobias like a tree did too. I exhaled, relieved that, once again, I'd managed to use the Opal with success.

"Our guess proved correct. Prince Asmodev rules here." Luca scrubbed his hand over the back of his neck. "Soon, we might see some salacious moments."

"I'll feel right at home," Rabi quipped.

Astonished, we stared at him until I broke the ice. "Did you make a joke, Rabi?"

"Of a darker nature." He offered a small smile, one of the few I'd seen from the air elemental.

He hadn't been with us long, and everything in this world was new to him, but if he could joke, maybe he was growing to trust us.

I hoped so. To do what we needed to do, trust was necessary.

We'd landed in an alley. Or maybe it was one of those narrow Italian streets. I couldn't tell the difference. It gaped open, empty of people, though voices came from not far off. Voices and . . .

Heat filled my cheeks as I registered the sounds of pleasure. Yes, Luca had been spot on. Were there to be orgies in the street? If so, we'd have to mimic those under the sin's power in case we came upon demon soldiers.

I hoped wherever the final *Vindix* was, I'd find them.

"Guess we should check it out?" Shay looked as uncomfortable as I felt. "Meredith can lift the magic from people we come across and, uh, question them."

Stopping people who might be in the middle of sex. *Goddess, kill me.*

However, there was no other option. We were close to the site of the escape and had to do what we had to do. So our group made its way down the alley.

Inside the wards of Hell's domain, the scent of water still permeated the air, but there was something more, something hot and sticky and reminiscent of mussed hair and wrinkled bed sheets. All of it set my nerves on fire in the most uncomfortable way. Had I been here with just my mate, it would be fine, but I didn't like that sex was on everyone's mind, and we were all together. I got the sense Tobias felt the same, partially because thinking of sex and others looking at me would not be okay in the world of a possessive vampire mate.

How awkward.

At the end of the alleyway, Luca glanced up to the sky and pointed. "Right there. That's where the dome cracked."

From the outside, it wasn't so obvious, but in here, the dome had clearly been cracked—shattered and pieced back together. The magic that sealed the broken bits glowed a different shade of black, as if it were reinforced.

Prince Asmodev isn't taking any chances.

"If anyone saw something, it would be the people in these apartments." Luca waved at the balconies lining a street that was only slightly larger than the alley we were crowded into. "It might be safer to try searching inside first. Keep us off the streets, away from soldiers."

I eyed the apartments. Some of the balconies had fallen off, likely from the wave of water that broke the dome. Would the people who had lived there be alive? Would they have stayed?

I was about to suggest we check those apartments first, when an old woman peered out an open window. She stared down at me. When she caught me staring back at her, she waved a hand.

My lips parted. Was she inviting me up?

I looked around, but no one else seemed to have noticed. Only Luca, Tobias, Giselle, and I were close enough to see the woman anyway, and they'd been examining other balconies.

"Guys, that woman waved me up," I whispered as I watched the woman staring at me with dark eyes lined with wrinkles.

Tobias found her instantly. He frowned.

She frowned back.

Tobias's shoulders loosened. "If she is under Prince Asmodev's sin, that's an odd reaction."

He was right. Someone giving themselves over to unquenchable lust wouldn't frown.

Again, this time with more exasperation in the flick of her wrist, the old woman gestured for me to come up, then pointed to the door. *Open,* she mouthed.

"Curious," Giselle mused. "But as she seems in her right mind, and I doubt many are in this city, I say we go."

"It's us against one old woman," Tobias said.

"That we can see," I corrected.

"True. Even so, I like our odds."

"Cocky vampire," I muttered.

Luca shook his head. "I don't love it, but you're both right. She seems quite in her own mind."

The woman glared at us with her arms crossed over her chest. She looked *pissed.* I supposed I would be too if I was in my right mind and had to hear people banging all day and night.

"Let's go talk to her." I slipped into the street.

As the woman had said, the door was open. Tobias and Giselle led the way into the apartment building. The old woman wasn't the only occupant, but the others were all *busy* —some so busy they hadn't bothered to shut their front doors. It creeped me out to see all that, but there was nothing to be done except close the doors on our way.

The old woman lingered at the top when we crested the stairs to her floor, her door cracked open, a wary eye watching. When she spotted me, she cleared her throat. "Come in."

Her accent was thick, and from the look of hesitation on her face, I got the sense that she might not know English well. That was fine. Luca and Shay spoke Italian. I wouldn't be surprised if Giselle, Serena, and Tobias knew enough to get by too.

We'd filed into the small apartment, one cluttered with stuff that screamed this woman was a witch. The cauldron on her stovetop was a giveaway, and if that hadn't been enough, the pulse of magic as we crossed her threshold would have given it away.

"Who are you?" she asked.

"We're hoping to help the city," I said.

"Covenant?"

"No," Luca replied. "Though we are in talks with them."

"You're not . . . looking for someone?" She spoke more clearly now, and I realized it wasn't that she couldn't speak English well. More likely that she hadn't spoken to anyone in days before we arrived.

My lips parted. "We are. Why do you ask?"

She waved out her balcony. "You're from the outside, and you come here? Where the magical ward has been broken, and you looked prepared to search for something, not break it again. It was a guess." She paused. "Also, he said you'd come."

"*He?*"

"The young man who broke it."

My heart rate sped up, but I tried not to jump ahead of myself. "Why did he think someone would come?"

"He said others like him would show up. That he thought they would've come a while ago, but he supposed he had to make the first move. He wasn't happy about it."

My mouth fell open. I didn't dare ask the woman about any stone or someone who might hold one. I needed more information.

"He took others too," she said. "His lover—the poor boy being used by the prince—and Kaito, that's the wizard's name, could not take it any longer."

"How are you speaking to us unaffected?" Giselle cut in. "So *normale*?"

CHAPTER TWENTY-THREE

"I'm old," the woman said.

Giselle lifted an eyebrow.

"Perhaps not as old as you," the woman conceded. "But old enough, and I've warded all my life. As did my mother and her mother and so on. Ask anyone. *Mia famiglia* is known for the talent, and we're the strongest warders in the city. We've also all lived here and, as such, my home is a fortress. Not even a demon from Hell can break my protections as they're borne of family and love."

"Good," I breathed. Goddess, being a warder was far more useful than I'd ever thought. "Now, you said the young man who left said we'd come for him. I think you're right—he's right. But he's gone now."

The woman grinned. "It's a good thing he told me where he was going, isn't it, *bella*?"

"Thank the Goddess," Hans murmured.

"That's why you stayed when you could have left with him?" If the man had taken others, why hadn't she escaped?

"One reason. The other being I can no longer swim well, and despite his impressive control over water, Kaito needed to know that everyone he took with him was a good swimmer. In case he lost control. Or had to fight off the devils. I would have held others up. It was best for me to stay here and wait." She sighed and with the dome moving a few feet each day, I wasn't sure it was worth it to try. I'm old, and this place is safe."

"Moving?" Luca asked. "The barrier around the city moves?"

"Sloth's didn't. Least not as far as I knew," Gunner said with a shrug.

"This one does. Not a lot, but since the prince took over, he's acquired another few homes. Progress is slow, but there," the woman assured us.

I drew in a shuddering breath. "I bet the initial land grab took a lot of energy and now Lust is moving more slowly, taking land inch by inch. Maybe Sloth didn't. Maybe he was too lazy?"

Gunner grunted. "Shoe fits."

This was not welcome information. Even if only half of the princes took more land by the day, that added up. And what if they were only biding their time? What if in two weeks, they undergo another mass expansion? Lust might be biding his time to overtake Italy and the others . . . one of the taken cities was London. What would happen to the *Abscondita* manor? I shuddered at the idea of losing our home base. Our one safe spot while we figured stuff out.

We had more investigating to do. That much was certain.

"Well, we can get you out," I said. "No swimming required. And then we can take you far, far away too. If we do that, can you tell us where to go?"

"If you are here to defeat the darkness, I would tell you, even if it meant staying in this cesspit till my dying day." The woman turned and opened a desk drawer. "Allow me to get my map of the islands."

CHAPTER TWENTY-FOUR

HARPER

THE SMOKE CLEARED, AND WE LANDED ON BURANO ISLAND, THE piece of land the old woman—Donata, she'd belatedly introduced herself as—pointed out on her aging map. Unable to help myself, I side-eyed the woman. Finding her, coming here, all of it, had been easy. Far too easy. A faint niggling told me not to trust this woman. Not fully, anyway.

The others, at least some of them, appeared of a similar persuasion. Notable exceptions being Meredith, inclined to believe we'd stumbled into good news and Gunner—the cinnamon roll oaf—like we deserved such good fortune.

Well, Old Ones love them both. They could be positive, but I wasn't trusting this old lady until we found the water elemental. Kaito, as Donata had identified him. I wouldn't put my guard down until Kaito was at the *Abscondita* Coven manor, and we were safe and alive.

"He said he'd be here." Donata found her balance with the help of a hand from Rabi. "Thought it safe after the devils scourged those who lived here off the face of the earth."

"I donnae see a single soul." Tana peered into the distance, past the buildings in front of us. They looked like rundown homes. According to Donata, Burano Island was residential and inhabited for many centuries, with few improvements to the infrastructure.

"I can help with that," I said.

We had vampires, and of course Gunner and I could sniff out people, but I didn't want to break up our group if I didn't have to. I had other methods of searching to help keep us together. I called my magic, and it took less than a minute for a spirit to find me.

"Can you fly around this island and find a young man named Kaito?"

Donata appeared confused, my first hint that the ghost wasn't showing himself to others.

"I'm speaking to a ghost," I explained when the ghost nodded. "He needs a description. What did Kaito look like?"

"About twenty-five. Asian. Spoke perfect Italian, though he was not from here. He had a nose ring." Her own nose wrinkled at that identifier. "Quite a short man."

"That's enough to go on." I gestured to the ghost. "So? Can you find him?"

"I'll look." The ghost disappeared.

As I'd done this many times with spirits, I knew it couldn't take long to travel one island and look for a man fitting Donata's description.

And I was right. We waited twenty minutes when the ghost reappeared. "He's an hour that way. At the old bay. Do you need a guide?"

"We can manage," I said. "Thank you." When the ghost left, I turned to the others. "Follow me."

Meredith swept a hand in the direction that I'd indicated. "Then, by all means, lead the way."

AN HOUR ENDED UP BEING MORE LIKE AN HOUR AND A HALF, BUT when I smelled the wood fire, I perked up. The ghost hadn't failed us.

We followed the scent, Tobias carrying Donata, as she was not spry enough to walk an hour plus at our pace.

"I hear them," Serena said when I estimated we were still a few minutes away. "Some of them anyway, walking the streets, some might be indoors? And the smell of fire is stronger—they're cooking with it because the island has lost electricity. Otherwise, they wouldn't dare use fire."

Giselle nodded, then Tobias, as they listened in.

"I estimate about twenty people," Giselle said. "Some might be sleeping in one of the nearby buildings."

It was daylight, but these people were living in fear. How could they not, seeing what had happened so close to their home? No doubt they were implementing watches, and some would have rested during the day.

"If this is the same group, there's at least one magic worker with them," Luca mused.

"There were more than him, at least fifty in total. Of course, some might not have made it," Donata supplied.

My eyebrows pinched as I took in her green appearance. Motion sickness? Or was she thinking she might have been among those who had not made it to safety?

"Let me down," Donata instructed.

Tobias did so, and the elderly witch brushed herself off.

"How many magic workers?" Rhianna asked. As we'd walked, she'd remained alert and fast-paced, all business. My kind of girl.

"A few of them tried to help Kaito break the barrier. Their

power did nothing, was nothing, especially compared to his, but they had it."

"Witches?" Luca asked. He was trying to gauge what we might walk into if the escapees attacked first and asked questions later.

Donata tilted her head. "Three might have been of my order. One was fae. Two vampires."

"They were all unaffected by the sin?" I asked. She'd told us as much in her home, but then I'd imagined a smaller group.

"Seemed that way. Even if one of them was a warder, it would be difficult. My home is protected through bloodlines and love as much as magic."

"Maybe compulsion helped?" Meredith murmured.

"We'll find out soon enough," Giselle said. "I'll approach them first. Tobias and Serena are with me. Unless there's a powerful fire witch, someone capable of lopping off our heads, or ash wood stakes, they can't kill us. We'll announce the rest. Tell them that we mean no harm."

No one opposed their plan, and the trio blurred off down the street, through the rubble lining road and turned right. They were out of sight, but we all heard the moment the escapees saw them. Cries rang through the air, and a boom gripped me.

Meredith's eyes widened. She looked about ready to sprint after her mate.

"Wait." Luca held up a hand. "We can't risk any *Vindix*. Trust in the vampires, they'll have been prepared for an attack."

I knew that. Mer did too. We *all* did. Still, tension thickened the air until Serena came racing back.

"They put up a fight," she brushed an invisible piece of

dust off her shoulder, "we handled it, of course. Kaito is ready to meet the other *Vindix*." Her dark eyes shone with excitement similar to the energy simmering in my bones.

"Lead the way," Luca said, and we followed Serena down the street and to the right, where the narrow road ended in a sort of circle.

Not ideal but defensible if . . . I looked up at the buildings and smirked.

Two archers peered down at us, bows not drawn, though I spotted four arrows smashed into the street. They'd shot at the vampires. Missed too.

"What the hell?" Meredith murmured. "Arrows?"

"Quieter than bullets, Stoney," Gunner said, coming to walk next to me. "That means you won't attract more enemies."

"They blew something up!"

"We did." A man stepped out of a home, his longish black hair swept back, and upturned eyes narrowed. "One among us panicked."

"They moved fast!" a woman of about thirty years of age threw up her hands. "I'm not used to vampires."

"It shows," the man replied, his accent American and familiar. If he wasn't from California, I'd pet Benedict. "I'm Kaito. About time you showed up. I've been waiting for you for a while." He gestured down to the bracelet on Hans's wrist. "Holder of the Pearl, huh? Our fearless leader."

Oh, thank the Old Ones. Like Rhianna, he knew who we were and what we were meant to do. Compared to most of us, this catch-up session would be a piece of cake.

"Hans. Yes, I hold the Pearl. Not sure how much of a leader I am, though. Meredith here," he gestured to Meredith, "was the first to know who she was, what she needed to do. She's a seeker and found most of the rest of us."

"I can't take much credit," Meredith said as Kaito took her hand. "Three of the *Vindix* worked together already."

"Convergence."

The word I'd heard so often, one that was its own kind of magic, echoed in my mind. I stared at the man, and perhaps feeling my gaze, he turned his attention to me.

"And you're the Diamond."

His eyes were unwavering, somewhat haunting, and I'd be lying if I said the man wasn't sexy as hell. Gunner picked up on the attraction and got closer. I hid my smile at the protective alpha gesture.

"I'm Harper, and you're correct, the Diamond is my *lapis caelesti*."

"You have ghost vibes." Kaito winked. "They're all over Venice, and while I'm not a spirit witch, ghosts have a thing for water."

The others introduced themselves, and escapees trickled over to meet us. A few introduced themselves too, and once that was done, we were shown around. They'd created a fortress out of a residential circle. Or as much of a fortress as one could manage with limited resources and crumbling homes as protection.

Donata took everything in, devastation on her face. "There aren't as many of you as I remember. Are the others resting?"

Kaito's face fell. "Only forty of us survived our escape— and some had wings, so they left. The rest . . . Well, I tried my best to control all the water, to get us here." He swallowed. "It wasn't enough. Not when the serpent showed up."

"Serpent?" Meredith squeaked, and I felt that sound reverberate in my bones.

"Turns out there's a monster from Hell in the lagoon," Kaito said. "Maybe more than one, but I for sure have spotted only the one. It ate some of those who escaped, and others drowned. I should have been able to save the latter, but—"

"Don't." A man who had introduced himself as Tomaso edged up to Kaito, threw an arm around his shoulder and kissed the water elemental's cheek. "Every single one of us understood the risks, and those who survived would be far worse without you. I know that for a fact, and so do you, amore."

The adoration in this man's eyes made me think he might have been the person Kaito rescued—the man who had been used by Lust. I shuddered, not wanting to mull over what a Prince of Lust would do to those he wanted to hold power over.

It didn't escape Kaito's notice. His face softened. "The monsters are a secondary concern."

The way he said it made me believe it, though I was still pretty concerned about monsters. I hadn't given it that much thought and wondered how many were loose in the world.

"The main island is a place of nightmares right now," Kaito continued. "The sin took over my coven. Tomaso was the only one I could save, but the things I saw will haunt me forever. I hope you did not have to stay there long." He cast the old witch a glance, and his eyebrows knitted together. "Donata, do you need to sit?"

I spared her a glance too and found the woman's grayish pallor had deepened. She was sweaty too. Before, I'd thought she might be motion sick from Tobias carrying her, but maybe she was experiencing lingering smoke-travel effects?

"I'm fine." The old woman waved off Kaito's concern.

Kaito gave an uncertain nod and turned back to me. For whatever reason, I wanted to open up to him.

"I understand what you went through. In my own way. Demons took over my pack—they're still controlling them." My throat tightened. To do what I needed to do, I had to push aside most thoughts of my pack, but from time to time, I'd think of them. The hurt never lessened.

"They're monsters," Kaito replied. "I welcome the day when we face them *and win*." From beneath his shirt, he pulled out a chain and showed us the gemstone on the end. The Sapphire of the Seas gleamed in the daylight, undoubtedly the final *lapis caelesti*.

Knowing what Kaito had done here, and that he held that stone, was enough for me to believe he was a *Vindix*. Though I was certain that the *Arcacustos* would still want him to jump in that Enchanted Pool. Hell, they'd made Rhianna do so as soon as we'd returned from New Orleans. The girl hadn't even had time to wipe demon blood from her hands. The elder witches took their jobs seriously, that was for sure.

"You've worked with the Sapphire before?" Giselle asked.

"Often," Kaito replied. "My family is open about our history. The Sapphire is part of the reason I came to Venice the first time—to study abroad. Then I fell in love with the city and Tomaso and returned after graduation. It felt right, being surrounded by water. I—" his brow wrinkled. "Donata? *Ti senti bene?*"

A gurgling sound hit my ears, and I looked at the old woman in time to see black smoke leave her mouth. The woman fell, her body limp against the broken stone ground. The others darted over to help her, but my spine went ramrod straight. I'd seen smoke like that enter my pack and take them over. Possess them.

As the smoke demon soared away, up and over the buildings and the expanse of water to the main island, my breath caught.

"Can't be," Gunner drawled, his eyes wide with fear. He'd been in California that day and had seen what I'd seen. He had to be reliving it too.

"She was possessed, which means we're about to have visitors," I said. "Arm yourselves."

CHAPTER TWENTY-FIVE

TOBIAS

Not even five minutes passed before a black-winged form burst through the magical barrier around Venice. Behind the figure, a retinue of at least fifty flying monsters surged, some as large as three men combined.

"Is the one out front who I think it is?" Serena asked, wide eyed.

"Prince Asmodev, in the flesh," Giselle murmured. "I never thought I'd live to witness one demon prince on this earth again. Let alone two."

We stood, a trio, a family, as the others dashed about gathering weapons and throwing on armor they'd cobbled together from boat parts and anything else they found lying around. My family and I had no need for such things, even against demons, but I was glad to see Shay fitting Meredith with a makeshift shield.

"We stick with the *Vindix*," I said.

And despite Luca trying to talk sense into them and have everyone flee, the *Vindix* had wanted to fight. Wanted to make a stand.

In a way, I could see their reasoning. It was unlikely more than one prince was in Venice, and if they could pick them off one at a time, that would be easiest. I only wished we had a full army at our backs.

"Of course." Giselle gave me a smile, one that came off both as warm and sly, my maker's specialty. "The most important people in this world, *non*?"

"It all rests on them." I looked again at my mate. "I need to speak with Meredith—make sure she's ready." I left my sister and sire and went to my mate.

"Take anything and everything they give you, love. That's the Prince of Lust flying our way, and he's bringing loyal soldiers with him."

Meredith looked to the sky, took in the demons flying our way, and gave a stiff nod. "Kaito told us there's an aerial barrier around this city circle. We can attack from within, but they can't. They'll have to fight through it first. That buys us time to pick them off so we can focus on the prince."

I was glad to hear about the warding system, but I didn't think for a second that Lust would hesitate to call for backup if he lost those soldiers with him.

"Then we stay behind the warding until we no longer can. You have your luxiter?"

"Yes, Tobias, I have it. Not that I'd use it without knowing the others are safe."

I stifled a sigh. What happened to the rocker chick that was in it for herself? My noble mate was going to be the end of me.

"Very well. We—"

An explosion shook the ground. I pushed Meredith behind me and looked up to find the magical barrier glowing.

"It held!" yelled a female from inside one of the dilapidated homes. "Working on re-strengthening it now."

"Allow me to assist!" Luca began adding his own magic.

So when the next boom came, one that flew from the impending army as a whole, the barrier only glowed once more. It did not crack. Nor shake or waver.

"Hey!" Meredith shouted. "Kaito!"

The water elemental had been about to rush by, desperate to make sure all were ready. He turned to her.

"How did you protect everyone from the sin?" Meredith asked. "If Prince Asmodev breaks through, which he will, he'll flood us with Lust."

"We had a fae with us who did that, but he had wings. He was one of the people who left as soon as he could."

Meredith swore. "The Opal allows me to keep the sin at bay, so I'll work on that. But with this many people." Her voice shook at the enormity of her task. "I don't know if I'll be successful."

"Do what you can." Kaito hefted two daggers. "I need to deliver these. Humans get first dibs on weapons."

"Right," Meredith's face took on an ashen appearance. "Go."

The moment Kaito was gone, I turned her to me. "You, my love, *you can* do this. It's what you were meant for. You will not fail them."

Meredith's eyes filled with tears. "Thank you. Since learning that Kaito was here, and this place is filled with water . . . Well, I should have known he was here! I should have been faster."

"You're too hard on yourself."

She drew in a long breath at the black storm cloud coming ever closer. "Do you think we can knock another one out?"

I wasn't sure. A demon had been living in Donata, who was now, regrettably, dead. Her possession told me Lust expected someone coming to look for those who had broken free of his kingdom. He knew someone among the escaped was special—maybe even that it was Kaito. Did the Prince of Lust know more? About the *Vindix* and that, one day, they'd come to fight?

One thing was certain: Prince Asmodev was far cleverer and more prepared than Prince Belhor.

"We fight with all we have." I pulled my mate close and kissed her, savoring the smoothness of her lips, her taste, her smell.

"To the stations!" Kaito yelled, and when he came running by again, he waved to us. "You and the other *Vindix* are with me, Meredith."

She followed, so I did too. Their scents told me that Giselle and Serena came along as well. Kaito twisted, saw that three vampires were following, and arched his eyebrows.

"Aren't you three better off up high? Fighting in the first wave?"

"Meredith is my mate," I retorted. "Where she goes, I go. Giselle and Serena are family—they will protect her—they will protect all of you, *Vindix*, for you are what's important."

"Fine." Kaito turned and continued on.

Meredith massaged my shoulder. "He doesn't look it right now, but I bet he's flattered to have a vampire protector. Just like I am."

"Oh? Just like you were *at first*?"

She snorted. "Well, you didn't make it easy."

"Nor you."

"No, I didn't. But we got there, in time."

We twined our fingers together as Kaito led us into a vast courtyard between two of the homes. I suspected it had once been used as a sort of garden area shared by two families. The courtyard had to be the size of a small gymnasium with a canal running along the far side.

"Vines." Kaito looked at Rhianna, who had been waiting in the courtyard, speaking with Tomaso.

She softened when gazing at the vines that someone had likely cultivated for their own visual pleasure. "I've already bonded with them."

"As for fire and air," Kaito waved his hand. "Do what you will. Hans is already above with Shay." From the rooftop, the pair waved. "Meredith, can you cast your magic to cover the entire circle? Soon Lust's sin will strike, and we can't be caught in that web."

She swallowed. "I might not have the range for everyone here. They're so spread out."

"Try," Kaito urged. "Just try."

Magic washed over us anew. I imagined Meredith's power spreading out, washing over everyone in the area.

"There," Meredith said after a moment and yet another explosion later. "I got it. Now I need to hold the heck on."

Kaito's eyes were steel when he spoke again. "Lust will come here. I'll make sure of it. We have to be ready. We—"

Another explosion rang through the air, this one larger and more violent than those preceding it. My skin tingled as the ward glowed from above and a crack formed down the middle. Pieces fluttered to the earth. Magic flew upwards, and the casters did their best to repair the crack on the fly, but the army was upon us.

"Here we go," Meredith exhaled as winged demons swarmed down, some of the larger ones carrying a smaller warrior on their backs. The smaller monsters dropped with weapons in hand. Bullets and arrows flew from our side, aiming for those who slipped through the crack of the shield.

Screams ripped through the air as another explosion hit from above, and this time, the shield shattered.

Magic blasted the side of neighboring buildings. Rocks flew every which way, and one balcony ripped off and flew into the side of another building. An arrow soared and hit one of the slower winged monsters. I exhaled. Within seconds, chaos had well and truly descended. Through it all, those in the courtyard stood still, waiting for the real threat.

"I'm going to draw him in," Kaito said.

Before anyone could pose the question if that was wise, the water from the canal rose thirty feet in the air and shot towards a pair of demons. The water blasted them into a wall, pulverizing their bodies and leaving blood marks on the building.

That signal was all it took. The air shifted, grew heavier. A black cloud appeared in the sky above, and a heartbeat later, a second cloud of smoke flooded the courtyard. When it cleared, Lust, Prince Asmodev, stood in the courtyard with a gleaming smile on his face, and a dozen soldiers at his side.

"*Bloody hell*," Tana breathed.

Tall and muscled with pale skin, a square jaw, and gleaming red eyes that somehow were not off-putting, the prince of the underworld was attractive.

His otherworldly aura and characteristics: two curled horns, a long, barbed tail, and black bat-like wings, only added to the allure. His clothing, a dark blue suit that exposed his chiseled chest, and fine leather shoes were also meant to attract. To seduce.

Even I, a male who had never been attracted to other males, saw the appeal. He was a creature that embodied lust and attracted it. He did both with every fiber of his being.

Those gleaming red eyes locked on Kaito, and Lust

grinned. "I'm so glad your little *plea for help* worked out. Now, I can be the one to garner the glory before my brothers realize the seven of you have found one another."

So, the Princes of Hell knew about the *Vindix*. After we'd met Sloth, I'd wondered. They were ancient and around during the last reincarnation of the chosen ones, but Wrath had not mentioned such a thing.

Then again, why show your cards? Wrath was a master tactician, after all, and I'd have done the same. A vampire knew better than anyone to keep things hidden.

"You knew who I was?" Kaito's question revealed how young he was compared to Lust.

"The moment you pulled your little water trick to save my toy." Lust leered at Tomaso. The young man glowered in response, and the prince wet his lips, excited by his fury.

"Keep your eyes off him," Kaito commanded, pulling Prince Asmodev's deadly focus back to him.

"Only with great, great power and the help of a *lapis caelesti* could a mere wizard do such a thing," Lust continued, unbothered by the ire he was drawing. "I hoped you'd be in my city. Water, water, everywhere—it seemed ideal for a person of your powers, so I took the gamble. Why else would I have chosen it when others would have sufficed just as well?"

Kaito's lips parted, and bloody hell, my heart sank for the bloke. He may have freed himself, freed his lover and others too, but he'd played right into the prince's hands. And he'd brought us along with him.

Lust moved on, his red eyes locking on Shay. "You beautiful morsel, you're an angel, if I'm not mistaken? How would you like to walk on the dark side?"

Hans growled, and Lust laughed as he twisted to him,

smoke undulating around him like deadly snakes. "Lilith's bastard! I can scent you from here."

More smoke bloomed from Lust, and as a fresh wave of the sin ran over us, I saw the gleam in Prince Asmodev's eyes. He thought he could take us down. But Meredith's magic held strong.

For the first time, Lust's face fell. "I suppose we'll have to do this the old-fashioned way." His tail, only about three feet long, whipped out, stretching and stretching until suddenly, it was around Tana's neck.

The other demons flew into action too, dropping to the ground and engaging whoever was closest in battle.

"We have to help her!" Meredith pointed Tana's way. "Rabi! Air shield us!"

I felt the air surrounding me harden into a shield. Rabi had been practicing this particular magic and though useful, I knew he did not yet excel at holding the shields in place. It was not enough for me to feel as though my mate was protected. I grabbed Meredith before she could move, intending to slow her only enough so that I could run in front of her. In that moment of delay, Giselle sprinted to Tana's side, a dagger in hand. With her face hard as stone, my maker stabbed Lust's tail. The prince snarled, and his tail snapped back like a whip.

Giselle turned, intent on making certain Tana lived. That she hadn't been too slow. So my maker did not see when Lust's tail flattened, thin as a blade, and launched for her.

"Giselle!" I shouted, but it was too late. The tail, now sharp as a sword, decapitated her.

Meredith stopped short in her sprint, and somewhere, I heard my sister scream. Giselle's head hit the ground, spun, and the world grew unbearably loud before it quieted to nothing. My vision darkened and the world around me ceased to exist.

I roared and became a whirlwind of destruction and death, fighting my way through the demons. Ripping off their heads. Punching my hand through their hearts.

Twice, a blade pierced my right side. Once magic pummeled me so hard I fell, but I staggered to my feet again, disoriented. Again, not seeing or hearing anything, just reacting. Killing.

Avenging.

And suddenly, I realized I'd left Meredith. I'd left *my mate.*

Fear gripped me in an absolute and horrible way, and my vision cleared as I searched the fray for Meredith.

It took me only seconds to locate her. She, along with the other *Vindix*, faced Lust.

Tears streamed down my mate's face. One might think it was for the visible effort she was expending, trying to protect every soul who was now attacking the prince with vengeance. I, however, knew better.

Giselle's head lay at Prince Asmodev's feet. Seeing her face again, her green eyes wide open and empty, made me feel as though someone was punching me in the gut.

But how were they not being attacked on all sides? The army he'd brought with him. I spun on my heel and sucked in a breath. A dozen bodies circled me, and not far away, Serena was ripping out the throat of Prince Asmodev's last soldier.

We'd both gone on a killing rampage, slaughtering two dozen soldiers in minutes. Leaving only Lust for the *Vindix.*

"That was for Giselle!" Meredith screamed, and I turned to find Tana had engulfed the prince in flames, her jaw set in a hard line.

Rhianna was closing in on the prince from behind, a stolen

sword in hand. He fought off the fire and didn't see her coming.

The earth elemental struck true, and the bastard's head ended up on the ground in a puddle of water, landing right next to Giselle's. Black blood mixed with red and churned in the puddle and suddenly, Serena's vision became terribly clear.

CHAPTER TWENTY-SIX

MEREDITH

I LOOSED A LONG EXHALE AS THE LAST OF THE REFUGEES FROM THE Hell-taken cities light-traveled away with Luca. Finally, the *Abscondita* manor echoed with quiet.

It had taken hours of healing on Hannah's part to ensure the injured gathered enough strength to travel. A few of us helped set them to rights, me included, but now the only people who remained at the manor were the *Arcacustos*, the *Vindix*, S&S, and Gunner's pack.

I looked about the yard, searching for my mate. I wasn't even sure if Serena and Tobias roamed the grounds. Earlier that day, they had left the manor, needing time to grieve the loss of their maker in private.

Giselle. Dead.

The pain that consumed me when I saw her head sliced from her neck ripped through me again, as fresh as the first time. In the short time I'd known her, I'd grown to love Giselle. I could only imagine the depths of pain suffocating Tobias and Serena.

A tear slid down my cheek. I wanted to check on Tobias. To

comfort my mate, in any way that he'd accept. So far, that hadn't been at all, but when grief was fresh, we often needed to sit with it. Alone. Or, in Tobias's case, with someone who experienced it as keenly as him.

I moved to the front door of the manor, opened it, only to find Rhianna and Kaito in the entry. They stopped talking when they saw me and offered me slight smiles.

Kaito, the man we'd set out to find. The mission succeeded in so many ways, but my heart hung so heavy that it didn't feel like a success.

"Everything alright?" I asked.

"Fine. We were getting to know one another. Outside of the healing sanctuary, you know?" Kaito shuddered. "I love Tomaso, but I had to get out of there."

"We're sharing intel too," Rhianna added.

I cocked my head. "Like?"

"The princes have colors associated with them," she replied. "Sloth wore a lot of light blue, almost like a baby blue. That color dominated his castle."

"And Lust was obsessed with dark blue. Navy," Kaito added. "I asked one of the *Abscondita* witches, the Irish one? There are so many. I'm still working on the names."

"Claire," I supplied.

"Right." He held up a finger as if her name had been on the tip of his tongue. "She said the Princes of Hell have colors associated with them. Those same colors Rhianna and I saw around the kingdoms tracked with the literature."

I hadn't read that. Nor was I seeing the importance of such information. Was I being slow? "How is that important?"

Rhianna shrugged. "Might be helpful if someone can sneak into their kingdoms and get a glimpse."

I let out a hum. The sin would be the first giveaway, and no one should go into a kingdom without me. Well, except for Hans, who based off Gunner's observations we were theorizing might be immune to the sin. Although they would never enter a dark kingdom without me, I would not say as much. I suspected that this sharing of information was about something more. Trauma bonding, possibly. Or they wanted to feel useful.

That almost made me laugh. Their mere presence was more useful, more *relieving*, than they ever could imagine. I was so grateful that they were here.

And no matter the reason, speculating and talking about their experiences brought them closer together. We needed that closeness.

"You'll have to write those colors down so I can review them later. I don't have the bandwidth to remember them right now," I said in an effort not to seem indifferent right before I twisted the conversation. "Do either of you know how Rabi is doing? Tomaso?"

"Both are good. Hannah is making them stay the night in the infirmary." Kaito blew out a long breath.

On our side, only six died. Among those in the courtyard, only Rabi, Tomaso, Tana, and Shay sustained injuries. Rabi's and Tomaso's were the worst.

Overall, though, the battle had been short and vicious. Largely thanks to Tobias and Serena going berserk.

I shuddered at the memory of the pair, two tornados of death, who sent heads flying and blood spraying in their wake. They'd decimated Lust's soldiers on their own. I didn't even think Tobias had noticed the injuries he sustained until the fight ended. Thankfully, none had been serious and healed on their own before we even got back to England.

I didn't regret that Tobias and Serena had ended the

fight within ten minutes, but their rage had scared me a little. It reminded me of the days when bloodlust fueled Tobias's hunger for me. Back then, before we'd both given in to what we needed—each other—he'd been unpredictable, violent, and terrifying. Not that I'd let him know, but still . . .

I didn't want to see that side of him, or Serena, again. Not even in battle. I didn't care how selfish that was either.

"How's your mate?" Rhianna asked.

"He spent most of the day with his sister, and I hope they're leaning on each other. I'm going to see if he's in our room now."

Rhianna chewed on her bottom lip. "They saved our asses big time. I didn't know her well, and wish it hadn't taken Giselle's death, but without their fighting, I'm not sure we would have won that battle."

"Don't talk like that," Kaito frowned. "We're trained."

Rhianna arched an eyebrow. "Yes, but Lust was much stronger than Sloth and that's concerning."

I recalled how much power flew through the air as the *Vindix* ganged up on Prince Asmodev. How each had taken a turn at pummeling him. How Harper and Tana had both collapsed from exhaustion, and I'd held a tenuous thread of free will running through everyone, sweating like a horse as I did so.

It had been *far* more difficult than our New Orleans win. Would defeating the other princes be as difficult? What if we had to fight more than one at a time?

The thought made my mouth dry up. I couldn't think about that now.

"I gotta go," I said, and left them in search of my mate. But when I opened the bedroom door, I didn't find him there. I sighed, shut the door, only to find Gunner poking his head out of his.

"Hey," I said. "How's Harper?"

Gunner wouldn't leave her side, so they were staying in the same room as she rested.

"Sleeping. You doin' alright, Stoney?"

"Sure. Have you seen Tobias?"

Surprising me, Gunner nodded. "A few minutes ago I was lookin' out the window and saw Toby and his sis go by. I think they're back by the Enchanted Pool."

"Thanks."

My feet felt heavy as I trudged back down the hallway, descended the stairs and went outside once again. Rounding the manor, I looked for my mate and Serena, and found them. The pair sat on a bench next to a pond.

I walked softly, even though they'd hear me approach. Sure enough, when I got but a few feet away, Serena turned. I swallowed.

Her eyes were ringed with red and puffy. Her face was sallow. She looked exhausted, and that was not a look I'd seen on her often. Or ever.

"Mind if I . . .?" I gestured to the bench.

"Not at all," Serena rose. "I need to clean up. Prepare for the ceremony."

"Ceremony?"

Tobias didn't turn to look at me. I wasn't sure he *could* move yet. The lines of heartache and grief were so obvious in his body. "I scooped some of Giselle's ashes before we left Venice. We need to have a farewell ceremony for her."

"Of course," I replied and went to join my mate on the bench, but before I passed by Serena, I reached out and took her hand. As a child who lost both of her parents, I understood their pain to some degree and goddess be, I wished I could erase it. "I know nothing I can say will help, but I'm so sorry. Both of you, I'm so sorry."

Serena swallowed. "I should have known. Blood and water —Giselle's blood is mine, there is no one closer. I could have stopped her from going. I should have . . ." she trailed off, and I let her.

We both knew that with such a vague vision, there was no way she could have known. And even if she did, would Giselle really have listened? The Laurent matriarch had been strong-willed and proud, and I wasn't sure if she would have let anyone boss her around.

Serena might have come to the same conclusion, for she left her sentence hanging and just left. I watched her walk away with sorrow heavy in my chest for Serena. I hoped that one day, she could forgive herself for something that wasn't even her fault.

I sat silently with Tobias, knowing if he wanted to, he'd talk. And for a while he didn't.

He sat there, watching the pond, watching as bugs landed on the water, causing ripples. A frog leapt in, maybe thinking he'd find a feast in that murky, shallow pool. I became increasingly aware of my breath, something that happened often when I was around my mate, who did not need to breathe except when trying to fit in among humans.

Goddess, I'm so noisy.

Was I bugging him? With my noisy breathing and intrusion into a relationship that I—no matter how much I loved him— couldn't fully understand.

In my mind, I'd compared Giselle to the loss of my parents, but she was not even quite that. Certainly not less, but more.

She'd saved Tobias from a horrible death and brought him

into a new life. One that he, as a poor sailor, could never have dreamed about. Giselle had given him forever and loved him fiercely all the way through it. She'd been with him for over a century, far longer than the rest of us got with our loved ones.

"There's a hole inside me," Tobias broke his silence. "Serena too. I never understood what would happen when, if, Giselle experienced the final death, but this gaping hole . . . it's *unbearable.*"

My throat tightened. "I'm so sorry that she's gone. That she died for us."

"That is something she would not be sorry for." He looked at me. "I think the only thing more painful for me would be losing you. This pain . . . it changes so much."

I scooted closer, took his hand. "Like?"

"Meredith, even if we survive the upcoming battles we must face, there's another that time will present us with. You're mortal."

I winced. This was an obvious issue in our relationship. One we'd spoken of only briefly, because what was the point? I might die in this war. Tobias too.

But if we survived, he'd have forever in front of him. And me? Maybe, *maybe,* I had eighty more years? Even those would be awkward. I'd look ancient next to him.

We could move to Isila—live in a fae court? Or with the wolvea? Surely such things wouldn't matter there?

Even as the thought arose, I brushed it away for being silly. At best, humans were second-class citizens in most of Isila. At worst, they were slaves. I wasn't sure witches were much better off. Kora, a witch and Queen of the Spring Court of the fae, aside, of course. Though she'd had to save an entire kingdom to win their love.

Plus I'd miss my life in this world. Miss the friends I'd made and S&S.

"I'm not saying we need to make a choice now," Tobias murmured. "Just that, after Giselle's death, I won't survive yours. I won't want to."

Either I turned into a vampire, or Tobias passed with me. Although I wouldn't be around, I hated the idea of him dead.

"I wouldn't survive your death, either." I kissed him on the cheek. "I promise, once all this is over, I'll think about changing."

He swallowed and fresh tears of blood ran down his cheeks before he wiped them away. "Thank you."

I nestled closer, my warm body pressed against his. "Can I do anything for you?"

"Be with me." Those emerald eyes that enchanted me from day one looked out over the pond, over everything, and into what, I wasn't sure. "Stay by my side."

So, I did.

———

THE MOON HUNG HIGH IN THE INKY SKY WHEN TOBIAS AND Serena proclaimed it time for Giselle's final farewell. Her ushering into her true death, as they called it.

Serena chose a spot at the back of the manor's property, a good fifty yards away from the pond. The area was clear, with the woods not too far away. Apparently, Giselle had meditated out here a few times. She'd thought it a pretty place, and that was as good a reason as any to spread her ashes here.

Not everyone attended the ceremony. Tomaso and Rabi were still bedbound in the sanctuary. Even if Rabi had not been injured, I wasn't sure he'd attend the ceremony. He hadn't shown an outward dislike of Giselle, but it was her family who had enslaved him, and unlike Tobias and Serena, Giselle had strong ties to Isila. She'd possessed property and a title, both of which I had no idea what would happen with. I didn't care either.

The rest of us were present though. For no matter how long people had known Giselle, she'd touched their lives. Helped them in some way. Even Gunner's pack showed up to honor Giselle, one of the people who had liberated them from Sloth's grasp.

"My sire." Tobias held out a white crystal bowl he'd borrowed from Claire, the prettiest one she had, or so the witch told him. "Giselle was a great vampire. She roamed this earth for thousands of years. She saw the rise and fall of empires. She touched many. Found, and lost, a mate." He looked at me as he said that, and I wondered at the strength Giselle had possessed to go on living for so long after her bloodbound died. "She created three new vampires, and I was honored to be by her side when the final death claimed her." He bowed his head.

Serena stood on her brother's other side. She cleared her throat. "Giselle found me in a moment of great distress and need. I was broken beyond repair, and yet, somehow, she fixed me. That was what she did, helped fix things, people too— especially those she loved. If she loved you, she stood by you no matter what."

In the circle, Tana let out a soft wail. She felt responsible for Giselle's passing.

A soft smile bloomed on Serena's face. "Our maker also had a softer side. She was sassy and frivolous and, moon above," her face tilted to the sky as she took in the moon's light, "did Giselle love a good designer dress."

Soft laughter cut through the flowing tears.

"All that to say," Serena continued, "I'll miss her until the day I meet my final death. My maker. My mother in this new world. My friend everlasting." Her hand landed on the bowl, overlapping Tobias's slender fingers. "I love you, Giselle, and I wish you peace. I hope you're seeing him again."

Red tears appeared on Tobias's cheeks again. "I'll love you until the world ends. Thank you for giving me this life."

My heart ached as the siblings each scooped a handful of ashes from the bowl. Tobias handed the bowl to me. "You're family. She'd have wanted you to spread her ashes too."

"You're sure?"

"Positive."

I took the bowl, scooped out the remaining ashes. Dry, so dry and soft and fine. It wasn't like the horror stories I'd heard of human cremation, where a tooth might have survived, and you'd find it in the ashes.

No, Giselle was pure ash. Nothing more.

"Stuart?" Tobias asked.

A soft wind filled the night. Stuart's magic whipped up the air, and Tobias lifted his hands. The breeze took the ashes. Serena followed. Behind us, I heard others crying, wailing, sniffling.

I allowed my own tears to fall as, third, I lifted the ashes I held, and Stuart's wind picked them up and carried Giselle away.

CHAPTER TWENTY-SEVEN

GUNNER

I saw Toby's back as I entered the hallway, and he disappeared into the room he and Stoney shared.

My first inclination was to go check on the guy. It had been two days since we spread Giselle's ashes, and he'd only spent time with Meredith and his sis. He wouldn't want me buttin' in. Since the world blew up, Toby and I had grown closer, but we weren't besties. Not yet anyway.

I had my plans to change that, just not right now.

No, right now, I needed to let the guy be. And for myself, I needed to get outside. To run.

I was pretty sure that fine she-wolf I was enamored with was outside too. So though my inner wolf was dyin' to talk to Toby and help him out, I walked right by his door and headed outside.

For once, the sun was shinin' and it felt nice. Crisp and cool. The leaves had changed, and the forest looked pretty as a peach. A slight breeze told me I'd been right. Harper was out here somewhere, and even better, so were some of the members of my new pack.

I followed my nose and found them chitchattin' at the eastern corner of the manor with big smiles all 'round. "Hey!"

They turned, and my heart 'bout stopped as Harper's face lit up at the sight of me.

"Hey, you," she said as I joined them. She stood on tiptoes and kissed me on the cheek, so casual, like we'd been together for months and not . . . whatever it was we were doin'.

Which, for the record, although we'd shared a bed every night since I'd been saved from New Orleans, I wasn't sure what we were doin'. Though I knew what I wanted. Her and me—together for reals.

More of her. *All of her.*

My cock twitched at the thought of takin' Harper like I'd been wantin' to. We'd kissed a lot, fooled around a little, but never taken it further. Never even been fully naked around each other. For two wolves to be so slow movin' said way more than if we'd already slept together.

We were bein' careful, even if inside, I was dyin' to take the next step.

"Hey, you back." I gave her a grin before nodding to my pack members—Jolie, Salem, Rubin, Farrah, and Ron. "What's goin' on?"

"I'm on a training break for the morning," Harper said. "The elders want to work with Rhianna, Kaito, and Rabi one on one. Even though they're all more advanced in magic, the *Arcacustos* are comparing their powers to what all those library books predicted."

"A free morning! I got an idea on how we should spend it."

"Running the woods?" Harper quirked a brow, and I got the sense she was thinkin' about the time in California when we'd raced, and I'd beaten her.

At least, that was the way I remembered it.

"Mind if we join, alpha?" Jolie asked, her eyes alight.

"Sure. The more the better when it comes to protectin' a *Vindix*." I hid my smile, hopin' to get a little rise out of Harp.

It worked, and chica whacked me on the arm. "Oh please. As if I need protection, and especially not here. This property is warded all the way to the afterworld. Luca and Shay check their wards every day and the *Arcacustos* already had a good foundation."

"Not good enough," I said.

The Ordo Aeternum had breached the wards, though I conceded the point that it hadn't happened since Luca and Shay had added their talents. Thank the Old Ones, since the Ordo had joined up with the demons. That was a lot of firepower we didn't want comin' to knock on our door.

"Don't tell them that," Harper sang. "Not unless you want to be on Gloria's or Miriam's bad side. Actually, add Aya to that list too. She looks sweet, but you don't want to cross her."

"Wouldn't dream of it."

"*So*," Jolie interrupted. "Running?"

"Let's do it," I said and, without further ado, shifted.

The others followed suit and soon 'nough, we were all fur and teeth and claws.

Let's go, I said to my pack and nodded to Harper, the only one not in on our mind-link 'cause she belonged to another pack. Still, she understood, and we took off into the trees.

Harper caught up with me right quick. I might have wolvea blood runnin' in my veins, but this girl was a born alpha too, and a chosen one to boot. She didn't like bein' left behind. Not that it happened often.

We wove through the trees, feelin' the leaves crunchin' beneath our paws and that chilly air blowing through our fur. I lifted my nose and let out a howl, lettin' loose, livin' the good life.

Harper howled too. Then the others, all of us bein' wild and free.

We ran and ran and ran. At one point, I saw one of the witches —Falak—walkin' through the woods, a basket on her arm. The earthy scent of mushrooms and herbs drifted to me on a breeze, tellin' me that the witch was foraging. Ma did that sometimes.

Warmer thoughts of my siblings and Pa quickly followed. Suddenly, even runnin' with the others through these amazin' woods with good and strong wolves felt a little less magical. I hoped my family was okay. Hoped Harper's siblings were too.

I shot the she-wolf a side glance and found her lookin' at me too. She winked.

That lifted my spirits a bit. I barked at her. She barked back.

Are you two official now, alpha? A voice entered my head. Jolie's.

Normally, a wolf wouldn't ask their alpha somethin' so personal, but my pack and I weren't normal. If I was bein' honest, I didn't feel like much of an alpha to them. I sorta felt like they might leave at any moment, though no one had said as much. All that was 'cause we'd become a pack under such weird circumstances. Out of necessity rather than true loyalty.

So instead of telling Jolie to mind her own, I answered. *Your guess is as good as mine.*

She wants it. Another voice, Farrah's, said.

Had the girls been talkin' about me and Harp?

How do you know?

How she looks at you. Farrah replied. *And how you two smell. Sort of like each other.*

Yeah, they kinda do! Jolie added.

CHAPTER TWENTY-SEVEN

My ears perked up. But that only happened when—

I ground to a stop as a small black figure leapt up and hissed at us all.

Benedict's amber eyes narrowed when he realized what happened. Who had nearly run him over. His tail stuck out, pointing to the right where none other than Rygor the wyvern lay in a bed of fallen leaves. "I thought the dragon was bad enough. Now I have to look out for you mongrels in the woods too! I can't nap in peace anywhere!"

"I'm *a wyvern*, cat," Rygor shot back, his green tail curling around him. "And these have been my woods for far longer than you've been around. If anything, you're intruding on my territory. Mine and Jon-Jon's." A cunning gleam shone in the wyvern's eyes. "I should call Jon—"

"Not the giant!" Benedict yowled. "He's so loud!"

Harper shifted back to human form. "Be for real, Benedict! You have a whole manor to sleep in, and these woods are vast. Go *somewhere else*."

Chica and the cat had beef. Sometimes I suspected the pair liked to get under each other's skin. This being one of those times 'cause Harper shouldn't care that much 'bout where Benny relaxed.

"The manor! The *manor*!" Benedict's pitch rose.

Old ones, he's hurting my ears, Rubin said dramatically.

Farrah laughed at that, and I chuckled too.

In New Orleans, Rubin, a heavy-set gray wolf, had been the first to talk to me, and back then, he'd struck me as serious. But now I knew him as the wolf who always had a joke to share. Most of 'em he directed at Farrah, a pretty wolf in her thirties that Rubin most certainly had a crush on.

Benedict hissed. "You mean where everyone is running

about like chickens and others are—*coupling*—so often that I can't help but hear? No thanks, I'll take the woods!"

Coupling? My pack howled, and I, too, 'bout died of laughter. Wantin' to egg the cat on a little, I shifted back to human form.

"Benny," I chuckled. "I didn't take you for a prude."

"Well, I guess I am!"

Harper shot me a grin before turnin' back to the cat. "Maybe you should try the tool shed? I bet you'll have privacy there."

"Tool—*a toolshed*! I need a proper bed to sleep in, you dog."

"Wolf."

"Same thing."

My pack growled, and Benedict seemed to realize he didn't recognize these other wolves. And they didn't take kindly to bein' called dogs.

But instead of apologizin', the familiar leapt into a tree, climbed up high, and disappeared into the mass of needles.

Rygor rolled his eyes. "Flames, he's insufferable."

"Agreed," Harper added.

I smirked. "He's mad 'cause he hasn't slept in a bed in a while. Guess he doesn't use Toby's bed anymore."

"That room is right next to Meredith's. They're too loud for him. I mean, come on Gunner, *we* hear them."

I nearly added that the vampire probably heard those sweet sounds I'd pulled from Harper's lips last night, but remembered we had an audience.

"That's true." I lifted my hands and cupped them around my lips. "Benny, stay in the trees, and we'll all be out of each other's way!"

No response.

Harper shrugged. "Back to running?"

I nodded, and we shifted again. It wasn't till we ran through the trees again, Harper pulling in front of me, lettin' me get a real good look at her, that Jolie's words took over in my mind again.

We smelled alike. Me and Harp.

I wanted to ask the others if they thought so too, but I was too embarrassed to. Among wolves, only mates smelled alike.

Wouldn't we know if we were mates? Unlike couples like Toby and Stoney or Shay and Hans, Harper and I were both wolves. Having a mate within one's own order was the normal way of things. And wolves' bonds snapped into place easily.

I'd known the she-wolf for years. Liked her a lot too, though she hadn't liked me much.

Or so she'd claimed.

The more I thought about it, the more I believed we couldn't be mates. That we must smell alike 'cause we were spendin' so much time together.

Kind of a bummer, but I'd take it. At this rate, I might want more, but Harper was under immense pressure and, really, I'd take anything the she-wolf gave me.

CHAPTER TWENTY-EIGHT

MEREDITH

Tana's bonfire flickered as it rose higher and higher, entrancing those who sat around it. Well, everyone except Benedict, who snoozed in my lap.

Such a primal thing, sitting in front of the fire. Even a bonfire that birthed little foxes and rabbits made of flame, thanks to the elemental controlling it. The fire made those who didn't know one another well feel closer.

And thank the Goddess for that because that was my plan.

Tobias and Serena were in the manor reminiscing about Giselle. Once I was sure my mate wanted only to be with his sister, I decided to get the *Vindix* together to bond.

Everyone except for Hans and Harper was already present. Hans should arrive at any minute, but Harper claimed to be too tired after running with Gunner's pack and having lessons with Aya in the afternoon.

Tired my round rear end. Pretty sure she and Gunner were making out, but that was okay. Most of the *Vindix* were here, and I called that a win.

"So Rabi," Kaito asked. The white lines the Enchanted Pool

had left when the *Arcacustos* demanded he hop into the water were still slightly visible on his forearms as he waved a hand around. "How're you feeling? Glad Hannah finally let you out of the infirmary." The air elemental shuddered. He really did not like spending time in the infirmary.

Rabi lifted a hand, blew the smoke up and away from the group. "Better, thanks. Tomaso was great company. I hope he's released soon too."

When no one else spoke, Kaito cleared his throat, seemingly uncomfortable in the silence that hung over our little group. I couldn't relate, but I had been the one to drag them out here, so I figured I'd put him out of his misery.

"What's everyone else's training like?" I asked. "Learn anything new in the library?"

The newest *Vindix* to come to the manor had been spending their mornings in the library and afternoons training, just like I had when I'd arrived.

"The library is *amazing*," Kaito answered, his eyes lighting up with academic fervor. "I hope we get to spend even more time there."

Rhianna shrugged. She'd claimed to know everything in the library, and though I found that hard to believe, she did know a lot and produced results when it came to magic, so I didn't bother pushing her. Miriam and the other *Arcacustos* could take up that torch. "The training sessions are fun. I rarely get to work magic with people who are so powerful. It's like a game."

I laughed and stroked Benedict's fur, so warm from the fire. "I can't relate. When I got here, most of my training sessions were hell. I can't tell you how many times I wanted to just leave."

"My parents trained me from the moment I took my first

step . . . not that those are related. That's what they always said, like it's lore or something." Kaito chuckled at the memory. "I guess I have a leg up."

"Same." Rhianna sipped at the goblet of wine she'd brought outside. "I can't imagine what it was like for anyone who didn't."

"It sucked," I admitted. "Everything was a steep learning curve."

"I can relate to you Meredith," Rabi said. "I feel like that every day here."

Yes, his past had been traumatizing too. More so than mine, which was saying a lot.

"You're doing a right fine job." Tana patted Rabi's knee. He'd been reluctant to open up, but the fire and air elemental had bonded well, and for that, I was grateful.

"You really are," I said. "And once all this is done, S&S or the *Arcacustos*, or one of us, can help you find your way in this world."

Rabi sat silent for a moment, then exhaled. "I'm thinking about returning to New Orleans. Living with my grandmother for a while."

A great idea. Lauretta would certainly want such a thing, and though family couldn't always be trusted implicitly, we'd met her, and I felt sure that she'd look out for him.

"It's an amazing city." Rhianna grabbed the unopened bag of large marshmallows, which had been hell for Gloria to find, and stuck one on a sharpened stick. "I can't wait to get back. I can show you around."

Rabi smiled. "I'd like that."

"We can go on a voodoo tour too! I've always wanted to—"

"Sorry we're late," Hans called out, dashing around the

manor and running at the firepit. Behind him, Shay ran too. She looked flushed, and I only needed one guess why.

I smirked, understanding the situation. After the soulmate mark appeared on Tobias and me, it had been difficult not to spend all day in bed. Too bad for us, we'd needed to go on a mission. Shay and Hans were far more lucky to have a few days here. A lull—for however long that might last.

Not as long as we might like.

"Glad you joined us," I said as Hans and Shay collapsed into side-by-side chairs. "Were you working out? You're so red in the face, Shay."

She blew me an air kiss. "Oh yeah. Working out *real hard.*" She pumped her eyebrows salaciously.

Kaito sniggered, and instead of getting to Shay, *my* face warmed. Should have known better. That girl was never embarrassed about anything.

"Goddess, help me," Hans murmured as he leaned over and kissed Shay.

"I don't know about your Goddess, but I'll help you, baby. Any time, any place."

"*Okay, stahp!*" I held up my hands. "Can someone please talk about something that Shay can't turn sexual? Seen any good paint drying lately?"

A titter rushed through the crowd and once it died out, Kaito began roasting a marshmallow and looked at Hans.

"I called you our leader in Italy, and I read about it here too, but I can't help but wonder, any reason why?"

Hans lifted a single shoulder. "I'm the oldest."

"Definitely that, but what if there's more? Like your connection to Hell?" Rhianna suggested, and it looked like she'd really thought this over. "Like maybe you have an in?"

Hans snorted. "I don't."

Shay leaned forward and placed her arms on her knees. "You mean, aside from your sister being married to Prince Rikel."

Rhianna arched an eyebrow. "Who's that?"

"Wrath's son. Hans's sister married him, even though she's far too young to be doing so."

Hans frowned. "Seventeen. Almost eighteen now."

"And you didn't consider that important information to share?" Rabi asked.

"My sister won't betray the Royals of Hell," Hans said. "She was honored to become one of them, even though our mother tried to dissuade her."

"Well, your mother is married to Lucifer," Shay said, "so that's kind of like saying do as I say, not as I do."

"Lilith didn't want to, though," Hans muttered. "Lucifer forced marriage on my mother. Nicoleta went to them willingly."

"All that aside," Rhianna held a finger up, "your connection to your sister can be useful."

"I don't see how. My mother yes, but Nic is lost."

"We'll have to keep our eyes open."

It was something I had not thought about—having long considered Nicoleta an enemy. Plus, Hans hadn't spoken of her in a while. I assumed he needed time to get over everything his sister had done. Valid, and I was willing to give it. Particularly if it meant he wouldn't screw up again.

But could we use that connection? Benedict shifted in my lap, and I moved to accommodate him as the others turned the conversation to other matters—lighter ones. Topics I should participate in because that was how you built trust, something Shay had taught me by example.

However, the thought of Nicoleta as an ally, no matter how

far-fetched, would not leave my mind. More than that, I thought of Raphael, who Tobias hadn't mentioned in some time. Was he still working with the princes? If working with Nicoleta wasn't in the cards, could we use Tobias's tie to his brother? We should definitely brainstorm how to contact Lilith . . .

I wasn't sure how it would all work out, but like Rhianna suggested, I'd be on the lookout for opportunities.

CHAPTER TWENTY-NINE

HARPER

GUNNER PINNED MY HANDS TO THE WALL ABOVE MY HEAD AS HE took my lips with his. "Old Ones, Harp, you taste so good."

My toes curled into the thick rug, gripping the ground for dear life. Since New Orleans, we'd stayed the night together. We'd danced this strange dance, one I quite enjoyed, but never knew how it would end. So far, the dance had included soft kissing, aggressive making out, some heavy petting, and once, Gunner making me come with those deft, strong, calloused fingers of his. But as much as I was sure we both wanted more, we'd always stopped there, curled into a big spoon and little spoon, and slept.

It was nice. It was also strange. I'd slept with men after knowing them for far less time. Had even had a one-night stand once, though I'd never admit that to anyone.

And the thing was, I *knew* Gunner. He was safe, and we cared for each other and wanted one another. Despite all my claims to the opposite in the past, I'd begun to fall for him.

We care too much, I thought as Gunner's lips traveled down my neck, and he showed the utmost attention to my right breast. My nipple peaked, straining against the fabric of my bra. Old Ones, I wanted to tear every scrap of material from my body!

I wanted to tear his off too.

I wanted *him*. Everything about him.

And as he ravished my breast and moved to the other, I thought it was about time I told him. I prayed that he felt the same—that I wasn't another one of those girls at Yale who fell all over him, but he just saw them as having fun.

"Gunner," I whispered. "We need to talk."

He lifted those stunning eyes to lock on me. "Talk?"

My lips pursed sassily. "I believe you're quite familiar with the concept?"

The alphablood let out a rumble of a laugh. "Guess I am." He took a step back, pulling my shirt into place and smoothing it. "What's up Harp?"

"Maybe we can sit down?" I gestured to the bed.

He arched an eyebrow. "Is this some complex scheme you cooked up in that big brain of yours to get me in bed faster? 'Cause all you needed to do was point and grunt. I'd have gotten the message loud and clear."

I snorted. "I don't think I'd even have to do that."

"Sassy she-wolf."

I tried to calm my nerves as we made our way to the bed, and I sat. Gunner weighed down the mattress a second later and caught me in that silvery gaze of his.

He was waiting, as he should. I'd asked for this, though now, with my heart racing and my skin tingling, I wasn't sure why. Couldn't I be content with hot make out sessions and whatever other fun times we might have?

No, you're not that girl. Not deep down.

I loosed a breath, ready to take this on like an adult even if it was awkward. "So, we've been having a lot of fun."

"I'll say."

His warm tone loosened me up a little. It was a specialty of his.

"And we care about each other. Am I right on that score?"

Gunner's face tightened a touch. To someone who didn't know him so well, hadn't been stealing glances at his face for weeks, and had not woken up to stare at him the last two nights, they might not have noticed it. But I did.

Did he sense where this was going and wasn't into it? He was the fun guy. The party guy. He—I cut that line of thinking off before it could take hold and dissuade me from something I needed to do.

You've seen the other side of him.

"I care a lot about you, Harper," Gunner said. "Are you havin' second thoughts 'bout what's goin' on? Did I go too fast?"

Oh . . .

"No! I—I mean, I care about you too. And neither of us went too fast. I want to get things out in the open. We haven't really talked and even though we're interested in each other, there's a lot to talk about." My teeth dug into my bottom lip. "Like our packs."

"Our—packs?"

I refrained from rolling my eyes at myself. He was right to question that because it had been stupid. And cowardly. I didn't want to talk about our packs. I wanted to talk about *us*.

"Actually," I said, trying to save face, "what I meant by packs is, where are things going between us, Gunner? Is this for fun? Or do you want more? Want me?"

His face cleared. "'Course I want you, chica. I have for years."

"But I mean, more than *physically*. Which is fine if you do. I want you in that way too, but I'm trying to set expectations. Things between us are so muddled and different from what I'm used to."

Even now, when I wanted to hurl myself out the window because I kept blundering the simplest things, I felt drawn to him. Drawn in a way that I hadn't for much of our relationship but had grown in the last weeks. Just like I had.

"So," I drew in a breath at the heart of it. "What's going on here?"

Gunner's eyes flashed as he took my hand. "Harp, like I said, I want you. Have for a long time, though I was sure you didn't like me much. Can't understand why, but sometimes we all make mistakes."

I laughed but let him continue.

"That bein' said, if you can handle me, I'd like to give this thing a try between us. Be official, 'cause chica, at the risk of soundin' too much like a lovesick pup, I'm fallin' for you."

I sucked in a breath as all the air seemed to have left the room. I'd hoped he'd say he wanted to date. To be exclusive. But that he was falling for me?

My heart gave a hard thump, and I swallowed down a lump forming in my throat. "I'd like that, and, for the record, Gunner, I'm falling for you too. At least since the day you left for Ireland."

"And knowin' that I was under the thumb of some evil prince made it hit home, eh?" He shrugged. "Guess my time in New Orleans wasn't a total loss. Not if it got me you."

I leaned forward, took his face in my hands, and kissed him.

Gunner met me right where I wanted to be, scooting closer, wrapping his powerful arms around me and pulling us together.

I moaned as the heat of our bodies met and swore that as my blood pounded in my ears, I could sense his, too, pulsing in rhythm with mine. It was like a tether was pulling us tighter and tighter. Like no matter how close we got, it would never be enough.

Though I was willing to try to prove that theory wrong.

"Back." I whispered into his mouth. "Lie down. On the bed."

"Knew this was all one big scheme to get me between the sheets."

"Oh shut up."

We pushed back, laying side by side on the bed, our lips dancing again, our hands roaming and hearts pounding. All the stress of the previous minutes was gone, as I got lost in the feel of Gunner's broad chest.

I slipped my hand beneath his shirt, which elicited a warm growl from the wolf.

"Gotta make things equal," he murmured as his lips shifted from mine to trail down my neck and one of his hands disappeared beneath my shirt.

His hands, large and warm and rough from time working outdoors, knew how to touch me, and while he was patient in many ways, right now, Gunner was done with waiting. He went right for the clasp, undoing it with one hand. He was back to my breasts, cupping it, tweaking, and pulling at my nipple in a way that made me whimper.

"Music to my ears." He showed the other breast equal attention.

"Take it off," I breathed back. "My shirt. Yours too."

He obliged, ripping his shirt off first and exposing a six-pack one could wash their clothes on. He took my shirt off more delicately, and I savored the expression of longing on his face as he got to see my breasts on full display.

"I've never seen a prettier sight." Gunner brought his lips to my right nipple and sucked.

My back arched, my toes curled, and my underwear soaked. Old Ones save me. We'd done this before, bared parts of ourselves, but why did it feel so much better now? Why did I seem on fire from his touch?

"Gunner," my hand dropped down, down to the buttons on his jeans. "These off too."

He lifted his eyes to meet mine. "You're sure?"

We'd only been about half undressed before, never fully bare.

"Positive. I want it all gone." And without asking, I unbuttoned the top button. "If you do, that is."

"Chica, you don't have to ask me twice." His pants were off before I'd even shimmied mine over my hips. I gaped when I realized he wasn't wearing underwear.

"Surprise." He threw his pants at the door, and laughing, I mimicked him, stripping bare and tossing my own clothes. I'd barely turned back to the alphablood when he pounced, his hand slithering down to cup my mound. "Already drenched. Old Ones, you're gonna be the end of me, chica."

I didn't answer, just gazed down, taking my first toe-curling look at Gunner in all his glory. I'd known from over the clothes dry humping that he was packing, but seeing him now, it was astonishing.

Long and thick, his cock gleamed in the light from the

roaring fireplace that warmed the room. A pearly bead glistened at the tip, and I wanted to lick it off, but Gunner took my chin with his free hand, lifted my face to meet his.

"You first, Harp. It will always be you first."

My stomach fluttered.

"Have your way with me," I choked out.

"I intend to." Gunner slipped a finger inside me.

I inhaled as his thumb circled my clit and slowly, so achingly slowly, he moved his fingers in and out. I was ready to beg for more when he slipped another finger in, stretching me deliciously.

My head tipped back, exposing my throat to him. He took the gesture in the way most wolves did, and leaned in, kissing, licking, softly nipping at the delicate skin there.

"You smell so good," Gunner moaned. "I wanna eat you up."

"Not off the table," I murmured back.

He chuckled. "You bet your fine ass it's not. I plan on doin' that. Tonight. Tomorrow. Any time you'll let me."

My ovaries threatened to burst, and of course, that was the moment he curled his fingers along my inner wall. Back arching, I let out a long, low hum of pleasure.

"More of that, eh? What the princess of the west wants, she gets."

His ridiculous nickname might have had me laughing, but Gunner chose that moment to infuse magic into his fingers. I gasped from whatever the hell he'd done and kept doing.

"Like that." Pressure built below and an ache grew in my pussy. "Like that, Gunner. Please."

"Mercy, I love it when you beg like that," he teased, but didn't stop, and from the look in his eyes, he would do this forever if I asked. But I didn't need forever. After our foreplay, I was close. Unbelievably close.

So—*Old Ones save me!*

The pressure came to a head, and my channel pulsed as heat and pleasure and pure magic flowed around me.

"Good girl, Harp. That's a good girl." Gunner pumped in and out, slower now. "So perfect."

My breath slowed, wobbled, as I came back to myself. I looked him in the eyes. "More. I want you inside me."

He locked eyes with me for only a moment before pressing up and positioning himself above me. I stopped him.

"I'm on top."

Gunner's face lit up. "You're the boss."

You bet your fine self I am.

I positioned myself over him, that easy, light euphoria of an orgasm left behind still flowing through me, my magic simmering below the surface. It had never seeped out of me before, but I suspected it might again soon. Tonight felt like a night for many firsts, a night that would bring us closer. I sensed a thread weaving through us, one that I might have been scared to let in before, but now I loved. I wanted.

I positioned myself over Gunner, preparing to take all of him. He was large, there was no doubt, and more than that, he was broad. My legs strained as I lowered and took him inside me inch by inch. Tomorrow I'd be sore in more ways than one.

Gunner moaned as I seated him inside me.

"You like that?" I whispered.

"Does a wolf love the moon?"

I rode the alphablood, relishing every inch of him I took and released. He stretched my insides and knew when to thrust his hips, when and where to touch me.

His hands gravitated to my hips, and he began to dictate our rhythm and moon above, it felt so good, right. My head tipped back, and again, my magic flowed out of me. The silver swirled and spun, reminding me so much of Gunner's captivating eyes as it surrounded us.

He barked out a laugh as we fell into our rhythm.

"Harp, I'm close," he growled. "What are you doin' to me with that magic, chica?"

"Not magic." I winked. "That's all me."

He smirked and reached around to smack my ass as I thrust down on him hard and deep.

My orgasm came even harder and faster the second time, and as I exploded, Gunner's cock twitched as he climaxed. He moaned, the sound music to my ears. I laughed and ground harder into him, wanting to be closer to him.

And suddenly, something inside me snapped into place. Was it magic? I gasped as a rush of something I'd never felt blasted through me, even more powerful than the orgasm making me see stars.

Beneath me, Gunner let out a sharp exhale, and though it was difficult to think with everything going on, I wondered if I'd hurt him.

"Are you okay?" I sounded breathy, unable to get a full gulp of air in. I tossed my head back, and my hair slithered down my back. "Gunner?"

"Harp, did you feel . . ." His voice was raspy too, as if he, too, was coming out of a daze. "Wait, what's that?"

My thighs trembled, weak from pleasure. Unable to take my weight any longer, I lowered myself onto his chest. "What's what?"

"There was somethin' on your chest."

I shoved myself back up and peered down to find a glowing crescent moon nestled between my breasts.

By the Old Ones . . . What is—oh!

Another light caught my attention, one on Gunner's chest. A twin moon to the one on my skin, glowing in the same place.

"Gunner." I looked up to meet his silver eyes. They were wide, like mine, and in them, I read his understanding. Our link.

The thing that shifted, that something snapping into place, hadn't been just in me. It had been between us, linking us.

We were soulmates. My mouth dropped open.

Our friends being soulmates and not knowing made far more sense. They were of different magical orders, but Gunner and I were both wolves. More than that, we'd been intimate before—not this intimate, but still, we'd bared our bodies, and ourselves. How had we not sensed this bond?

Gunner grinned, the shock vanishing from his face far faster than mine. "I dunno for sure, but I think it's 'cause you're not full wolf, chica. And you've accepted all of you. All of me too. So the bond—it snapped."

I sat there staring down at his chest, his dick still inside me. It made sense, but what did not was how I hadn't seen it coming.

"You've had a lot on your mind, Harp. I gotta say, though," Gunner shifted, and a rush of pleasure pulsed through me. He was still partially hard and deep. "I wondered 'bout this a few times. You didn't?"

"I—no. I thought if I ever met my soulmate, it would be obvious. I didn't take into consideration that I might stand in my way."

Had I accepted my magic and gone all in from the get-go—

had accepted my feelings for Gunner too, I could have known. And this was something everyone wanted.

"Well, looks like you're stuck with me, chica," Gunner winked. "What are you gonna do about it?"

As he spoke, he hardened inside me again. His desire flared, and mine rose to meet it.

I rocked against him. "Why don't I show you?"

CHAPTER THIRTY

MEREDITH

I was Miriam's idea, but the moment she spoke it out loud, we had to see it through. Because I'd seen this moment—this moon ritual, as Miriam called it—in a book in Yale's Beinecke Library. Way back before I even know who I was, who the other *Vindix* were, I'd seen this moment and now I felt deep inside that we should partake.

"Does it matter that it's not a full moon?" I asked Miriam as we tramped to the backyard, or the garden, as the *Arcacustos* called it. I pulled my leather jacket tight around me and zipped it up, wishing I'd worn something warmer.

"You think the moon doesn't hold power in all of her glorious phases?"

"I—no, I'm sure it does," I said. "That's just what I saw in a book. An image that caught my attention and stuck."

"Well, it's more impressive that way as an illustration," she conceded. "But this will work as well."

I took her word for it. I didn't even know if Miriam was right and the moon would give us some extra magical juice, but I *was* sure that rituals like this bonded people. And that was my current fixation. I cared that the *Vindix* felt close to each other. We would soon rely on one another to stay alive. To save the world.

Everyone was already assembled outside: the *Arcacustos*, the *Vindix*, S&S, Serena, and Benedict. My eyes caught on Gunner and Harper, both looking at each other and smiling in a super lovey dovey way. I had to wonder if they'd gone all the way, but I hadn't gotten Harper alone to ask. Then again, even if I had, she was pretty private. She might tell me to stick my question where the moon didn't shine, or some other wolfy saying.

"Everyone has been debriefed?" Miriam directed her question to Claire and Gloria, her right and left hands in the coven.

"Hans knows what to say. The rest is up to the magic of above." Gloria looked up and smiled at the celestial orb above. The gesture was sweet, an adjective I didn't use to describe the old witch who often liked to sass people and egg them on.

"Right then. Meredith." Miriam pointed to an opening in the circle between Hans and Kaito. "Wolf, you need to leave the circle." She nodded to Gunner, who released Harper's hand and took a step back.

I took my place.

"Hans," Claire spoke more softly than Miriam or Gloria. "Whenever you're ready."

"Before that," Harper cleared her throat. "I have something to say. Or, rather, show." She pulled down the front of her shirt to reveal a white crescent moon on her pale skin.

My eyebrows pulled together. Was that an Enchanted Pool marking? And if so, why was she showing us? All the *Vindix* had them, though they weren't as obvious as that one.

My questions disappeared when Gunner unbuttoned the top three buttons of his shirt, revealing the same marking. My mouth fell open, but before I said a single word, Shay let out a squeal that could be heard as far away as the village.

"*Soulmates!* Heavens, you've got to be kidding me!" Shay leapt into the circle and squeezed Harper, who beamed back at our friend. "I can't believe this! Harp, if you didn't push him away for years, you could have known way before, but . . . *Oh!* I'm so glad you found out!"

Gunner grinned. "Me too. Coulda done without all those haughty looks, but my ice-queen mate finally figured out I'm quite the catch."

Harper rolled her eyes. "Oh shush."

Gunner laughed, and Shay let out another squeal and hugged him too. I clasped my hands to my chest. Not long ago, I'd never have imagined having such close friends. Now those in S&S were bound by fate and a web of friendship. I didn't see how I could have gotten luckier.

"I'm happy for you two." My voice joined the chorus of others who had already said as much. "It's a gift."

"It is." Harper's hand drifted back and squeezed Gunner's before letting go and turning to the circle. "Should we get started?"

I winked at her. "Reading my mind, roomie. Shay, get outta here, okay?"

The nephilim still looked about ready to pass out from happiness, but she stepped out of the circle, leaving only the *Vindix* in the sacred space. We grasped hands, and Hans cleared his throat.

"We gather here tonight, in sacred ritual. A rite formed by seven families, long ago. Some of us share their blood. Others have been gifted their fate." His eyes closed briefly, and I wondered if he still wished he hadn't been given the Pearl when the original family line died out. "A fate of seven to save all. To defeat great evil, to defeat seven lords of the underworld."

Two down, though. We all knew that no matter how good it felt to have ended two Princes of Hell, it wasn't enough. It wouldn't be, not until they were all gone.

Hans exhaled, long and low. "We ask the stars to bless us in our task, our destiny. We request that as seven, we be bound in more than friendship and duty. We beseech the stars and those with greater magic than ours to bless us as we face a great war of good and evil."

Hans tipped his chin up to the stars, and one by one, the rest of us followed suit.

"To the magic that came from above, we beg your blessing. We request any extra help you may give, whether it be strength of mind, magic, or body. With such gifts, we will fulfill our destiny." Hans let out a long breath. "So mote it be."

The last line echoed around the circle, as we'd been told to do. I couldn't say I expected much of anything, though the instant the final syllable left my lips, a jolt of electricity flooded through me.

I gasped, my eyes flying open in time to see a flash of light rush around the circle, haloing each witch before moving on to the next. When it had completed the circle, the light pulsed, illuminating us all at once.

And that wasn't all. Above, seven stars shot through the sky.

My hands trembled, but no one spoke. I wasn't even sure anyone dared breathe as the stars blazed across the night sky and disappeared, and the light in the circle vanished too.

"A sign," Gloria's voice broke the silence.

"An omen," Claire agreed, her Irish lilt soft and hopeful in a way that stopped the pit in my stomach from expanding.

"Good or bad?" Luca asked.

"No one can say," Claire replied. "But a celestial event started all this—when the *Vindix* were born. To me, it's clear the stars are saying one thing and one thing only."

"The end is near," Gloria whispered.

Chills ran down my spine. We'd all known a true battle was coming. It had to, after what we'd done—after we'd already killed two princes. Once the living brothers learned of the deceased fates', they'd band together to end our lives. To make their rule over Earth complete.

"What about the light?" Tana asked. "It ran through me, electrified me." She scanned each in the circle. "I feel more of you all. Like we're connected deeper, or the like."

The moment she said it, I sensed it too. Almost like if I closed my eyes, and they moved, I'd still be able to feel them.

"Above gave us a gift of awareness," I said. I was sure of my correctness in a way that rarely happened. "We need to test it."

"Tomorrow," Miriam said. "Tonight, you have had enough. Rest is needed for the effects of your gift to settle."

There was wisdom in her words, and as badly as I wanted to test out the new power, she was right.

"Then we rest." I released Hans and Kaito. "And tomorrow, we learn how best to use our new gift."

The circle broke, and I sought Tobias's eyes, his familiarity and peace. Instead, I caught a blur of white streaming through the night sky. A yelp escaped me, and I leapt back, right into Harper—only for the blur to pause in front of us.

I blinked. A man dressed in an overcoat and page boy hat floated there. A ghost.

"There you are!" Harper exclaimed as if she'd been waiting for him.

Understanding dawned. This was the ghost she'd sent out to learn which prince ruled where. My heart began beating hard, like a drum, in my chest.

The ghost peered at the others as if he questioned his choice in coming.

"You can speak in front of them," Harper said. "They're in this with me."

"I've been to each city, learned who rules where," the ghost said.

"By all means," Harper replied. "Spill everything."

CHAPTER THIRTY-ONE

TOBIAS

Water had seeped into Seattle's underground tunnels, filling them with a dank scent that made my nose wrinkle. I had not wanted to come to the Covenant debrief, but Luca wanted me here with him, Gunner, and Shay. Many of us were representatives of powerful lineages and organizations. And mates to *Vindix*, of course, which I suspected was the real reason.

This time away from the manor gave the *Vindix* time to test out their new ability, which, as my clever witch had guessed, was indeed an increased awareness of each other, something that would be invaluable in battle. I understood where Luca was coming from. Mates could be quite distracting to their counterparts.

Still, the sooner we returned to England, the better. After the death of my maker, being away from Meredith was even more tortuous.

An hour, no more, I reminded myself. *Meredith is a powerful witch, and safe behind many wards. Not to mention many other skilled witches, a wolf pack, a giant, and a bloody wyvern. She'll be fine.*

"Here we are," Luca muttered as he reached the entrance to the Covenant's most secure hideout. "Time to see who is still around."

The mage traveled here to provide updates, and according to him, each time, another Covenant Seat had either left or just arrived. Artem Kovalenko remained the only constant. The wizard remained through it all.

So it was no surprise when we entered the underground headquarters to find Artem sitting at the meeting table. Not alone either.

Nina Tyche was the phoenix Seat, Liliana Valori represented the vampires, and Susan Chappel spoke for the witches. In the back rooms, others—at least three people—were milling about.

Most shocking of all, however, was the body laid out on the large table.

"Richard Brons," Gunner breathed. "What happened to him?"

Artem stood. "I apologize for the ghastly sight. We were discussing where to put his remains."

"Remains?" Luca asked. "He's *dead*?"

Nina cleared her throat. "Arrived here half out of his mind. There are markings of demon possession, and we think they tortured him for information. He died only about two hours ago."

I stiffened. "What kind of information?"

While the Covenant had been informed of Egor Drago's death, no one here knew that we'd been the reason Brons had not joined the government the moment he should have. That he'd been our prisoner.

Or at least, they *hadn't* known. What if when Brons arrived here, he told them, and we were about to be reprimanded? Worse, what if we lost information sources because the Covenant believed we could not be trusted for what we'd done?

I didn't regret keeping Brons captive, but I would regret the repercussions, should any come our way.

"We don't know." Middle-aged Susan frowned down at her fellow witch Seat. "He spoke gibberish. Though he did say something about light and traveling. I can't say we saw eye-to-eye, but I found it disconcerting to see him like that."

Shay stepped forward. "He spoke of light-traveling?"

Susan shrugged. "Light and traveling, but I guess he might have been trying to say that."

"Did you search him?"

Artem arched an eyebrow. "I presume you're interested in this?" He pulled the luxiter Shay had bargained with from his pocket.

In response, the other Seats glared at Artem.

"You hid that from us!" snapped Liliana, a Seat for my order and a personal vote of mine.

"I did. I was interested in what S&S might have to say about it. Especially seeing as we could not acquire luxiters, but Brons, of all people, possessed one?"

Bloody Shay and her foolish deals.

Shay sighed. "I made a deal with Brons. I gave up my luxiter, and he gave Hans his power back. That's why he had it."

"Nothing more?" Artem asked.

Silence rang through the headquarters.

"Nothing that you need to know," Shay replied.

Artem tilted his head as though he wished to press, but

Luca took the reins. "As horrible as it sounds, Brons's loss is your benefit. The Covenant may have that luxiter, which I believe will be beneficial for all." Luca exhaled. "We've come to catch up again. We learned valuable information last night."

Now we knew exactly where each prince ruled. Valuable information indeed.

Artem lowered the luxiter to the table. "Fine. Let us move the body, and we'll proceed."

Luca levitated Brons into a back room and placed a stasis spell on the body. I wasn't sure what the Covenant would do with Brons in the end, but at least he wouldn't stink up the underground headquarters as they decided.

After the meeting table was scrubbed, and others, including Shay's mother, had joined us, we reviewed what was happening in the world. Told them what Harper's ghost had learned. As Luca had done well to keep the Covenant up to date on New Orleans and Venice, it didn't take long to relay our information.

Then it was their turn. According to Artem, human and magical forces were fighting demons around New Orleans and Venice, trying to regain ground. Human communities were doing what they could and creating ties with magical communities too. I wondered how things would go once the danger passed—if we'd continue to work together and get along—but that was a worry for another time.

A time after we've won.

"Next steps?" Liliana asked once the catching up was done. "Any idea where the *Vindix* will attack next?"

I looked at the list of cities and the corresponding princes' names that Artem had jotted down. Those who still lived.

Prince Orien - Washington DC

Prince Lucifer - Los Angeles
Prince Bale - London
Prince Levi - Sydney
Prince Mon - Las Vegas

The idea of Meredith having to enter any of those places and fight again was enough to make me go feral—even if I also fully understood that it was her destiny. I despised not controlling this narrative. Nor protecting her as well as I wanted.

"We don't have a plan for our next steps yet," Luca admitted.

"That does not sound promising," Angelina looked to her daughter, worry plain in her eyes.

I agreed.

"Let me be plain. *Nothing* about this is promising." Luca stood. "But whatever happens, I would like to be sure that the Covenant still has forces in place and is ready to move when we are. We will need help. As will the people who are trapped if and when we can shatter another dome around a taken city."

"We are with you. And speaking of with you." Artem held up the luxiter. "Show me how to use this before you go? Then I can travel and transport others."

Shay stood. "Of course." She shared a glance with me. "After that, we'll go. We're needed elsewhere."

With our mates, I added in my head. Of those around the table, only Luca wanted to go slow. To stay here. Gunner, Shay, and I, however, had important people in England. People we loved and needed to protect.

"Hurry," I said to the nephilim.

"Plan on it, stiff," she shot back, and the moniker did not annoy the hell out of me. For once, we were on the same page.

CHAPTER THIRTY-TWO

HANS

I ROAMED THE WOODS, SENSING THE OTHERS CONVERGING IN space, but not yet seeing them.

Claire had placed a short-term invisibility spell on each *Vindix*, then an *Arcacusto* led us deep into the woods and told us to find one another.

We'd done this three times already and managed it each time with the power the moon, or the stars, or whatever was in the sky, gave us.

I push aside a fern. Someone approached from behind. Who? From our other attempts, I'd learned I could tell who I was coming up upon.

And this one was Meredith? No, Kaito?

Both! A bush rustled behind and to my right, at the same time as a twig snapped to my left.

"Meredith? Kaito?"

"Hans?" Meredith asked back.

I heard the smile in her voice. She'd sensed me too.

"We did it again," Kaito sounded elated. "And if I'm not mistaken, someone is nearing. Rabi."

Rabi felt like a breeze, light and airy, and as such, he was the most difficult to track in the woods. But as he neared, seeking us like we sought him, I knew Kaito was right.

We waited until the air elemental closed in. His soft voice cut through the relative silence of the woods. "There are three of you—Hans, Meredith, and Kaito."

"Hell yes there is," Meredith said. "Let's search for the others!"

We set off and though we couldn't see one another, there was no worry about losing one another. Not when we felt each other's presence.

Following our connection, we'd found the other three, and, victorious, the *Vindix* trekked back to the manor, where Miriam and Claire would be waiting for us.

As we were all cloaked in Claire's magic, she felt us first and grinned.

"All seven?" Her Irish lilt sounded so hopeful.

"Yep," Meredith replied. "We were faster that time too?"

"You were," Miriam gave a small smile which was practically elation from the likes of her. "By a good three minutes. That counts for a lot."

"Minutes, even seconds, might be the difference between life and death," Harper agreed as we stepped out of the forest to join the elder witches. "But I think I'd like a break. Anyone else?"

"Dinner would be amazing," Meredith replied.

I wasn't hungry. Not for food, anyway. Shay had returned from Seattle two hours ago, and I craved her presence. Like all new mates, I also craved her body. I hoped to convince her to push back her meal so I could feast on *her* first.

"We'll try twice more tonight." Claire waved her hand, and

the invisibility magic around us disappeared. "Then—what in the bloody hell!"

A blaze of smoke shot down from the sky, setting us all on edge. That was until the smoke and a presence I recognized closed in.

Mother? Is she smoke-traveling through the wards?

But no, when the smoke settled to the ground and cleared, no Queen of Hell stepped out. There was no body, not a physical one anyway. Instead, the smoke took the shape of a woman and spoke.

"Hans, darling, I have information for you. Listen, for I cannot stay for long."

I stiffened, nodded, which was stupid because my mother could not see me. Not that it mattered as the smoke person continued.

"My husband and I are in DC with Wrath. Plans of expansion and vengeance are being made with the brothers. Mostly the latter. They will attack—it might even be coming now. They wish to cut off the head of the serpent, your rebellion, before you inflict more damage upon them." She paused, longer than one would need for a breath.

Was she speaking to us now in real time? Or was this recorded?

"I'm imprisoned for killing Lust's son in LA. Soon, I will die—be made a spectacle of, but you needed this information," she said, her pace of speech picking up. "If you move quickly, you might kill them all at once, for the more you kill, the weaker they all become."

I swallowed. The princes had imprisoned my mother in DC. For a crime she'd committed for us. "Mother, I—"

"I love you, Hans. Remember, I love you with all my heart."

The smoke disappeared, the message delivered, and my knees buckled at the implications, and a hand—Rabi's, I thought—caught me. Mother was imprisoned, soon to die. The princes were meeting to discuss how to kill us and soon they'd send an attack.

"We need to move first," Kaito spoke. "Attack before they can. She might have bought us a chance. Might have bought the areas around DC a chance too. If we move before the kingdoms expand a second time, think of how many we could save."

"Like her," I added. "We're going to save my mother."

No one looked convinced by that, and really, I didn't blame them. As Lilith's son, I would do anything in my power to save her, but we were up against literal gods of the underworld. Five of them in one place—when we'd barely been able to kill one with our powers combined.

And my heart told me Wrath and Pride, Orien and Lucifer, were far more powerful than Lust or Sloth.

"We should go tell Luca," Meredith said. "And the other *Arcacustos*. If someone is coming, they—"

Boom!

Above us, the wards shook like I'd never known wards could shake before and everyone except for Miriam and Claire dropped and covered their head.

The older witches, however, stayed standing, looking up. Fire raged in Miriam's steel-blue eyes.

"They're here already," she growled. "It's too late."

The *Arcacustos* looked at one another, and Miriam nodded. "I'll go."

"I'll remain and protect." Then Claire looked at Harper. "Miriam is going to the library to ensure those protections are up. Send ghosts to tell the others to come outside. Now. The rest of you have your stones, correct?"

Everyone did, and we said as much. Harper called spirits and sent them into the manor. I watched them streak off, my heart racing.

Only seconds passed before Tobias and Serena blurred outside. Shay, Luca, Gunner and his pack were not far behind.

The older witches arrived last and when they did, Gloria was wheezing. "An attack?"

Claire's chin was tilted to the sky. "I can sense them up there. Hundreds, maybe a thousand swarming and bombarding."

Luca went pale. "But the wards—my magic, yours, and Shay's combined—will it hold?" He raised his arms, and Shay, now at my side, was only a second behind. White and gold light streaked from them, up, up, and up, to the barrier that protected us.

When I saw Shay's face fall, I knew things weren't going well.

"Many of ours are dismantled," Claire said. "Miriam would know exactly how many, but she's gone to put extra protections on the library."

"Mine are disabled too," Luca confirmed after a moment of assessing. "At most, we have ten minutes to prepare to fight."

"Which you won't be doing," Gloria snorted. "You all must leave. Hannah and Stuart, you as well. The rest of our coven will remain to protect the library until we no longer can. I'll make it my final act."

My stomach dropped. A witch's final act, or as some called it, a final spell, was powerful. Miriam's protections would go far in keeping the library safe, but if Gloria wished to protect the library and made it her final act, few creatures could break that protection. For six witches of such power to do so?

The library would stand until the end of time.

"*Vindix*, give me your hands," Claire said, as though Gloria hadn't announced their suicide mission.

"Wait!" Hannah cried out, and only then did I see tears streaking down her face. "I'll stay too. It's my duty."

"You will not," Olga cut in. "You're young and the *Vindix* will require a healer. The world too. And Stuart—you must stay with Hannah. She needs you, and you're the very last of your line. The rest of us have family to take our place if they must."

Again, the wards above shook. This time, I swore I heard the shrieks of demons above, the flapping of wings, and a trickle of dark magic. I shuddered.

"*Hands*." Claire produced a blade. Where had that come from? She didn't walk around with knives on her.

It hit me then that the moment Harper sent that message, Claire had known what they were going to do. That they'd stay and defend. All the eldest witches had.

Judging by the looks on Hannah's and Stuart's faces, they hadn't. Just like the rest of us.

Hannah continued to fight Gloria, but the rest of us produced our hands for Claire. She cut deep into our palms, but I barely noticed the blade digging into my skin.

My mother was in the dungeons. Demons were above us, not visible but there, beyond a veil of curated wards, waiting to break in and kill us all.

Claire took her own hand, drew blood, and allowed two drops of her blood to land on our cuts. "There, when this is over, when it is safe to return, you all will have access to the library. Promise me, you'll keep the books safe. Should another tragedy occur after all our deaths, the next *Vindix* will need them. Hannah and Stuart, you live and shepherd those books to the next generation."

"You should come," Meredith said, her voice choked as the droplets landed on her skin, giving her access to the library no matter the protections put on it. "Please. We can all leave."

"We cannot leave our home unguarded." Claire shook her head. "The oldest will remain and fight for as long as we can. The rest of you take the luxiters and go. Seek safety and when you can, fight. Save us all."

"We will," Luca spoke up, though even his tone was raspy, emotional. "Thank you for what you've done. Your sacrifice."

"We were born to do it," Claire said and in a display of affection the witch rarely exhibited, she pulled Meredith into a hug. "You made our lives meaningful."

Mentor and mentees said brief goodbyes. As I had not had a mentee among the *Arcacustos*, I hung back, nauseous. Shay and Luca, the best at light-traveling via luxiters, were discussing where to go when Hannah approached me. Tears streaked her face.

"I'm sorry," I said as the wards shook again. This time, I spotted a crack.

"I want to stay, but I also cannot leave you guys. You're our last hope."

I didn't know what to say. Shay saved me from having to say anything at all.

"Gather!" my mate instructed. "Link up! Get your asses here, like now! *Hans!*"

"Come on." Hannah spared a look back at the older witches preparing for battle.

We joined up and linked hands.

"Close your eyes," Shay said, her voice shaking. "My wards have shattered. Luca's too. They're close."

No sooner had she spoken than the first demons poured in through a hole in the wards, much like the night they'd entered our world in Italy. Hundreds of demons of all shapes and sizes, and the flow did not slow. Did not stop.

No one can survive such an onslaught, I thought, as the *Arcacustos* blasted the demons, one after the other, from the sky.

The last thing I saw before the light took us was Gloria's vicious snarl and Olga's surge of fire as a thousand devils swarmed them.

CHAPTER THIRTY-THREE

MEREDITH

My feet slammed into the ground and the light receded, leaving me blinking, my heart rate thrumming at a speed that had to be dangerous.

We left them. Left the Arcacustos *to die.*

There was no other way to look at it, no way one could spin a sweeter, more palatable story. Five elderly witches were up against thousands of demons. No one would be so delusional to think they'd survive.

A sob ripped up my throat, and a hand, Tobias's, pulled me in close for comfort. I nestled into him, relieved to have both my hardened vampire and my familiar, who was still in Tobias's grasp.

In a sweet gesture, Benedict put his paw on my shoulder. It was only then that I noticed he was trembling. That I was trembling too.

From the sounds of it, we weren't the only ones who needed a rock in our corner. Hannah bawled loudly. Tana only slightly less so. Her fire witch mentor, Olga, might not have been a warm person, but she'd transformed Tana from a witch with vast raw power to someone who could control and unleash that power with a thought.

And if I pulled my head from my mate's comforting shoulder, I suspected I'd find Harper in a stunned state. She and Aya had bonded, and Harper respected the old spirit witch.

The rest of the *Vindix* didn't know the *Arcacustos* well at all. They'd barely been around them, but no one could feel untouched by such a sacrifice.

So many deaths for the library.

And for us. My heart clenched. I hoped it wasn't all in vain. We wouldn't know until we won this war, *if* we won it. Surely, a contingent of demons would remain at the manor and wait for us. Returning to a place that, despite the questionable decor, had begun to feel homey was far too dangerous. There was too much on the line.

"Is there a place where Hannah and I can be alone?" Stuart asked. "Even just for a mo'?" He looked up, then all around, his eyebrows pulling together as he took in the area. "Where are we anyway?"

Great question. One that cut through the pain of loss enough that I lifted my head.

"This is the headquarters of the Coven of Shadows and Secrets," Luca replied.

So it was, though it looked *different*.

I pulled away from Tobias and scanned the large atrium, the very place where a shade attacked me before I knew who I was and what I was meant to do.

The tomb, always busy, was empty, but there were signs that people had been around. *Many people.* My eyebrows pulled together as I gazed up at the intricate light fixtures above. It was dented?

"What happened here?" I asked, noting the damage to the

stairway banister and that one door leading into a room I'd never entered was cracked right down the middle. My anger grew with every new blemish I spotted. I hadn't been a coven member for too long, less than a year, but this tomb had quickly become a place that I loved. A place where those I loved gathered.

"Demons attacked a few times," Luca said.

My mouth fell open. "*What?!*"

"Why are we here, then?" Harper asked, echoing my horror.

The rest of S&S nodded in agreement, though Gunner's wolves seemed too preoccupied by the opulent tomb to notice our objections.

"They never entered the building but shook it, and there have been no attacks since the OA learned we were in England. Maybe they assumed the entire Coven was there." Luca swallowed. "But in the wake of the last attack, S&S members have also been reinforcing wards. Setting up technologies too. The tomb is better protected than ever before, and we didn't have many choices. We needed space for many, and headquarters can provide. At least for a little while. If we end up staying here too long, I can ask the Covenant for a safe house."

"I don't think we'll need that," Hans spoke up. His face was ashen, his blue eyes haunted. "I have news from my mother."

Luca listened as Hans relayed what Lilith's smoke form had said.

"I assume you want to go to DC?" Luca asked.

"And soon," Hans said. "Not just to save my mother, but if the princes are gathering there, this could be our best chance to beat them in one go."

"Or their best chance to kill us all," Kaito muttered.

They both had points. Good ones too. Hans knew it would be difficult for us to kill five of Hell's princes at once. That wasn't even factoring in the difficulty we'd undergo sneaking into Wrath's territory and not being caught by who-knew-how-many monsters.

"Well," Luca spoke slowly, probably carefully weighing out the options presented to us. "We can't go now. We're not ready, and if we're to attempt a last stand, we need help."

"Call our allies then," Hans said. "Call the Covenant. We can make a stand at the capital."

"You forgot one important part, Hans." Harper held up a finger. "Your mother said that the princes are weakening. The more we kill, the weaker they become."

"What?" Luca blinked. "That's what she said?"

"It was," Hans agreed. "I'd been more focused on my mother and forgot, but that works to our advantage too."

"So they're all connected?" I asked, trying to piece it together.

"That means that if we kill the others, Orien and Lucifer will be weaker at the end," Shay said, as though it were a given that Wrath and Pride were the strongest of the brothers. To be fair, I agreed on that point. Others nodded in agreement too.

"I think so too," Luca said. "We—"

A door opened from above. We turned and looked up to find Lisha, a female vampire, peering down at us.

"You're here!" She smiled, but then it fell from her face. "Why?"

"We needed refuge," Luca replied. "Has all been well here since I last checked in?"

"Everyone has been staying here, safe and sound."

CHAPTER THIRTY-THREE

"The entire coven sleeps here?" Tobias rubbed my back.

"It's the safest place." Lisha replied flatly. "Most of them are out demon hunting now, but they'll return tonight. Many sleep together in the larger rooms for protection. I'll admit that the tomb is not the most comfortable of places to sleep, but it can offer great protection."

Goddess. What had the greater New Haven area been like since we left? I'd been so focused on Hell's seven kingdoms and the princes within them that I hadn't considered smaller cities and towns. Were demons running amok everywhere?

"Lisha? Who are you talking to? Sara and I are trying to research." Another figure popped out of a door and my eyes bulged.

Josiah.

"Oh, hey guys." The necromancer looked nervous to see us, and for good reason. He was supposed to be our spy in the OA. "I had to leave my post. Someone saw me snooping, and they were gonna out me. I didn't want to die."

My frustration fizzled, and from the looks of it, the others' did too. Any tightness or anger in their bodies or faces vanished.

"Sorry," Josiah added smally.

"Considering what we learned and what we need to do, it's for the best," Luca answered after a beat. "In my eyes, you're redeemed."

Josiah's face brightened. "Really?"

"The Night Circle might not agree, but yes." Luca let out a long breath. "However, we might have need for you soon. And others." He turned his face to Lisha. "We need a meeting, and to prepare to call all our allies to battle."

Night fell in New Hampshire and still the hours marched on as we light-traveled people into the safety of S&S's tomb.

Covenant members. Other covens who had expressed wanting to fight alongside us. Vampire clans. Two wolf packs. And so many more.

Having to explain who we were and our plans over and over proved exhausting. And yet, I always offered to light-travel to someone, somewhere. With Tobias at my side, we ventured to every corner of the globe to bring back allies.

Difficult though it might be, I welcomed the distraction. Not only did connecting with these new people help me push aside the enormity of our plan, but it also kept my mind off the *Arcacustos*—all of them undoubtedly dead by now.

Not Hannah. Not Stuart, I reminded myself.

Not that they found that any consolation. I wasn't sure that the youngest members of the *Abscondita* Coven would ever be able to live with the guilt of leaving the older witches to fight and protect the manor. But the truth was, we needed the youngest *Arcacustos*. Just as we needed every single other soul we brought back to the tomb.

Tobias and I finished showing a new group of witches to a sleeping room when I spotted Artem still working. The wizard had been the first Luca brought back. Since then, the Ukrainian wizard gathered information on people brought in to fight. He'd also been tasked with connecting with the human military around DC.

"Artem." I gave a small wave. "Have a moment?"

"For you, of course." He shook Tobias's hand before pulling me in for a hug.

I should have guessed that Artem was a hugger. While I wasn't the same, I couldn't lie—it felt good to be held. To feel close to others. Soon we'd have to rely on each other in a way I'd never had to rely on near-strangers before.

At least my close friends would be with me too. At this point, they were more like family. Tobias certainly was, and though I'd grown up guarded, I felt like Shay, Harper, Gunner, Hans, and Luca were too.

"What can I do for you, Meredith?" Artem asked as we pulled apart.

"What's up with the military outside the capital?"

"They're preparing for our arrival, and other forces are being mobilized to join. We should have a sizable force when we make our move."

Tomorrow night. We would fight tomorrow.

Hans wanted to move sooner, and seeing as his mother's life was on the line, I didn't blame him. But the consensus was that we had one chance and one chance only to end this in a single blow. If we needed a few more hours to shift things in our favor, we had to take them.

"Great," I said, though it came out on the back of a yawn. "I think things are coming together."

Artem's face softened. "You need rest."

"Agreed," Tobias murmured. He'd been saying as much for the last hour.

"Everyone does," I replied.

"You and the other *Vindix* most of all," Artem retorted in that kind way of his.

"He's right, love." Tobias's hand landed on my shoulder. "Give your luxiter to someone else so they can continue to bring people in, but you need to sleep."

Though I should have argued, I didn't have the energy. "A few hours. Then I'll do whatever needs to be done."

We parted from Artem, and Tobias and I walked the halls

of the tomb until we found an S&S witch willing to use the luxiter and keep it safe. A sense of unease went through me as I left the priceless object in her hands, but Tobias assured me of her trustworthiness.

He led me to an empty room. From what I could tell, the tomb was bursting at the seams. How was no one sleeping in here already?

I turned to Tobias, the question in my eyes.

He rubbed my arm. "I had Hans make it invisible to others." He pointed up to the threshold above the door where runes glowed. "I wanted time alone with you."

I understood, but was it right? My teeth sank into my bottom lip.

"It's the smallest room. We could barely fit four more people in here," Tobias added. "And if Shay and Hans can't find another space, they'll join us. Gunner and Harper too."

My shoulders loosened. Fine. That was reasonable. Plus, I also wanted time with him. Alone. Even for only a few moments.

"Here," Tobias ushered me into the glorified closet and gestured to a bed mat at the end. "Lie down."

I did as my mate asked, groaning as my body hit the thin and lumpy mat. It felt amazing to rest.

"On your stomach."

I sighed as Tobias straddled me and began to knead my shoulders.

Goddess, I hadn't even known how tight I was.

"Good?"

I laughed. "I bet my heart rate slowed so much."

"It did."

For a few minutes, he worked on my muscles in silence, allowing me time to process the day, and the day to come. That was one amazing thing about having a vampire as a mate. He didn't mind prolonged silences. His kind lived in them. They were comfortable saying nothing. They had so long to say whatever they wished.

I might have that too. One day. If I lived through tomorrow.

I hadn't voiced my concerns about dying to Tobias, though it had to have been on everyone's minds. Soon, we'd face the crux of the war. We'd aim to kill five of the most powerful beings to ever live.

Would we be enough?

I didn't let the question take hold, and instead allowed my mate to manipulate my body, to force relaxation. And when he bent down and kissed my cheek, I needed more. More *of him.* What if tonight was our last?

I twisted my neck and caught his lips in mine before they left. He let out a little noise, one that made my toes curl. "You know what else releases tension, Tobias?"

The vampire's emerald eyes twinkled. "If the others walk in?"

I shrugged. "A gamble I'm willing to take."

Tobias laughed and hefted himself off me, only to pull me up and kiss me again. "Then let's lose ourselves to the night, love."

CHAPTER THIRTY-FOUR

HANS

"Be careful," Shay whispered, rolling over and taking her lips in mine. "We need you. *I* need you."

"I will. And remember, I'm taking an invisibility potion."

"They might still feel you," she replied knowingly.

My mate wasn't foolish. Far from it. She was clever as hell. The most beautiful woman, *and* funny too.

How did I get so lucky?

I only wished we'd discovered our mate bond sooner, but that would have meant me coming to terms with myself. With accepting my demon side, something I hadn't been able to do before walking through the fire.

Sometimes, I wasn't even sure if I'd gone all the way, but at least I'd traveled far enough. For that matter, Shay had too. In the past weeks, we'd both changed so much, and yet, we were still the same people at heart.

"Wish we had a lot more of the invisibility potion." Shay stroked my face. "A whole cauldron of it."

I did too, but invisibility potion was difficult to brew. Not only that, but it had a time limit. Even if we possessed enough to give to an entire army, it would wear off.

"We make the best of what we have," I said. "Enough to scout. Enough for the *Vindix* later. Just in case."

In case we needed to flee for our lives.

She swallowed, tightness crinkling her face in a way I hated to see. If I didn't have to cause her so much pain, I wouldn't. Alas, there was no way I couldn't go to DC. Even if my mother did not need rescuing, I was among those destined to bring down the Princes of Hell and they were there, together. A chance like this was once in a lifetime.

We needed to play it smart. To prepare. Which meant me leaving my mate and journeying into Hell's dominion to get the lay of the land.

I pulled Shay into me and kissed her thoroughly. At any moment, Luca would knock on the door to his office. He'd graciously given us the room the night before, when we'd heard Meredith and Tobias screwing in the room we'd originally said we would share.

Another might have been mad, but I understood. I'd wanted to make love with my mate too, and thanks to Luca, I was able to enjoy her, and she enjoyed me. I tried not to think that last night might have been our final night together.

"I can't wait until I can protect you," Shay whispered.

I smiled into her lips. "I can't wait for that either. I—"

Two knocks came at the door. "Are you decent?"

"One sec, Luca! Let me jump off your desk and grab my bra!" Shay shouted back, a devilish grin overtaking her plump lips. Goddess, I wanted to bite them, to suck them, to ravish them.

A long pause followed before Luca cleared his throat. "I

hope you're joking, but I suppose I can't blame you . . . Just for the love of my sanity, clean it, Shay?"

She laughed, and we rose from our makeshift bed. I unlocked the door and found Luca frowning.

"*Was* she joking?"

"We kept any funny business to the ground."

"Thank god." Luca walked into his office and veered to his coffee machine. From Isila by birth, but Italian-grown, Luca didn't have many vices, but the mage was addicted to his espresso. "One espresso, and we'll go. Do either of you want one?"

Shay and I declined, and Luca went to work, humming happily as he prepared his drink. He hadn't had proper coffee in a long time, which had been difficult for him in England, where the witches weren't as particular about the quality of their brew.

I cringed at the thought of the *Arcacustos*, no doubt all dead by now. They'd sacrificed for us. For their legacy. I'd never forget them.

But today, I had to move on. Put them out of my mind and venture into Wrath's kingdom.

"You have the potion?" I asked Luca as he prepared the milk he kept in a small refrigerator near his machine. Milk that Lisha had been kind enough to keep stocked for the coven master, who, unlike the rest of us, had traveled back and forth from headquarters many times.

"I do. You'll wait until the absolute last minute to take it though, so it lasts longer."

I nodded, familiar with the drill. Most recently, I'd taken the potion to venture into Hell and retrieve a plant to save Luca from poisoning.

"Right," I said. "In that case, I'll go grab a bite from downstairs. Then we'll leave."

General McNair spread out the map of the city on a dented wooden table. We had an idea of where Wrath would raise his castle, so I focused on that area.

"Right here, this street is quiet. Normally, that is. And it is close to the White House." McNair pointed. "Land there, inside this building, for your best chance of not being noticed. Can you do that?"

"I can." My smoke-traveling abilities had progressed greatly. I no longer doubted I could span Hell's barrier or land exactly where I wanted. And since I'd soon be invisible, I wasn't worried about arriving in a home where others were present. The only issue was the possibility of landing on top of someone. I'd deal with that if it happened.

"Useful," the general murmured. "Why haven't your kind shared this magic with us?"

"We don't want to be used," I retorted. "And my ability to smoke-travel is very rare."

I didn't say that smoke-travel, like light-travel, was limited to those with demon and angel blood. He'd only appreciate one of those magical orders.

The humans didn't need to know all our tricks. I didn't know the exact numbers, but humans greatly outnumbered all the magical orders and had weapons of their own. Until now, they had been fine, and if we succeeded in killing the princes, they'd be fine again.

"You're sure you don't want assistance?" McNair jerked his

head toward a group of soldiers, all special forces. "Any of them would have your back."

"No," Luca replied. "Not even I can go with Hans, not without Meredith. The sin would overtake me."

"Then where is Meredith?"

Luca arched an eyebrow. "Practicing extending her powers over increasing numbers of people, so that when we make our move, she'll be ready."

"And he doesn't need the girl?" McNair gestured to me as though I wasn't even there. I brushed it off. The man was helpful in the sense that we needed forces here. I would not rock that boat.

"We believe Hans might be naturally protected."

It had been Gunner who brought it up. He noted that in New Orleans, the demons who worked the castle and the city were unaffected by Prince Belhor's sin. Maybe Sloth had singled out those who worked for him, or maybe they'd been immune simply because they were demons.

When we thought about it, those demons in LA hadn't seemed prideful. Nor my mother. And though Meredith had acted fast in both New Orleans and Venice, covering me with her magic so I wasn't overcome with sloth or lust, now I wasn't sure that I'd needed it at all. The others had been affected within seconds of entering the dark kingdoms, but I had not.

Demon blood might be a protectant. Something we had not considered before. Only I could enter the taken cities without Meredith's help. Or so the theory went.

The general looked like he wanted to push, but Luca's chin lifted. "I'll say no more. But only Hans can enter. I'm here in case he needs help getting back to headquarters."

The general nodded, and I took one last look at the map,

noting the red lines drawn on it, the indicators of where the magical barrier covering DC was and how far it moved. Not far, but there had been movement, just like in Venice. We needed to stop this before the princes took more land, and as a result, more lives.

I caught Luca's waiting gaze. "I'm ready."

"To the barrier, then." We strode to the barrier, shimmering and black and oily from the outside. "Wait until you enter to take the potion."

Of course. We didn't need McNair knowing about that, either. I patted the bottle in my pocket, assuring Luca.

"Be careful. Come back, or Shay will kill me."

"She'll kill *me* if I don't return," I joked. "Take a couple of steps back."

Luca did as I requested, and I called my power. Smoke billowed up, consuming me, and seconds later, the prickle of magic that allowed me to traverse space took over.

I thought about the place the general had pointed out, one I assumed he knew well from time in the city. Trusting others in this endeavor was difficult, but I'd learned that putting my trust in others wasn't just a good idea—it was vital.

The smoke cleared, leaving me in an abandoned building. Broken windows, the roof had caved in, and bullet holes riddled one wall. Aside from all that, though, the room had an air of luxury. Nice furniture, even if it was ripped and torn and smashed. From where I stood, I spotted a kitchen, and I recognized high-end finishings when I saw them.

The home wouldn't be large enough to land everyone inside, though, so I crossed to the window and looked out. The street below stared back, empty. I cast a spell into it, trying to detect humans or others that might be hiding in the area.

Nothing. Perfect.

I popped the cap off my vial and downed the invisibility potion. This brew worked instantly, not always a given with potions, but we'd made sure to only gain the best for our expedition and my scouting. If things went south during the real mission and the *Vindix* needed an out, they wouldn't have time to wait for a potion to kick in. They would need to disappear and run.

Tingles erupted along my skin, telling me the potion had kicked in. I unfurled my wings and soared out of a smashed window. I spotted the castle. It was where we'd thought it would be—on the White House lawn, over where that stately presidential building once stood. Wrath wouldn't want a single icon competing for his show of dominance.

My gaze crept out, taking in the surrounding crumbling buildings, some demolished. It tore at me, though I took heart that if we landed in this exact position, then we would be only about three blocks from the castle. A good distance in which to create a diversion and make an approach. First, though, I needed to prepare us for a safe landing.

From above, I took in the street. One end curved sharply, so I could not see past it, and the other went on and on.

After a brief assessment, I began my work, casting protection spells, warding the area. They weren't the strongest wards —nothing like those over the *Abscondita* manor or S&S's tomb. However, they were strong enough to deter enemies and could last a few hours. Or so everyone hoped. There was the chance that someone would find my protections and dismantle them, but that was another factor that we could not control.

I'd done my best to prepare a landing area and scout a way into the castle. So that's what I did. After I'd thrown every protective spell I knew at the street and set a repellent charm above the area to deter flying creatures, I warded the area with runes. Those in place, I soared toward the castle.

A few other demons littered the skies, but thanks to the invisibility potion, no one saw me, or seemed to sense me either. I flew right above the castle, taking in a bird's-eye view.

The castle looked a lot like the ones in LA and New Orleans, even larger than Lucifer's castle. That same flame burned in a tower too, though this one appeared weaker than the one in LA. Maybe because the two brothers were dead?

Harper brought up that theory. The clever wolf-witch had noticed Sloth's flame was dimmer than Lucifer's, and Kaito confirmed he'd witnessed when Lust's flame dimmed.

Were the flames connected to the princes' life forces?

We weren't sure, and as it wasn't my job to figure that out, I got on with scouting, flying over the structure, looking for weaknesses.

There were few. Not that I'd expect anything less from Wrath.

A courtyard, like the one in LA, was wide open. I might be able to smoke-travel us in there. Secondly, there was an entrance that might be for servants, judging by the appearance of those coming in and out. That was it. Two entrances. I found no others during my search, which, due to the constraints of the invisibility potion, was limited to an hour.

I watched the clock as I studied the landscape, but it slipped away. At five till the hour, I needed to leave, or risk being spotted.

I prepared to soar upward, back to the home I'd warded and draw a map, when I saw them.

Raphael Laurent, Tobias's brother, and Nicoleta, my younger sister, walking out of the rubble of the city and back to the castle.

A flash of need to swoop down and grab Nicoleta, to take her away from all of this, flared within me. But Shay's face filtered into my mind, stopping me.

My mother thought my sister was lost. And Nicoleta hated Shay, my mate—the most important person to me in the world.

Though it made my heart hurt, I twisted to soar away, to leave Nic to her chosen fate, but of course I couldn't help sparing a last glance.

I nearly fell out of the sky when I found my sister staring up at the sky, staring right *at me*, as if she felt something.

CHAPTER THIRTY-FIVE

SHAY

THE MOON SHONE DOWN ON US AS HANS PULLED ME CLOSER TO him. With Luca in the lead, the *Vindix* and select S&S members wove our way through the military base just outside the magical dome that surrounded Washington DC. *Thousands* of soldiers strode about the camp, ready to make their move. I suspected if Hans had it his way, my mate would carry me, curling his large black wings around me so those same thousands of soldiers waiting for battle could not see me.

Since our mating bond had snapped into place, he'd become increasingly protective over me. Though I considered myself a feminist, I relished his care. It was pretty freaking hot.

Plus, I felt our bond too, and was just as protective over Hans. Wanted him biblically all the time too. That had never been more evident than last night when we'd spent hours making love.

Thank the Heavens Luca had given us his office.

Given that death loomed in the shape of a black, sparkling dome of demon magic, I wished we had more time to do it again and again and again.

"Shay, I can sense you getting turned on." My mate's hand fell to my ass, and the tension in his fingers, the want, sent a shiver up my spine. "If you don't stop, I'm going to steal a tent from one of these poor saps and embarrass us all."

Hans's words sounded more like a promise than a threat, and yet, I pulled myself together. Luca would be super pissed if we disappeared to screw. We would enter Wrath's territory within the hour. Distractions, no matter how pleasant, needed to be eliminated.

"Sorry. I'll turn down the filthy thoughts." I beamed at Hans, who looked like he regretted what he'd said. And yet, instead of jumping each other's bones again, we acted like total suckers and continued to follow Luca to General McNair's tent.

The general and Luca had been in talks all morning, and those talks had only grown more frantic when McNair informed us that the dome had expanded five feet in all directions. The princes were, as Lilith said, making moves, but before we entered the dark kingdom, McNair still wished to see us all and pair us up with select special forces members. Those military personnel would venture into the dome with us.

Truthfully, though they were trained in the art of war, I wasn't sure they'd be anything more than a liability. None of them had ever fought against magical beings.

I thought of the vast green yard and the big white house sitting on it. According to Hans, it was rubble now, crushed by a black castle topped with scary spires.

We reached the tent, large enough for at least thirty people. Luca ushered the *Vindix* inside along with their mates. Serena too, but everyone else waited outside. Anything of importance would be relayed to them if they couldn't use their supernatural hearing to eavesdrop like Gunner instructed his pack to do.

"Luca." General McNair, in a military uniform, stood from behind a large table covered in maps and battle plans. He peered behind the coven master, taking in the rest of us. "These are the witches who need to enter DC? I thought you said there were seven."

"Not all witches. Not all are Vindix."

"Is it wise to include so many in military plans?"

"Their mates are among them, and you don't separate mates. Not if you value your head on your neck." Luca gave a charming smile that offset the violent truth of what he said.

General McNair's lips flattened. "Very well then. I recognize some of you. Might I get a rundown on the rest?

Luca did the honors, introducing the *Vindix* to the general, who in turn offered two soldiers to protect every one of them. It went this way until it was Meredith's turn.

Tobias held up a hand. "I am all that she needs, but my sister is offering to assist as well."

Not to mention Rooms had a pistol. As the *Vindix* most concerned with protecting others, we wanted her to use her magic to keep the sin from invading us, rather than fighting. So my witchy sis got a gun.

Gunner stepped forward. "Me and my pack have Harper's back."

McNair arched an eyebrow but must have sensed that arguing was not worth it. When he turned to Hans, the last *Vindix* in line, Hans smirked.

"I'll be fine."

"That one is your protector?" McNair cut a doubtful glance my way.

"She is," Hans said matter-of-factly. "But I have a wide

range of powers that make me doubt anyone will get close to me."

"Which is?"

"I can torture people with a thought."

The general's face blanched.

"We have coven members and me as well," Luca added, trying to soften Hans's words. "So thank you for the soldiers, General, but that's enough. Anymore, and Hans might have trouble transporting. Or Meredith will not be able to keep us all covered, safe from Prince Orien's sin floating about inside the dome."

What he didn't say was that the humans might also get in the way. Luca was walking a fine line here. He knew better than to deny the general's help. Relations between humans and magical people were good now, but later? When this was over? Who knew how they'd turn? Especially if we did not allow them to help reclaim our world.

I suspected Luca included the soldiers to enhance a sense of camaraderie, but he was right. No matter how trained they were, the soldiers knew nothing of our world. Of magic and the horrors it beheld. We'd learn how they'd react inside the dome.

The general nodded. "They're outfitted with comms, so we'll be in communications—"

"They won't work in there," Hans interrupted, his tone gruff. I had a feeling that they might have gone over that before, and he was over the general ignoring the importance of magic in this scenario.

"These are the top-of-the-line comms." McNair's eyes narrowed.

"They're permitted to wear them," Luca interjected, "but

like Hans said, electronics don't work inside the princes' king-doms. Not the ones we've been in anyway."

McNair let out a low breath but nodded. Not appeased, but clearly not going to fight it any longer.

"Did any of you fight demons or their allies after the libera-tion of New Orleans or Venice?" Luca asked the eight soldiers who would accompany us.

None of them had, but four had shot winged demons outside of DC's dome, so they'd at least seen the creatures.

Maybe they'll survive.

We went over a few more last-minute details, preparing the general for when the barrier fell—if it did.

"We'll be going then." Luca shook hands with the general.

We left the tent and joined those outside. Luca looked at them.

"I listened," Lisha spoke for the group as Benedict wove around her feet, on edge, "and relayed the important informa-tion to those going with us. No need to reiterate."

"Everyone knows what to do," Artem agreed. He was among one of the Covenant Seats who would join us. Cuan O'Malley for the wolves, Susan Chappel for the witches, Nina Tyche for the phoenixes, were also coming with.

"Good," Luca said, and we made our way to the spot cleared for us—a large area in the middle of the army camp. One warded and cleared and covered in an illusion the previous day so that if anyone was watching from inside the dome, they wouldn't see us gathering. Instead, they saw static tents. No one would see us coming.

"You're clear on where we land?" Luca asked Hans.

My mate's jaw was set in a hard line. "I've prepared the site."

"Meredith, you're certain you can protect so many?" Luca asked, clearly going through his last-minute checklist.

"I'm sure," Meredith replied, not a speck of hesitation in her voice. In the carrier she wore, Benny's eyes glowed amber. Rooms hadn't wanted her familiar to join us in battle, but Benny had been adamant. So he was stuck in the carrier until we got inside DC.

"Good." Luca sighed. "And Artem, you're sure the Covenant has people stationed outside the city too? We don't know everything regarding what's inside."

Demons certainly, but they weren't the only creatures that called Hell home. The hounds we'd seen in New York would likely be the least of our worries once inside.

"All around the dome. Seats are helping organize magical armies." Artem replied.

My mother was one of those Seats helping to organize fighters in other areas. I couldn't say that was her forte, but with me going inside Wrath's kingdom, there had been no talking her out of it.

Luca nodded, apparently out of questions as we reached the launch point, ready to smoke-travel.

Hans held up his hand. "For those who have not done this, smoke-traveling can be disorienting. But I have you, and we will wait to move until every one of us has our bearing." He looked at the humans, though they weren't the only ones we were concerned about. Many S&S and Covenant members had light-traveled but not done so by smoke.

At least they're kinda similar. I grabbed Hans's hand, which wasn't necessary. Physical touch was needed when one used luxiters, but not smoke or light-travel. Still, it made me feel better to touch him. That we were together in this, our hearts still beating.

We assembled, and Hans's smoke billowed out like a million black, formless spiders, covering the ground, our knees, our hips and then—darkness took my vision.

I held my breath. Smoke-travel had always been uncomfortable for me, but now it was less so. Not just from experience, either. Now that our mate bond had snapped into place, Hans's demon magic had less of an effect on me. Same with my angel magic upon him. It was like the bond smoothed over what should have been insurmountable differences.

Hans squeezed my hand, a sign that we were about to land. I prepared my wings, spreading them for balance, and released him, both of us aware we might need to catch someone less accustomed to traveling in this manner. As the smoke cleared, Artem lunged, and as he was close, I saved him from falling flat on his face. I heard others, the humans, being saved too.

"Many thanks," Artem said with a wince.

I suspected that he, like me, was feeling the effects of the sin in the air. A nudge of anger tried to burrow inside me. I ignored it, knowing that Meredith and the Opal would allow no such thing. "Similar to the luxiter, but I'm still not great at using those."

"Some people never get it. Meredith, for example."

"I heard that," Meredith muttered as her magic took hold, covering us and keeping the sin that was in the air away before it rooted deep within. "Don't talk about me, Shay. I'm working."

I shut my trap, knowing that even with her morning of practice against Serena, Tobias, Lisha, and any other vampire who had the time to help Meredith strengthen her powers, the sheer number of people here would stretch Rooms's talents.

And it was a good thing that I did. If I'd been yapping, I wouldn't have heard the click of talons above. My heart jumped into my throat, and I looked up to find five winged demons descending, bows drawn. Arrows loosed.

Two pierced through human soldiers. They fell, and another arrow hit Cuan O'Malley, wolf shifter Covenant Seat, through the eye.

I bent my knees to launch into the air when Hans pushed me aside. The *thwack* of a fourth arrow hitting cement and splintering racketed my heart rate ever higher. I'd almost joined Cuan and the humans. Heavens, they had to have been waiting for us.

"Air team!" Luca hollered, my cue.

I launched into the sky alongside Hans and Nina Tyche. Below, Rabi took hold of the winds, blowing the demons off course as Kaito shot torrents of water that could rival small rivers at the devils.

One fell to the ground and died seconds later. I blasted light at the one closest to me, well aware that a third was still drawing arrows, shooting below.

Please don't hit the Vindix. No one knew what would happen if one of the fated fell. I didn't want to find out.

But I couldn't focus on that as the demon I was up against struggled out of Rabi's grasp, regained control, and aimed his weapon at me.

Too slow, though. I'd already sent a second blast of light at him. That time, I hit dead center. The angelic light ate through him, riddling holes in his leathery skin. The devil shrieked as he fell to the ground.

"Get his weapon!" I spun, ready to take on another but discovered there was no need. We had already taken the other three demons down—with the help of Rabi and Kaito.

Still, we hovered above, scanning the area, the surrounding

buildings. Hans had landed us where he'd meant to, three blocks from the White House.

From where I flew, I could see the iconic building no longer existed. Instead, a black castle, so similar to the ones we'd seen in LA and New Orleans, rose. A flame burned in a tower.

"Clear," I said, not spotting another demon.

The others echoed me, and we descended. As I neared the ground, my mouth went dry. A third human had been hit, leaving us with five special force soldiers. Cuan was dead. As was Susan Chappel.

"They were waiting for us," Meredith said when Hans and I landed next to her. "They found your protections and disabled them and waited."

Hans's eyes narrowed to slits. "Correct. We have to proceed with extreme caution toward the castle."

"They wore armor," Luca added. "Green leathers. That color represents Envy, and if each prince now has forces out here, that could make things far more difficult."

"Should we split?" Meredith asked. "We can sense one another."

"No," Hans retorted more forcefully than he normally would. "*Vindix* stay together. The diversion squad should help us get there."

I swallowed, hating that he was right, that this was the best move. It put others in immense danger.

They knew that coming in, though. I—

Growling hit my ear, and I turned to find blazing red eyes and elongated canines round the corner. A pack of at least fifty.

"Hellhounds," I whispered, my voice trembling. "Everyone run!"

CHAPTER THIRTY-SIX

GUNNER

WE SPRINTED AWAY FROM THE HELLHOUNDS, ONLY SHAY, HANS, and the fire-winged Nina Tyche flying above, doin' their best to cull the pack of beasts at our heels. Though the alpha in me wanted to protect, to stop the beasts chasin' us, I darn well knew my limits.

Those things were *enormous*, at least double my size as a wolf, and their teeth were filled with poison. One bite and any of us were done for.

Fifty of 'em, I thought, casting a glance at Harper before makin' sure my pack was right behind us. How were we gonna get rid of 'em?

"They're too agile!" Nina yelled. "We've only hit two! We need to stop them! Trap them!"

"Harper!" Meredith screamed. "Shield the street!"

My eyes widened. Now that was an idea, though had Harp made a ghost shield that large?

"Any warders?" Harper shouted back, her arms pumping at her sides as we ran with all that we had. "To help divert them? Or slow them while I work?"

I winced at how loud she was. Any other day, I'd relish my mate being all loud and authoritative, but we were supposed to be quiet. Stealth gave the other squad a chance to implement the diversion at a safe distance from us. We'd also be able to sneak into the castle more easily.

We're blowin' that now.

Then again, the hellhounds weren't bein' quiet either with all their howlin' and growlin' and gruntin'. I could only hope something big was happenin' at the castle. Somethin' to keep the royals busy.

"Warder here!" a witch somewhere behind me yelled. The lady already sounded winded, which I wasn't sure boded well for her doin' magic on the fly. "What do you want me to do?"

"I don't know! Slow them down!" My mate tossed a look over her shoulder and those pretty eyes widened. "They're gaining."

"We need to split into our teams!" Luca shouted. "We're making too much noise! And it will split the hounds."

"At the intersection!" Artem, the leader of the diversion squad, shouted back. "The other warder is with us. You have Harper. Go at least a block before shielding!"

Harper sucked in a breath. My poor chica, this was all gonna be on her.

"You got this," I growled loud enough so that only she could hear me.

Luca leapt over a fallen street post. "At the next intersection."

My stomach tightened as we neared the splitting point. I was with my mate, my pack, the *Vindix,* and S&S. The remainin' humans would come with us too, as well as Seats from the phoenix and vampire orders.

Powerful groups, both of them. Too bad now that we were

here, now that we were doin' the thing, it didn't seem like enough.

The turn off was fast approachin', and my ears told me that the hellhounds were gainin'. I wasn't sure we'd get too far before Harper had to initiate a shield.

"Can I help?" I asked her.

"Watch my back. Let me concentrate. I'm calling right now, but I'm going to need a lot of spirits to block an entire street." She gasped, tryin' to catch her breath after explainin' so much.

I shut up. Let her breathe and think and work. My she-wolf was amazin', and I wouldn't be the one to stand in the way of her greatness.

"Ready!" Luca yelled. "Veer to your sides!"

Everyone runnin' did, and I tried not to notice the sheer terror in so many eyes. This was crazy, and we hadn't even gotten to the castle yet.

The turn came hard and fast. I ran to the right, makin' sure my mate was beside me. When we cleared the turn, Luca spun and shot a barrage of power behind him. It went off like fireworks, streamin' and explodin'.

He had to have bought us a few seconds. Guessin' that the diversion squad hadn't been so quick thinkin', I sent a prayer up to the Old Ones to watch over them. They were the most vulnerable out of our two teams.

That was what I thought, at least until a female screamed. A shout for help.

I recognized that voice.

"No!" a man bellowed.

My stomach fell to my knees as I twisted and watched Farrah scrambling back up. Somehow, against all odds, 'cause wolves had amazin' agility, she'd fallen. Worse, her man Rubin had turned to help her, only to find the hellhounds were upon both of 'em.

They sprinted, gave it all they had, but neither were fast enough, and I had to watch as two hellhounds leapt on each of 'em and tore their limbs off their bodies. Tears pricked my eyes as one hellhound latched onto Farrah's neck, endin' her life in a second.

Close by me, Jolie let out a garbled sound. She'd seen Farrah's death too.

"Gunner! Don't look!" Harper wheezed, bringin' me back to her—to this moment.

They were my pack. No matter how little time I'd known them, Farrah and Rubin had bound themselves to me, and I couldn't even try to save them. Not without goin' to my death.

Not without leavin' my mate, cleavin' her soul in half right when she needed support the most.

So, though it killed me to do so, I faced forward, knowin', just missin' when Rubin let out a garbled scream.

"The plan worked!" Nina Tyche yelled. She, Hans, and Shay flew with our group, each of 'em shooting fire, spells, and light behind us. "They split. Twenty are with us!"

"Harper!" Hans cried out. "When? We'll be ready to attack!"

"Give me one more minute!" my mate gasped for air as she replied. "They're coming."

The moment she said it, I saw 'em. Ghosts streamin' above us. There musta been at least a hundred and Harper needed more?

Another scream behind us felt like a knife to the gut. I didn't need to turn to know who it was. The blood must have sprayed, and I caught the scent in the air. Another human soldier was gone. Not one of mine, but after my failures to protect my pack, it still hurt. Someone that I normally coulda protected.

"Okay!" Harper gasped. "I'm ready. I need to stop to make the shield, and I need a second, so everyone attack."

"Say when!" the mage replied.

"On three!" My mate counted down, and we spun on the pack of monsters. Those who had magic blasted it off. My remainin' wolves and I shifted—prepared to defend with teeth if one hellhound got through.

But my clever mate was right. She needed only seconds, and the magic workers had done well, slammin' another ten hounds down. By the time five leapt to their feet again, the spirit shield was in place.

Gleaming white, it stretched across the entire road. The monsters threw themselves against the barrier. I doubted they were used to being stopped, but Harper's magic held strong.

"I can take them from above," Hans said, his chest rising and falling rapidly.

"No, you rest. Allow me." The phoenix spread her fiery wings and soared above the shield, where she began rainin' blue fire down on the hounds. The buggers were fast, but not as fast as her many fire missiles.

"How terrifying," Tana whispered.

I swallowed as I caught Jolie cryin' not far away. Another pack member comforted her and though I wanted to be there for them, I did my best to push the memory of what I'd seen from my mind. I'd mourn Rubin and Farrah and everyone we lost later, but right now, I needed to keep my head on straight. Otherwise, I could lose a hell of a lot more. "I wish I could say that can't happen again, but I know better. This place is gonna be full of surprises."

"More like horrors," Rabi panted. Out of all the *Vindix*, he was the most out of shape. Blood slaves didn't need to be on an exercise routine.

Nina fired off her last missile, and the final hellhound fell.

"Nina," Hans called, "can you estimate the blocks from the castle while you're up there?"

"There are four blocks. Well, four and half," Nina replied and turned in the air, graceful as a swan in the water. "And then I—oh shi—"

The phoenix exploded. A gasp flew up from the crowd and once again, everyone was on alert, searchin' for the threat. A stinkin' blast of sulfur filled my nostrils right before they appeared.

Two devils, twenty feet from us, with a pack of wolves and other people who might be human or other behind them.

I hadn't seen these two before, but judgin' by the power rollin' off them, their big black bat-like wings, and those horns, one of whose towered at least two feet high, these had to be Princes of Hell.

"I must admit, I expected Orien's prize dogs to last longer." The prince with the straight, towerin' horns brushed an invisible piece of lint off his dark green tunic, as if unimpressed. "Perhaps Lucifer's pups will do better?"

"To be determined," the other wore dark yellow robes of silk and loads of gold jewelry. The color matched his eyes and his eerie gaze devoured everythin' in its path, as if he couldn't get enough of what he saw.

What the hell?

Rhianna sneered. "Stealing your brother's things, you pieces of trash?"

The girl had already been captured by a Royal of Hell and no doubt she had balls, but she was too important to garner notice like that. Luca seemed to think the same and put his body in front of Rhianna.

"When I covet something, I take it," the prince, wearing a dark green tunic, replied with a shrug. "It's in my nature. Both of ours, though the roots differ."

"Covet," Hans murmured, his attention ping-pongin' between the two as he took them both in. "You must be Envy. And . . . Greed."

Ah, right. The colors.

The prince in green, Envy, or more formally known as Prince Levi, revealed teeth as sharp as Toby's fangs. "Correct, Lilith's spawn."

"Why are you here? Just the two of you?" Hans's eyes narrowed, as if realizin' maybe the devils weren't alone. They'd appeared outta nowhere, after all. Were the others hiding?

That felt out of their nature, though. Especially Pride and Wrath. I didn't think those two would hide from us. Nah, they'd come at us, guns blazin'.

"For once, *we* want the glory. We *crave* it, so we took what we wanted from our brothers to make it happen." Prince Mon, also known as Greed, forced a pout and gestured to the charred hellhounds behind us. "So far, we've failed, but I think that won't happen a second time." The prince lifted a hand, loosed a whistle.

The wolves beside him parted, and a big one with gleaming red eyes prowled from the crowd.

Harper's knees buckled, and I caught her before she hit the ground.

"Chica? What is it?"

"Gunner, that's my father."

CHAPTER THIRTY-SEVEN

HARPER

MY BLOOD POUNDED IN MY EARS, ELIMINATING ALL OTHER sounds. This had to be an illusion. A nightmare.

Father was on the West Coast, trapped under Lucifer's thumb, yes, but still. Far, far away. Not here.

But then a mind-link pressed against my head, someone trying to connect with me. Only an alpha held the power to initiate such a link when a pack member was in human form and the alpha in wolf form. My stomach fell to my knees.

Dad, I whispered in my mind, trying to put on a brave front. Failing, probably.

Like you failed at being alpha apparent. Like you failed your dad. Your mom. Tears sprung into my eyes. Since arriving at the *Abscondita* manor, I'd rarely had a moment to dwell on my many failures, and I'd been thankful for that. Now, though, they came rushing back. Filled me with nearly as much dread as the scene in front of me.

Dad, can you hear me?

His eyes blazed red as he prowled forward, but for a moment, no more than two seconds, they dimmed. He was fighting the possession, trying to reach me. His push into my mind would have been stronger if he controlled his own thoughts.

Dad, you can do it. Please, speak to me. I stepped forward and heard Gunner tell me not to go closer to my father. I didn't listen.

Gunner would understand. If this was his pa, he'd get it, and my mate would do the same thing. He'd fight for his pa to come back. He'd—

"Meredith, help him."

"I—I've been trying," my friend replied, her voice strained. "The possession is powerful."

"Our brother's sway is *unbreakable*, witch," Greed drawled.

"Yes, useful now, though normally, it can be quite annoying," Prince Levi, known as the Leviathan in the most ancient of texts, added.

The pair had stayed back, happy to let others do their work of destroying us—no, destroying *me*, from the inside out.

But I wouldn't let them. I might have failed so many times, but I was not weak, and if there was one thing Harper Mace Ferenz excelled at, it was learning. I'd excelled at sparring as a pup, excelled at Yale, and most recently excelled at harnessing my new magic. I could do this. I'd pull my father through. So, I ignored the princes and focused on the alpha wolf in front of me. "Try again, Mer."

A wave of warming magic that I recognized as Meredith's washed over me anew. My breath clung in my chest, and I kept my eyes on my father. That red dimmed as he pushed on the mind-link again. This time, I opened my mind.

Dad?

Harper, my father sounded exhausted, beaten down. Not like himself at all.

Fight it, Dad. Please. We're here now, we can beat them.

Kill me.

The elation coursing through me at this one small win fizzled.

Dad, you can't be serious.

Do it, Harper. You must. Under their control, I've done horrible things. I don't deserve to live, don't deserve to lead. Please, it would be a mercy.

I swallowed. My father could count on me for anything. Anything but this.

I can't. Dad, where's Mom?

She's alive. She—the red blazed back into his eyes, and my breath hitched as my father leapt for me.

"Meredith!" I shrieked.

"Trying!"

"Get away from her!" Gunner roared, placing himself in front of me and shifting.

"Don't hurt him, Gunner!" I shouted, all the while trying to contact my father again. To break through.

The two alphas met in the air with their teeth bared. I winced as my father sank his teeth into my mate, then vice versa. Though Gunner was of the wolvea, with Dad being possessed by a god of the underworld, they appeared matched.

They'd tear each other to shreds. Or, more likely, my father would tear into Gunner because my mate would be more care-ful. He didn't want to hurt someone I loved, not unless neces-sary. I couldn't have that, but I wasn't a real match for either of them in wolf form. So, I called ghosts as I tried to reach my father again, tried to talk sense into him.

Under the commotion, the princes gave the signal. Their

wolves ran for us, and those on my side shouted and cursed as they spread out, ready for battle.

Tobias placed his body in front of Meredith's, for she had to be protected at all costs. Meredith was the weakest fighter in our group, but also the only one keeping us from succumbing to the sin in the air. Or maybe *sins*, I wasn't sure, as she'd done such a good job of keeping our minds and bodies as our own.

If only she pushed a little harder, I thought, as I tried again and again to reach my father and failed. Thankfully, that wasn't the only trick up my sleeve. The ghosts had arrived. I pointed to the pair, my blood and my mate.

"Don't let them hurt one another.

The ghosts soared between Gunner and Dad and created an impenetrable shield not even the strongest of wolves could break. They were safe.

I realized my mistake an instant too late, when my father turned to me. He was closer to me now, not Gunner. I barely had time to shield myself before Dad was upon me, eyes blazing like rubies.

Dad! Stop! This isn't you!

Tears streamed down my face. Others fought all around us, and I'd penned Gunner in with a ghost shield, protecting him. I wouldn't release him either. If it was me or my father, he'd kill Dad to save me. No one got between a wolf and their mate.

The evil gleam in Dad's eyes dimmed again. Meredith had gotten through.

Kill me! Dad commanded; his alpha tone powerful. *Do it. Let your mate kill me if you won't!*

"I can't!" I wailed.

You must! I can't control myself for long. They're telling me to end you. Please Harper.

An impact struck my father, and he fell to the side. As he

hit the street, the red disappeared from his eyes, leaving them flat and lifeless. For a moment, I thought he was back, but then I saw the spear piercing straight through him, the tip obsidian, with a sheen of green magic. Blood pooled beneath my father, his chest still. Dead. He was dead. There one second, gone the next.

Body vibrating, I fought the urge to go to him, and instead, searched for the killer. All around, others battled, but my target wasn't difficult to discover.

Twenty feet away, still keeping his distance like a coward, Envy, clad in dark green, watched me with disdain. "I have no need for a servant who cannot listen. Even a borrowed one. I might have done Lucifer a favor, culling his weak."

"You bastard!" I summoned spirits with all that I had, and an onslaught replied. In a blink, ghosts surrounded me.

Envy's green eyes widened, and it took a moment before I pushed past my own emotions enough to place his. Fear.

A Prince of the Underworld *feared me.*

As he should. I flung my hands out, and the spirits followed my unspoken directive, racing for the prince, shredding through him.

He cried out in pain. I hadn't known that ghosts could harm him. They never harmed me or anyone around me, but I realized how stupid that correlation was. The princes weren't human or anything like the demons and hellblooded in this world. They were their own race—different from everything but one another. The brothers who'd ruled the underworld for millions of years were both closer and farther away from death. And while I hadn't killed him, I could weaken him, that much was plain by the visible graying of his skin.

"Hans!" I yelled, pushing the ghosts through the prince. "Help!"

Faster than I would have expected, Hans dropped from the sky. Blood dotted cheekbones, and his jaw was set tight as he began to help me pummel the prince with his demon magic.

Against our powers combined, Prince Levi doubled over, but didn't die. He might not be the most powerful of his brothers, he'd said as much, but they were made of stronger stuff.

Not indestructible though. No one was. Not even a god.

"Someone take his head!" I pummeled the prince again and again and again, never letting up, disarming him. With each attack, Envy weakened, but he remained standing, those green eyes burning at us, promising vengeance.

A promise he'd never keep, as Serena, wielding a sword she got from the Old Ones only knew where, flew at Prince Levi and severed his head from his neck in one clean blow.

The head flew, landing at my feet, eyes up, staring sightlessly.

I spit on the prince's face. "We're going to finish all of you. I swear it."

"Harper," Hans gasped. "We need to help the others."

I twisted, understanding what Hans meant right away. The other five *Vindix* were ganging up on Greed, who looked grayer and weaker than minutes before.

I blinked, recalling Lilith's words. Was Prince Mon weaker after Envy's death?

Though I was dying to know the answer, I wasn't sure it mattered too much. The prince still fought like a fiend, whipping and whirling with magic the likes of which I'd only seen come from Hans. And he didn't just use his own powers. Most of the wolves surrounded Greed, their teeth bloodied.

One glance told me the *Vindix* were fine. Protected at all costs. But we'd lost the rest of the human escorts and one more from Gunner's pack. They'd trimmed our forces, whereas we'd only killed three wolves.

Three wolves and a prince, I corrected. *Time to even the odds.*

"Harp!" Gunner screamed as Hans battled with the others, leaving me the only *Vindix* out. "Let me help!"

Though I wanted to keep him safe behind my shield of spirits, I'd be an idiot not to use Gunner's strength. But that didn't mean I had to make it likely that he'd fight.

I released the ghosts shielding my mate and directed them at the prince. They tore through him like the other spirits had ripped through Envy.

Again, I noted the spirits weakened the prince. Why that happened, I did not know, but I was pleased to the moon that I had another weapon at my disposal. One that the others were taking full advantage of.

Tana engulfed the prince in flames as Rhianna wound a lasso of vines around his neck and squeezed.

Vines weren't a sword, but when wielded by the strongest earth witch in the world, they were darn close. Greed's face turned red as he fought for air, for life. But Rhianna bore down against that iron will and pushed her magic so hard that her knees buckled. Behind her, Luca caught the earth elemental. She thrust her hand out, and brilliant verdant magic flew from her. The vines cinch so tightly that Greed's head separated from his neck.

The head fell to the ground to land in a puddle of blood and above, I caught the flame in Wrath's castle dim. Had he seen it too? Did he know that two more of his brothers were gone?

The questions disappeared as it became clear that while we'd beaten two princes, we weren't out of the woods yet. The wolves followed all the prince's commands, but it seemed they were controlled by another. Lucifer was my guess. Their eyes still gleamed red and though they'd frozen at the death of Greed, now they turned on us.

"Cage them!" I yelled. "Don't kill them!"

I had to believe these wolves were innocent. Even if they'd done terrible things, like my father had said, it had to be on the word of the princes. Until I heard for sure, I couldn't see them die too.

"Luca, please!" Just thinking about my father sent a sob up my throat, choking my words.

"On it." Magic whipped from the mage's hands, filling the air. Tana blasted fire at five approaching wolves, sending them running back, helping to corral them.

"Get them closer together," Luca instructed. "I'm ready!"

The *Vindix* leapt into action, working as one to create a cage using our gifts. When the last wolf backed up against the others, a cage materialized around them.

"Thank you," I said, and went to my father's body.

CHAPTER THIRTY-EIGHT

GUNNER

My mate fell to her knees before her father. While every instinct told me to join her, to comfort her, if that were even possible, I waited.

She needed a moment with her alpha, her father. A moment to say goodbye the right way. She wouldn't be able to grieve the way she deserved. Not now. She had seconds—minutes, at best.

So I placed myself in front of Harper, in case others weren't on the same wavelength as me, and scanned the area.

Luca had caged the surviving wolves. There had to be at least sixty of 'em, still growlin' and barkin'. Thank the Old Ones my clever mate had come up with that idea. I couldn't bear it if more wolves died, even those who weren't in my pack.

My pack.

Like when I'd seen them fall, the pain barreled through me again. Two more had died fightin' Greed. Four in total. At this rate, by the end of the day, I wouldn't have a pack.

I had to be the worst alpha in existence.

As if she sensed my pain, Jolie appeared at my side. "You're injured."

"It's fine." I spared a glance down at the gash along my right tricep, given to me by Mace Ferenz. "Nothin' to what others got."

"No, but they're dead, and we're not. We have to keep fighting." She jerked her head to where Harper was still cryin' over her dad. Though I tried to give her privacy, I heard my mate's whispered promises to her father.

The woman carried the weight of the world on her shoulders.

"She needs you," Jolie added. "Needs you to be strong."

"Don't tell me what she needs and what she doesn't." My tone was snappish, and Jolie reared back. Immediately, my stomach twisted. The woman was tryin' to help. More than that, she was right.

"We got a healer 'round here?" I added, softer this time.

Hannah stayed back at the human base, waiting for those with the worst injuries—those seconds from death—to be brought back. Many other healers, magical and otherwise, were at the magical camp waiting.

"We had a medic. One of the humans, but they're all dead now," Jolie swallowed. "Serena and Tobias are offering blood."

I inhaled. Vampires didn't do that lightly, and my kind, the wolvea especially, didn't accept it lightly either. Though, I'd done so before and this time was more important.

"Get Serena for me?"

"You got it, alpha. I'll be right back." She left, but Hans took her spot right away.

"I'm taking those with the worst injuries and the dead back to base," he said. "We can't leave them here. I can't."

I agreed, and I understood why he approached me and not

my mate. "I'll tell her. I'm sure she'll want to take her pa away from all this."

Hans nodded. "I'll get Harper's dad last. Give her as much time as possible."

"Appreciate it."

"Also, people are moving in there while we regroup," Hans pointed to where Luca ushered people into a nearby building. An old museum, or somethin' like it. "If she'll let you move her dad in there, I'd go. It's safer. Less out in the open."

Safer. What a freakin' joke. Until we killed the last three princes, safety didn't exist. And even then, this world had a hell of a lot of healin' to do.

Still, Hans was tryin' to help and be as expeditious as possible 'bout it.

"Thanks man." I held up a hand. "Go do your thing."

He'd no sooner left than Serena arrived. She offered her arm. Silently, I brought it to my lips and took three drags of vampire blood.

"That's enough," she said. "Your healing abilities will take care of the rest. And I think your mate needs you now."

I twisted to find Harper watchin' us, her beautiful eyes ringed red.

"Gunner," her little croak broke my heart in half. "*Hold me.*"

I went to her, dropped to my knees, and pulled her close. Harper pressed her face into my chest and soon enough, my shirt dampened with her tears.

I didn't say a peep though, just let her work through it. Let her feel. Soon enough, she'd have to be on the move again, but until that moment, I'd shelter my she-wolf with my body, heart, and soul.

People disappeared into the buildin', hidin', finishin'

healing fast as heck thanks to the vampire blood. None of the *Vindix* approached us, and I got a feelin' Stoney and Shay told 'em not to. Smart women, all of 'em.

While she cried, I stole glances at her pa. I wasn't mind linked with him, but even I could tell he'd been fightin' some sort of order. Probably one to kill his daughter.

It felt like forever but wasn't more than a few minutes before my mate lifted her head. She looked me in the eye. "What did Hans say?"

"You saw that?"

"I see everything."

Any other day, I would have joked that she was fancying herself a goddess, and that was my job. But not today. "He's taking the injured and dead back to base. Wants to move your pa, if that's what you want."

Harper looked down and to the side of us where her father lay. "Yes. He can't stay here in this nightmare."

"I was hoping you'd say that." Hans appeared right in front of us in a billow of smoke. "I can take him back to the base, if you're ready?"

Harper swallowed. "I'll see you again, Dad. I love you." She released me and bent over to kiss her pa on his furry head.

I helped Hans with the body, lifting the alpha wolf and situating him so that Hans didn't topple.

"They'll take the spear out too," Hans said. "Do you want a witch to shift him to human?"

"Yes," Harper said.

It was a rare, specialized talent, and I was thankful some witches possessed the power to do it, and we had one here.

"See you soon." Hans disappeared again.

"Let's get in there." I pointed to the buildin' the others had disappeared into. Luca watched us, along with a few others, lookin' for enemies that might sneak up on us. "We'll be less out in the open."

Harper allowed me to support her as we made our way to the building. We were halfway there when the sky lit up with magical fireworks. Ten blocks away.

I sucked in a breath. The diversion team had beaten off the hellhounds, and our plan was underway. They were tryin' to catch the attention of the prince's armies.

"Hurry," I said as a sound arose from the castle and winged demons took to the skies.

We ran the rest of the way, and Luca shut the door after us, sealin' it with a ward. Meredith and Shay were waitin' close by, their eyes wet with tears.

Harper didn't say a thing. She stumbled over to her friends, and they held their arms open to her. I watched as the three women comforted one another as they dropped to the ground to better cover Harper with love and, most shockin' of all, Benedict joined them.

The cat sat right in front of my mate, bowin' his black furry head. "We aren't always on the best of terms, but I am sorry for your loss, Harper."

My mate sniffed as she took in the cat. "Thanks fleabag."

The cat's tail twitched, but he said nothing as he lay down right in front of her. A cat and a wolf, as if they were the best of friends.

The sounds of risin' armies outside made me hope such a thing could happen, and that it could happen real quick because in here, everyone needed to have each other's backs or none of us would survive.

CHAPTER THIRTY-NINE

MEREDITH

Ten minutes. Fifteen tops to pull ourselves together after killing Envy and Greed. That wasn't enough time for *anything*. Not for Harper to grieve. Nor for me to come to terms with the fact that I'd failed one of my best friends.

I hadn't been able to completely lift the possession over Harper's father, and he'd died, still in Lucifer's grasp. I hated myself for failing Harper, and though I wouldn't say out loud that I was the reason her dad died, the thought was still stuck in my head. It was an anguish I'd have to live with for the rest of my life.

So no, we hadn't had enough time to deal with the trauma we'd gone through, but with the diversion well underway, we had to move. The fighters led by Artem were giving us the best chance to enter Wrath's castle. We couldn't allow their sacrifice —because there was no way in hell everyone would get out of this alive, maybe not even us—to be in vain.

I wrestled with that possible fate as we waited for Hans, listening to the sounds of the city. Quieter before the diversion team set off the fireworks, the night was now filled with screeches and screams and gunshots. Once, I thought I heard a bark that was so loud, it couldn't have come from a hellhound or wolf. Thanks to Kaito seeing a water serpent in Venice, we knew that monsters had come over from Hell along with demons. Had that been a cerberus? Goddess, I hoped not.

Hans reappeared from transporting the last dead and seriously injured back to the human camp, and we quickly gathered around him.

"Ready?" Hans looked at Harper when he asked.

She drew in a long breath. Her eyes gleamed red and puffy, but the wolf-witch had regained her composure in a way that I'd never be able to mimic. Goddess, she was a tough one.

"The sooner we kill them all, the better."

Smoke curled upwards all around our squad, much smaller than before. Fewer than twenty people when we'd started with over forty fighters. Goddess, we'd already lost too much.

Before I could let another negative thought claim my mind, darkness sucked us in, transporting us to the castle.

Within the smoke, my hand was on the gun, given to me by a soldier back at the base—a small pistol. I wasn't too keen on shooting it, and not because I wasn't an excellent shot. Working for the Ringmaster, I'd shot a gun many times. However, with so many allies around, I worried that when things got hectic, someone would get in my shot.

Still, I gripped the cold metal tight. Hans was aiming for the servant's entrance and seeing as Hans's smoke trailing abilities had only gotten better, I was sure we'd touch down where he intended. If demons milled in the area, I'd be ready.

Thank the goddess I was. The moment my feet touched down on the grass, I spotted a demon, one of the more human looking ones, leaning against the castle and smoking a cigarette.

I aimed, shot, and the sucker dropped to the ground before most of the others had even seen him.

Shay spun. "Holy Heavens, Rooms!"

"One of my witch's many skills," Benedict drawled, the delight undeniable in his voice.

During the fight and our run from the hellhounds, he'd stayed close to me, running at my feet. I wished he'd either go invisible or allow me to carry him in the harness, but my familiar was too prideful for that. Seeing as he'd clawed an eye from one enemy wolf in our fight against Greed, I didn't think that ego was going to diminish soon.

"We can't afford to waste time fighting peons and lose anyone else," I said.

"No, we can't," Luca agreed. "Be ready to attack and kill the moment you see a demon. Princes aside, of course."

Those were for the *Vindix*.

Four down, three to go. I exhaled but did not allow pride to bloom inside me. The Prince of Greed had gone far more easily than I'd expected. I put that down to the fact that Harper and Hans had annihilated Envy, and Greed had been in pain from that loss. That shock of pain had helped us overcome Greed.

While I was sure the Princes Bale, Lucifer, and Orien would now be weakened too, we believed the final two of that lineup to be far more powerful than the rest. Even if we offed Gluttony before facing Pride and Wrath, it would be a gamble. Especially seeing as the princes weren't the only ones running low on steam.

We were all sensing the strain of using our powers, and we'd already lost so many, so that wasn't a good sign.

Should we not save Lilith and live to fight another day?

That wouldn't be ideal. Hans would be furious. Plus, we hoped to end this today. But if we weren't strong enough, retreat might be the only option—hence the invisibility potion each *Vindix* carried.

"Prepare to enter," Luca said.

We already discussed where we should be, so Tobias and I positioned ourselves behind Serena, Luca, and Hans, the first wave into the servant's area. The door was small, meant for people no more than five feet tall, so when Luca blasted it open and we rushed in, we had to duck.

The moment I got a good look at the inside, however, my breath caught. We entered a kitchen worked by ten humans.

They grabbed knives, their eyes were red and gleaming. As they worked in Wrath's castle, it was fair to assume they were under his control, filled with his sin. Now they looked to be turning that rage on us.

"Innocents," Rabi breathed. "I don't want to pull air from their lungs."

And I didn't want to shoot them.

"Let me try to lift it," I said.

"Not if it means the sin slipping into one of us," Hans growled as the humans approached.

"I know," I shot back. "I won't slip, I'll stretch."

I made it sound so easy, but it wasn't. My magic felt as thin as Benedict's patience for Harper, but I couldn't kill these people. Too many deaths weighed on my shoulders already.

I called on the Opal and pushed the magic of free will out there. The magic already covering everyone in my group spread further. When it met the closest human, I pushed it inward.

I exhaled when her eye color changed from red to brown. She blinked, but when the possessed shuffled past her, she let out a little scream.

"Shield her," I murmured, trying to concentrate but also

clocking the gleam in one of the possessed's eye when he realized the human was not like him.

A shield appeared right when a knife would have found the woman's throat. I swallowed and moved on, freeing another human, another, and so on until all ten were blinking back at us.

One dropped the knife and held his hands high in the air. "We don't want to die."

"We're not here for killing," Rhianna said, her tone reassuring. "Well, not you, anyway."

That didn't seem to comfort the man. His face, already pale, blanched.

"We're here for the princes," Kaito spoke hurriedly. "Do you know where they are?"

"And Queen Lilith," Hans added.

The man's eyes widened at the queen's name. "She's in the great hall. The princes, well, I only know where Prince Orien sleeps. Not the others. They've not been here very long, and I only took food to my lord once."

You could tell the words *my lord* did not sit easily on this modern man's tongue. That he'd been conditioned to speak with such reverence that he did not feel in his heart.

"He's not your master any longer," I assured the man. "We can get you out of here alive, but we need your help. Can someone lead us to the great hall?"

With everything going on in his kingdom, I doubted that Wrath was just chilling in his room. Sloth had lounged on a throne while his kingdom was being bombed, but Prince Orien was likely commanding forces from afar—and even more likely waiting to see if we'd been spotted.

After all, the Prince of Lust had known who we were. Greed and Envy hadn't seemed surprised to see all seven of us either. As we'd suspected after previous battles, the princes knew about the *Vindix*, even if they hadn't recognized us as such when we'd met before.

The first woman I'd pulled from possession stepped forward. "I can show you the way to where Queen Lilith is being kept. And if I do, can you please get me out of here? Right away?"

All eyes landed on Hans, who nodded. "I can get you out, and you'll be among the first, but after we fight."

Two other humans raised their hands, eager to leave as well, but Luca shook his head. "Only her. The rest of you should be safe from what's going to happen in here. Once we're done, military forces will come to save you all."

Their shoulders slumped, but the tone in Luca's voice brooked no argument. The woman slipped between Luca and Hans, Serena right behind her, and we left the kitchens.

Thankfully, the hallway to the kitchen was long and deserted. When we reached an intersection dominated by a wide set of stairs, the human turned to Luca, correctly discerning him as the leader.

"This leads up to the main castle. If you want to fight, we climb now. But we can get most of the way there using servant corridors beneath the main ones. Then we go up a different staircase, straight into the grand hall where they're keeping the queen. It's how we served food at the first feast. It's less direct that way, but safer."

"Less direct is fine," Luca replied. "We all want to get there in one piece."

The woman set off to the right, her shoulders looser. I wondered what she'd been imagining she'd have to do. If we'd make her fight.

My hand tightened around the pistol. No doubt, the

humans had lived in constant fear since Wrath took DC. I'd lived that way once, for years, I'd lived in fear of the Ringmaster. I hated that so many were experiencing such a foul existence. No one should have to live this way.

The woman led us through the servant corridors and there wasn't a soul in sight. No one to fight, or to pull from possession, or to even worry that they might raise an alarm on us. I took advantage of our stroke of luck, doing my best to even out my breathing and harness what energy I could. Around me, I felt the *Vindix* running alongside me. When the woman got to a set of steps, she paused, swallowed.

"The queen is being kept up there. Do I have to—"

"Stay down here," Hans spoke softly, as if to a frightened doe. "We'll get you when it's safe."

She exhaled and wordlessly, we ran up the steps, two by two. Benedict darted ahead of me, trying not to get caught underfoot. When Hans and Luca reached the top, we found the door closed. Magic burned in Luca's hands as he wound up to tear the door from the hinges and everyone prepared to rush in.

Boom!

The door flew, and we sprinted into the room, flags of red bearing a crest that had to belong to Prince Orien lined each wall. Benedict swerved right as Tobias and I went straight. I took in the sweeping room, large enough for at least five hundred people to feast and dance, if such an occasion occurred in this kingdom of darkness. Large though it was, the room held only six. One of whom actually mattered. The queen we'd rushed here for, hoping if we saved her, she might help us take down the princes in one fell swoop.

But Lilith was in no condition to help us because the Queen of the Underworld was sitting in a cage, her head in her lap.

Dead. Already dead. My heart dropped to my knees.

A roar filled the cavernous black hall as Hans unleashed himself. Black magic shot at the demons surrounding the dead queen's cage. Why they were even there, I had no idea, but I didn't miss when one disappeared. I used the power gifted to us by the moon, felt the *Vindix*, knew they weren't anywhere near where the demon had just been.

"Where—"

A feline yowl, followed by a slapping sound of flesh on stone, cut through me. I twisted to find the demon had teleported to the right. He'd landed by Benedict, and my familiar had leapt at him. Benedict had clawed the demon's face, only to be hurled into the closest wall.

He lay there, unmoving. Breathing?

"Tobias." Dread threatened to drown me.

My mate sprinted to my cat as Luca and Serena tagteamed the teleporting demon. But I couldn't focus on the demon, barely noticed when others joined in on the fight, when growls and the shooting of bullets filled the room. My eyes locked on the black cat in my mate's arms as Tobias sprinted back to me and pulled me into the stairwell.

"Breathing," Tobias said. "He's alive, just knocked out."

"Thank the Goddess." I pulled Benedict close, kissing him on the head. If he were conscious, such a gesture would earn me a good bat with a paw. "Should I put him in the sling?"

Benedict had been adamant about not using it, but I'd had a feeling we might need it.

"Leave him tucked here," Tobias footed at a little alcove in the stairwell. "He's so dark no one will see him, but we need to get back to help."

"Right." Though I didn't want to leave Benedict, he'd

survived, and he would be fine. No one could kill my sassy little familiar so easily. And the others needed me.

I nestled Benedict into the alcove, exhaling when I saw that Tobias spoke true. Thanks to his black fur, my familiar was very hard to see, and I doubted anyone would come up these steps. These were for servants, and the woman who'd shown us here was at the bottom listening to the roars and growls and gunshots. No doubt she'd warn others away.

With my familiar safe, I gripped my pistol. "Let's go help."

But as it turned out, our friends didn't need us. We entered the grand hall again, and I located the other fated six with my magical senses. Felt that they were fine—safe—seconds before I watched the final demon suffocate at Rabi's hands right before Lisha lobbed his head off with a sword.

"For good measure." She shrugged as the head rolled across the room.

"It's always good to do a thing properly," a voice, the accent Italian, filled the air as one of the heavy doors to the grand hall swung open.

The man appeared, handsome in a devastating and dark sort of way, his eyes going straight to Tobias. "Brother. I see you've found your way in. We've been waiting."

Oh Goddess. This is Raphael!

No, wait—another person followed. Not a person, a demon. This one was dressed in orange robes that reminded me of a monk's robes. He was at least fifty pounds overweight, though beneath the padding was visible muscle, and his large bat-like wings spread behind him, imposing as the tips ended in three-inch long talons.

"And I see that you've expanded your circle of monsters, Raphael." Tobias sneered. "Wearing orange, so you're Gluttony, I presume?"

"Prince Bale," Gluttony corrected. "You *will* address me properly, as you'll soon be working for me, vampire."

Off to the side, Hans seethed. He hadn't even had time to go to his mother before these a-holes arrived, and he'd had enough. The rage rolling off him attracted Bale's attention.

"Lilith's brat. Ah, good, we can even the score. Blood for blood, as we like to say below." A tendril snapped out of the prince and before anyone so much as breathed, it lashed around Hans's throat.

CHAPTER FORTY

TOBIAS

SHAY SHRIEKED, THE SHRILL SOUND ECHOING THROUGH THE cavernous great hall, as she launched herself at the Prince of Gluttony.

As we were still quite far away, Prince Bale turned his attention to her, releasing his power over Hans, who dropped to the ground. I watched the hellblooded demon twitch as he fell. Injured, but still alive, and as Harper formed a shield around him, I knew he'd be safe. For now, at least.

"Attack!" Luca commanded, and Meredith sprang into action, sprinting ahead with the rest of the *Vindix*.

"Tobias," Serena had waited, her dark eyes watching me.

It killed me to say these next words, but I had to. Prince Bale was a threat, that was certain, but he wasn't the only one in this room who was a threat to me and my mate, my family. "He'll scent her on me. He'll hunt her." I swallowed, thinking of Giselle, dead at a prince of Hell's hands. "He betrayed our family."

"Understood." Serena shot forward to run behind Meredith.

For the first time since we entered this infernal city, I'd separated from my mate, and for good reason. My older brother prowled my way, his eyes gleaming, a wicked smile on his lips. The last time he'd smiled at me, I'd been at his villa in Italy. We'd talked like brothers should and shared wine and bonded, but mere days prior, he'd changed Denz, Meredith's old partner, from human to vampire. He might have even known that he would send Denz to find Meredith, to kill her. Even then, when we'd spoken with love between us, my brother was working with our enemies.

Since that night, he'd done things that harmed my mate. I would not let him do so again.

We stopped twenty paces from one another. Raphael held out his hands, as if in supplication. A farce, if I ever saw one.

Behind him, the *Vindix* were already fighting Prince Bale. In my stolen glances, it was easy to see that he was shockingly agile and powerful for someone whose sin was overindulgence.

"I hear we have a dukedom up for grabs?"

I scowled at Raphael. "Is that how you'd like to address our maker's death? By claiming her title?"

"I'm the oldest."

"You know full well, brother, that is not how titles pass down in Isila."

In that land, might and magic ruled, birth order being a secondary factor to who was the most powerful among the children of the titled.

"I do." He patted a sheath containing a stake on one hip. From the other hip hung a dagger. Raphael preferred them to guns. He'd always enjoyed the rush of hand-to-hand combat. "It's even ash wood."

Ash, the only wood that when fashioned into a stake,

possessed the power to kill someone with royal blood. Someone like me and Raphael. Serena, too, for that matter.

"You'd kill your kin for a title?"

He snorted, as though it were obvious. Serena and I had desired nothing to do with Giselle's lands and holdings, so such a thought hadn't entered our minds.

Raphael was a different breed from Serena and I. Always wanting more. More power. More notoriety. Just *more.*

"How did you even learn of her death?" Behind him, Gluttony struck Shay. I forced myself not to wince as his attack hit and she fell. Only for a moment, though. The nephilim was back up and fighting, protecting her mate who had also managed to rise from his attack.

"I have my ways." He gestured behind him, and my jaw tightened at his elusive manner. "You should have joined me, you know. Sided with *true* power. When they're done here, they'll move on to other worlds. To Isila." He spat out the name of the other realm as if it were a bad taste.

"That's right, you still hate that they looked down on you there." I laughed, which visibly infuriated him. "It seems that I now share their disdain. You're a small, bloody *worthless* creature, Raphael, and you'll find no alliance with me."

Raphael moved, shooting toward me with such speed that he was little more than a blur. I spun out of his way, caught the flash of fang, scenting the sulfur that covered his skin. Evil had permeated him so deep he even reeked like the demons.

"I wish I could say I'm surprised. Or that I'll miss my brother and sister," Raphael twisted, a snarl marring his traditionally handsome Italian features, "but we haven't loved one another in decades. So I'll soon be the only one of Giselle's children alive. I can't say that I'll hate the prospect. Nor being able to mold our line into something great."

He came at me again, but this time I was ready. My fist found his face, and Raphael stumbled, fell. He rose quickly though, and we became a whirlwind of fang and claw and fist, fighting in the way of our kind. True monsters.

Raphael took advantage of every weakness I possessed. Each time I so much as glanced at the others, still fighting for their lives, he capitalized. And when I saw Luca take a blast for Meredith and fall to the ground, Raphael sent a stake toward my heart.

I gasped, shot back in time to feel the brittle wood graze the skin of my arm. For a while now, I'd been the better fighter, but he had been training.

Punch. Kick. Lunge. The snapping of fangs.

We landed blows, but never came close to ending our fight. Knowing each other too well meant we could anticipate much of what the other would do. Even with the obvious training Raphael had done, I knew my brother, and he knew me.

I needed to do something new, something he wouldn't expect. A plan had formed in my mind when a shriek—Meredith's—cut through me.

My gaze slanted to her. That was all the advantage he needed, and a moment later, I found myself on the ground, his foot pressing down on my chest.

Raphael sneered. Blood dripped down his face, and he looked more hideous for it. "When I'm done here, I'll finish off your witch. You won't have to wait long for her."

I fought to get up, but Raphael was as strong as me, and I was in a disadvantaged position. Below, not above. Worse, I could not see beyond him to discover what had caused my mate to scream.

"I'll make it quick, Tobias," Raphael said. "Not for her, but for you. Brothers do that—*ahh!*"

Blood sprayed, and I caught the whiz of a bullet as it blew through my brother's arm.

"*Tobias!*" Meredith bellowed my name, as though it came from the very depths of her soul.

I leapt up, taking advantage of the seconds in which my brother was disarmed. I gripped his head, twisted, and tore his head clean off his neck. The body fell, and I dropped my brother's head.

When I looked up next, I found Meredith sprinting toward me, covered in blood and tears streaked her face. "You idiot! You shouldn't have done that alone, you stupid vampire!"

I went to her, held out my arms. She leapt into my embrace. Our lips met, hers salty with blood. Not her blood, though, rather, demon blood. I pulled away.

"Are you hurt?"

"This is all Gluttony." She wiped at the blood covering her front. "I was close when we killed him, and he exploded." She swallowed, and tears filled her eyes again. "Tobias, Luca . . . He . . ."

"Hans will take him back," I assured her, understanding that the blow Luca had taken had likely injured him.

"No, Tobias. Luca isn't injured. He's d-dead."

I stiffened and cold rippled through me, all-encompassing and horrible. "Are you sure?"

She squeezed her eyes shut. "He took a curse for me and never rose. We checked him over. He's not breathing."

No. This couldn't happen. I refused to believe that a soul as good and pure as Luca could die.

"Hans needs to get him back to base. He can take Benedict too. Maybe the curse is making it look like he's dead. There's still ti—"

My words died on my lips as above, the roof exploded.

CHAPTER FORTY-ONE

HANS

Rubble cascaded down, and acting as one, Shay and I threw our bodies over Luca's before protecting our heads with our arms.

His *dead* body, already growing cold. My throat, sore from where dark magic had wrapped around it, tightened painfully as that fact sank in. First, they murdered my mother, then Luca . . . and so many innocents.

Maybe it's time to take the potion. To run. Doubt crept in like a poison, weakening my resolve. If the best among us had died, then who were we to think we'd live through another fight? I took a deep breath to calm my racing heart, which only resulted in me inhaling so much dust that it resulted in a coughing fit.

A hand hit my back, Shay's. "Are you okay?"

"Fine," I choked out as the coughing ebbed, thinking I was crazy for giving such a blatantly false answer. Nothing about this scenario was fine.

"Okay, we—oh Heavens . . . Hans. Look up." Shay's voice shifted from worried to positively trembling and knowing I wouldn't like what I found, I still did as my mate said and looked up. At that moment, any spark of positivity that might have remained inside me flickered out.

Above the grand hall, hundreds of demons swarmed the night sky, filling the air with the reek of rotten eggs. Smaller creatures rode on their backs, weapons in hand. I thought I caught a shade or wraith flying in the night sky too.

In the forefront, four more prominent figures sneered down at us: Prince Orien, Prince Lucifer, Prince Rikel, my sister's husband, and of course, Nicoleta herself. The scent of sulfur intensified as a wind came up from behind them and blew into the castle, bringing with it the reek of Hell's notorious royals.

One might have expected one of the princes to speak first, to relish in finding us on the ground, covered in dirt and rock, and most of us wounded. Instead, my own blood extended a fine-boned hand to us as she smiled a smile that promised malice. "Your diversion put up a good fight, but not good enough." Nicoleta snapped her fingers, and a body fell from the swarm of monsters.

It landed on the cage my mother sat in, dead, her long red hair streaming down her legs, caking to them with the blood that dripped from Lilith's decapitated head.

"Not Artem," Shay whispered, sending dread flooding through me as I recognized the wizard.

Goddess. Had anyone in the diversion squad survived?

Luca hadn't. Mother hadn't. Harper's father hadn't survived either. All of them were powerful in their own rights. I felt a strong sense of responsibility for every death. After all, I'd been the one to push this mission. *An opportunity*, I'd called it. Not only would we save my mother and use her magic to help us defeat the princes—but the royals were all here. We could try to kill them all in one go.

I'm a fool.

"Not looking so hot, are you?" a rebellious, *furious* voice shouted.

Kaito, I registered the water elemental's voice, felt where he was and prepared for the attack on his person.

"Gray, aren't you ol' Oreo and Lucy?" Kaito added, seemingly not terrified for himself like I was. "As if you might be dying already? That's what it is, isn't it, you ugly devil!"

I looked up again to find that Kaito was right. Wrath and Pride appeared gray like Greed, Envy, and Gluttony had. Weakened. Nothing like when we'd seen them before.

"You're the last ones," Rhianna taunted, bold as hell, just like Kaito. "We killed the rest. We'll add you to the list too."

I expected Wrath to rage, to hurl dark magic at her. Instead, he smiled and the sight of it chilled my bones.

"Our brothers' faults could always be counted on."

What?

"Oh my god," Shay breathed. "That's why they didn't help them. Why they let their brothers fight alone. They *wanted* to be the last ones standing."

Goddess. I'd always assumed that the Princes of Hell were tight. That nothing could tear them apart. But I'd been wrong. Each thirsted for power, a larger share of the pie.

"With them out of the way, there's more of this world for us," growled Lucifer.

If there was one Prince of Hell I hated the most, it was Lucifer, the person who ensured my mother was bound to the underworld. The one who forced her to marry him, and the reason she stayed beneath when she loved my father with all her heart.

"And why would we need their sins?" Lucifer shrugged. "The humans exhibit such weak sins all on their own."

"We will divide the world in a new way," Rikel, Wrath's heir, shouted. "To usher in a new age!"

Demented, all of them. And they might become our overlords.

Their overlords, I corrected. If the princes and their offspring lived to rule, I'd be dead. We all would. We'd be like my mother. Unable to stop myself, I cast her body another glance. How long ago did the execution take place? Had Nicoleta watched?

My stomach hardened. I didn't want to know the answer to that.

"So?" Lucifer asked, as though he were inquiring about the time. "Any last words?"

Behind him, the demon swarm grew closer, as if they were being telepathically commanded. Maybe they were. According to Gunner, Sloth had possessed that power.

"Shield. We need a shield," Shay whispered.

I jolted. Wait, she hadn't given up?

One sidelong look at my mate told me that no, unlike me, Shay had not given up already. Feeling wondrous at her strength, I twisted to take in the others covered in the dust of rubble and blood, though determination still lined their faces.

How was I supposed to be the leader of the *Vindix,* yet I'd given up and they hadn't? Probably because, unlike the others, I knew intimately what was inside the devils. I wasn't that far from being one of them.

But I'm not one of them. I never will be. What I am is a Vindix, a mate, a son, and a brother to a monster.

I pushed myself up, caught Harper's attention. She was our best chance at large-scale protection. "Shield the army. Keep the swarm away from us. Rabi, shield us."

An air shield wrapped around me, and I assumed everyone else in our group. It felt stronger than the one Rabi had made in Venice. Thanks to Stuart's help, and Rabi's increased familiarity with the Amethyst of Air, his shielding had improved greatly. I only hoped that it would hold against whatever the princes threw at us.

Harper worked more slowly, sucking in a breath, likely sizing up the area she'd need to work in. The gaping roof was big, but she'd already shielded across a street. She *could* call enough spirits for this to work. I had faith in Harper.

"We need to buy her time." I called my magic. We didn't stand a chance against hundreds of flying demons, the princes, Rikel, and Nicoleta. Hell, we might not even win against the princes, but we could even the score. Keep away the lesser beings and make it a fairer fight.

The princes sneered down at me, likely thinking that I'd attack them. That was the logical thing to do—but logic would not win us this war.

Feeling the other *Vindix* gather around me, I pushed my torture magic on Rikel. He hadn't been expecting the move either, and the young prince writhed right away.

Nicoleta shrieked. "Let him go! Let my love go! I—"

Light slammed into her, Shay stepping it up and helping me. My sister's scream ripped through the night, and Pride's and Wrath's eyes glowed brighter.

We had seconds before they attacked. Wrath might wish to play with me, just for giggles, but I was attacking his blood, his heir. He would not stand for that.

I pushed so hard that Rikel's wings faltered, and he fell twenty feet. Nicoleta cried out and dipped to help her husband. The princes followed, though slower, as if not wanting to show how much they might care for the heir.

I didn't care for their reasoning. All that mattered was that dip, bringing them closer to us, widening the gap between our targets and their army. "Harper!"

"They're coming!" Sweat dripped from her chin. Once the ghosts were here, it would be all that she had to keep them in place. To protect us, like Meredith had been doing all along.

"Elementals ready!" I yelled, and they came closer. No doubt they, too, understood it would come down to me and them with Meredith and Harper as support.

The elementals aligned with me when hundreds of ghosts streamed down from above. As they were busy snarling down at us, the flying demon army didn't see them coming. Sounds of shock and fear and anger muddled the skies as spirits flew through them and solidified into a shield between the demons and their masters.

The princes spun in the air, taking in our move, and when Wrath turned back to face us, his face was red with fury.

"You think we need our army, Lilith's bastard?"

Forcing myself to appear unbothered, wanting to bait them, to rile their emotions so they'd be more likely to make a mistake, I picked an invisible piece of lint off my shirt. "Kind of desperate, showing up with an entire army when we have such a small force. But who am I to presume that I understand the inner workings of the likes of you?"

"*To your detriment.*" Lucifer's face twisted in a way that told me I'd succeeded in pissing them the hell off.

As one, the pair beat their wings and soared downward. Nicoleta was still assisting her beloved halfway between us and the princes. She sneered at me, her expression promising pain.

"Rabi, knock the younger ones from the sky," I said.

"My shields will falter."

"Do it," I instructed, knowing that if all four of those royals made it down here, they might be able to shatter the air shields around us anyway.

Of those on my side, few possessed wings. I didn't know the full scope of Rikel's powers, but it didn't matter. We needed to even the score and get them all on the ground. Hopefully injure one too.

I pushed aside the faint guilt that bubbled up in me at the idea of harming my sister. She'd chosen her side. She might have even been the one to kill Artem—a wizard known for his kindness as well as his strength. Knocking Nic out of the air was the least she deserved.

And Rabi proved he understood the assignment because as soon as the air shield weakened, a hurricane force gale of wind ripped upward then tore back down. The gust yanked Rikel from my sister's grasp, down, down, down.

I winced as the heir to Wrath's kingdom slammed into the ground. The crack of a skull against the stone twisted my stomach and as soon as blood began pooling from his skull, I recognized that Rabi outdid himself. Rhianna compounded that effect when she sent a scrap of sharp metal soaring towards Wrath's heir. The makeshift blade skittered along the prince's neck, severing it, and Rikel's head rolled lazily an inch away from his body.

Nicoleta screamed and tendrils of black filled the sky above us. My heart stopped. I knew how deadly Nic could be, and that was before she'd been living with literal demons from Hell.

But she didn't get the chance to prove how deadly she was, as Wrath's far more detrimental power exploded over us.

My feet left the ground as I was hurtled through the air. I slammed into the back wall, sensing the others hit too. I groaned as I slid down. At my side lay Shay, her expression fierce, though I didn't miss the scratch on her face.

"Harp! Chica *wake up*!" Gunner said from somewhere past Shay, his voice frantic.

Shay sucked in a sharp breath. "Gunner, she's alive. I can see her breathing. Stop freaking out. We need you to keep your head on straight."

"What happened?" I said as I rose to my elbows and blinked back the stars in my vision.

"Harper's unconscious, which is bad in more than one way," she replied, but instead of turning back to our friend, her finger drifted up.

My stomach clenched. The ghost shield was gone, freeing hundreds of lesser demons as Orien, Lucifer, and Nicoleta stalked towards us, fire sparking in their eyes.

CHAPTER FORTY-TWO

MEREDITH

The army of darkness swarmed closer, waiting for their princes to give the word to annihilate us. And unfortunately for us, that might happen. Harper was just behind me, lying on the ground, unconscious.

How can we beat them back without her?

I wasn't sure that we could, so we had to buy ourselves time until Harper awoke. The others seemed to still be getting their bearings after being thrown into the wall. For now, it was up to me. Goddess, help us.

My hands, bleeding and cut up and sweating, trembled as I called my hedge magic. As I prepared to use it in any way that I could to slow the princes. To harm them. But before I could rein in that innate power and hurl it at our enemies, Kaito let out a long groan.

My stomach dipping, I cut him a glance. He gripped his head right before a dark presence shoved at the magic I wielded with the help of the Opal. I sucked in a breath, understanding. Calling my hedge magic had loosened my control with the Opal and sins were slipping in, already threatening to take over. In one second, with a single panicked choice, I'd nearly given the princes the chance to control us all. To win.

I backpedaled, knowing full well I couldn't let that control slip another time. And I certainly couldn't lose consciousness like poor Harper. If I did, we were *all* dead—lost to Wrath's sin and his influence. Maybe Lucifer's too.

But could we last long enough for Harper to wake up and help? Or had we gotten as far as we were going to get?

Should we run to Hans? Have him smoke-travel us out of here?

I almost called it, but then remembered Benedict, still likely unresponsive in the alcove. My heart rate spiked. I should have kept him closer! There was no way I would leave my familiar in this house of horrors.

Tobias must have sensed the battle going on inside me. He took my hand. "I can get him. I—"

Tana's fire bloomed like a ravenous flower in front of her. The flames grew by the second, morphing through shapes until the flower became a dragon. "*Go!*"

The fire dragon shot into the sky, growing in size by the second and heading straight for the army. I gasped as it opened its maw, engulfing ten demons in one blazing gulp.

Lucifer hissed. Those particular soldiers must have been his.

In response, Tana glowered back at the princes and Nicoleta, still stalking our way like menacing serial killers in a movie. "You think we'll stop! Then yer fools! You cannae make us stop!"

Great gales gusted into the sky to join the flames. Above, demons spun, and some fell and hit the ground as Rabi pulled air from their lungs. "I've been a slave before. Never again."

His words left his lips far softer than Tana's, but they were just as powerful.

Rhianna's magic rose in the form of thorns, dagger sharp and deadly. Then Hans and Kaito. I looked back at Harper, still unconscious, but maybe with a little more color in her cheeks? My resolve strengthened.

We were fighting. I was fighting. For the world, and even more so, for the lives of those who were here fighting with me. As crazy as it felt to say such a thing, many of them were now my chosen family. The others I was close to in a different way —fate decreed our shared destiny and that was a bond none of us would break. I would fight with them, *for them*, and do my best to defeat the princes, to make sure we all lived to see another sunrise.

"Wake Harper," I said to Jolie who was closest to my fellow *Vindix*. Gunner wasn't far off, but he wasn't hovering over his mate either because he didn't want any enemy getting close to her at all. "Protect her. We'll take care of the rest until she can join us."

I sounded far more confident than I felt. Even with Tana's fire dragon and Rabi's wind dispersing the princes' airborne forces, they outnumbered us.

But we'd already come so far. Lost so many. Though unspoken, I suspected we all believed our last stand had arrived.

Grabbing my magic, I pushed it all into the Opal, strengthening my protection over the others. While I still breathed, we'd keep our minds through this.

The *Vindix* received the power I gave, and we formed a semicircle. A wall facing the princes and Nicoleta.

"You think you're strong enough to defeat us?" Lucifer mused. "I can admire the guts. The pride. Even if it is foolish."

"Foolish maybe," Kaito shouted, "but we have something you don't!"

Lucifer arched an eyebrow.

"Each other. We can trust one another, whereas your brothers shouldn't have ever trusted you!" A fifty-foot wave of water appeared out of nowhere and rushed to the princes and Nicoleta.

The princes appeared unfazed, but Hans's sister soared to the left. Rabi caught her in his element, and though Nicoleta fought, Rabi's Amethyst glowed brightly on his wrist, hinting that he was working hard to control her.

I didn't even have time to wonder what he planned to do with her when Rabi launched Nicoleta into the sky, back toward the demon army.

She tumbled through the air, wings flapping to regain purchase, to seize control. It wasn't working though, and she went higher and higher and—a gasp caught in my throat as Nicoleta rammed right into an unsheathed sword.

Though impossible with all the commotion, I imagined I could hear the sickening sound of the blade tearing through Nicoleta's slight frame as one of her own army impaled her.

Her body went limp on the blade, and the demon's face registered what he'd done. He dropped the sword. Nicoleta fell.

"Rabi, catch her. Capture her or something!" My voice was shrill.

Hans loved his sister. Despite all that she'd done, who she'd become, he couldn't help but continue to love her. It was the most frustrating, and probably also the best thing about him—his ability to love. And he'd seen his sister, a girl he'd grown up protecting, impaled—it was unlikely that she lived.

The last thing Hans needed to witness was her splatting to the floor.

Rabi did as I said, confusion in his dark eyes. He didn't know the full story behind Nicoleta. He might not even know who this girl was, and that was for the best. I hated the girl, but even I would have found it difficult to kill her because of Hans. Though leaving her alive was not an option, either.

Nicoleta's body drifted toward the ground far away, far enough to where no one got a good look at her. Her small body landed just as black magic parted Kaito's onslaught of water.

The princes strolled through the water, wet but unaffected. They smiled and the expressions were wrong, promising pain and death. Rhianna retaliated, growing a wall of thorns, but as I saw black tendrils weaving through those, I knew it was only a matter of seconds before that defense fell too.

A groan and two mumbled words came from behind. *Harper.*

I twisted to find that her eyes were still closed. Still, groaning had to be a good sign. Goddess, I hoped she regained consciousness soon. Something told me that while we might fight these two for a while, we wouldn't end them until we joined forces.

We needed her.

"Tana, keep the dragon going," Hans's voice sounded strangled, no doubt from the death of his sister. Yet he remained with us. Fighting. Leading. "Rabi, rip the air from their lungs. Rhianna, hold them."

Rhianna bound one of the brothers with thick green vines that grew from the stone. Rabi's magic was more subtle, but when Wrath began to choke, I cheered inside. The air elemental was suffocating them, and my hope rose. That was until Lucifer broke free of the vines, and Wrath sent forth tendrils of dark magic to attack Rabi, lifting the air elemental twenty feet high.

Rabi fought with his own element, and Hans struck at

Wrath. The torture magic proved effective. Prince Orien doubled over, releasing Rabi, who with quick thinking drifted to the ground, unharmed.

Tobias growled low in his throat, and I saw the predator in him rising to the surface. "The rest of us, our turn to make a diversion. Love, get Harper ready. You might only have one chance."

Before I uttered a single protest, Tobias, Serena, Shay, and Gunner, and everyone else who wasn't a *Vindix*, shot forward and took on Orien and Lucifer in hand-to-hand combat combined with magical strikes.

My heart rate spiked. Desperate to keep Tobias alive, I turned to Harper, knelt at her side, and shook her.

"Wake up! Please, wake up." If Gunner wasn't busy trying to kill Lucifer, he would have told me to be gentler on his mate. And I got it, I really did, but she needed to wake the hell up!

"Kaito, splash water on her face! Someone *do something*!"

The water elemental obliged, and to my utter shock and relief, Harper coughed. Slowly, her eyelids fluttered open. They landed on me, then searched behind.

"Where's Gunner?"

"Fighting the princes." From behind, I heard Shay scream in pain. A second later, darkness struck my back. I hissed and shielded myself. The magic left, but when I looked at Kaito, he was shaking himself.

"I felt weird," he said. "Furious."

Wrath had tried his hand at regaining control, and he'd put a dent in my magic. Had other opponents not distracted him, it might have worked.

Oh my Goddess, we needed to end this and end it now. I

could not allow Wrath to engulf us in his sin. If I did, it would only be a matter of time before we were goners.

"Shay and Tobias are out there too," I added, trying to center her as much as I was centering myself. "Harper, I know you hit your head, but we need you. We need to fight together."

She took my hand, gripped it tight, and I helped her rise. She slumped, as if standing was as good as she could do.

"Someone, take her other hand. She needs support," I instructed. "As a matter of fact, all of us link up. We need to work together."

Together, we became stronger. Together was the only way to win.

We assembled into a semicircle. I stood between Harper and Hans and watched as Tana's dragon ravaged the army above us that waited for its princes' commands. Below, a dozen fighters took on Wrath and Pride. One of our own had fallen—an S&S member—and before my eyes, Lucifer almost succeeded in taking off Serena's head.

I swallowed and made sure my magic covered us. The others blinked, and with their minds fully their own, rolled their shoulders back.

"Harper first," Hans said. "Like with Greed."

She could make a shield, but I was fairly sure the princes wouldn't call their army to defeat us. If they were going to, they would have done so. They were, after all, Pride and Wrath. They wanted that honor. Needed it.

So we only need to focus on them.

Harper called the ghosts, and they swarmed the fighters, defending some while others began shooting through the princes. Like their brothers, Lucifer and Wrath screamed. I didn't understand why spirits affected the devils, but I'd be lying if I said I didn't relish in their pain.

"Fire, air," Hans ground out.

Rabi and Tana unleashed their magic on the princes. Rabi once again working from the inside, Tana by surrounding the princes in rings of flame.

Rhianna didn't wait for a command as she strapped them down with vines and grew a cage of thorns around them. I watched in amazement as the princes lost their focus second by second. Their magic dimmed.

And when Kaito was ready to push, when I thought we had it, a demon fell from the sky. The creature stabbed Rhianna in the side. She crumpled, breaking the chain, and I felt that loss of power, that loss of connection. But there was nothing to do for it, as the demon made a move for Kaito. The latter twirled out of the way, encasing the devil in a bubble of water, rolling it away.

Tana's dragon was still terrorizing the demons, but some had broken off, and seeing that their princes were now losing, they'd trained their weapons at us.

"Harp! Up!"

She shifted her magic upwards, forming a shield. A heartbeat later, bullets and arrows pinged off the shield.

"*My turn,*" Hans growled and unleashed himself.

A harrowing sound came out of the princes. Sheer horror and pain.

Lucifer crumpled to the ground, and I watched with wide eyes as Shay took her sword of fire and light and lobbed off his head.

My heart sang, and I held my breath as she spun to take the other prince down, but Wrath's magic was already upon her.

CHAPTER FORTY-TWO

Tendrils wrapped around Shay, choking her. She dropped her sword.

Hans roared and broke the chain of *Vindix*, soaring toward Wrath. He dipped, scooping up a sword dropped by a demon guard, but from the looks of it, kept control over his magic.

Wrath might have Shay in his grips, but the prince was still writhing beneath Hans's power. More than that, the gray color of his skin had deepened. This was our chance.

Hans didn't hesitate as he flew to the prince, didn't pause as tendril after tendril came for him. And he sure as hell didn't hesitate in swiping the sword at Wrath.

The blade met skin, cut through it, and I watched, mouth agape, as Wrath's head flew across the room.

Above, demons screamed in anguish. The magical wards around the city lit up and cracked, then broke down, the oily black turning white, flaking away.

My heart raced. *We did it! We—*

The momentary pain of the demons had lifted, and they turned on us, revenge sparking in so many eyes.

"There are too many. We need to leave," Tobias yelled. "Get to Luca's body! We're not leaving him here!" He blurred off in the opposite direction. I was about to call after him, to ask where he was going, when I realized he was retrieving Benedict.

My shoulders slumped as a wave of exhaustion came over me. We'd done our job in killing the princes, and it had taken much from us. I felt tapped out and assumed others did too. Rhianna was seriously injured, and others were covered in scrapes and bruises I hadn't noticed before. We looked like we'd been run over repeatedly by semi-trucks and needed to leave, to let the military and gathered magical forces handle the other demons. At least for a while. Once I was strong enough, I'd come back. I'd fight. I'd never stop.

"The woman too!" Hans screamed after Tobias as the rest of us sprinted for Luca's body.

I wasn't sure he'd heard, not until I saw my mate blur back. When he stopped, the terrified servant who'd shown us to the great hall was tucked under one brawny arm and Benedict, still out cold, in the other.

Ever helpful and considerate, Rabi used air to collect our other dead. He floated them closer as the demons soared down, ready for vengeance against those who had killed their masters.

But they were slow. Far too slow.

We vanished into smoke.

CHAPTER FORTY-THREE

SHAY

WE LANDED IN THE ARMY CAMP, AND A GASP TORE UP MY THROAT.
Helicopters soared above, and on the ground, soldiers were already on the move, streaming into the city, guns blazing. I imagined that in the magical base, those forces had also leapt into action.

"Not a second wasted," Meredith murmured, her shoulders slumped, probably with relief from being here and not in the midst of fighting again.

"Good. Who knows how many monsters are still in there, not to mention people who need help?"

And speaking of people, my gaze went to Hans, then down to the body in his arms.

Nicoleta.

Rabi had levitated the dead from our side to us, allowing us to bring them with us, but Hans retrieved his sister.

She exemplified so many vile qualities my kind despised about hellblooded beings. I could barely believe she shared blood with my mate, for he was the opposite.

Blood ties bound them, though, there was no doubt, and

while Hans had promised me he wouldn't go off protecting his sister in battle again—a promise he'd kept today—he never stopped loving her. Not deep in his heart.

I placed a hand on his shoulder. All around, others had leapt into action shuttling the wounded into tents and asking where to take the dead. One of those deaths was weighing on me, but Hans was still here, still alive, thank the heavens. At the moment, he needed me more than Luca.

"I'm so sorry Hans."

He lifted his handsome face. Tears streamed down his cheeks and, heart clenching, I brushed them away.

"She hated you. And you hated her—most people I love did," he closed his eyes briefly, "and in no way do I blame them for that. Nicoleta, the version of her at the end, was horrible." His gaze fell upon his sister again. "But she wasn't always like that, and I'm going to try to remember that part of her. Just to myself, I want to think of her in a better light. Don't think I expect others to, though."

"I can understand that." I inhaled softly, amazed by his capacity to love even when the person did not deserve it. "We should move out of the way, though. Into a tent or something? You can set your sister down and—"

"I need to find Tana," Hans said. "And I'm not leaving Nic's body. Not until . . . I need to find Tana. Can you do that for me, Shay?"

I'd seen Tana helping Rhianna into the tent where the wounded were being treated. "I'll find her. Move to the side for me, okay? I don't want you to get trampled."

I didn't think Hans possessed the mental capacity to look out for himself and not get run over by soldiers as they streamed into the city to fight demons and protect citizens.

He did as I asked, and I rushed over to the infirmary tent. I spotted Tana off to the side, drinking water and looking shell-shocked.

"Hey, Tana. How's Rhianna?" I asked as I approached.

"Fine, they're already working on her. She was in a poor way, but she'll survive."

"Good. Hans needs you."

She swallowed a sip of water. "What happened? What does he need?"

"I-I'm not sure."

Of course, I had *an idea* why he requested the fire elemental. Nicoleta was dead and not beloved, and Hans wouldn't leave her body alone. I didn't blame him. Soldiers had been known to do horrible things to the dead on opposite sides of a war. Most wouldn't even see Nicoleta as human. But if I told Tana my suspicions, she might not come. She had every right to despise Nicoleta too, but that didn't change the fact that Hans needed this. If there was one person I'd pull strings for in this world, it was him.

"Right then." She tossed a paper cup into the trash. "Let's go."

I led her back to Hans, approaching him slowly. My mate was still staring at his sister, still grieving. As if he knew he wouldn't have very long at all.

I cleared my throat. "Hans."

He looked up, eyes finding mine first, then Tana's. He exhaled. "Tana, I need you to burn my sister, and I need you to do it now."

She took a step back. "Hans, I'm exhausted. I cannae—"

"Please," his voice broke on the word. "*Please,* for me. I can't leave her alone. She has too many enemies. I need to be sure her body isn't abused."

"Wha' about yer da?"

Hans swallowed. "I'll take my sister's ashes home. Explain what happened. He'll understand. Maybe not right away, but one day, he will."

"Yer ma? Do you want to wait for her body?"

I swallowed. Tana was brave, or maybe foolish, in bringing up Lilith.

"I couldn't get to her and save you all. Maybe when the fighting is done, I can do the same for her." Hans's voice cracked.

"We will," I assured him. Nicoleta had created only chaos, but Lilith had helped us, and I wanted to see her body properly buried or burned, whichever Hans wished.

Tana went silent before exhaling loudly. "Fine, but I'm doing this for *you*. Not yer sister. Let's find a quiet place."

Hans pulled his sister close, and as a trio, we made our way through the base. At one point, I flew above, checking it out from a bird's-eye view. In the air, I saw an area where there were fewer tents, and navigated us that way. Finally, we reached a quiet street lined with trees.

Hans looked around and carefully set his sister on the grass between two oaks. He bowed his head. "Nic, I love you. I'm sorry that I failed you."

I wanted to protest but held my tongue. Hans was doing this for himself. I would not intervene.

"I hope you're at peace now, and know I never wanted things to end like this. I love you, little sister." He bent, kissed her on the forehead, and when he rose to find us watching, he nodded to Tana. "Burn her to ashes."

Tana extended her hand, and the ruby flared on her wrist as she called her power. Suddenly, Nicoleta's body caught, and the fire took over, covering her completely, climbing five feet high.

"This will take a while," Tana said. "My fire runs extra hot, but there's a lot of tissue."

"I'll wait. Shay, you should go find your mother. Let her know you're alive."

A pause stretched between us for a heartbeat. "Are you sure?"

"I'll be fine." Resolve fortified his voice, and I got the sense that, though he was far from being fine, this step of burning his sister was already helping. He needed time, like so many of us would when we could stop and breathe a full breath.

I took his hand, kissed his cheek. "I'll find you later."

He squeezed my hand before letting go, turning back to the bonfire. Tears pricked in my eyes, and I decided that instead of walking through the chaotic base, I'd fly. Mom would be easier to spot that way. Plus, it would give me a moment alone to pull myself together.

I soared the skies above the camp. I saw at least two soldiers spot me and aim, but my white wings were a dead giveaway that I wasn't a demon, so they lowered their weapons. Nerve-wracking, though. I couldn't fault them for such trigger-happy behavior. They'd had little to no idea of what would come out of the barrier, so the humans remained, understandably, on edge.

From my vantage point, with the shield gone, I could also see much of DC. The flame that had been lit in the castle's tower had disappeared. Demons took to the streets and the skies, though many were quickly shot down. Some might escape, but they wouldn't get far. We'd find them. It was only a matter of time.

After ten minutes of searching from above, I spotted my mother. Even in a crowd of thousands and the aftermath of a battle, she stood out. More than that, she was using her powers to heal—to the degree that our kind could do so.

I fluttered to the ground behind her, trying not to distract her as she poured her light into someone. When the golden glow faded, and she straightened, a victorious smile on her face, I knew it was safe to announce my presence.

"Mom."

My mother spun, her eyes wide as her hands flew to her mouth. "Shaylina! You're alive!"

She raced to me, engulfing me in such a tight hug, it was difficult to breathe.

"I'm alright, Mom. A little beat up and tired, but fine."

"*Mi preciosa hija!*" Mother wailed so loudly I was sure that we were drawing eyeballs. "You're so brave and strong, but—oh!—I worried so!"

My chest tightened. Mother was hard to impress, and though I suspected this praise was largely a result of stress, I'd take it. Heavens, I felt I deserved a little something after all I'd been through.

Mom pulled away slightly and took me in. Then, her eyebrows knitted together. "Where's Hans?"

I blinked. Did she really just ask about him?

I'd told my mother that Hans and I were mates, and she'd stopped referring to him in a derogatory manner, but asking after him? It showed she cared, and that made my throat tighten in a good way.

"He had to take care of some things. Family things."

"A good man, that one," Mom pulled me in close again. "And he's so lucky to have you. *I'm* so lucky to have you, Shaylina."

Warmth spread through me. Smaller battles might rage for some time, and there was still the question of monsters—how many and what kinds—roaming the earth, but with the death of the Princes of Hell, we had a great chance at reclaiming our world.

War aside, there were more changes to come too. A lot of things were up in the air, new ways of life to bloom. Magical orders to be accepted, or not, among the humans. As I breathed in my mother's distinct spicy scent, I wondered if maybe more than I'd ever dreamed was about to change.

EPILOGUE ONE

TOBIAS

One Week Later

"Knock, knock!"

I glanced up from Luca's desk, my desk for the time being as I was acting as coven master until S&S voted someone else into the position. Shay leaned against the door frame, her arms crossed over her chest and a thoughtful expression on her face.

"You actually look like you might fit in there. Not as much as Luca, of course, but that sort of grace is impossible to come by nowadays." The nephilim winked and sauntered into the room, veering toward the espresso machine I hadn't the heart to put elsewhere, though the scent of coffee was far too strong for me. "Maybe I'll vote for you to keep the top spot, after all, stiff."

"I still feel as if he'll walk in at any moment." I wished it were true.

Having lost Giselle tore me apart. Losing Luca, a dear friend, so soon after, made me ache with grief. It was even worse knowing that Luca had died taking a curse for my mate.

He'd saved Meredith, and even if he were still alive, that was a debt I could never repay. I swallowed down the lump climbing my throat. I knew from experience that, given enough time, we could heal from pretty much anything, but healing this degree of agony and regret and sorrow seemed a long way off.

I looked aside at Shay, she picked up a tiny cup, then set it back down and exhaled.

"Anything new?" she asked, her tone falsely chipper.

In the aftermath of DC, we were all doing our best. Shay put on a better front than most. Hans came to the tomb only once—when Ginevra, Luca's twin sister, arrived to grieve her brother and help us plan for his funeral in Italy. Even then, I'd strong-armed Hans into coming and accepting the passing on of Luca's magical vault to him, Shay, Meredith, and me. Gunner and Harper had also been options, but they'd declined. A wise move as Harper had been in California since DC. She'd found her mother in LA, and parts of their pack and, with Gunner's help, they were working to rebuild a life.

Though we now had the power to open the vault and investigate the objects—all of which had been found by S&S members over the years—we hadn't. No one wanted to delve into the dark artifacts we were in charge of. We did not have the energy. Not yet.

"No sighting of Hell's heirs." I said, knowing that would interest her. "I expect they'll lie low. No new monsters popping up and wreaking havoc either."

We'd seen hellhounds during the war, but apparently, they hadn't been the only creatures who roamed Earth that didn't belong. Monsters like three-headed dogs, hydras, reapers, and more continued to terrorize the planet. In Sydney, London, and around Las Vegas, conquered cities we had not gone to, there were, apparently, many such hellborn monsters that had taken to the sewers or the forests and deserts around the cities. That water beast outside Venice was still on the loose too.

Add that to the unfortunate fact that, apparently, all seven gateways to Hell—the Eyes of Darkness—were still open, and I didn't see the monster problem disappearing. As long as the gates were open, more would slip through. Unfortunately, no one knew of a way to close the gates. The magical community was doing our best with wards but they weren't completely secure. Perhaps there wasn't a method, and this was simply our new reality.

"It's been quiet today," I finished and considered it a great victory to have one quiet day in the aftermath of war.

"We deserve it." Shay slouched into the chair. "What about Benny?"

"Still recovering. And being a total pain in my arse."

"Well, that's his job! Let me guess, he's demanding the fanciest tuna in a porcelain dish and some elevated posh bed?"

I chuckled. "You do know the beast."

"Too right I do." Shay grinned. "So, is Rooms going to meet us in Tuscany?"

"You won't be able to call her that for much longer, you know."

"Says who?"

"She's moving in with me at the end of the month."

Which was only a few days away. It would be odd sharing my home, though I couldn't say I was not looking forward to such a future. Even if I still had a lot of remodeling to do to suit my warm-blooded mate's many, *many* needs. My sassy, lovely witch had told me as much when she'd stayed the night for the first time and found my home *'unsuitable'* for her needs.

"Unless Rooms tells me otherwise, the nicknames are staying." Shay stretched her long arms, and I caught a glimpse of her soulmate mark. "Where is she, anyway?"

"The *Abscondita* manor—or what's left of it." With Hannah, Stuart, Tana, Rhianna, and Kaito. Rabi had traveled to New Orleans and planned to live with his grandmother for a time. He needed the quiet. The wizard was a bloody wreck after DC, and I didn't blame him for needing distance. To have gone from being a blood slave to a war must've been beyond traumatic.

"Oh." Shay swallowed. "This is the first time they've been back, right?"

I nodded. I was sure my mate, the other *Vindix*, and the remaining *Arcacustos* would find a gruesome scene at the manor, but they'd claimed it was their duty. I couldn't have been more proud of Meredith for stepping up in such a manner.

"Like Harper and Gunner, they will all meet us in Tuscany. Meredith has her luxiter."

"Hans too." Shay pressed her lips together. "He went to Romania two days ago to see his father. But he promised he'd be in Italy."

"Then he will. He loved Luca too."

We sat in silence for a while, a feat I hadn't known Shay was capable of.

War changes us all, I thought, as the nephilim stared out the window, twirling her hair around her finger and pondering.

I returned to the paperwork, a task I despised. Luca never mentioned the mountains of the stuff. As far as I was concerned, the man had been a miracle worker—doing all this and remaining sane. More than sane: noble and kind and fair to the end. I could only hope to do the job half as well, even if for a short while.

Before I knew it, the alarm I'd set beeped. I looked up to find Shay already holding her luxiter.

"Ready to see him off?"

I stood and shut the office door before joining hands with the nephilim. The light took us, and a moment later, the luxiter deposited us on a grassy hill. It was cold out, but sunny, a perfect day to see a great friend off.

"Over here!" Meredith's voice rang out.

Shay and I twisted, looked up, and my heart, still as it may be, swelled. Our friends were already there. Hans too, just as he said he would be. They were accompanied by the rest of the *Vindix*, much of S&S, a few Covenant members, and others I did not recognize. Probably Luca's friends from other areas of his life. There were many.

In the middle of them all, Ginevra stood by a pyre with Luca's magically preserved body atop. He would be burned and bathed in mage magic. According to Ginevra, this ritual sent the soul to the starry halls of the afterlife that mages in Isila believed in.

Releasing Shay's hand, we walked up the hill to meet them and see our dear friend and leader off on his next adventure.

EPILOGUE TWO

MEREDITH

Seven Months Later

GUNNER SCOOPED HARPER INTO HIS ARMS AND GAVE HER A thorough kiss. Above them, rose petals were released to rain down on the newlyweds. The air was warm, and the sun shone bright in North Carolina, the perfect day for a wedding.

"He's always *so much*," Shay said, but with a ridiculously happy grin on her face.

All around, wolves stood and applauded the marriage of their friends and alphas—the beginning of the joining of two dominant packs.

Shay laughed. "She said I drove her crazy. I don't know how Harp is gonna handle that guy for the rest of her life."

Beneath the flowering arch, the groom set his bride back on her feet. Harper glowed, her cheeks as red as the roses in the arch, her eyes twinkling.

"They'll be fine." I laughed as Harper waved her bouquet.

In the front row, her mother and siblings beamed. Just as Gunner's family—biological mother included—did the same on the other side of the aisle. But two spots in the front had been left notably empty. In a perfect world, Harper's father and Luca would have been standing there too, celebrating the new couple. While the world was still far from perfect, this day was about as close to it as one could get.

The bride and groom walked back down the aisle, Gunner exclaiming to everyone in attendance that it was time to party as they went. I spied the other *Vindix* in the crowd, all looking happy and clapping. Rabi had transformed in the past months, and had a confidence about him that made my chest swell with pride. The two wolf packs howled at Gunner's exuberance, and we followed the crowd to the reception area. A sense of lightness like I hadn't felt in a long time overtook me and tears pricked my eyes.

For months, the world had been in a rebuilding phase. Rebuilding *and* restructuring. As most humans had only recently learned about magical beings during the war, there was a lot of image building to do.

Though I wasn't one for the spotlight, fate thrust me into the center of it—a Covenant Seat for the witches. At least until the next election cycle.

At least I have Serena to cling to, as she was now a fellow Covenant Seat too.

We weren't the only ones in leadership positions, either. Though he'd hemmed and hawed about it, Tobias was officially elected as Coven Master of S&S and accepted the position. He was doing well, making me proud.

Harper was now the alpha of the Midnight Pack, and as Gunner was her mate and husband, she was in constant talks with Gunner's father about the intricacies of merging the packs in the future. Neither of the pair would return to S&S, but that was okay. Others had filled their spots, three of my fellow *Vindix*. All except for Rabi, who was still living a well-deserved quiet life with his grandmother in New Orleans.

"Hey Rooms! Want some champs?" Shay said as we entered the wooded area where the reception would take place.

Fairy lights hung above, a dance floor as large as a school gymnasium had been constructed, and multiple mobile bars waited on the edges of the dance floor. Not too far away, dinner tables sat dressed and waiting for what Gunner promised would be some of the best barbecue we'd ever had. Judging by the mouthwatering scents in the air, I didn't doubt it.

It looked like it might rain, but even if it did, the party would go on. Hans had charmed a shield above to keep everyone dry. Nothing would ruin Harper and Gunner's day.

"Yes to champagne." I grinned at my friend. "Thanks."

"Babe?" Shay ran her hand up Hans's arm.

He smiled, and I was relieved to see it was genuine. For a while, Hans had switched back and forth, from happy to depressed back to happy only to sink into the depths of sadness once more. Not that I blamed the man.

He'd seen his mother dead in a cage, and then watched his sister die too. That would do a number on anyone. I was glad that Shay stuck by him, and he'd come out of his dark period. I really hoped he was only on the up and up from here.

"Please." Hans kissed Shay. "I'll come with you."

"How chivalrous," Shay purred. "We better hurry, though. There's already a line at the closest bar. Dang thirsty wolves!"

They dashed to the bar, leaving me with Tobias. I turned to my mate, and he read my mind as he bent down to kiss me.

"Do you want this?" he asked as our lips parted.

"This?"

"A wedding."

My eyes widened. *Unexpected.*

"I-I don't know?" I admitted. "I haven't thought much about it. I've considered other things more."

Namely, him changing me into a vampire.

Tobias arched an eyebrow. "And?"

"I've come to a big decision," I admitted.

He waited, patient as ever.

"I want to turn thirty as I am. I want to be a witch for a bit longer," I said. "And having a wedding before that might be fun."

I said the words before examining them, but they sat right in my gut. Just like choosing the age when Tobias would turn me into a vampire had felt right. I still had eight years and a few months as a witch. Then it would be off to another adventure with my mate.

"Thirty. A good choice."

"What wouldn't be a good choice?"

"Whatever choice you make is good. Even if you wanted to turn a hundred as you are, I would wait. And if you never wanted to turn, I'd understand. We'd make the most of our time and when yours was up, I'd go with you."

"Tobias, I might end up being a hot one hundred-year-old, but can you imagine our dates? The looks we'd get? That's beyond cougar level!"

His emerald eyes twinkled with mirth, and the day we'd met came back to me.

Him prowling towards me while I watched from behind the bars of an Egyptian prison. Even then, I thought he looked dangerous. Dangerous *and* hot as hell.

Some things hadn't changed. Others had changed a lot.

Like the world we lived in. Still overrun by demons and monsters who'd escaped taken cities.

It's a good thing we like to keep busy.

"Here you go!" Shay reappeared, flutes in her hands. "We beat the wolves. And look who we snagged!"

Behind her trailed Hans, Gunner, and Harper.

"Congratulations," I said when the newlyweds joined us.

"Thanks, Stoney," Gunner beamed down at me. "Doesn't my wife look hot as heck?"

I laughed. "Always."

Harper rolled her eyes, but the way she smiled up at Gunner broadcasted she loved his over-the-top style of loving her.

"We should make a toast!" Shay exclaimed. "Before they have to go say hello to all five hundred guests that Gunner invited."

"Five-fifty," Harper corrected. "Combining two packs means big wedding ceremonies. Why else do you think we have a million bars?"

"What do you want to toast to?" I asked.

Shay's head tilted in thought, but it was Hans who lifted his glass.

"To friendship. And our next adventure together."

My heart warmed. It was so perfect. Even for me, a loner who had found my friends—my family, as well as love. Dang, I was one lucky witch.

So we toasted to our friendship, to the next adventure, and while the glasses remained aloft, I held up a finger.

"One more thing," I said, all soft and mushy inside.

Hans made the 'go on' motion with his free hand.

"To the family we became and the ones we lost along the way."

My toast echoed all around.

ACKNOWLEDGMENTS

I truly hope that you loved the Coven of Shadows and Secrets Series! These characters are near and dear to me, so while this series is complete expect to see them pop up occasionally in other books in the Crowns of Magic Universe.

There are a few people to thank so let me get on with it.

As ever, thank you to my husband, my biggest cheerleader and best friend. We're so lucky to have one another and I think we'd totally be fated mates.

A big thanks to April Stacey, Donna Diagle, and Saundra Wright for typo hunting. I really appreciate your keen eyes and kind words of friendship.

And a huge thank you to any reader who has spread the word about this series. I may not know all that you've done, but talking about books really helps me out and allows me to keep writing. This is a dream job, so I'd like to do it for as long as possible.

All the magic,
Ashley McLeo

ALSO BY ASHLEY MCLEO

<u>The Winter Court (Crowns of Magic Universe)</u>

A Kingdom of Frost and Malice

A Lord of Snow and Greed

A Hallow of Storm and Ruin

A Crown of Ice and Fury

<u>Standalone Novels</u>

Curse of the Fae Prince (The Spring Court: Crowns of Magic Universe)

<u>Coven of Shadows and Secrets (Crowns of Magic Universe)</u>

Seeker of Secrets

Hunted by Darkness

History of Witches

Marked by Fate

Kingdoms of Sin

Bound by Destiny

<u>Spellcasters Spy Academy Series (Magic of Arcana Universe)</u>

A Legacy Witch: Year One

A Marked Witch: Internship

A Rebel Witch: Year Two

A Crucible Witch: Year Three

The Spellcasters Spy Academy Boxset

<u>The Wonderland Court Series (Magic of Arcana Universe)</u>

Alice the Dagger

Alice the Torch

<u>The Bonegate Series</u>

Hawk Witch

Assassin Witch

Traitor Witch

Illuminator Witch

<u>The Royal Quest Series</u>

Dragon Prince

Dragon Magic

Dragon Mate

Dragon Betrayal

Dragon Crown

Dragon War

ABOUT THE AUTHOR

Ashley lives in the lush and green Pacific Northwest with her husband, their dog, and the house ghost that sometimes makes appearances in her charming, old home.

When she's not writing fantasy novels she enjoys traveling the world, reading, kicking butt at board games, and frequenting taquerias.

For all the latest releases and updates, subscribe to Ashley's newsletter, The Coven. You can also find her Facebook group, Ashley's Reader Coven.

www.ingramcontent.com/pod-product-compliance
Lightning Source LLC
Chambersburg PA
CBHW061540190726
48289CB00004B/1106